THE
LITTLE
PRETENDER

Barbara Cartland

▲ PYRAMID BOOKS • NEW YORK

TO RAINE,

whose beauty and sweetness are
a continual joy and inspiration

THE LITTLE PRETENDER

A PYRAMID BOOK

Pyramid edition published January 1971

Copyright 1950 by Barbara Cartland

All Rights Reserved

Printed in the United States of America

PYRAMID BOOKS are published by Pyramid Publications
A Division of The Walter Reade Organization, Inc.
444 Madison Avenue, New York, New York 10022, U.S.A.

Author's Note

No author, especially one of Scottish blood, would dare to give too free a rein to fiction in connection with Prince Charles Stuart, because his memory is sacred to every Scot and the story of his exploits, so exciting, dramatic and heart-stirring, is as clear and familiar as if the events took place only yesterday.

I have therefore in this tale of 1750—four years after the Prince led the Rising of the Clans and had been defeated—contented myself with making use of only two historical facts: the first that the Prince lost his bonnet as he fled from the battlefield of Culloden Moor, the second that he visited London secretly in September, 1750, and at a house in Pall Mall asked the Duke of Beaufort and the Earl of Westmorland to raise him 5,000 men.

The rest of this book and its characters are entirely a product of my imagination, including the Clan MacCraggan and their position on the map of Scotland.

1

"*Bonjour, Mademoiselle! Vous êtes trés charmante!*"

Iona stopped and looked up, for her eyes had been on the ground as she picked her way carefully over the dirty, cobbled street. In front of her, barring her way, stood a gentleman. He was dressed in the height of fashion, but neither his clothes nor the rouge and powder with which his face had been carefully embellished could hide the fact that he was elderly.

But if he would disguise his age, the wrinkled Lothario made no attempt to hide the question in his peering, lecherous eyes or the invitation which twisted his thin, reddened lips.

Iona drew herself up to her full height, which was not very high, and in a voice as disdainful as she could make it she replied in French:

"You have made a mistake, Monsieur! Permit me to pass!"

But her gesture of dignity had perhaps been a mistake, for as she threw back her head, the dying light of the afternoon revealed the whiteness of her skin, the surprising colour of her eyes and the delicate features which had been half-hidden by the darkness of her fur-trimmed hood.

The rake's smile broadened and he took a step forward over-eagerly. He had not been mistaken; here was loveliness. His sudden movement made Iona shrink away from him. She was not really afraid, for she had moved about Paris alone since she had been a child and was accustomed to the *roués* and the *vieux marcheurs* who thought that any young woman who walked the streets unchaperoned was theirs for the taking. Usually she could deal with them effectively and with little trouble to herself, but this evening she was in a part of Paris which she did not know well and she was uneasily aware that she was inviting unpleasantness by walking alone in such a neighbourhood.

But she had no choice in the matter, and now she looked swiftly round her to find the best means of escape. It was not easy to know what to do. The street was very narrow and in the centre the cobbles sloped to a deep gutter where the water from recent rains strove to flow against the piles of sewage, refuse and rotten vegetables which were flung out daily by the inhabitants of the tall, dirty houses.

It might be possible to cross the gutter, Iona thought, and proceed down the other side of the street, but the cobbles were wet and it would be easy to slip and fall ignominiously should she try to move swiftly. There was nothing for it, she decided quickly, but to face her persecutor defiantly.

She pulled her dark cloak further round her, then clearly and in a slightly louder tone, so that he should not think her afraid, she said:

"I am on business of the utmost importance, Monsieur. Be kind enough to stand aside."

Perhaps it was her tone, perhaps the haughty carriage of her head or maybe the look of utter contempt in her eyes which told the reprobate all too clearly that here was someone he could neither entice nor threaten into obliging him. Almost instinctively he started to move aside, and then perversely changed his mind.

"If you must leave me, most beautiful Mademoiselle," he said, "at least allow me to kiss your lips before you go."

His voice was silky, but there was an undercurrent of lust in it which warned Iona of the danger in which she stood. Unwisely perhaps, but impulsively, she attempted to push past the man who barred her way, and instantly found herself clasped in his arms.

She was so slight and slender that he seemed to enfold her, his white hands covered with glittering rings having a surprising strength, and the folds of his velvet cloak went swirling around her so that she felt that he both suffocated and overpowered her. She fought against him frantically and in terror realised that his desire had given him the strength of the youth he had long lost.

"*Au secours! Au secours!*" she cried, and then in her extremity called in English: "Help! Help!"

Already she could feel the hot breath of her captor on her cheek, could see his dark eyes looking down at her as he forced her head back against his shoulder; and then, when she felt almost faint from the horror of it, help came unexpectedly.

Quite suddenly a dark shadow seemed to blot out the light as she struggled, panted and cried. One moment she was captive, the next moment she was free; freed so quickly that she staggered and almost fell. But to her surprise she saw that he who had held her at his mercy was now at the mercy of another—a tall man, so tall, so broad shouldered that the old *roué* seemed but a pygmy in his hands.

"This man is molesting you, Mademoiselle?" the newcomer asked.

"*Oui Monsieur.*"

Iona's answer was barely a whisper between lips which were quivering.

The Frenchman struggled like a rat held beneath the paws of a cat.

"*Lachez-moi, Canaille! Lachez-moi!*" he cried; but he was as impotent and powerless as Iona had been but a few seconds before. He screamed, a scream of rage and terror as the big man picked him up by the scruff of the neck and the seat of his breeches and flung him into the gutter. There was a splash and a squelch of mud and filth as he sprawled on his back in the dirty, polluted water, his silk-stockinged legs in the air.

He looked so comical with his face distorted with rage, his wig askew revealing his bald head, that for a moment Iona felt the laughter swell in her throat, and then she was aware that her heart was beating quickly and that she was still trembling a little from her fright.

She turned towards her rescuer.

"Thank you, sir, thank you," she said, and even as the words fell from her lips she was aware that unwittingly she had spoken in English. She was answered in the same language.

"I am glad that I could be of assistance, Mademoiselle."

If the words were formal, the tone in which the stranger spoke them was even more so. Instinctively Iona felt that though he still stood there, he had withdrawn himself from her presence.

She glanced up at his face and knew that, having been of service, her rescuer was anxious to efface himself. She could not have explained why she knew this, for the man who had saved her from the unwelcome attentions of the Frenchman made no effort to withdraw into the shadows, nor was his three-cornered hat pulled low over his eyes, and yet Iona was convinced that there was some mystery about him.

He was handsome, she thought, perhaps the most handsome man she had ever seen, yet there was such an air of aloof frigidity both in his expression and in his chiselled features that the words of gratitude which she would have spoken died on her lips. She felt somehow that they would sound false, for there was something so cold and imperious about this stranger that she felt only humiliated that it should have been necessary for him to champion her.

His clothes were plain, so plain that Iona was sure that they had been chosen for that reason. He wore no jewellery and yet she was sure that this, too, was deliberate. She had looked at him for but a second, and yet she felt that she had taken in so much and yet had learnt nothing. Without speech or gesture she knew that he was urging her to go and compelled by some force which she could not attempt to understand or explain, she obeyed.

She curtsied, he bowed, and then Iona was hurrying down the street with not even a backward glance at the spectacle of the amorous voluptuary picking himself out of the gutter. She moved so quickly that she was breathless when, after taking a turning to the right, she found herself at her destination.

She raised her hand to the knocker on the door and then waited until she got her breath. For the first time she looked behind her to see only another street as dingy and as dirty as the one she had just left.

She knocked on the door. It was opened almost immediately as if someone had been waiting there for her arrival. Iona stepped forward and, as she did so, the door was shut behind her and bolted, She stood uncertainly in what seemed to her a vacuum of darkness, and then a wheezing voice said:

"*Ici, 'moiselle!*"

A door was opened ahead, and now there was light, the light of four candles on a table in the centre of a room. There were six men seated round it, and as Iona entered, blinking a little after the darkness of the outer hall, two rose, one moving into the shadows at the far end of the room, while the other turned towards her.

With a little smile of pleasure she recognised a friendly face.

"I have come, Colonel," she said simply.

"I knew you would not fail," he replied.

He was a big man, red-faced and jovial, and there was something reassuring in the warmth and strength of his hand, so that Iona felt her fears and apprehensions of the last few days slip from her.

She had lain awake at night worrying, and had gone through the days haunted by an aching fear of her own incompetence; and yet now at the clasp of Colonel Brett's hand all that seemed fantastic and impossible became quite reasonable and possible.

Instinctively she took a deep breath and raised her hands to throw back the hood from her head. Colonel Brett turned towards the table.

"Gentlemen," he said. "This is the lady of whom I was speaking."

As the four men rose and bowed, Iona was aware that she was being scrutinised minutely and searchingly. Then before it could embarrass her Colonel Brett drew her to the table and pulled up a chair.

"Sit here, my dear," he said kindly. "Will you have wine or coffee?"

"Coffee, please," Iona replied.

It was set down in front of her and she lifted the cup to her lips. It was hot and strong, and as she drank, Iona took stock of her surroundings. Now, counting Colonel Brett, there were five men at the table, but still one chair was empty. It was an armchair at the head of the table, and in the shadows by the mantelshelf the sixth man was standing.

She could see nothing of him, but she knew that he was there and that he was listening. The men at the table were middle-aged or elderly, and Iona only had to look at them to know that they were all Scots, that they were exiles even as her guardian had been.

Quite suddenly a homesickness, a nostalgia for the years which had passed, came over her so strongly and so vividly that she felt as if she would choke. It was the familiarity of the scene, the darkened room, the lighted candles on the table, the half-empty wine glasses, the air heavy with tobacco smoke. How well she knew it. How well she recalled the lowered voices, the heavily shuttered windows, the servant on guard at the outer door. Yes, she knew it all, the talk which would go on in to the early hours, the arguments which would wage backwards and forwards across the table, the problems to which there would never

11

be a solution, the sadness—or was it yearning?—which seemed to overlie the expression on every face until they seemed to appear almost alike, related one to the other by a mutual suffering.

How much she missed all this. She only knew now how long the last two years had seemed and how utterly lonely she had been. She sat there very still and quiet in her highbacked chair, but her hair shining in the candlelight was fiery red and seemed to draw the men's eyes as if it were a torch.

At last Colonel Brett spoke.

"Iona," he began, and his voice was low and deep. "I have told these gentlemen of your coming, but I have waited until your arrival to go deeply into the matter which concerns us all. One thing I want to make quite clear, and that is this—if you have changed your mind, if you feel that you cannot undertake what we ask of you, then do not be afraid to say so. We shall understand, all of us."

There was a little murmur from the other gentlemen as if of approval, but Iona merely lowered her eyes, the long dark lashes seeming almost to touch the paleness of her cheeks.

"Well, gentlemen," Colonel Brett went on, "the position is briefly this. Most of you will remember James Drummond. He was one of us whom we loved and trusted, who fought with great bravery for the Chevalier de St. George in '15 and who was exiled for life. James Drummond died two years ago. I went often to his house and I know what Scotland meant to him and that he died as he lived, wanting only the return of our rightful King. He had living with him his ward, Iona, whom you now see before you. He had brought her up since she was a tiny child. He was her guardian; he never acknowledged any other relationship; and there is in fact no record of who Iona is. Of one thing only are we certain, that she is of Scottish extraction and that, although she has never been to Scotland, it is indeed her native land."

Colonel Brett paused and looked at Iona.

"Is that not true, my dear?" he asked.

But Iona could only nod, for the references to her guardian had brought the misery of her loss all too vividly before her. For a brief moment she raised her eyes, bright with unshed tears, then lowered them again.

"That is Iona's background," Colonel Brett continued, "And now, gentlemen, comes the second part of my story.

A few weeks ago Father Allan MacDonald, who was Chaplain to Clanranald's Regiment at Falkirk, came to me with a strange story. A French priest, with whom he had become friendly, had called upon him one evening and asked him to attend a parishioner of his who was dying and wished to make her last confession. Father Mac-Donald quickly gathered that the parishioner in question was a Scot and the priest, whose knowledge of our language is very limited, was appealing to him because he was unable to cope with the old Scotswoman's distress. Father MacDonald followed the priest to a shabby, poverty-stricken house where he found a very old woman making an almost superhuman effort to cling to life until her story had been told. Her delight at seeing Father Mac-Donald was pathetic, and drawing on her last remaining strength, she told him that she was Jeannie MacLeod who had been nurse to the infant daughter of the Duke of Arkrae.

"Seventeen years ago, in 1733, the Duke and the Duch-ess and their family had crossed the Channel to visit Vienna as the guests of the Emperor Charles. On their return, traveling in the Duke's private yacht, they were overtaken by a terrible storm. At this point, Father Mac-Donald said, Jeannie MacLeod became somewhat in-coherent, but it is easy to understand that in the confusion and terror she had lost her head, as perhaps had many other people aboard. It appears, however, that she had for many years been in love with the Duke's valet, and it was therefore with a sensation of relief that she found herself safely in a boat with this man at the oars and her charge, the Duke's little red-haired daughter, in her arms.

"But her relief was short lived, for after a few hours at sea the child died. Heavy with grief, sea-sick, hungry and thirsty, Jeannie MacLeod did not realise what was hap-pening until after three days adrift they were picked up by a French fishing-boat and brought to the Coast of Brittany. By her account she was ill for some time, but when she recovered she learned with horror two things. First, that the valet, whose name was Ewart, had drawn away from the yacht without taking any trouble to find out if the Duke or the Duchess or any other members of the party were safe; secondly, that he had in his possession all the Duke's jewels.

"Father MacDonald said that he had no reason to doubt that Jeannie MacLeod had been an honest woman. She

13

was shocked and horrified at what Ewart had done, but she loved him and she was utterly dependent on him in a strange land. The child she had nursed was dead. She had, to put it bluntly, little to gain and much to lose by exposing Ewart to the authorities, so, as most other women would have done, she made the best of a bad business. She married the man and the sale of the Duke's jewels enabled them to set up a small shop on the outskirts of Paris.

"They remained there until he died of a fever and then she supported herself as best she could by taking in washing. But the sin her husband had committed and she too in condoning it lay heavily on Jeannie's heart, and she begged Father MacDonald for absolution and also that he would convey the truth to the Duke. The child had not suffered, she said. She was but three years old and unconscious almost from the first moment that they had found themselves adrift in the boat. Two things only had Jeannie kept which she asked should be returned to their rightful owner. One was a miniature, the frame of which, set with diamonds, had long since been sold, and the other a little bangle of no particular value, which the child had worn round her wrist. They are here."

Colonel Brett put his hand in his pocket and drew out the two objects. The bangle was of gold set with very tiny pearls. He placed it on the table and beside it he put a small frameless miniature.

Iona glanced at it curiously and saw that it was of a woman. Colonel Brett cleared his throat.

"You may be wondering," he said, "how this concerns us all, so I now come to the point. When Father MacDonald gave me the miniature and the bangle, I had no other thought in my mind but to get someone who was going to Scotland to return them to the Duke of Arkrae. Then looking at the miniature I was astonished, for the picture painted a good many years ago reminded me of someone I knew very well. Jeannie MacLeod had not told Father MacDonald whom the miniature portrayed, but there is no doubt in my mind that, as it was in the Duke's possession, it is a picture of the Duchess of Arkrae—mother of the child who was drowned. I will now, gentlemen, pass this miniature amongst you and ask you if it reminds you, as it did me, of anyone you have seen before."

Colonel Brett pushed the miniature across the table to the man on his immediate left. He stared at it for several seconds, then looked up at Colonel Brett from under bushy eyebrows. Without a word he passed it to his immediate neighbour. Almost in silence save for one exclamation of astonishment the miniature was passed round the table until it reached Iona.

She had known what to expect, but now as she looked at the pictured face staring back at hers, she, too, felt inclined to give an exclamation of astonishment, for it was as if she looked in a mirror. The miniature was very delicately executed, but the colours were unfaded and the pictured face was clear, its colour undimmed.

It might easily have passed for a portrait of Iona. There was the same red hair curling riotously back from the white forehead, the same big green eyes with long, dark lashes. It would be impossible for anyone to look at the miniature and then at Iona and not to see the resemblance. It was impossible, too, not to imagine that the delicate, heart-shaped face was hers, and the narrow white pillar of her neck was carried just as proudly.

A man at the far end of the table cleared his throat.

"Well, Brett, continue," he said.

The Colonel looked down at the small bracelet and touched it with the tip of his finger.

"So far I have spoken of this to no one save Iona. Father MacDonald must remain in ignorance, as must everyone else outside this room. My suggeston is that Iona goes to Scotland carrying the miniature and the bracelet and presents herself at Skaig Castle as the present Duke's sister."

There was a sudden movement and somebody said gruffly:

"A wild scheme!"

"Daring if you like," Colonel Brett said, "but not wild. You gentlemen here know as well as I do that we have for months now, nay years, been trying to get in touch with the present Duke. The old Duke, his father, died in '45. He was eighty-one and on his deathbed when Prince Charles landed. The Clan MacCraggan therefore took no official part in the Rising, although several members joined individually.

"The present Duke was abroad, and as he did not return to Scotland until our armies were defeated and our Prince forced to take refuge overseas, we do not know where his sympathies would have lain had he been there. You, gentlemen, and I both know what the support of the MacCraggans would mean to our plans for the future, but at

15

the moment we are unable to say whether they will be for or against us.

"Twice during this past year we have sent messengers to Scotland with instructions to get in touch with the Duke. The first was caught by the English and beheaded before he got to Skaig Castle, the other has never been heard of since. We have heard rumours of all sorts. The old Duke was supposed to have been in touch with the Hanoverian Usurper of the British throne but it is difficult to know if this is the truth or no. He inherited from his uncle and was therefore not important enough for us to have a record of his sympathies in the Rebellion of '15. The present Duke has great power. He has increased his territory since he inherited the title; his Clan, unlike many others, has not been persecuted. We want him on our side; but if he is to be our enemy, then let us know it and be forearmed."

"And this lady will undertake such a dangerous quest?" someone asked.

"When I have finished Iona shall answer that for herself," Colonel Brett replied. "There is one more thing. You all know of the 'Tears of Torrish', those fabulous diamonds which were given to our Prince before the Battle of Culloden. For safety they were sewn inside his bonnet, but when His Royal Highness was forced to fly from the battlefield, the wind blew his bonnet from his head. Thus the 'Tears of Torrish' were lost. For years we have been making what inquiries we could. The bonnet may have been trampled in the mud or it may have been preserved as a precious keepsake by someone who is still loyal to the Prince. We had almost given up hope of hearing of the diamonds again, when three months ago a rumour reached us, alas, merely a rumour, that the MacCraggans knew something of the gems. If Iona goes to Skaig Castle, that is the second thing she may discover for us. There is no need for me to tell you what the 'Tears of Torrish' would mean to the Prince at this moment. Five years ago they were valued at fifteen thousand pounds, today they may be worth a great deal more."

Colonel Brett drew a deep breath and laid both his hands face downwards on the table.

"That, gentlemen, is my story. You have seen the miniature, you have seen Iona. If she will undertake this adventure with all its risks, with all its dangers, with all its penalties, I can tell you she will do it for one reason and one reason only—because she believes in our Cause. She believes, as we do, that Charles Edward Stuart should reign over England and Scotland. . . . as now and for all time he reigns in our hearts."

There was a sudden silence, a silence in which Iona knew they were waiting for her to speak. Her eyes went to the miniature, to the tiny gold bracelet, somehow pathetic in its very smallness; and then suddenly she got to her feet. She stood there in the candlelight looking so fragile and so delicate that for a moment those watching her felt that she had not the strength to undertake anything, not even to make the speech for which they waited. Then suddenly her eyes were open and they saw the fire within them, a fire which seemed suddenly to light her whole body as if it were a light shining through her.

"You have spoken of this, Colonel," she said softly, "as if what I have promised to attempt were a very great undertaking. Surely it is but a small thing to do for the Prince we love?"

There was a little sigh from the assembled company, a sigh of relief as Iona spoke. Then from the shadows of the fireplace someone came walking towards the table. He stood for a moment behind his empty chair. The gentlemen rose and Iona looked across the table. Though she had never seen him before, she knew him even as she had known that he had been all the time listening in the darkness.

In silence the men drew aside to let her pass, and then she was beside him, sinking at his feet in a deep curtsey, her lips against the hand he extended to her. Then he drew her to her feet, and she looked up into his blue eyes and saw in his handsome, whimsical countenance that strange, compelling charm which made men even against all logical conviction be ready to fight and to die for him.

"Thank you, Iona," he said, and at the sound of his voice her heart swelled within her with a joy which she could neither explain nor contain. Still holding Iona's hand, the Prince turned towards the assembled company. "Gentlemen," he said, "if this lady will undertake such an adventure on our behalf, then we can only offer her both our blessing and our faith in her success."

His fingers tightened for a moment on Iona's and then he released her hand.

"A toast, Colonel," he said, and lifted from the table the glass of wine which had stood in front of his empty chair.

Five men lifted their glasses and turned towards Iona.

17

She felt full of an excitement such as she had never experienced before. She felt a power within herself to achieve whatever was asked of her, because it was for his sake she attempted it and because of his faith in her.

She clasped her hands together tightly. This moment was beyond happiness. The glasses were raised.

"To Iona—The Little Pretender!" His Royal Highness said softly.

2

A church clock struck six as Iona got out of bed and pulled the curtains. The window of the hotel bedroom looked out over the grey roofs of houses hardly distinguishable from the sky.

There was something drear and sombre about the scene and Iona shivered before she turned hastily to the room and began to dress. It had been after sunset the night before when the little French shipping packet *La Petite Fleur* had nosed its way slowly up the Moray Firth and into the harbour of Inverness.

Iona had stood on deck since the first moment when she was told that the coast of Scotland was in sight. She had felt excited beyond expression at the thought of seeing the land which, since her earliest memories, had been a part of her heritage. And then when she beheld the mountains rising peak upon peak against the crimson splendour of a setting sun, she had felt such a soul-stirring elation sweep over her that she could only stand trembling with the sheer intensity of her feelings, her face reflecting some of the glory which shone in the sky.

The spray of the waves breaking against the bow of the ship glistened in her hair and on her cheeks, but she felt neither the damp nor the sharpness of the wind, and was so enthralled that she was unaware that Hector MacGregor, coming in search of her, watched her for some moments before he spoke:

"Is it what you expected?" he asked at last softly.

She turned to him with an effort as if he dragged her spirit back into the confines of her body.

"Scotland at last!" she said softly. "My land, your land . . . and his land!"

She spoke the last two words softly and it was a physical pain to think of their Prince exiled among foreigners, eating his heart out with yearning for the mountains and the heather.

"Four years since I was here last," Hector said gruffly, "and God knows it's lovelier than ever."

There was so much pain in his voice that Iona threw him a quick glance of sympathy. She knew his story only too well, how his father and his two brothers had been killed at Culloden and a price put on his own head.

After months of privation and incredible hardships he had managed to escape and join the Prince in France, but of all the exiles in the Royal entourage Hector MacGregor was the most restless, the most untiring in his plans and plottings for a triumphant return.

Lean and wiry, his big bones and sandy head making it impossible for him to disguise his nationality, Hector was only twenty-seven though he had acquired in those years experience enough to last the average man a lifetime. He had a natural severity of expression which was transformed by his smile, and which changed him from a taciturn Scot into a charming young man. A man, moreover with an irrepressible spirit and an unquenchable optimism. In a tight corner, in an odds-against fight in all times of danger, Hector was an invaluable companion and a partner without compare.

It was the Prince who had insisted that someone should escort Iona from France to Scotland. She had been willing to make the journey alone, but His Royal Highness had been adamant on the point that someone must accompany her until she was safely on the Scottish shore.

His chivalry had touched Iona, but she had lived in France long enough to know the dangers which would beset any young and pretty girl setting forth alone on a French packet which did not ordinarily carry passengers. Although she was prepared to brave the dangers, whatever they might be, it was with a sense of relief that she heard that Hector MacGregor had offered himself as her escort.

It was dangerous for him, she knew full well, to go to Scotland and should he be recognised, there would be only one ending for the journey—the executioner's axe. But when she spoke to him of her fears, he laughed.

"I have taken graver risks," he said, "and what's more, it would be almost worth dying to see Scotland again, to smell the wind blowing across the moors and to hear persons talking in a civilised tongue."

Iona laughed. It had not taken her long in their acquaintance for her to realise with what bitter contempt Hector, like many other of his countrymen, held the French. Nevertheless her fears for his safety increased as they grew nearer to the Scottish shore and she begged him to be careful.

"I'll be careful enough," he answered. "Do not trouble your pretty head about me. I have friends whom I must see and work that I must do for the Prince before I return. Nevertheless, remember that from the moment we leave this ship we know nothing of each other. Speak of me to no one or if by any unfortunate chance you learn that I am in any predicament, deny any knowledge of me. To admit an acquaintance, however slight, would be to draw suspicion on yourself and your enterprise which, as you well know, is of the greatest import."

Iona had not needed Hector's confirmation of what she already knew. Colonel Brett had spoken without undue emphasis of the task before her, but in the days that followed, when she had seen much of the Colonel and the gentlemen surrounding the Prince, she had begun to learn just how much value they put on the information she might obtain for them regarding the Duke of Arkrae.

Expressions of loyalty reached the Prince continually from the Clans who had supported him four years earlier in his ill-fated march south; but many of them were but ghosts of their former selves, their leaders beheaded, those of their clansmen who had lived after the terrible Massacre at Culloden being hunted relentlessly and continuously by the victorious English troops. The Duke of Cumberland had countenanced the most bestial cruelty. Wounded Highlanders had been dragged from their hiding places and tortured or clubbed to death, their crofts had been burned to the ground and their women and children left to starve. In some cases a Clan had to all intents and purposes been wiped out, in others the survivors, scattered and impoverished, lived pitiable lives under the tyranny of the English Governers who watched suspiciously their every movement.

The Clan MacCraggan, strong and wealthy, with its lands untouched and its Clansmen unintimidated could, the Prince's advisers thought, be strong enough, should they prove loyal, to carry His Royal Highness to victory.

Iona had tried to imagine what the Duke of Arkrae would be like, but failed because no one could give her any clear details of him. The men who had been exiled after the Rising in '15 as her guardian had been, had, of course, never met him, and the younger men who had fled to France after the defeat in '45 were equally ignorant. Hector MacGregor, whom she had questioned on the journey over, could tell her little more than she knew already.

"His Grace is of consequence," he said, "firstly because of the strategic position of his land. Secondly, from all I hear he is the rising power in Scottish affairs. So many of our great men are lost to us—Kilmarnock and Balmerinoch executed, Keppoch and Strathallan killed in battle, Lochiel and Elcho in exile. If Arkrae is of the right way of thinking it may be the saving of Scotland."

"And if he isn't?"

Hector made a grimace.

"Then let us know the worst," he said. " 'Tis better than hoping against hope."

He looked at her, shook his head, and she sensed the pity in his eyes.

"They have set you a herculean task, my girl," he muttered. "I'm not sure that I approve, it's too risky."

Iona raised her head proudly and smiled at him.

"I am not afraid," she said, then hesitated, and added honestly: "Well . . . not very."

Hector MacGregor put his hand on her shoulder.

"Of course you're afraid," he said. "We are all afraid when we go into battle and that's what you are about to do, and the Lord knows I hate to see women fighting."

"But not in a battle of wits," Iona replied.

"There's more to it than that," Hector retorted. "What if you are caught? If they find out who sent you on this journey, it will be prison and perhaps worse."

"Torture?" Iona asked, her eyes wide.

"Maybe," Hector answered. "The English would give a great deal to know where the Prince is at this moment. He is, as you know, banished from Paris since King Louis signed the Treaty of Aix-la-Chapelle; but most Frenchmen have a sneaking fondness for the Stuart cause and would look the other way if they met him. But the English would make trouble if they could. They're afraid of another rising and so long as they're afraid, they will do everything in their power to keep a check on the Prince's movements."

"I am thankful I know so little," Iona said. "His Royal Highness may have left Paris by now and be anywhere in Europe. How am I to know where he is?"

22

"To be a Jacobite is enough to damn you!" Hector said. "But let us look on the bright side—even if all goes well, you will have to get away before you are proved an imposter. I suppose you have made plans for returning to France?"

Iona nodded.

"Colonel Brett has given me the name and address of someone I can trust in Inverness."

"Then let's pray they are trustworthy and will be able to help you. Brett's all right, but he is always full of schemes and ideas, many of which are impracticable when it comes to putting them into operation. Don't rely on him too completely when it comes to details, Iona; check up where you can on your own. It's your neck you're risking, not his."

Iona looked startled.

"But of course I trust the Colonel," she said. "I have known him for many years and he lives only to serve the Prince."

"Yes, yes," Hector said testily. "I'm not questioning his loyalty, I'm just saying that sometimes he is so carried away by his grandiose schemes that the details are often forgotten or ignored. But attention to detail is often the difference between success and failure. Take, for instance, this plot in which he has involved you. The Colonel sees a miniature, decides that you resemble the lady in question and without further inquiry packs you off as a claimant to the title and identity of a child who he has been told was drowned seventeen years ago. Has he made absolutely certain that the girl was drowned? How does he know that the miniature is a picture of the child's mother? Suppose the Duke carried a portrait of his favourite mistress with him, where do you find yourself then?"

Hector spoke vehemently, but Iona threw back her head and laughed.

"Oh, Hector! Hector!" she said, "What a basket of bogies you are carrying! I swear that your imagination easily exceeds the Colonel's. Why, the old woman, Jeannie MacLeod, said that the child died in her arms and they buried her at sea. She would not have lied on her deathbed. And the child had red hair! Someone said—I can't remember who—that it is a characteristic of the MacCraggan's, so the Colonel's assumption that I might be accepted as the Duke's sister is not so wild as you would pretend. After all, the drowned child would be just my age if she had lived."

23

"Yes, that's true enough," Hector said reflectively. "And the MacCraggans are red-headed—but there are many red-headed folk in Scotland."

"I won't listen to you," Iona declared. "You're trying to frighten me, but what purpose will it serve? The adventure has begun and I must go through with it to the end."

"I know that," Hector said, "but be on your guard. Promise me?"

"I promise you," Iona answered with all sincerity. She did not really underestimate the dangers which would be waiting for her at Skaig.

Now in the chill of the morning Hector's words came back to frighten her. Her hands trembled as she dressed herself and she knew it was not only with the cold. She had made inquiries the previous night and they had told her that there was a stage coach leaving at seven o'clock for Fort Augustus, which would bring her within some ten miles of Skaig Castle.

Iona put on her travelling dress of dark green silk and arranged a clean white fichu around her shoulders. She had but few clothes. Colonel Brett had given her a small sum to fit herself out for the journey; but although Iona had expended it with meticulous care, her wardrobe was limited and the trunk in which it was carried was light enough to cause comment along the porters at the hotel.

Such frugality was fitting, she thought, for a girl who was supposed to have been brought up by an impoverished nurse. All the same, she was feminine enough to wish that she could have arrived at Skaig Castle beautifully and fashionably garbed in gowns which would have given her courage and been a fitting background to her pretension to ducal lineage. She thought sadly of some of the lovely things she had owned before her guardian died; not that her gowns and manteaux had been exceptionally expensive, but she had been able to dress as befitted the cherished ward of a gentleman.

Her guardian had denied her little and she always understood that some of the money on which they lived was her own. James Drummond's money was principally an allowance paid by his relatives which Iona was well aware would cease at his death. But he had some capital in France and with her own dowry she would certainly not be left penniless.

But when eventually James Drummond died, things

24

were very different. Iona found then that he had lent his own small capital and hers to one of his relations who had been banished in '45. It had not been a tremendous sum—in fact the gentleman who received it had thought it so negligible that he spent it both speedily and lavishly in keeping up his position at the French Court. But it was all that stood between Iona and absolute penury. James Drummond had trusted the exile and had believed his repeated assurances that sooner or later the money would be returned. It was left to Iona to find on her guardian's death that the money was lost beyond recall.

James Drummond had been dead only a few days when his debtor and relative was arrested and thrown into prison because he could not pay the thousands of francs he owed the tradesmen. Iona had known then what it was to have no security, to be alone in the world without money, without a home or even a name.

For perhaps the first time in her life she had felt humiliated and ashamed of being herself. When she had been old enough to understand, her guardian had told her that she had been brought into his keeping when she was but a few months old.

"I gave the person who brought you my most solemn oath," he told her, "that I would never reveal to you or anyone else who you are. You were christened Iona because you were born on the small lovely Island of that name which lies on the west coast of Scotland. That is all I can tell you. But I can promise you one thing, my dear—you need not be ashamed of the blood which runs through your veins, and you need never be anything but proud of your nationality which is Scottish."

James Drummond sighed, then added:

"I have tried to make a home for you, Iona; if I have failed it is not for the want of loving you."

Was it surprising that then and at other times when the subject had arisen Iona had assured her guardian that she loved him better than anyone else and that she wanted no other home? They laughed together when, finding a surname essential, she had chosen to call herself "Ward", because she was his ward and he was her guardian.

"Iona Ward!" she dimpled. " 'Tis a pretty name and one day perhaps I will make you proud of it."

But when their home was sold and the sale of the furniture and the pictures brought Iona only enough to pay

25

for a granite headstone over James Drummond's grave, she wept bitter tears because she had nothing left—not even the knowledge of her own identity.

Who was she? Where had she come from? And where should she go?

Eventually she found a job in a milliner's shop where once she had bought her bonnets, and had rented a tiny attic in a respectable lodging house nearby. She had never realized until then how few friends her guardian had made in France.

He had not been a young man when in '15 he took an oath of allegiance to the Chevalier de St. George. Banished from Scotland a few months later, James Drummond had found it hard to start life anew in a strange country. He had hated his life in Paris and had been too homesick even to be particularly sociable with the other exiles. Occasionally he paid his respects to his exiled King, occasionally he spent an evening with some other Scotsmen or they dined with him and they passed the hours making plans which they knew in their hearts, even while they agreed over them, were doomed never to be anything but dreams born of wine and tobacco smoke.

The years passed; James Drummond's friends thinned out as they died or were pardoned and returned home to Scotland. He was an old man when Prince Charles set sail in '45 on his gallant bid for power. When the fugitives and exiles of that ill-fated enterprise came flooding into France, James Drummond would not bestir himself to make their acquaintance.

With the selfishness and egotism of one who has nearly reached the end of his life he was complacently content with the companionship of his young ward, and it never entered his mind that she might need friends of her own age. Iona never complained, and having never associated with young people, did not miss them. But when her guardian died, she was appalled by the barren desolation of her own loneliness.

Now, as she dressed in the austere and ugly little hotel bedroom, she wondered why she should be afraid. Nothing in Scotland, she thought, could be worse than what she had experienced in the last two years in Paris after James Drummond's death.

She was engaged in adjusting her travelling hood over her hair when there came a knock on the door. She bade whoever it might be enter and a maid came into the room, bringing a cup of chocolate which she set down on the table.

"Will ye be wantin' breakfast afore ye leave?" the girl asked.

She was a skinny creature with big red hands and large, clumsy feet.

"No, thank you," Iona replied.

"The coach will be in the yard at a quarter to seven, if ye be wantin' a guid seat," the girl volunteered.

Iona was grateful for the information and when the maid had left the room, she picked up the chocolate and began to sip it. It was badly made and tepid, but it was all Iona had ordered. Her guardian had always eaten what he called "a proper breakfast"; but Iona, reared in France, had a native taste for hot rolls, coffee or chocolate, and could not contemplate anything more substantial.

She finished the chocolate and was gathering together her small pieces of luggage when suddenly she dropped everything and stood still in utter horror, the blood receding from her face. She had remembered something almost unbearably disturbing. While she and Hector were travelling from Paris to the coast, she had given him for safety the miniature and the pearl bracelet which were to establish her identity when she reached Skaig Castle.

Colonel Brett had also written out an account of the confession Father MacDonald had heard from Jeannie MacLeod, with the alterations and additions on which they had agreed. He had not, of course, been able to sign it with Father MacDonald's name; instead he had added a fictitious one.

"They will make investigations, Iona," the Colonel warned her, "but before anyone can have returned from France with the information, you will, pray God, have learned all we want to know and have made good your escape."

The letter had been bulky and the miniature and bangle so precious that Iona had been afraid of losing them or having them stolen from her. She had given them to Hector for safe keeping, and now with a kind of sick horror she remembered that he had not returned them to her. They had both been so excited at seeing Scotland, and he had talked so much of the evening he was going to have with his friends that they had left their farewells until the last hurried moment.

"I shall drink whisky tonight, Iona," Hector had said as

the ship neared the quayside. "That's real drink, and it will be a welcome change from the gallons of sickly wines I've quaffed these last five years. Doubtless I shall be gloriously drunk. If you hear me come singing to bed, remember you have no acquaintance with such a vulgar, roistering fellow."

Iona had assured him laughingly she would have no desire to claim acquaintance with him under such circumstances, and then their smiles had faded and they had looked at each other, their faces suddenly serious.

"God keep you!" Hector MacGregor said quietly, his eyes on Iona's shadowed face. "I shall be waiting to welcome you in France on your return."

He raised her fingers to his lips. Iona felt an almost insane desire to cling to him, to ask him to come with her and to tell him that she was afraid to go on alone. As if he sensed what she was feeling, he suddenly put his arms round her and drew her close to him. For one moment she leant her head against his shoulder and shut her eyes. Here was security and protection. For a moment Iona told herself that everything else in the world was unimportant. Then Hector let her go and his face was turned towards the shore.

"I will go first," he said in a low voice. "We must not be seen together."

With an intolerable sense of loss Iona watched him leap from the deck on to the stone quay. Hector was her first playmate, her first friend of her own age and class. He had teased her and bullied her and looked after her during the journey as if she were the most precious person in the whole world. They had argued together, quarrelled a little and laughed for no better reason than that they were young and light-hearted. Iona knew now that the voyage from France had been for her a time of extraordinary happiness—but it was over.

If Scotland was full of unknown fears for her, it was home for Hector and he walked away from the ship with his head held high and whistling a gay tune which Iona heard long after he was out of sight.

It was only now that she remembered that he had stridden away from her with her most precious possessions still in his keeping. Agitatedly she looked round the room. Should she write a note and send it to his bedroom? That would be to invite comment amongst the servants, and besides, there was so little time.

It was nearly a quarter to seven, the coach would be waiting. Whatever happened she must get a seat. There was only one thing to do. Risky though it might be, she must go to Hector's bedchamber.

The hotel was small and the guest rooms were all on one floor. Coming up to bed, Iona had seen a porter ahead of her with Hector's trunk on his shoulder. He had entered a room at the far end of the passage.

Quietly she opened her door. There was no one in sight. Picking up the voluminous folds of her skirts so that she could move quickly, she ran across the landing and down the passage. She reached Hector's room and knocked on the door. There was no answer.

Apprehensively she wondered if, after all, he had not returned to the hotel the night before. Perhaps his friends had persuaded him to stay with them, although more than once he said it was unfair for any man with a price on his head to shelter under a friendly roof, for should the English start to hunt for him, the consequences for those with whom he stayed would be serious.

Iona knocked again, but there was still no answer. Desperate and almost faint with anxiety she lifted the latch of the door. It was not locked and peeping in she saw with a sense of utter relief that Hector was lying on the bed. He was snoring with his mouth open and Iona guessed that his friends had been as hospitable as he had anticipated. She only hoped the whisky had not been too potent.

Iona crossed the room and saw with amusement that he was still fully dressed save that he had pulled his nightshirt over his coat and breeches and his nightcap was perched precariously on the side of his wig. She touched his shoulder.

"Hector," she whispered, not daring to raise her voice. "Hector!"

He grunted and tried to turn over on his side, but Iona shook him again, this time roughly so that he opened his eyes. He looked at her in a glazed way.

"Wake up, Hector! For Heaven's sake wake up!"

The alertness which comes instinctively to a man who has once been hunted cleared his brain and almost immediately he sat up.

"What is it?" he asked, and though his voice was thick the words were clear.

"The miniature! My letter!" Iona said urgently. "You forgot to give them to me and I have to go now."

29

Hector pushed his wig and his nightcap a little further back on his head.

"Fool that I am!" he said.

He got to his feet a little unsteadily, walked across the room then stared around him.

"My coat," he said at last. "Where is it?"

Despite the urgency of the situation Iona wanted to laugh. A little chuckle escaped her lips.

"You have got it on under your nightshirt."

"I must have been more tipsy than I thought last night," Hector said ruefully, and thrust his hand through the opening of his nightshirt and into the breast pocket of his coat.

"They're here safely," he said in a tone of relief, drawing out both the letter and the small sealed packet which contained the miniature and the bracelet.

Iona almost snatched them from him.

"Goodbye, Hector," she said. "I must go—the coach leaves at seven."

"I'm sorry I forgot them, Iona. I'm a dolt and you have every reason to be angry with me."

He looked so contrite that once again Iona had to laugh.

"It's all right," she replied. "There's no harm done if no one sees me leave this room."

She went to the door and opened it cautiously. There was no one in the passage. She turned to smile at Hector who still stood in the centre of the room watching her go. As she did so, the latch of the door caught in her cloak.

Iona had not been able to afford a new one and the material of the one she had worn for some years, which had never been expensive was wearing thin. She tried to free herself and the stuff tore. Ruefully she surveyed the triangular tear where it was most noticeable on her shoulder, and as she did so a door opened on the opposite side of the passage.

It was too late to do anything. A man came out of the room and stood within a few feet of Iona, having her in full view, her wide skirts filling the doorway while behind her was Hector in his nightshirt, his wig askew.

Without thinking Iona glanced up. She saw a young man with a strange dark, secretive face. He wore a cloak trimmed with sable, his velvet coat was richly embroidered and ornamented with jewelled buttons.

She met his eyes, saw the faint smirk of amusement which twisted his lips as he looked beyond her, and the blood flooded into her cheeks as she realised her position

30

and he suspicioned. She turned her head aside and the fur which edged her hood fell forward to shadow her face. But she knew that it was too late, too late to do anything but watch the man who had taken her at such a disadvantage walk slowly and with an innate dignity away down the passage.

It was only when he was out of sight that Iona collected herself. Without a backward glance at Hector she shut the door and ran to her own room.

She was alarmed and panic-stricken at what had occurred, but there was no time for retrospection or trepidation. She gathered up her belongings and sped down the stairs. The clock in the hall told her it was five minutes to seven and she sent a servant hurrying for her trunk. She passed through the hotel and into the yard. The stagecoach was waiting and already a number of passengers had taken their places.

There were also two private coaches in the yard. One drove away just as Iona came out from the hotel. She noticed that it was drawn by four finely matched thoroughbreds and that the servants' livery was resplendent with gold braid. She had no time to notice more, for the stagecoach was filling up and she must be certain of a seat.

She found one, but it was none too comfortable, for she was squeezed between a fat woman with a basket of baby chicks and an elderly man who smelt unpleasantly of raw spirits. Iona's trunk was stowed away with the other baggage, then the coachman appeared from the side door of the hotel, wiping his lips. He climbed up on the box and took the reins. With much jostling and creaking the coach moved slowly from the yard of the hotel out into the street. Only as the horses quickened their gait did Iona feel herself relax and begin to lose the tension which had made it difficult for her to breathe.

She was not even sure of what she had been afraid—of being denounced perhaps, of being prevented from going further, of being taken prisoner. Those were but a few of the misgivings which had invaded her mind since she had been discovered in the doorway of Hector's room. Fool that she had been to linger for one moment. Better to have torn herself free regardless of the damage to her cloak and rushed headlong down the passage.

But after all, she reassured herself, Scotland was big. Why should she ever again meet the man who had come from the opposite bedchamber? Besides, he might be just an

31

English visitor going south. Firmly she tried to reassure herself and gradually the frightened thumping of her heart subsided and she felt the burning flush die away from her cheeks.

This should be a warning both to herself and to Hector. They had been careless, both of them, in not remembering the precious package. More especially she was to blame, for Hector was not so directly concerned with it. How could she have been so stupid?

Bitterly Iona blamed herself and then with a burst of common sense tried to put the whole incident from her mind. It had happened; what was done could not be undone; it would only make things worse if she was to allow it to make her timorous and weak hearted. Unpleasant things should be forgotten. Then insistently the last unpleasant thing which had happened to her came to her mind. That encounter with the ancient libertine but a week or so ago when she had been on her way to that most momentous meeting with the Prince's advisers.

How frightened she had been when she realised the strength of the Frenchman's arms and the nearness of his face! But she had been rescued. Once again she thought of the tall stranger who had come like a knight of old to her rescue, but who, having vanquished the dragon, had appeared cold and disinterested.

He had been English, and she thought that though she hated the whole race for what they had done to her Prince, she had reason to be personally grateful to one of them.

Yet, she queried, how could she be certain that he was an Englishman? His voice had been aristocratic and distinguished, but might he not have been Scottish? She hoped he was, and as the coach jolted and swayed through the town and out into the open countryside Iona smiled to herself. Here in Scotland she was carrying partisanship to its logical conclusion in believing that nothing good could come out of England and nothing decent be expected of the English.

Yes, she was convinced now that her rescuer must have been a Scot!

3

Iona was never to forget her first drive through the Highlands and the thrill of seeing the mountain peaks, some still showing patches of white from the snows of last winter, of beholding the moors purple with heather stretching away on to the horizon, and of watching a fall cascading down the hillside to join the swift flowing waters of a river golden with peat.

At the first halting place Iona left the stuffy confining atmosphere inside the coach and climbed on to the roof, glorying in the sharp air as it whipped the colour into her cheeks, and quite unmindful of the stares of the other travellers who were all men. She was indeed oblivious of everything save the beauty of the scenery. She did not even notice how hard her seat was or miss the warmth of a rug which sheltered the legs of more experienced voyagers.

She felt as if a psalm of thanksgiving were rising within herself. This was Scotland, and thank God it was as beautiful and as wonderful as she had imagined it; no, more than that, for her imagination had fallen far short of the truth.

The heavy morning mist had risen and in an hour or so the sun came out. How often Iona had heard her guardian talk of the lights on the hills! Now she understood what he meant as the sun and clouds cast a pageant of light and shadow over the landscape, while the waters of Loch Ness, beside which the roadway ran, varied from a blue, vivid as the Madonna's robe, to the cool depths of a great emerald.

The road surface was bad and the stage-coach was slow. There were frequent halts to set passengers down or take more aboard. Half-way through the morning they changed horses and the travellers took the opportunity to buy food at a wayside inn. Iona found that after such a light breakfast she was both hungry and thirsty and she ate with relish a big scone made of oatmeal and drank a small glass of ale.

It was while they were waiting to go aboard the coach again that Iona noticed something strange. Two men were approaching along the road. Big men, gaunt faced and bearded, they were strangely dressed. Their coats, ragged and dirty, were ordinary enough, but round their waists, dropping to their knees, they each wore a piece of coarse camlet. Iona wondered for a moment if these were the kilts of which she had heard so much; then to her astonishment she saw that each man carried suspended from a stick a pair of breeches. She was so surprised that she turned to a man standing next to her and said:

"Forgive my asking you, sir, but why are those men carrying their nether garments over their shoulder?"

The man gave her a sharp glance of suspicion; then as if reassured by the innocent inquiry on her face, he replied gravely:

"Dinna ye ken that the kilt has been forbidden and the English law says that a mon just tak' tae breeches?"

"No, I have not heard that," Iona replied. "I have but just arrived in this country. I thought all Scotmen wore the kilt."

"Aye, we did that," was the answer. "There's nae doot but that it was the sensible dress for a mon who has to live in this climate an' who has to climb hills an' ford rivers. But the English hae decreed that every man must hae a pair o' breeches. Only the law dinna specify on what part o' the body the breeches are to be worn. So there ye see my gallant countrymen obeying the law."

The two men passed by at that moment and went on down the long dusty road, their breeches dangling from off their shoulders like scarecrows in the wind.

Quite unexpectedly Iona felt the tears come into her eyes. Despite the dire punishment, cruelty and tyranny of their English masters the spirit of independence was still alive in Scottish breasts.

She spoke to no one else until at three o'clock in the afternoon the coach arrived at Fort Augustus. It was but a small place. A few stone crofts were clustered round the pompous authority of the stone fort built after the Rising in '15. Outside this lounged several English soldiers in their red coats and white breeches, uncomfortably conscious of the dark looks and sidelong glances of enmity which every countryman gave them in passing.

The coach drew up at the inn which was low built and had a drear, unwelcoming appearance. It was here that Iona had been told in Inverness that she must hire a private carriage to take her to Skaig Castle.

She made inquiries of a dour innkeeper who appeared to think her request a peculiar one, but grudgingly promised that a conveyance of some sort would be ready in half an hour. To pass the time Iona seated herself in the parlour, a dismal, sparsely furnished apartment without a fire and with only the comfort of an embroidered text to cheer the wayfarer.

Iona had not waited there more than a few minutes when she heard a loud-voiced altercation going on in the next room.

"I tell ye, dolt," said a woman, "that it is taemorrow His Grace sent word that her ladyship was a-comin', not taeday."

"Weel, please yersel', but either His Grace or yer ain hearin' was at fault, wooman, for the lady is here."

"It canna be the same," was the reply, "for why would her ladyship be arrivin' on the stage-coach. Do ladies o' quality travel on the stage-coach, I ask ye?"

"I ken naething of their doings," a man's voice replied, "but there canna be twa ladies a-goin' tae the castle."

"Why not?" the woman asked sharply. "Dinna blether; I'll go an' see for mysel'."

As Iona expected, there was the sound of footsteps and a moment later the door of the parlour was opened. An elderly woman stood there, her greying hair drawn back sharply with almost undue severity from her lined forehead and wrinkled face, giving her a look of age in strange contrast to the bright, alert shrewdness of her blue eyes. She wore a white apron and her arms, which were bare to the elbow, showed signs of flour as if she had been busy baking. She looked at Iona and dropped a curtsey.

"Yer pardon, m'lady, but ye required o' m' husband that a conveyance should be made ready tae tak' yer ladyship tae the castle. His Grace wasna expectin' ye until taemorrow when a carriage was to hae been sent frae the castle tae carry yer ladyship the last part o' the journey."

"I think you have made a mistake," Iona replied, "I have indeed asked for a conveyance to carry me to Skaig Castle, but I am not expected."

The woman's expression seemed to alter.

"Then ye are not Lady Wrexham?"

35

"Indeed not!"

The woman came further into the room.

"Ye must pardon me for the mistake, ma'am," she said. "We hae but few visitors o' quality save guests for the castle, an' His Grace is kind enough tae notify us when they are expected."

"As I have said, His Grace is not expecting me," Iona answered, "but I would be grateful indeed for your assistance in reaching the castle."

The woman kept looking at her and Iona was well aware that her curiosity was growing.

" 'Tis strange," she said at length, "an ye must pardon ma presumption, ma'am, but I canna help thinkin' that I hae seen ye somewhere afore. 'Tis nae the first time ye hae come tae Skaig?"

"Indeed it is," Iona answered, "and my first visit to Scotland, though I am a Scot myself."

"There's nae doot about that when I looks at yer bonny face an' the colour o' yer hair," the woman replied. "Yer parents must hae had guid Scottish blood in them."

But Iona was not to be drawn into discussing her ancestry.

"I have come from France," she said. "The ship in which I travelled only reached Inverness last night."

"Frae France!" the woman said strangely. She crossed the room and shut the door. Then she turned and asked in a low voice:

"Hae ye heard aught o' *him* in France?"

There was no need to ask who "him" was, and Iona's heart warmed instantly towards the woman to whom the very mention of France meant news of the Prince. At the same time she knew she must be cautious. This might be a trap. Whatever she did, she must not jeopardise her position by unwary speech.

The woman saw the hesitation in her face, and as if she understood what Iona was feeling, she crossed the room to stand near her.

"Ye needna fash aboot me, ma'am," she said. "I was a Mackenzie afore I were wed. Ma brother was killed at Prestonpans, an' after Culloden the English set fire tae his hoose an' farm an' turned his wifie an' the bairns oot tae starve. Ma husband took nae part in the Risin', but once a Mackenzie always a Mackenzie, an' it's a Jacobite I'll be tae ma death."

There was no mistaking the woman's sincerity, and she

spoke with a passion which seemed strangely at variance with her austere, Puritan-like appearance. Impulsively Iona put out her hand and laid it on the older woman's arm.

"The Prince is well and in good heart," she said softly.

"God be praised!" the woman answered. "Maybe afore I die I'll see him come tae his ain agin."

She picked up the corner of her apron and wiped her eyes with it. Iona considered a moment and then, daring the question, she asked:

"Are there many that are still loyal to him round here?"

The woman glanced over her shoulder as if she suspected someone might be listening in the corner of the room.

"Aye," she answered, "but many are fear't an' the English hae spies everywhere."

"As bad as that?" Iona asked.

"An' worse," the woman said sharply. "Be careful wi' whom ye speak, ma'am, especially in the castle."

"In the castle?"

Iona repeated the words almost in a whisper. The woman nodded.

"You mean . . . with the Duke?" Iona questioned.

"I'm saying naething, for indeed I ken naething," the woman answered. "I'm only warnin' ye, keep guard on yer tongue, ma'am, when ye reach Skaig."

She turned briskly away and Iona thought that perhaps she was offended, but a second later she realized that the woman's quick ears had heard her husband approaching. When she opened the door, he entered the room.

"There's a vehicle ootside," he said gruffly. "If it's nae what yer ladyship's accustomed tae, dinna blame me. His Grace was expectin' ye taemorrow."

"This is nae Lady Wrexham, ye fule," his wife said sharply; "it's . . ." She turned toward Iona. "Indeed, ma'am, I hae forgotten. What were ye sayin' was yer name?"

Iona smiled.

"I did not mention my name," she replied, "but I am not Lady Wrexham."

She gave both the innkeeper and his wife a sweet smile, then moved with dignity from the parlour across the hall to the open door.

The coach they had produced for her was old and creaky, the upholstery stained and torn, the glass in the windows cracked and patched with paper. Indeed the whole conveyance was sadly in need of a coat of paint and

37

the handle was off one of the doors. But it had four wheels and as the two horses which drew it were sturdy, well-fed creatures, Iona was able to thank the innkeeper with a note of real sincerity in her voice.

She stepped into the coach, which smelt of musty hay. The coachman whipped up the horses and they were off. They turned north and were soon climbing uphill over a narrow track flanked by purple moors which rose higher and higher until they merged into rocky, barren mountains.

Soon after they started there was a sharp shower of rain which proved the roof of the coach to be anything but rainproof and the wet trickled through the ill-fitting and cracked window panes to run in little streams on to the floor. But when it was over, the sun came out again and the countryside seemed even more lovely than it had been before. There was a glistening radiance over sky and moor; and when Iona saw a golden eagle hovering against the translucent heavens. she felt as if her whole heart leapt out towards it and was one with the brilliance and beauty of this new world.

After an hour's pull uphill the coachman drew his horses to a standstill. Iona put her head out of the window.

"Where are we?" she asked.

In answer the man pointed with a whip.

"Yon's the castle," he answered.

Iona stared in the direction in which he pointed and turning the handle of the door, got out.

For a moment the wind took her by surprise. It seemed as if it would carry her off her feet. It swept her cloak around her, the sharp sting in its violence making Iona feel as if she were dressed in paper; and then what she saw below made her catch her breath and forget everything else.

She stood on the summit of a hill, and the road wound downwards to a great loch bounded by mountains, their steep sides reflected in the still water. The rays of the setting sun pointed across the centre of the loch like a finger of light, turning to sparkling gold the turrets and towers and massive keep of a castle. Built on an island and joined only to the mainland by a narrow bridge, it appeared to Iona at that moment to be a fairy palace of almost ethereal loveliness.

It stood there proudly, not overawed or dwarfed by the

height and majesty of the surrounding mountains, its massive stone bastions seeming a part of the landscape.

How long Iona stood staring at the castle she had no idea. She was conscious only of some strange emotion within herself, something she did not understand, but which stirred her to the very depths of her soul.

The wild beauty of the whole scene, the dark bareness of the mountains, the depth, length and breadth of the loch and the golden glory of the castle itself seemed to impress themselves into her consciousness so that she could forget everything but her sense of kinship. It was the coachman who recalled her to the urgencies which lay ahead.

"Whit aboot gettin' along, mistress?" he asked, and Iona climbed back into the coach.

Slowly, the horses holding back the heavy vehicle with difficulty, they descended. The road wound backwards and forwards across the heather-covered hillside. As they dropped lower, the mountains seemed to get higher. They were no longer in the sunshine. It was dark, and one had to look upwards towards the sky for light.

They drew nearer and nearer still to the bridge connecting the island with the mainland; and when at last Iona heard the horses' hoofs clatter over it and looked out to see the castle towering above her, she felt the blood drain from her face and almost a paralysis sweep over her.

It was bigger, far bigger and far more frightening than it had appeared from the top of the mountain. They passed under a watch tower and into a great courtyard, and now the castle was no longer golden and ethereal. The walls were grey and foreboding, the windows were narrow, some of them mere arrow slits in the massive towers.

The coach stopped. At the top of a flight of stone steps was a huge oak door studded with iron nails. It was closed and Iona had a sense of panic. She must go back! She could not go through with this! It had been easy enough in France to agree to arrive unannounced and present her credentials. Colonel Brett had thought she was more likely to gain an entrance this way than if she wrote to the Duke and waited at some adjacent town or inn for his reply.

It had seemed easy to be daring when they had talked about it at a comfortable distance, but it was hard to do what they had agreed now that the moment had come to put their plans into action.

Iona sat very still in the coach, her fingers pressed

together as if she must take courage from herself. The coachman descended and pulled at the bell-chain hanging on one side of the door. Minutes passed; then at last the door swung open and the coachman let down the steps for Iona to alight. Iona opened her lips to speak; but when her voice came it sounded strange even to her own ears.

"Leave my trunk on the coach," she said. "I may wish to return."

The man looked surprised, but Iona gave him no time to answer. She stepped in through the front door and the flunkey closed it behind her.

"Your pleasure, ma'am?" he inquired.

"I have called to see . . . the Duchess," Iona replied.

She meant to ask for the Duke, but at the last moment her heart failed her. It would be easier to talk with a woman—especially a woman who might still be grieving for a child she had lost many years ago.

The servant preceded Iona through a great hall and up a magnificent staircase then opened a door off a wide landing hung with tapestries.

"Your name, ma'am?"

Iona had been anticipating this question.

"Will you tell Her Grace that I have come from France especially to wait on her. My name would convey nothing."

The servant bowed and Iona was alone. She was in a huge room, and even though its size and magnificence awed her, she could not help responding to the beauty of its furnishings. Never in her whole life had she seen anything to equal the heavy velvet hangings of crimson and gold or the highbacked needlework chairs, the polished furniture, the great gilt mirrors and fine portraits in carved and decorated frames. Four big windows reaching almost from ceiling to floor opened out on a balcony, and beyond Iona could see the loch, misty now in the evening twilight, the mountains black against the sable sky.

She stood waiting, too tense to sit, too frightened even to move from the position she had first taken up on entering the room. Then the door opened. She gave a little gasp and turned towards it, only to see not a woman, as she expected, but two footmen resplendent in claret-covered livery with silver buttons, bearing lighted tapers.

There was a massive crystal chandelier hanging from the centre of the room. At the footmen's touch each candle sprang into life. There were candles too in glittering crystal sconces on either side of the mantelpiece and on the other walls.

The footmen moved quickly and silently. When the candles were lit, they drew the curtains, shook up the cushions and one man placed a log on the fire before they withdrew. Iona felt as if she must be invisible for they did not even glance at her, intent only on arranging the room as if they were setting a stage for a drama that had not yet begun.

Now that the curtains were drawn, she felt enclosed, a prisoner. Yet it was impossible not to appreciate the beauty of the prison. For the first time she thought of her own appearance. A few steps brought her to a gilt table above which hung a mirror. It was carved with cupids supporting a crown and the glass was slightly iridescent with age, but Iona could see herself clearly.

Her face was small and white beneath her dark hood, yet the curling riotousness of her hair, which would never lie smooth, caught the light of the candles and gleamed vivid as a flame against her forehead. Her eyes were very wide, the pupils dilated. Her lips were red—a vivid contrast to the pallor of her face.

Iona gave a little sigh. She wished she dare open the small packet which contained the miniature and compare it with her own reflection here in the castle. Had they been mistaken in thinking there was some resemblance? Was it just imagination and the wish for an excuse to bring her over here? A thousand fears seemed to whisper themselves in her ears. The whole scheme seemed at this moment ridiculous and crazy. Perhaps this very night she would be unmasked and taken to the prison at Fort Augustus. Then she stilled her imaginings. She was afraid of prison, but even more afraid of failing the Prince and those who trusted her.

She moved from the mirror across the room to where she had first stood. At any moment now the Duchess might be coming to her. At least she had not refused to see her! Now for the first time Iona thought of the Duchess as a person. Until now she had been so intent on thinking of the Duke because of his importance to the Cause that she had given little thought to this woman whose daughter she must pretend to be.

Quite suddenly she was ashamed. Supposing the Duchess believed her story, supposing she welcomed her with joy as the child she had mourned. Could anything be more

41

cruel, more bestial than to deceive a mother? Iona was in that instant horrified at what she was about to do. It was wrong, wrong, because her pretence might hurt and deceive another woman!

Wildly Iona looked round her as if for some way of escape. It was then that the double doors at the far end of the room were opened by two footmen, who bowed as a woman passed between them.

For a second Iona could not look up. Her hands were clenched together tightly and she felt as if her heart lay heavy as a stone in the centre of her body. At last she forced herself to raise her eyes.

She had a quick impression of a slight figure with powdered hair dressed high in the latest fashion, of a thin face with a down-turned, petulant mouth, of glittering jewels, of rustling silks and velvet bows, and of long white fingers holding a lace handkerchief; then confused she swept the ground in a deep curtsey.

Only as she rose was she aware that she was looking into a face which bore no resemblance whatsoever to the miniature. The Duchess scrutinised her with narrowed eyes.

"They told me you had come from France," she said, "I was expecting someone else. Who are you?"

There was a sharp note in her voice which better than anything else seemed to bring Iona to her senses. Her heart-searchings and fears were swept away. Here was no bereaved mother to be deceived and hoaxed. There had been a mistake somewhere, what it was she did not know, but of one thing she was certain—the sharp, metallic note of the Duchess's voice hid no aching, anxious heart.

Resolutely Iona spoke up.

"I hope you will forgive my troubling you, ma'am, but I have come to Skaig Castle with a strange story and one to which I believe in justice you will grant a hearing."

"They said you came from France," the Duchess repeated. "You have a special message for me? An introduction?"

There was something insistent about her questions. Iona shook her head.

"No, ma'am, I have no introduction. I know no one in France who has the honour of your acquaintance."

The Duchess made an impatient gesture as she turned and walked across the room to sit herself in a high-backed chair.

"It is intolerable that I should be deceived by such

messages," she said. "Strangers are not admitted to my presence without good reason."

"Please believe me, ma'am, when I say that I have good reason," Iona answered. "Here is a letter which I would beg Your Grace to read. I have also two articles to show you."

"A letter? Then you have been sent to me?" the Duchess said eagerly. "Who is it from?"

"A priest, ma'am. Father Quintin by name."

The Duchess sank back in her chair and the eagerness faded from her face.

"I never heard of him," she said petulantly. "Well, since you are here, you had best explain your presence and be quick about it for we dine at six o'clock."

"Yes, ma'am."

Iona was calm now. Her mind was clear. Perhaps the Duchess had once been good-looking, but any beauty she possessed had faded and her whole face contained only a querulous expression of nervous irritation. Her eyes were sunk in her head and there were deep lines from her pinched nose to the corners of her thin lips. Unattractive, despite the elaborate coiffure and expensive gown, it was obvious that the Duchess was nevertheless but a middle-aged woman, perhaps in her early forties.

Iona knew now that there had been some mistake. It was impossible for this to be the mother of the child who had been drowned, and she remembered Hector's warning that Colonel Brett was not always accurate about details.

"Well, hurry, girl," the Duchess commanded, "and explain your business."

"Seventeen years ago," Iona said quietly, "the Duke of Arkrae's yacht was sunk in the English Channel."

"That is true enough," the Duchess interrupted. "What of it?"

"Aboard that yacht," Iona went on, "there was the Duke's little daughter, Lady Elspeth MacCraggan. She was, I think, aged three at the time."

"That is correct," the Duchess agreed.

"The Duke believed that his daughter was drowned that night at sea," Iona continued, "but in actual fact the child's nurse—Jeannie MacLeod—and the Duke's valet escaped in a boat to the French shore. The child went with them. I have evidence here in this letter which gives me to think that I am that child."

The Duchess stared at her.

43

"A nonsensical suggestion," she snapped. "The child was drowned."

"Was her body recovered?" Iona asked.

The Duchess put out her hand.

"Let me see that letter."

Iona handed it to her. The Duchess slit open the envelope and drew out the closely written sheets of paper. She read them through carefully, then lifted a small gold bell from the table beside her. It made a musical tinkle as she shook it. She looked again at the sheets of paper in her hand and then up at Iona.

"A pretty story!" she sneered. "You have a great deal to gain if this is proved to be the truth."

"I suppose so," Iona agreed gravely.

"There is no need to look so innocent," the Duchess said sarcastically. "You are doubtless well aware that the eldest daughter of the Duke of Arkrae on reaching twenty-one inherits special privileges and a fortune. Now that I think of it, I wonder there have not been more claimants to be the poor lost Lady Elspeth."

Her tone brought the blood to Iona's cheeks. She felt incensed by it and realised with a sudden flash of humour that she was genuinely offended at the Duchess's attitude.

A footman came to the Duchess's side.

"Inform His Grace I should be grateful of his presence here," the Duchess said.

The footman bowed and went from the room. Iona felt her heart begin to beat a little quicker. Now at last she would see the Duke, see the man who was of such vital importance to the Prince.

They waited in silence. The Duchess did not speak again and Iona felt it would be presumptuous for her to say anything. She still stood, for she had not been invited to sit. Uncomfortable in the heat of the fire, she pulled back the hood from her head and was conscious, as she did so, of the contrast between herself, plainly dressed, her red curls rioting rebelliously over her small head, and the Duchess's elegant gown and elaborately waved and powdered hair. There was a chain of emeralds and diamonds arranged by skilful fingers on the Duchess's coiffure and they matched the wide necklace of emeralds and diamonds which was clasped round her thin neck.

A sudden idea presented itself to Iona's mind. Might this lady be the Duke's wife? But surely, she answered herself, the Duchess was too old for the Duke if Colonel Brett was right in supposing him to be about thirty? Yet men did marry women older than themselves. If this then was the reigning Duchess, was there a Dowager Duchess who was the mother of Lady Elspeth? How many possibilities there were, how many problems? And again Iona remembered Hector's warning.

The door at the end of the room was opening. She felt her eyes drawn towards it and awaited expectantly the Duke's entry into the room. She saw a tall, broad-shouldered figure wearing a coat of blue velvet embroidered with silver and sparkling with decorations. His hair was powdered and it was perhaps this last fact which for a moment blinded Iona to the truth. Then, as he came nearer, crossing the room slowly with an unhurried dignity, she recognised him: recognised the handsome features, the cold aloof air, the dignity which was almost an arrogance and the irresistible authority which once before had made her obey his wordless command.

It was difficult for her to prevent herself from giving a cry of astonishment. Incredible though it seemed, the Duke was the tall stranger who had rescued her from the odious attentions of the amorous French *roué*.

For a second she thought wildly that already her plot was discovered. He had been in France, he was here. He knew then why she had come, what planning and scheming was behind her visit. Then desperately she pulled herself together. It was a coincidence, a chance encounter, that was all. The Duke could not have known where she was going that evening and had indeed shown little interest in her. He performed an act of mercy and that was all.

From a long distance it seemed to Iona she could hear the Duchess's voice.

"I have something to show you, Ewan," she said. "It is a letter brought by this girl from France purporting to show that she is your half-sister, Elspeth, who was drowned seventeen years ago."

The Duke took the letter which the Duchess held out to him, but did not look at it; instead, he looked at Iona.

It seemed to her there was no recognition in his eyes and she said nothing. She only met his glance, her head thrown back a little because he was so tall, her gaze steady beneath his, though something quivered within her.

"What is your name?" he asked.

His voice was quiet and courteous.

"I have been called Iona."

Her answer seemed to satisfy him and he looked away from her to the sheets of paper he held in his hand. Impatiently the Duchess broke in.

"It is, of course, a preposterous tale," she said. "Elspeth was drowned, there is surely no doubt about that? Who is this Jeannie MacLeod? I have never heard of her."

The Duke raised his eyes from the paper.

"There is no reason why you should have," he said. "She was my sister's nurse—and mine."

The Duchess shrugged her shoulders petulantly. The Duke merely glanced at her and then turned to Iona.

"Won't you sit down?" he asked. "If you have indeed come from France, you must be fatigued for it is a tiring journey."

With a gesture of his hand he indicated a chair opposite the Duchess beside the fireplace. Iona went to it, hoping that she held herself gracefully. She sat down. The Duke stood with his back to the fire between the two women and read the letter carefully, a quizzing-glass raised to his eye. When he had finished, he folded the pages together.

"It speaks here of a miniature," he said. "You have it with you?"

Iona held out to him the little packet containing both the miniature and the bracelet. The Duke opened it and took out the miniature, then stared at it for some seconds.

"Whom does it portray?" the Duchess inquired. "Let me see."

"It is a miniature of my grandmother," the Duke said quietly. "I cannot remember seeing it before but it is a good likeness. There is a portrait of her with which you can compare it in the State Dining-room."

The Duchess took the miniature from his hands, looked at it and then across at Iona.

"I suppose," she said slowly and reluctantly, "that there is a . . ."

". . . distinct resemblance." the Duke finished.

"Then. . . ." the Duchess began, and stopped. "But this is nonsensical. We must have more proof of this."

"Of course! Who has suggested otherwise?"

The Duke turned to Iona.

"I think we should express our thanks to you for coming all this way from France with information which is, of course, of the greatest interest to me and my family, and I would ask you to accept the hospitality of Skaig while investigations are made and your claim established. You will be aware that this will take time, but I can only hope that it will give us the opportunity of getting to know each other."

"But, Ewan . . ." the Duchess protested, "aren't you assuming that this girl of whom we know nothing is indeed Elspeth?"

"I am assuming nothing," the Duke replied. "This lady has made a claim which appears to be, on the face of it, a very reasonable one. It is for our attorneys to examine the proofs of its authenticity. In the meantime this lady will, I hope, accept our invitation."

Iona found her voice.

"I thank Your Grace," she said, "but perhaps under the circumstances it would be better for me to return to the inn until you have decided what would be the best course to pursue. I have kept the coach which conveyed me here and it can take me back."

She was conscious as she spoke of going against Colonel Brett's instructions, but somehow she felt that she could not force herself upon the Duchess. Hospitality, unless freely given, would stifle her. It was then that the Duke smiled. To Iona's surprise it transformed his face. The coldness vanished and he looked in that second younger and far more human.

"I cannot recommend the inn at Fort Augustus," he said. "You had best stay with us at least until you have time to rest after your journey."

"Thank you," Iona said.

The Duchess got to her feet.

"I fail to understand your attitude, Ewan," she said. "It seems to me all very peculiar. And what, may I ask, are we to call this . . . this person until we learn if she is indeed your half-sister or an imposter?"

Again the Duke smiled.

"This lady has already told us her name, my dear, and to be sure it is a very charming and a very Scottish name. To us, for the time being, she will be Miss Iona from . . . Paris."

He looked at Iona as he spoke and now she knew that he had not forgotten. He, too, remembered that strange encounter in Paris.

4

My Lady Wrexham was bored. She shut her eyes against the swaying of the coach, but her mind was active and she found it impossible to relax. It seemed to her that she had been jolting over bad roads, fording swollen rivers and being held up by floods for an endless length of time. She felt bruised and battered and utterly fatigued, and her red lips tightened ominously as her head rested against the blue satin upholstery of her coach—a sign, her maid thought, watching her timidly from the other side of the coach, that boded ill for somebody.

A bad rut in the road caused the coach to bump more than usual and Beatrice Wrexham sat bolt upright.

"A plague on it!" she exclaimed. "Will this journey never end?"

"The coachman was certain that we should reach Aviemore by five o'clock, m'lady," the maid ventured timidly.

"Aviemore!" Lady Wrexham made the name sound like a swear-word. "We have many miles to go beyond Aviemore and we are a day late as it is."

"The floods were uncommon bad in Yorkshire, m'lady."

"I know that, you fool. Heaven knows why I was insane enough to undertake a journey such as this."

Beatrice Wrexham threw herself petulantly into the corner of the carriage. She—as well as Heaven—knew the answer to her own question. The reason she had undertaken the long journey from London to Scotland was because, success or failure, what she would receive would make it worth while.

Yet now she wondered if any sum of money, however vast, or any jewel, however valuable, was worth the endless exhausting monotony of being a traveller. Few people journeyed in such luxury; but then, if Beatrice Wrexham, the most beautiful and by far the most notorious woman in England, could not command comfort, who could?

Beatrice yawned; then taking a small gold-framed mirror from her reticule, she scrutinised her face. She might be tired, but her reflection showed no sign of it. There was no doubt that she was beautiful. The milk-white skin, the deep blue of her eyes, the almost classical perfection of her features seemed to have no flaw in them, and her hair, which was the colour of ripe corn, rippled, unpowdered for the journey, high upon her head, making a halo for the exquisite heart-shaped contour of her face.

Yes, she was beautiful! But how cleverly and successfully had she exploited that beauty!

Beatrice yawned again, her red lips parted to reveal her even, pearly teeth. She held out the mirror to the maid.

"Put it away, woman," she said sharply, "and take good care of it. I am told that Scotland is full of thieves and robbers."

"Oh, m'lady, are our lives likely to be in danger?" the woman quavered.

"I swear I would welcome danger at this moment," Lady Wrexham answered, "if it did ought to relieve my ennui."

The maid sniffed and quivered with fright at the thought of what lay ahead of them, but Beatrice Wrexham closed her eyes again and for a moment there was a faint smile on her lips. She had never been afraid of danger. She had supreme belief that her own plausible tongue and the enticement of her beautiful body would carry her through any difficulty, however perilous, however unpleasant.

And she had just cause for such confidence. For ten years she had used her womanhood as a man might use his sword—a weapon to gain her whatsoever she desired.

At twenty-five Beatrice had come to the full blossoming of her beauty. As she closed her eyes, she could see herself as a child of fifteen, innocent, unsophisticated and unpolished, yet already lovely and with a promise of still more beauty to come.

Her mother had brought her to the Court of St. James', openly defying her father's wishes in the matter. He was an unimportant, impoverished country squire, the owner of a dilapidated manor and a few acres of land in Kent. Beatrice had neither noble birth nor wealth to assist her, but she had an ambitious mother and a magnetic, irresistible beauty.

Her mother was friendly with one of the Queen's ladies-in-waiting; and presuming on that friendship, she pleaded and implored the unfortunate lady until she obtained permission to bring Beatrice to St. James's.

Beatrice might have been innocent in some ways at fifteen, but she would have been deaf and an idiot if she had not understood very clearly and without pretence what her mother desired for her.

They had taken a stage-coach from Sevenoaks to London as they were too poor to afford a postchaise. Every penny they could scrape together or borrow from their equally impecunious relations had been expended on Beatrice's wardrobe. Even then they were heavily in debt, but supremely confident that the future would enable them to pay their dues.

They were not mistaken. Beatrice's beauty did not go unnoticed and within a few weeks of their arrival in London it was obvious that her most eligible admirer was Lord Wrexham. That he was over sixty, a licentious, dissolute man, was of no consequence. Younger men waited on Beatrice, flattered her and avowed themselves to be her most devoted slave, but the majority were seeking a bride with a dowry. Lord Wrexham could not only afford to marry, he was wealthy enough to be a matrimonial catch. The fact that he had sworn, when his third wife died ten years earlier, never to take another did not depress either Beatrice or her mother.

They played their cards carefully. Lord Wrexham was encouraged to call and Beatrice was paraded before him. He was tantalised and tempted by her beauty, but he soon realised that the price of making her his was the cost of a plain, gold wedding ring.

His lordship paid and was the first of Beatrice's triumphs, although by no means the last. Those who were shocked by the marriage and the disparity of age between the bride and the groom, and who knew the unsavoury reputation of the latter, foretold the future with gloom. They were disappointed. Beatrice showed no sign of being disgusted or affronted by her husband's licentious ways. Gorgeously dressed, wearing fabulous jewels which even the Queen would have been proud to own, she became the toast of London.

For so young a girl her self-assurance was phenomenal. Her beautiful face was a mask to hide her real feelings, whatever they might be. There were those who said that Wrexham, entranced by his young bride and converted by her innocent purity, had turned over a new leaf; there were others who averred that he had merely drawn her into the vortex of sin and vice in which he himself wallowed.

It was hard to know the truth. One thing only was certain—Lady Wrexham enjoyed her position as the wife of a nobleman.

Four years later Lord Wrexham suffered a stroke. He retired to his country seat, but his wife did not accompany him. She remained in London and there were those who said that she was preparing to make a much more important marriage as soon as she became a widow.

But Lord Wrexham did not die; he remained in the country half paralysed, his senses somewhat impaired, enjoying, it was true, many comforts but not the companionship of his wife.

Beatrice Wrexham began to be talked of in a hushed voice. It was not only scandal which surrounded her, it was the aroma of intrigue. Still the most beautiful and the most extravagantly dressed woman in London, she appeared to demand more of life than the social gaiety of Ball, Masque and Rout. Her ambition was insatiable. Once she had craved money, jewels and a title, now she wanted much more—that insidious, delectable, but dangerous possession of all—power.

It was noticeable that among the beauties at court, Beatrice was unique in that she chose her lovers not for their physical attributes, but because they were of political consequence.

The ladder Beatrice had chosen to climb was by no means an easy one, but beneath her soft yielding femininity lay a backbone of steel. Slowly, step by step, she climbed until with the triumphant ecstasy of one who reaches the summit of a mountain, she captured the attention of the Marquis of Severn. Earl Marshal and Hereditary Marshal of England, the Marquis was also the King's chief adviser. He was a clever, ruthless and extremely able man, and George II with his heart and his interests firmly fixed in his native Hanover, was content to leave State affairs in Severn's capable hands. The Marquis's influence was everywhere, his position unequalled.

Beatrice became friendly, too friendly some people said, with the aide-de-camp. Having learned from him who were Severn's enemies, she made it her business to discover certain information about them and had it conveyed to the Marquis with her compliments.

51

The Marquis's life had been singularly barren of women. Married when he was quite young to a simple but dull young woman of noble birth, his family consisted of two sons and three daughters. The Marchioness was an admirable housekeeper and an excellent mother. The family place in Hertfordshire was kept up with the pomp and splendour which most people averred surpassed any royal palace and easily eclipsed the drab formality of the Court at St. James's.

But the Marchioness seldom came to London, while pressure of State affairs made it difficult for the Marquis to visit his country seat save at irregular intervals. Strangely enough, there was little evidence of any feminine influence at Severn House in Berkeley Square, for the Marquis was happiest when immersed in the machinations of statecraft and had a contempt for the frivolous, empty-headed chatter of fashionable society.

He liked the company of men, he enjoyed intrigue as other men might enjoy a game of faro. He was singularly astute and he was well aware that Beatrice was stalking him as an animal stalks its prey. He watched her with amusement and when finally he took her in his arms, she was uncertain whether he had succumbed to her beauty or had decided that she was too useful for him to lose.

It was enough in some ways to know that she could hold him, the most powerful and most feared man in England, but at times it had its disadvantages.

The Marquis was no voluptuary as Lord Wrexham had been, to be beguiled with exotic delights and to be enticed into the whirlpool of passion. If Beatrice worked hard to get him, she worked much harder to keep him. He was insatiable in his desire for knowledge of other people. His agents and informers were spread like a spider's web across the length and breadth of England, but now his tentacles were reaching out towards Scotland.

Beatrice had been taken by surprise when the Marquis had sent for her and told her that he wished her to visit Skaig Castle. She had planned various amusements for the month of August, among them a visit to Italy. But the Marquis had swept her plans aside without even listening to them.

"Arkrae is important," he said. "I have reason to believe that the Jacobites are trying to gain access to him. If he should decide to support the Pretender, the consequences might be serious."

"What do you know of him?" Beatrice asked.

"He is young, handsome and wealthy. That at least should make your journey worth while, my dear," he said, a faint smile twisting his hard lips.

Beatrice turned her shoulder to him petulantly. She had been about to leave for a Ball when he had demanded her presence. She was dressed in a gown of shimmering silver brocade trimmed with lace and velvet ribbons. There was a fabulous necklace of sapphires and diamonds round her neck, and the same stones glittered in her ears and on her wrists. Her beauty was almost breathtaking as she stood there, her big eyes raised to his. But the Marquis seemed hardly to see her.

"Yes, you should be able to manage Arkrae," he said reflectively.

Beatrice pouted a little.

"And if he is pliable, what do you want of him?"

"His assurance of absolute loyalty to the throne, his enmity towards the Pretender and all those who support him."

"And when he has promised me that, I can come home?"

"Of course."

"And you will miss me?"

The very feminine question seemed to remind the Marquis that he was dealing with a woman. He put out his hand and put it under her chin, then he tilted back her head and looked into her eyes.

"I shall not allow myself to think of you," he said quietly, "or I might be jealous."

It was the most revealing thing he had ever said to her and she was unable to prevent the elation she felt at his words from shining in her eyes. He saw she was triumphant at what she imagined was a revelation of weakness, and he laughed.

"One day, my dear, you may fall in love," he said. "It might be an amusing experience."

"But I am in love," Beatrice protested, "with you."

The Marquis shook his head.

"You are in love with what I stand for and what I can give you."

She would have protested, but he lifted his hand to silence the words which came to her lips.

"You have not yet asked what payment there will be for this journey."

Beatrice dimpled at him.

"If I told you I was not interested, you would not believe me."

It was rogue speaking to rogue, and the understanding which passed between them seemed to draw them closer. The Marquis named a sum which made even Beatrice looked surprised.

"And also those emeralds which belonged to my grandmother. The corsage is considered by those who know to be exceptionally fine and of some considerable value."

Beatrice was excited. She had wanted the emeralds for a long time. She gave a little exclamation of delight, but the Marquis interrupted her.

"There is, however, a condition attached to the emeralds. They are yours if you bring me the 'Tears of Torrish'."

"The 'Tears of Torrish'? What are they?"

"A necklace of diamonds, a magnificent collet given by old Lady Torrish to the Prince on the eve of the battle of Culloden. After the battle they vanished, but they did not accompany the Prince to France. Recently I have had information that the Pretender's spies are making inquiries about the necklace, and a few days ago a whisper came to my ears that the 'Tears' may be at Skaig. It was that which decided me, Beatrice, to send you on this very difficult mission."

"I should be flattered, I suppose; but the idea of visiting an uncivilised country so many miles away has few attractions for me."

"You forget the Duke," the Marquis said with a smile.

Beatrice shrugged her white shoulders.

"He is doubtless as uncivilised and crude as the rest of his countrymen."

"I think you will not be disappointed when you see him," the Marquis said; "and while fulfilling the first part of your task, do not forget the second."

"But why are those diamonds, whatever they are called, so important?"

The Marquis turned suddenly and she saw the steel in his eyes.

"Because diamonds mean gold and gold in the Pretender's hands means weapons—weapons and soldiers, and the chance of another rebellion. We have defeated him once, we have driven him into exile, we have killed and

54

tortured and rendered homeless those who followed him; and yet, fanatical fools that they are, the Scots still wait for his return and there are those who are ready to rise again and follow him."

The Marquis's voice seemed to echo round the room. Beatrice, alive to his every mood, sensitive to the merest inflection of his voice, thought she had never seen him so moved before. She must obey him, she knew that; but even as she accepted his command, she shivered and felt strangely perturbed.

In her mind's eye she saw the long road leading north and at the end of it a darkness, a cloud sombre and somehow threatening. But she knew it was useless to argue. If she failed in what she set out to do, the Marquis might forgive her; but if she refused his command—for that there would be no forgiveness!

She left him and went to the Ball, and when later that night he visited her and her head lay against his shoulder, she whispered:

"Why do you send me away from you? I am happy and so, I think, are you. Must we risk our happiness?"

He silenced her with a kiss, but his lips, passionate and possessive, were also masterful to the point of tyranny. She knew then that any plea she might make was useless. Once the Marquis had set his course, no one on earth could make him change it.

The long lonely hours in the coach had given Beatrice time to think. For the first time she considered her life as a whole, not just as hours and days to be lived fully and excitingly as she schemed and plotted towards some particular objective. For the first time she asked herself where her adventuring would finally lead her—what lay ahead? She had gained so much, achieved in a few years more than most women attained in a lifetime; yet now she wondered if she had missed something by the very speed at which she had traveled. Had the Marquis been right when he inferred that she had never been in love?

She had known delirious moments of passion which had seemed to burn their way through her body like a flame, but which like a flame had died away to ashes. She had been loved by a hundred men, but had she ever really loved one of them in return? She asked herself the question, but she did not know the answer.

Again she saw herself at fifteen, coming to London, her heart beating quickly beneath the budding outlines of her breasts, her eyes starry with anticipation, her lips parted. She had expected so much of life. She had dreamt that there was a man somewhere—a Prince Charming—who would awaken her heart. She had thought that she would know him instantly, that she would surrender herself to him in rapture, and at his touch she would savour heaven.

How very far from her imaginings had been reality. She recalled Lord Wrexham on their wedding night—his eyes bright with lust—leering at her from a network of wrinkles, his thin sensuous lips wet, his old hands outstretched. . . .

A deep sigh seemed to echo from the very depths of Beatrice's soul. The voice of her maid interrupted her reverie.

"I think we have reached Aviemore, m'lady."

Beatrice opened her eyes. She saw several grey stone crofts, and a crowd of children in tattered clothing with bare feet who stared open-mouthed at the splendour of the coach and its attendants.

The postilions riding ahead turned into the courtyard of an inn, the coach followed them, the opening so narrow that the wheels almost scraped the sides of the walls. Ostlers came running, the landlord bowing an obsequious welcome as he hurried to the door.

Pulling her ermine-lined pelisse around her, for the air was chilly, Beatrice slowly descended the steps of the coach.

"You were expecting me?" she asked the landlord in a haughty manner.

"Your ladyship's bedchamber has been ready these last two days," he replied.

"The roads were so excruciatingly bad that we were delayed," Beatrice said.

She swept in at the door of the inn, the width of her silk gown brushing against the side posts.

"See that dinner and the best wine in your cellar are served to me immediately in my sitting-room," she said.

The landlord coughed and stammered.

"Your ladyship's pardon, but we were expecting your ladyship yesterday. All was prepared and the fire was lit, the dinner was half cooked, but your ladyship didn't come. We thought you might be further delayed and . . . and that your ladyship would understand and . . . be gracious."

"What are you trying to say, my good man?" Beatrice asked sharply.

"The private sitting-room, m'lady . . . it was reserved for you but a gentleman came but a few hours back . . . a gentleman who said."

"Turn him out," Beatrice said briefly.

"But, m'lady, he is a gentleman of quality, a nobleman, of the greatest import in this part of the world. If your ladyship would only understand, it is impossible for me."

Sweating with discomfort, the landlord failed to complete the sentence, his words seeming to trail away into an incoherent whisper. Beatrice drew herself up. She was about to be angry with an anger which her servants well knew could annihilate those who encountered it. Then suddenly she changed her mind. She had been alone for so many days that "a gentleman of quality", "a nobleman", might well prove a distraction.

She hesitated, and the landlord, seeing her hesitation, felt relief surge over him.

"This gentleman . . ." Beatrice asked, "he is young?"

"Indeed he is, m'lady. Young and of handsome countenance. If your ladyship would only condescend."

"Her ladyship will," Beatrice said. "Pray give the gentleman in question my compliments and ask him if he will do me the favour of dining with me."

She turned and went upstairs. The chambermaids were sent scurrying to and fro as soon as she reached the bedroom.

"More candles for her ladyship!" "More towels for her ladyship!" "Send up her ladyship's trunks!" "Another blanket for her ladyship's bed!" "A bottle of wine for her ladyship immediately!"

The inn seemed to buzz with the voice of retainers like a beehive that has been disturbed.

Beatrice, washed and robed in a dress of oyster-tinted satin, sat at the small muslin-frilled dressing-table and sipped a goblet of wine while her maid dressed her hair.

"A simple style, woman," she said crossly. "For God's sake use your intelligence if you have any. I have no wish that this stranger should imagine that I bedeck myself for him. And now my pearls."

The maid opened the massive jewel box with difficulty. There, lying in velvet, was a priceless collection of gems, each one a tribute to Beatrice's beauty. She took up a great rope of pearls.

"I will wear these," she said, "and the pearl earrings."

She put a patch—a tiny star—near the corner of her

mouth; it was fascinating and provocative against the magnolia texture of her skin, and for a second her red lips smiled at her own reflection. Perhaps this nobleman might relieve her boredom and the inescapable depression which had followed her peregrinations into the past. How foolish she had been to try and recapture the thoughts and feelings of an inexperienced, idealistic child! What had she to regret? She had beauty, wealth and influence! What more could she ask, what more had life to offer?

Beatrice finished her glass of wine and rose from the dressing-table. Slowly, her skirts rustling silkily against the dark stair boards, she descended to the private sitting-room. It was a small panelled room, dark with age and, as she well knew, a perfect background for the shining gold of her hair and the opalescent sheen of her gown.

She moved regally into the centre of the room. A man was seated before a big log fire, his feet stretched out. As he heard Beatrice enter, he rose hastily to his feet. Her eyes flickered over him, noting the rich embroidary on his coat, the sparkle of his buttons, the diamond brooch at his throat. She raised her eyes to his face.

Yes, he was young. The landlord had not lied. He was young, and not unattractive. She had always thought that her fair beauty was best offset by dark, sardonic man. She held out her hand and felt his lips on her fingers.

"You will honour me by being my guest, sir?"

The nobleman straightened himself. He was taller than Beatrice, and after days of being alone she noticed with satisfaction the undisguised admiration in his eyes.

"On the contrary, madam, I beseech you to honour me. I have presumed to order dinner, and I pray that you will sample the wine that I have brought with me. This poor hostelry has nothing worthy of your patronage."

Beatrice laughed, and seated herself beside the fire.

"I infer that you travel in comfort, sir."

"Invariably," was the reply, "but most especially so when there is a reason for my journey, a reason such as dinner with the most beautiful woman in England."

Beatrice raised her eyebrows.

"Can it possibly be that you were expecting me?"

"It is indeed. I waited for you last night in Inverness, but when you did not come I journeyed here with all possible dispatch. I feared an accident."

"I am flattered at such attention," Beatrice said. "May I know your name, sir?"

"But of course! We have overlooked the formality of introduction. May I present myself, Lord Niall MacCraggan, at your service."

He bowed.

"Then of course you know who I am," Beatrice said, "without my telling you. It was most gracious on the part of your brother to have sent you to meet me."

Lord Niall's dark eyes met hers.

"No one has sent me. In truth my brother has no knowledge of my intention to intercept your ladyship."

"Really?"

Beatrice's surprise was not simulated.

"No, I wanted to meet you, Lady Wrexham; but above all things I wanted to talk with you before you reached Skaig. I think there is much that we might say to each other . . . of advantage to both."

Beatrice's eyes narrowed. There was a hidden meaning in his voice and it did not escape her.

"Shall we dine first?" she asked quietly.

"But of course," he replied. "You must be fatigued."

He rang the bell and almost immediately food was brought to the table.

Lord Niall had ordered cleverly. The meal was simple and not beyond the culinary efforts of the inn cook; but each dish had a special quality about it, and the wine that his lordship had brought with him surpassed anything Beatrice had ever sampled even in London.

"I had not realised until now how hungry I am," she said approvingly.

When the meal was finished, the servants withdrew and Beatrice crossed the room to an armchair by the fire.

"May I offer you a glass of brandy?" Lord Niall asked.

He poured it out and Beatrice took the goblet from his hand. His fingers touched hers and looked down in to her face.

"You are far lovelier than I remembered," he said.

"You have seen me before then?" she asked, her eyes searching his strange, dark, somewhat secretive face to recall it to her memory.

"Yes, I have seen you in London," Lord Niall replied. "I have watched you in your box at the opera on two occasions."

"But we have never met?"

"Never until now."

He turned to the table and poured himself out a glass of brandy.

"My stepmother told me she had a letter from you suggesting a visit to Skaig Castle. I was surprised."

"I have always wanted to visit Scotland," Beatrice said somewhat unconvincingly, "and the beauties of Skaig are talked about even at St. James's."

Lord Niall smiled.

"Shall we be frank with each other, you and I?"

"Why not?" Beatrice replied lightly.

"I would hate you to think me a fool," Lord Niall said. "I know why you are here."

"You do?" Beatrice questioned.

"My brother's position in the Highlands concerns two people very deeply. One is the Pretender, Charles Stuart, the other the Marquis of Severn. I will not say His Majesty, King George II for I doubt if he is aware even of my brother's existence."

Beatrice was interested and intrigued, but she had no intention of declaring her own hand in this game of hazard.

"I am extremely interested in what you say," she said, "but frankly I know nothing of your brother and less of where his loyalties lie."

Lord Niall gave a little chuckle.

"Nor does the Marquis of Severn," he said, "and that, my dear Lady Wrexham, is exactly what you have come to find out."

Beatrice sipped her glass of brandy before she replied, and then she said slowly:

"I am wondering if you are a very impertinent young man or a very impudent one."

"I am neither," Lord Niall replied. "Like yourself, madam, I am merely ambitious."

"Would it be indiscreet to ask where your ambitions lie?"

"It would not," Lord Niall replied; "and once again I will be devastatingly frank with you. I want to be the Duke of Arkrae."

His reply was so unexpected that Beatrice could only stare at him. Utterly composed, he smiled at her and put his glass of brandy down on the table.

"Have I shocked you?" he said. "I cannot believe that Lady Wrexham is shocked where a man is honest and truthful. So very few people are either. I will repeat, I would like to be the Duke of Arkrae. If anything happens to my brother, and as you doubtless know, he is only my half-brother, I should inherit the title and the territories of Skaig. I should also be Chieftain of the Clan. Is it necessary, after saying that, to tell you that my sympathies are wholly and completely English, and my loyalty to His Majesty, King George II, unswerving?"

Beatrice felt a little breathless. In all her experience things had never happened so swiftly or so strangely as this.

"How can I trust you?" she asked at last.

"I will answer that question," he replied. "Because I love you."

Beatrice got to her feet.

"This is absurd," she said. "I think your lordship goes too far. You are making fun of me."

Lord Niall looked down into her face.

"I have loved you since the first moment I saw you at the opera," he said; "when I said I had seen you but twice, it was an understatement. All this spring, wherever you went, I went too. I could have gained an introduction to you, but what good would that have done me? Severn can offer you far more than I can . . . at present. I have walked the streets at night beneath your window, thinking of you. I have waited hour after hour in crowds for the privilege of seeing you pass by. I came back to Scotland hoping that somehow I would be able to forget the beauty of your face, the carriage of your head, the way your little hands seem too small for the great rings you wear. Then your letter arrived. My stepmother showed it to me and I knew that we were meant to meet, that this had all been planned by a fate which was stronger than circumstance."

His voice was deep and he spoke slowly. His words seemed somehow all the more poignant because he did not hurry over them.

Beatrice looked away from him. There was something about him which frightened her, something almost sinister in his very directness, a frankness which seemed to her at variance with the dark secretiveness of his face. And yet she did not disbelieve him. He was not lying to her, she was certain of that.

Lord Niall looked at her averted face.

"Why are you afraid, my sweet?" he asked softly. "I can help you, even as you can help me. Besides, I know now we can never escape one another."

She turned to look at him, prepared to say something

61

light, to laugh perhaps at the very seriousness of his tone; but the words died on her lips. His eyes held hers magnetically, compellingly. She felt the warmth of a sudden flame awaken within her, she felt her lips part, her eyes suddenly heavy with desire. There was no need for words, the magnetism between them was expression enough.

She felt herself sway a little towards him before his arms came out and took her. Then his lips were on hers and he carried her away into the shadows.

5

Iona came slowly down the carved oak staircase. It was morning, and with the elasticity of youth there was no sign on her face that she had passed a restless, sleepless night, beset by fears and apprehensions.

After her arrival the evening before, she had retired to her bedchamber and her supper had been brought to her there. The Duchess had suggested this, not only from consideration for her fatigue after a long journey but because, as Iona well knew, she wished to discuss her story with the Duke and doubtless to express her quite obvious scepticism of Iona's claim to be the long lost Lady Elspeth.

Last night Iona had been too tired and too frightened to care what was said of her; but now this morning she felt ready to defy the Duchess and to begin the task she had been set and on which so much depended. In the small hours of the night, lonely and fearful in the darkness of her bedchamber, she had felt that the whole plan was impossible. Humiliated and abashed by the Duchess's attitude she had also been disconcerted and confused at finding that the Duke was the stranger who had come to her rescue in the streets of Paris.

The morning sunshine brought Iona renewed courage. It brought her, too, a sense of excitement and the return of that exhilaration she had first felt on seeing the natural beauty of her native land.

"I am a Scot! I belong here!" Iona said, looking out of her bedroom window on to the loch, misty blue in the morning haze, and at the mountain peaks, indomitable against the cloud-tossed sky.

Here in this neighbourhood were many of the places where the Prince had lain concealed after the Battle of Culloden. Iona thought of the dangers and the terror of those months in hiding when, despite a price of thirty thousand pounds on his head, no one would turn traitor and betray him.

What courage he had shown, what fortitude and how gladly those who met him had risked their lives and everything they possessed in an effort to help him! How little, Iona thought, she had to risk. A life of loneliness and drudgery in a milliner's shop in Paris, a life without even the hope of change or improvement. Then unexpectedly as if by magic she found herself here, in Scotland, entrusted with a precious mission, honoured and enriched by the Prince's own faith in her.

"I am lucky, terrible lucky," she told herself as she reached the wide landing off which lay the salon where she had waited for the Duchess on her arrival at the castle.

She had a chance now to look about her. Last night she had been too bewildered to gain any impression save one of massive, overpowering grandeur. Now she saw that the castle had not only majesty but charm.

Built hundreds of years ago, it had gradually accumulated an atmosphere of mellow maturity. It had been a fortification and a stronghold for generations; it had repelled aggression, defied its enemies and been a refuge and shield for those it sheltered. It had also been the habitation of the chieftain of the MacCraggans and the point of convergence for the clansmen. To them the power and majesty of the castle was a part of their heritage. Childlike in their trust and dependence on their chiefs, loyal to the very core of their being, they were proud of the magnificence of Skaig and as jealous of its traditions and privileges as they were of their own.

When Iona reached the first floor, she could look below into the Great Hall. This was the most ancient part of the castle; the walls were four feet thick and constructed to withstand the most violent assaults of an enemy. Decorating them were flags and banners captured in battle, and until four years earlier they had also displayed a unique collection of spears and claymores, shields and battle-axes. These had all been confiscated by the English after Culloden, when the Scots had been required to hand over their weapons of every sort and description. Iona did not know of this and she wondered at the bareness of the walls and at the marks where the weapons had been torn down from their resting place of several centuries.

The stone floor was covered only with skins of animals and at one end of the hall was a high-backed, carved oak chair set like a throne on two stone steps and canopied by curtains embroidered with heraldic designs.

Turning from her contemplation of the hall, Iona walked towards the salon into which she had been shown the night before. It was empty save for the sunlight flooding through the windows which overlooked the loch. In one of the gilt mirrors Iona could see her own reflection. She was wearing a gown she had made herself of grey muslin, its severity relieved only by narrow ribbons of emerald green velvet which laced the tight bodice and were tied in a bow at the waist. It was a demure dress which she had chosen deliberately to make herself appear unobtrusive and modest.

But she would have been a hypocrite if she had not realised that the puritanical colour of the gown only accentuated the brilliance of her hair and revealed the almost transparent quality of her skin. The ribbons she had tied so carefully echoed the vivid green of her eyes and made it of supreme unimportance that she owned no jewels and that the round perfection of her neck was therefore left unadorned.

"Good morning," a grave voice said behind her.

She turned swiftly and saw the Duke standing in the doorway. For a moment she stared at him, wondering why he seemed different, and then she knew. Last night his hair had been powdered. That day in Paris when they had just met it had been hidden by his three-cornered hat, but now she saw that he too was red-headed, his hair a deeper and more chestnut tone than her own, but undoubtedly red.

She stared at him, then sensed that he was awaiting her reply, and the colour rose in her cheeks at her abstraction. She swept to the ground in a graceful curtsey, and was aware as she raised her head again that the Duke was looking at her closely, examining her face, it seemed to her, feature by feature.

She waited in silence for him to speak, conscious that her heart was beating a little quicker under his scrutiny, but remembering to bear herself proudly despite an almost overwhelming shyness.

"My attorney is in the library," the Duke said at length, "He called to see me on business and I took the opportunity of relating your story and of showing him the proofs of your identity which you brought with you from France. But there are several matters on which he would wish to question you."

65

"I will do my best to reply," Iona said quietly.

She moved towards the Duke and he waited for her to reach his side. She looked up at him and realised how exceptionally tall he was. There was, too, something strong and reliable about him. Iona thought that like the castle he gave her a sense of protection and security.

"Shall I lead the way?" he asked. "You will find the castle a trifle puzzling until you have been here some time. That is because my forebears all had a passion for building and each generation has added to the original structure."

His Grace's tone was cold and aloof—a manner which Iona had begun to believe was characteristic of him. She glanced at him sideways underneath her dark lashes and wondered if he disliked her. He had not expressed any personal doubts as to the veracity of her story; in fact he seemed inclined to accept it at its face value; and yet Iona was sure that underneath his icy, indifferent manner he must have decided opinions on a matter which affected his family and his household.

It was impossible, she thought, for anyone to be so inhuman as the Duke appeared on first acquaintance; and yet she doubted if her experience had been varied enough for her to be a competent judge of the Duke or any other man for that matter.

In silence His Grace led her down several passages until they came to the library. It was a huge room lined from floor to ceiling with books. The windows looked out over the loch, but at a different angle from those in the salon. From here one could see moorland and mountains stretching away to the west, while in the foreground the hillside fell sheer to the edge of the loch to form a perpendicular cliff above which stood massive black rock jutting out over the water below. Iona had no time to notice anything else for the Duke's attorney, a wizened, white-haired old man of nearly seventy, rose from a chair by the writing-table. The Duke introduced him and he peered at Iona with short-sighted eyes for some seconds before he said grudgingly:

"The young woman looks a MacCraggan, Your Grace."

"There you can certainly speak with authority, Tulloch," the Duke said.

"Indeed I can, Your Grace, having served your family for over half a century."

"Miss Iona is not unlike the miniature," the Duke said.

"Aye, but that doesn't prove that she's the Lady

66

Elspeth," the attorney replied, peering again at Iona and then down at the miniature which lay on the writing-desk.

"I have some questions to ask you, ma'am," he said at length, drawing a notebook from his pocket.

The Duke drew up a chair for Iona and she sat down. The attorney began his questions. He was irritatingly slow, writing both his questions and Iona's answers out laboriously.

Iona, while on her guard against making a mistake, found his questions easy as he gave her so much time for consideration before she need reply. But as she spoke or sat waiting patiently for her words to be inscribed, she was acutely conscious of the Duke. He had withdrawn to a seat near the fireplace, but she knew he was listening and watching her. It was with the greatest effort that she did not turn her head and look at him. She wanted to see his face and the expression in his eyes. She had never known that anyone could have so strong a personality that she could feel it physically. It was almost painful to force herself to attend to the attorney.

Finally the last question was put to her.

"You are anxious to prove yourself to be Lady Elspeth MacCraggan?"

"I am anxious to prove that I have a name," Iona answered in all sincerity. "I have never had one."

As she spoke she wondered if by any strange unpredictable coincidence she was in truth a MacCraggan; but then she remembered that her guardian had never spoken of them. Could that have been intentional? She thought not. He had been a blunt, unsubtle person. He had talked continually of his own family, the Drummonds, of their deeds of valour, of their successes and failures. Had he been in any way closely connected with the MacCraggans, she felt he must have talked to her of them, for he was interested only in Scotland and its people and could wander on by the hour, the past events of history being more real to him than the present with its limitations to his freedom.

With a little sigh Iona remembered that to be a Scot and red-headed was commonplace enough. In France she had been outstanding because of the colour of her hair, but here every other person had hair the same colour.

The attorney shut his notebook with a snap.

"That will be all, ma'am, for today."

He rose to his feet and turned towards the Duke.

"With your permission, Your Grace, I will send

67

someone from my office immediately to France. We must, of course, interview the priest, make inquiries among the neighbours, and find, if we can, the fishermen who rescued the shipwrecked valet, nurse and Lady Elspeth seventeen years ago."

"It will not be easy," the Duke said.

"It will not be easy; it will take time and be extremely expensive," the attorney agreed.

"I would wish, of course," the Duke said, "that no expense should be spared."

"I can understand that, Your Grace. May I take the letter with me? I will have a copy made of it in my office."

"Yes, take it," the Duke replied, "but leave the miniature and the bracelet."

"Very good, Your Grace."

The attorney bowed to the Duke and to Iona; then hesitated;

"The lady . . . will be staying here?"

"Certainly! At least until the inquiries in France are complete."

The attorney bowed again and left the room. Iona looked towards the Duke a little shyly.

"It is kind of you to offer me your hospitality until my case is proven."

"It appears you have nowhere else to go," the Duke replied.

"That is true," Iona answered, "but . . . I was thinking of the Duchess. I feel she would not be entirely agreeable to my remaining here."

"I think you will find that the Duchess will not oppose my wishes," the Duke replied.

His tone was final and there seemed nothing more to say. Because she was nervous, Iona impetuously asked the question which was uppermost in her mind.

"Have you been married long, Your Grace?"

The Duke's eyebrows were raised in surprise.

"I am not married," he said.

Iona felt the colour rush into her cheeks.

"Oh," she said in confusion, "I am sorry. I thought last night that . . . that. . . ."

". . . the Duchess was my wife," the Duke supplied. "No, you are wrong. She is my stepmother. Perhaps it would be wise for me to outline briefly our family relationship. It is somewhat complicated for a stranger."

Still confused by her mistake Iona murmured something incoherent and the Duke went on:

"My father, the late Duke, married three times. My mother, his first wife, was married to him for twenty years before they had a child. She was over forty when I was born, and my coming into the world killed her. My father married again the following year. His second wife was a distant cousin. She was a MacCraggan and she bore him two children—my half-brother, Niall—who is years younger than I am—was born in 1722, and my half-sister, Elspeth, eight years later. My father's second wife was drowned when the yacht was wrecked in the Channel, and we believed that Elspeth was drowned at the same time."

"How terrible!" Iona exclaimed. "But you and your half-brother were saved."

"My father saved us," the Duke replied. "Although he was not a young man he was a powerful swimmer. He guided both my brother and me to a raft. We drifted for two days and two nights, then we were picked up by a man-of-war. When we reached port we learned that two sailors had been drowned of the crew, the rest had been saved in one way or another. Altogether it was calculated that six lives were lost, counting the sailors: the other being the Duchess, Elspeth, her nurse, and Ewart—my father's valet."

Iona felt her eyes drop beneath his. Quite suddenly she wished with all her heart and soul that she was the Lady Elspeth and that there was no deception in the part she had to play.

"A year late," the Duke continued, "my father married again. He was over seventy and I think he hated to be alone. His life with my mother had been, I am always told, a very happy one. He craved companionship and my brother and I were not old enough to give it to him. His third wife, the present Duchess, was an Englishwoman."

"English!"

Iona was startled into repeating the word.

"Yes, English," the Duke repeated. "My present stepmother, was a Miss Howard. She was only twenty-five when my father saw her and fell in love with her. She came of a well-known and distinguished family who lived in Kent. She had never been to Scotland before and she found it uncongenial. In fact she has never been happy here."

"Then why, now that she is a widow, has she not returned to England?" Iona asked.

Her question was obviously one that the Duke was not prepared to answer. He rose to his feet and Iona realised that their conversation was at an end. She felt that in not answering her question and merely ignoring it he had been, if not deliberately rude, almost unbearably autocratic.

"Shall I escort you to the salon?" the Duke asked. "My stepmother should be there by now."

"I thank Your Grace."

Iona's tone was almost as frigid as his. As they reached the door, he paused and looked down at her.

"You will oblige me," he said quietly, "if you will not mention to my stepmother that you saw me in Paris."

Iona glanced up at him quickly. She was surprised by his request, yet the expression on his face was as reserved and autocratic as always. If he was forced to ask a favour, he was not prepared to unbend or be friendly about it.

"I will not mention the incident," Iona replied briefly.

"Thank you."

The Duke opened the door. In the passage outside a footman was on duty. The Duke beckoned him.

"Show Miss Iona the way to the grand salon," he commanded.

"Very good, Your Grace."

Iona dropped the Duke a curtsey and as she moved away feeling that he was relieved to be rid of her, she heard the library door close decisively and firmly behind him. She felt that the sound was an answer to all her hopes and plans. How could she learn anything from a man like that?

Iona reached the drawing-room and found the Duchess sitting before the fire, a glass of wine in her hand. She acknowledged Iona's curtsey with a curt nod and asked the footman:

"Has Lord Niall returned yet?"

"Not yet, Your Grace."

"You are certain?"

"I will inquire again, Your Grace."

"Then do so. If his lordship has not arrived yet, bring me tidings immediately the carriage is seen descending the hill."

"Very good, Your grace."

The footman closed the doors behind him. The Duchess looked at Iona and in almost a friendly tone asked:

"How long did it take you to come from Inverness yesterday?"

"I left at seven o'clock in the morning, ma'am. The stagecoach is slow and stopped continually. We did not reach Fort Augustus until three o'clock in the afternoon."

"The stage-coach!" the Duchess said with contempt. "It is hopeless to compare that creeping hearse with the pace of well-bred horses drawing a light chaise."

She put down her glass of wine and shivered.

"It is cold this morning," she said pettishly. "Is there a window open?"

Iona glanced round the room.

"No, ma'am, but the sunshine is warm."

"It is never warm here," the Duchess grumbled.

She put out her hands to the blaze. The veins showed startlingly blue.

Iona looked at the Duchess's face. She was rouged, yet it could not disguise the unhealthy pallor of her skin. She must be anaemic or ill, Iona thought, for the heat of the fire was almost overpowering.

The Duchess thrust her hands into a little ermine muff which lay on her lap.

"Have you regaled His Grace's attorney with your sensational resurrection from a watery grave?" she asked disagreeably. "What did he think of your fairy tale?"

"He expressed no opinion, ma'am," Iona answered. "But with His Grace's permission he is sending someone to France to make inquiries."

"And if they prove you to be an imposter, what then?" the Duchess asked.

"In that case I shall return to France," Iona answered calmly. "I can always find work in Paris."

"Work? What sort of work?"

"I have been a milliner these past two years."

"A milliner in Paris?" the Duchess mused. "It makes a good story; but you can hardly expect me to believe that with your looks and hair you live a life of honest toil."

"I am sorry to disappoint you, ma'am, but it happens to be the truth."

Iona felt her temper rising. The Duchess's sneers were hard to bear.

"Then if that is the truth, you must indeed be a Scot," the Duchess said. "There is a streak of the Puritan in all of them, though it's my belief it is not because they wish to be good but because they are sore afraid of the fires of Hell."

Iona managed to smile.

"I am not afraid of Hell, ma'am."

The Duchess looked at her speculatively.

"Doubtless in time we shall learn of what you are afraid," she said.

"I hope not!" Iona parried.

The Duchess took up her glass again and sipped the ruby wine.

"Do you know many people in Paris?" she asked.

Her voice was almost affable and Iona was instantly on her guard.

"Very few, ma'am. I lived in straitened circumstances."

"But even so," the Duchess went on, "you must have heard talk of the great personages. The French people are fluent talkers, aren't they? They must have gossiped about the King and Queen, the Court, and those who visited France."

"Yes, I suppose one heard gossip of that sort, ma'am."

"Did you hear them speak of the Young Pretender, Charles Stuart?" the Duchess asked casually.

"I have heard talk of him, of course," Iona replied slowly. "Did you ever meet him when he was in Scotland, ma'am?"

The Duchess glanced sharply at Iona, but her eyes were wide with innocence.

"I did not," the Duchess said quickly, then added, this time in the disarming tone she had used before: "But perhaps you have seen him in Paris? Is he there now, do you know?"

"I heard tell," Iona answered, "that the Prince was not allowed into France by order of King Louis."

"Yes, yes," the Duchess said, "but there are rumours that he returns when it pleases him."

"Are there?" Iona questioned. "But surely, ma'am, that would be rash of His Royal Highness?"

The Duchess shrugged her shoulders.

"You have heard naught of this?"

"Nobody has ever spoken to me of Prince Charles's return to Paris," Iona said in all truth.

"It would be amusing to know if he dared defy the French King, wouldn't it?" the Duchess asked. "You have friends, perhaps, who could find out if such an escapade were likely?"

"I am afraid not, ma'am."

Iona spoke decisively. The Duchess shrugged her shoulders again and leaned back in her chair.

"How industrious you must have been in your milliner's

shop," she said sourly. "It is a wonder you ever consented to leave it."

"I thought it my duty to come to Scotland," Iona answered, "and I wanted above all things to see the country which I have always known was my own."

The Duchess gave a derisive sound.

"You will be disappointed." she said. "It is a bleak land, comfortless and unfriendly. When I first came here, I thought to find it charming, but I was mistaken. You will find out your mistake and you will wish to go scuttling back to the gaiety and warmth of Paris."

"I think that is unlikely, ma'am," Iona said quietly. She glanced out of the window and added: "It is sad that Your Grace does not like Scotland."

"Like it," the Duchess's voice was strangely shrill. "I hate it!"

The words seemed to fall like a naked sword between the two women. For a moment there was silence and then the Duchess said:

"Yes, I hate it! I hate the cold and the loneliness, the dreary monotonous life I live here, and I hate the people, too, with their sanctimonious expressions and their underlying treachery."

The Duchess spoke vehemently with a kind of smouldering passion; and when she had finished speaking, her mouth twitched and her whole body seemed to quiver, Iona felt there was nothing she could say. She realised the woman was a mass of nerves, that her body was tense, and that her eyes were dark with the tempest of her emotions. After a moment the Duchess finished her wine, put down the glass on the table and took up the golden bell which stood there. She shook it violently.

The door was opened almost instantly and a footman appeared.

"I told them to bring me tidings the moment Lord Niall's carriage appeared on the hill," the Duchess said.

"The order has been given, Your Grace," the footman replied, "but there is as yet no sign of his lordship."

"He should be here by now," the Duchess said.

"It is but half after noon, Your Grace," the footman replied.

"Go and see if there is any news in the stables," the Duchess commanded. "A postilion may have been sent ahead with instructions."

"I will inquire, Your Grace."

73

The man left the room. The Duchess got to her feet and walked restlessly towards the window.

"Niall promised to return yesterday," she muttered, speaking, Iona felt, more to herself than to anybody in particular. "He is late; he should be back by now. Something must have happened to him."

There was a sudden pain in the querulous voice, and Iona wondered why the Duchess should care so deeply about the movements of her stepson.

The door opened and the Duchesss turned eagerly, but the expression on her face altered as she saw it was the Duke who entered. Iona rose to her feet at his entrance, but he looked only at his stepmother.

"You have remembered that Lady Wrexham is arriving today?" he said. "I have sent a coach to Fort Augustus as arranged."

"Her room is prepared," the Duchess said indifferently. "I cannot think why a woman with the whole of London to amuse her wishes to visit an outlandish spot like this."

"Doubtless she has her reasons," the Duke said evasively.

"I should be surprised if she hadn't," the Duchess said, and there was an unpleasant undertone in her words.

The Duke looked at her.

"I have heard a great deal about Lady Wrexham," he said. "Have you ever seen her?"

"Not since she was a baby in arms," the Duchess replied. "Her parents lived close to my home, as she reminded me in her letter inviting herself to stay. But I cannot believe it is my *beaux yeux* which have drawn Beatrice Wrexham from St. James's to Skaig."

"And I am not conceited enough to imagine it is mine," the Duke said impassively.

The Duchess laughed unpleasantly.

"Perhaps the Marquis of Severn is curious about you, my dear Ewan. I am told that his favourite method of inquisition is to send Beatrice Wrexham ahead of his executioner."

"That is indeed interesting," the Duke said, "for you have put most ably into words something I have suspected, but hesitated to formulate even to myself."

Iona watching closely thought that the Duchess's expression changed and she looked disconcerted. Then she shrugged her thin shoulders and turned towards the fire.

"I am but funning, Ewan. Beatrice Wrexham has no ulterior motive in coming here other than to admire the Highland scenery and to enjoy the hospitality of Skaig."

The Duchess's change of tone was entirely unconvincing and left both her listeners with the impression that she was anxious to cover up a previous indiscretion.

The Duke glanced at the clock on the mantelshelf.

"At any rate her ladyship will not be arriving until the afternoon," he said. "The road from Inverness is in bad repair and I should not imagine she will leave particularly early."

"I had forgotten she came from Inverness," the Duchess exclaimed, and there was suddenly a strange and wary look in her eyes as if she found the knowledge strangely perturbing.

6

"There must have been an accident! Niall is three days overdue," the Duchess said for the thousandth time.

"His lordship may have been held up by floods or by a bridge having been washed away," Iona replied.

She had made the suggestion before; in fact in the past three days she had put forward every possible explanation of Lord Niall's absence in her efforts to soothe the anxiety of his stepmother.

"If the Duke had any natural feeling in him," the Duchess said, disregarding Iona's remark, "he would send a groom to Inverness to discover if there is any news of his brother."

The Duchess had made the same request of His Grace at dinner the previous night, but the Duke had merely replied that Niall was old enough to look after himself and he would not thank his relatives for being over-anxious about him.

Iona had noticed that the Duchess was not half so insistent in her fears for Lord Niall's safety when the Duke was present; indeed she kept her complainings and her unceasing speculations as to what had happened to him for when she and Iona were alone.

After three days at the Castle Iona had begun to think that the subject had been exhausted in all its possibilities; she was growing tired of the very sound of Lord Niall's name. The Duchess was interested in nothing else and Iona was beginning to wonder if the days were to pass endlessly with her doing little but listening to the Duchess's querulous, grumbling voice and getting no better acquainted with the Duke.

She saw him at meal-times, when he sat at the head of the wide dining-table; but with a footman behind every chair intimate conversation was impossible, and Iona was well aware that the Duchess thought it both forward and presumptuous on her part if she spoke without being addressed.

When they were alone together, the Duchess behaved as if there were a kind of truce between them. She was obviously quite pleased to have someone to whom she could grumble incessantly and who was forced to spend many hours of the day in her company. But when the Duke was there, the Duchess allowed her enmity to reveal itself quite plainly; and making no pretence of politeness she made a practice on every possible occasion of taunting Iona with being an imposter.

The situation, Iona felt at times, was almost impossible; but she hoped that, when more people arrived at the castle, it would perhaps be easier for her to find occasion to speak with the Duke and to be alone with him. She was growing exceedingly weary of the Duchess with her doleful forebodings, her whining voice which seemed to run on endlessly, her questions needing no answer, her remarks inviting no comment.

"What can he find to interest him in Inverness?" the Duchess asked, holding out her hands as usual towards the warmth of the fire. "It is a poor, dingy little town, for all these uncivilised Scots are proud of it. Heavens above, as I have told them often enough, if they saw London or York or Canterbury, they would laugh to think a few scattered crofts and vermin-ridden inns should dare to style themselves a town. But then these poor, uncouth barbarians know nothing better."

There was venom in Her Grace's voice, as always when she spoke of the Scottish race; but although she was expressing her genuine conviction about the Scots in general, Iona was well aware that the sneering criticism was meant also for her personally. She was wondering what to reply when the door opened and a footman came into the room.

"What is it?" the Duchess asked impatiently as he approached her.

"His lordship's carriage is approaching the bridge, Your Grace."

"The bridge?" the Duchess exclaimed. "Then he is nearly here? Why wasn't I told before? Go at once to the front door and ask his lordship to wait on me immediately."

"Very good, Your Grace."

The footman withdrew and the Duchess started to her feet. She turned towards a miror and patted her elaborately arranged hair with anxious fingers, then drew a small pot of salve from her reticule and reddened her lips. There was a sudden light in her eyes and for the moment she looked younger and not unattractive.

"She loves him," Iona thought with sudden clarity and wondered if Lord Niall reciprocated the affection of his stepmother.

There was the sound of footsteps outside and the Duchess turned eagerly towards the door. Embarrassed and anxious not to intrude, Iona withdrew into an embrasure at the side of a window and was half hidden by the draping folds of the crimson silk curtains. She stood looking out on to the loch, wishing that she could have retired to her own room; but it was too late now for her to suggest it. She heard the door open but did not turn her head. Then the Duchess's cry of relief rang out:

"Niall! At last! What has happened to you? I vow I have been nearly demented with anxiety."

"You flatter me, *Belle-mère*," replied a low, smooth voice.

"You told me you would return on Wednesday," the Duchess scolded. "Do you realise it is Saturday today and I have had no word from you, no explanation of what happened to prevent your return?"

"I had no idea my absence would perturb you so unnecessarily."

"You know full well it would," the Duchess replied. "If you had not come today, I would have sent a groom to Inverness to make inquiries, though it is beyond my comprehension to imagine what interest you could find there."

"The groom would have returned as ignorant as he went," Lord Niall said in a tone that was unmistakably bored; "for I have not been to Inverness."

"Not been to Inverness?" the Duchess queried. "But you said you were going there!"

"I changed my mind," Lord Niall replied, "instead I turned off the road at Glen Urquhart and stayed with some friends of mine."

"Who are they?" the Duchess asked suspiciously.

"You have never met them, so their names are not important," Lord Niall answered.

"Then you have not been to Inverness at all?" the Duchess insisted.

There was an obvious note of relief in her voice.

"Have I not said so?" Lord Niall asked impatiently. "Why the cross-examination?"

The Duchess answered him truthfully.

"I thought perhaps you had encountered Lady Wrexham."

"Lady Wrexham?" Lord Niall repeated in surprise. "But is she not here?"

"She too has been delayed," the Duchess replied.

"How strange!" Lord Niall said; "but then it is to be expected when she is coming such a great distance. Now that I think of it, someone mentioned to me that the roads from England were in a bad state and that there had been floods in Yorkshire."

"Who told you that?" the Duchess asked.

"I have not the slightest idea," Lord Niall replied. "The subject was not of any interest to me, but now it seems to account for Lady Wrexham's nonappearance."

"Well, it is of no consequence," the Duchess said quickly, "and now that you are here, Niall, I have a thousand things to tell you."

There was a low and intimate note in her voice and Iona was uncomfortably aware that Her Grace had forgotten her presence.

For the first time she turned and looked into the room. The Duchess had her back to her, but Lord Niall was facing her, and as she moved she attracted his attention. Her heart gave a startled beat and she felt the blood drawn away from her cheeks for she recognised him instantly—recognised the sardonic face and the air of authority and distinction, the glittering magnificence of his coat and sparkling diamond buttons. She had seen them all before and she knew, as their eyes met across the room, that he also remembered her.

"So we have a visitor, *Belle-mère!*" he said softly.

The Duchess turned impatiently towards Iona.

"I forgot that you were here, girl," she said. "If you wish to withdraw, we will excuse you."

Iona curtsied demurely, but Lord Niall's curiosity was not so easily circumvented.

"I beg you to present me," he said, and it was a command.

The Duchess tossed her head.

"Indeed it is a difficult thing for me to do, for I have not the slightest idea who in truth this person may be. She

79

claims to be your sister Elspeth, who was drowned seventeen years ago, but I vow I have no credence in such a tale. In the meantime until her claim—presumptuous as it is—is proven to be false, she is called Iona. 'Miss Iona', if you can credit such an appellation."

"You believe that you are my sister Elspeth?" Lord Niall asked.

His eyes narrowed and somehow Iona found it impossible to meet his gaze.

"His Grace has the proofs, if it will interest you, my lord," she stammered.

"They interest me greatly," Lord Niall said; "but I would rather hear your story from your own lips."

Iona wondered wildly how she could refuse him, but the Duchess came to her rescue.

"There is plenty of time for that," she said impatiently. "Come with me to my boudoir, Niall; I would talk with you."

Before Lord Niall could answer, Iona curtsied and hurried from the room. Outside the door she stood for a moment with her hands raised to her hot cheeks into which the blood returned tumultuously; then she lifted her skirts and ran up the stairs.

"Was there ever such a tangle?" she thought. That it should be Lord Niall of all people who had seen her coming from Hector's bedroom in Inverness! What must he have thought, she wondered? And in shame she knew the answer.

Desperately she tried to think what she should say when he spoke of the incident. Then she remembered that he had told the Duchess he had not been to Inverness. Why had he lied? What was he hiding by such a falsehood? Could not his desire for secrecy be turned to her advantage?

She felt her embarrassment and confusion forgotten as she tried, with every instinct alert, to sort out the hard facts from a chaotic muddle of coincidence, suspicions, fears and distrust.

There were too many mysteries, too many secrets for which she had no explanation. The Duke's presence in Paris which he did not wish known; the Duchess's probings with regard to the Prince; her own unfortunate encounter with Lord Niall at Inverness which fortunately—or so it appeared at the moment—he could not disclose without revealing his own presence there.

"What does it all mean?" Iona asked herself a dozen

times, and felt that the more she considered everything that had occurred the more complicated and bewildering it all became.

She had been in her room but a few minutes when there came a knock on the door. She bade the person who knocked to enter and a maid came in. Her name was Cathy and she had maided Iona since she first came to the castle. Bright-eyed and smiling, she was wearing a frilled cap of starched linen over her hair and an apron which rustled as she walked. She shut the door behind her and crossed the room to Iona's side.

"Theer's a body below who wad speak wi' ye, mistress," she said softly.

"Someone to see me?" Iona asked in surprise. "But who can it be?"

" 'Tis Dughall, mistress, an' he has brocht a message for ye."

"A message?" Iona echoed, feeling that she was being stupid, but cudgelling her brains fruitlessly to think who could be sending her a message.

Cathy glanced over her shoulder.

" 'Tis important, mistress, tha' Dughall should talk wi' ye alane. He told me no tae say he wae here if onybody was wi' ye."

"I will go to him at once," Iona said. "I will not be seen?"

"Not if ye'll let me lead ye, mistress!"

Iona picked up a light woollen shawl and put it round her shoulders, then she followed Cathy from the room. The maid avoided the main staircase and led the way along the passage until after several twists and turns they reached a narrow, winding stairway. It had obviously been built inside a tower and the only light came from arrow-slits in the massive stone walls. More than once Iona stumbled in the darkness and would have fallen but for Cathy who put out her arms to save her. After some minutes they reached the bottom of the stairs and Cathy hurried along another passage. They were now, Iona could see, in a part of the castle which was not in use. There was a close, musty airlessness in the atmosphere; the windows were shuttered, the pictures covered, the chairs and furniture protected by dust sheets.

At last, after walking what seemed to Iona a long way, they came to a small oak door in the outer wall. It was bolted and locked. Cathy drew the bolts and they squeaked

81

and wheezed as if they had not been used for a considerable time. Drawing a key from the pocket of her apron, Cathy turned it in the lock and the door opened. Fresh air and sunshine came flooding in.

Iona looked out on to a terrace bounded by a balustrade which opened immediately ahead to reveal a steep flight of stone steps descending to the loch. There was no one in sight and she realised that they were on the east side of the castle and out of sight of the bridge which joined it to the mainland.

Cathy whistled and almost immediately there appeared the head and shoulders of a man coming up the steps. He climbed quickly on to the terrace and came to Iona's side. He was a big man, roughly dressed and wearing a tattered bonnet on his greying hair.

"This is Dughall, mistress," Cathy said, and added. "He is ma uncle an' a guid mon. I'll be leavin' him tae talk we' ye, an' I'll be waitin' by the door."

The Highlander waited until Cathy was out of sight, then he drew his bonnet from his head and feeling in the headband with toil-worn fingers, he drew out a piece of paper. Without saying a word he passed it to Iona. Quickly she opened it and saw it contained one sentence.

"I must see you; you can trust this man.—Hector."

She read it two or three times until she was quite sure she had not been mistaken. It was from Hector MacGregor, of course, but what was he doing here? She had thought by now that he would be on his way back to France. She looked up at Dughall.

"Where is the . . . the gentleman who sent this note?"

"I'll tak ye tae him."

"Now?" Iona asked.

"Aye."

"But how?" Iona inquired.

Dughall pointed towards the steps.

"I hae ma boat."

Iona hesitated for a moment, then turned towards the door and called to Cathy. The girl was waiting in the passage.

"Your uncle wants me to go with him," Iona said. "I hope not to be long. If anyone asks for me, say I am resting and cannot be disturbed."

"Ye can trust me, mistress," Cathy replied.

"But when I return, how shall I get in?" Iona inquired.

In answer Cathy handed her a key.

"I'll leave the door unbolted," she said. "Ye hae but tae turn the lock."

Iona knew that this was not the first time this door had been used as a secret way of leaving or entering the castle, but she had no time for further speculation. She went out through the door, locked it behind her and put the key in her pocket, then slipping her shawl over her head she followed Dughall down the cliff-side. Below them she could see a small boat.

When they reached the end of the steps, Dughall jumped into the boat and reaching up took Iona in his arms and set her down in the stern; then moving his oars with an astonishing silence, he rowed away, keeping under the lee of the land.

It took them a few seconds to cross to the mainland. Trees russet and gold with their autumn foliage grew right down to the water's edge. Dughall edged his boat in amongst them and Iona saw that they were effectually sheltered from being seen by anyone in the castle. In a silence which Iona realised was not essential but due to Dughall's native reserve they left the boat tied to a tree stump and started to climb the mountain side. There was a suspicion of a path which wound sharply uphill beneath pine trees. It was hard walking because the ground was soft and sandy and Iona's feet, clad only in house shoes, slipped or sank with every step she took.

She was soon finding it difficult to get her breath. Dughall sprang along with the tireless gait of a countryman who was used to covering long distances. Up and up they climbed until Iona felt her lungs were bursting; but just when she felt that she would be forced to sit down and rest Dughall turned inland, and after walking on the level for a few moments they came unexpectedly upon a house. It was only a small croft roughly built of stone with two wooden shuttered windows, a door and a thatched roof; but there was smoke coming from the chimney and Iona guessed that they had reached their destination.

Dughall opened the door and Iona, entering the cottage, saw Hector sitting by the fireside, his long legs stretched out in front of him, the expression on his face serious as he contemplated the flames. He jumped up at the sight of Iona and held out his arms; she had only the breath to gasp out his name.

"You have come!" Hector exclaimed, hugging her. "I was certain Dughall would manage it somehow and that you would not fail me. Sit down, you look exhausted."

He offered her his chair and she was glad to obey him, for she had an agonising stitch in her side from the speed with which she had followed Dughall.

"You are out of breath," Hector said and added laughingly as Iona nodded at him. "I should have warned Dughall to bring you slowly. Many a time he's walked me off my feet, and I know what you feel like."

"Wad the mistress tak a sup o' someat?" a voice asked, and Iona looked up to see a little old woman, wrinkled and bowed with age but with bright eyes which seemed to peer at her like a wild bird's.

"I would be grateful for a drink of water," Iona replied, and the old woman bustled away into the shadows at the far end of the room, to return with a rough earthenware pot filled with water.

It was cool and delicious and when she had drunk Iona could at last speak easily.

"Why are you here, Hector?" she asked; and even as she spoke she glanced around her as if afraid they would be overheard.

The old woman had disappeared and Dughall was standing outside the door. There was something in his attitude, relaxed and yet alert, which told Iona he was on guard.

Seeing her glance around, Hector understood.

"It's all right, Iona," he said. "Dughall and his mother are my friends and you need not be afraid of anything you say in front of them."

He set himself down at her feet, his legs crossed, his back to the fire.

"I have something of the greatest import to tell you," he said.

"But surely it is madness to come here," Iona protested. "Every minute you spend in Scotland is fraught with danger. I thought that by now you would have already returned to France."

"My plans are changed," Hector said. "I am making my way to Skye, but it is not for that reason I wanted to see you. Listen, Iona, for we have not much time."

He felt in the pocket of his coat, drew out a little black notebook and said:

"This concerns you."

"Why me?" Iona asked.

"That is what I am here to tell you," Hector replied. "The night after you left Inverness I was sitting in the bar of a drinking house down by the quay, waiting to see someone with whom I had an appointment, when a man came in. He had just landed and was drunk—very drunk. He had been drinking, he told me, for days as he was miserably sea-sick. He insisted on talking to me and I was wondering how to shake him off when after another drink he began to boast.

"He said that he had been sent to France to find out various things and because he was so clever he had succeeded in discovering all that was asked of him. 'The information I have got here,' he bragged, producing this little notebook, 'is worth a pocketful of gold to me, I can tell you that. Gold, me boy, and I'll make her pay me all right. And why not? If you can't get money from a Duchess who can you get it from?' 'A Duchess?' I asked curiously. 'Don't tell me that the Duchesses in Scotland are reduced to paying their lovers?' He laughed at that, as I thought he would. 'It's not love the Duchess will be paying me for—but information. Shall I tell you something?' He leaned forward in a tipsy fashion and whispered: 'She's English and she hates the Scots! What do you think of that? But, do you know who she hates the worst of them all? I tell you, it's a belly-laugh; but women are like that. She hates the Duke himself. Yes, poor Arkrae, how she hates him!'"

Iona drew an excited breath.

"This man was a Scot?" she asked.

"Of course not," Hector answered scornfully; "he was an Englishman."

"Go on."

"Faith, but you can imagine that by this time," Hector continued, "I was determined to get possession of the notebook and see what was in it. I did my best to draw the fellow out. I paid for further drinks and he told me how the Duchess had sent him to France to follow the Duke. Arkrae has been in Paris, Iona."

"I knew that," Iona said.

"You knew it?" Hector exclaimed.

"Yes, but that is another story," Iona said. "Go on with yours, Hector."

"Well, he hinted at this and hinted at that, and kept telling me that he had got it all written down, until I was nearly frantic with curiosity. Then just as I was wondering how I could best knock him out and get hold of the book, he began to get truculent and with a sudden burst of shrewdness and sobriety he accused me of spying on him. Yes, he insulted me although for that matter I was quite prepared to make the first move. It ended, of course, with us going outside. There was just enough light in the moon for us to see what we were doing. He was drunk, but even so he was not a bad swordsman. We fought for ten minutes—then I left him."

"You killed him?" Iona asked.

"If he's not dead I promise you that he won't be seeing the Duchess for a long time," Hector replied grimly. He opened the little black notebook. "There's a lot in here which the Prince must know and Brett, but I'll show you the entries which concern yourself."

" 'July 5th:' That was after he arrived in France, sent by the Duchess to follow the Duke. 'Followed the Duke to the Rue Marie. He spent two hours in No. 27. Discovered later it is the house of Estelle Dupret, mistress of the Jacobite exile, Rory MacCraggan, who died in the spring.' "

"The Duke called on a Jacobite!" Iona exclaimed, her eyes round.

"Rory MacCraggan was dead, don't forget," Hector said. "If he hadn't been, we would have consulted him about Arkrae and the family before you came here. He was exiled after the Rising in '15. He was pardoned about five years later, but he never went back. I remember hearing the others talk of him, but I never met him. He drank like a fish and found the amusements of Paris very much to his liking. He was not a young man when he was exiled and he must have been very old when he died the other day. He always lived with the woman Estelle Dupret and she was the chief reason why he did not return to Scotland. Of course, those who would have given their right arms to return home were angry that he did not avail himself of the opportunity. He lost touch with his friends and just vanished into the slums of Paris, where he spent every penny he possessed in drink and debauchery."

"He sounds horrible," Iona said. "Why should the Duke go all that way to see his mistress?"

"Rory was related to Arkrae, of course," Hector said, "but even so you can see the construction the Duchess's spy was putting on the fact that the Duke visited a Jacobite household."

"Yes, I see that," Iona said. "What else did he discover?"

"He got in touch with a man whose initial was 'K'. He is also a spy and one, I gather, who has an intimate knowledge of France and the Prince's friends. He knows Brett by sight and has trailed him on various occasions. You see the danger in that, Iona. If the Colonel is being watched, he should know it or else eventually they will discover the whereabouts of the Prince."

"Who is paying 'K'?" Iona asked.

"I don't know. The English Government as likely as not. But here's where it concerns you. It's the very next entry after July 5th. *'July 6th: Met "K" who tells me that some days ago Colonel Brett visited a milliner in the Rue St. Honoré and talked for some time with a girl called Iona Ward, known to be a Jacobite. "K" suggests Colonel B. may be procuring I.W. for the Prince in which case it is worth keeping a watch on her.' "*

Iona put her hands to her cheeks.

"How dare they think such things?" she cried angrily.

"It doesn't matter what swine like that think," Hector said soothingly. "What is important is that if, as the man had intended, he had taken this book to the Duchess, the game would have been up as far as you were concerned."

"But, of course," Iona exclaimed. "I hadn't thought of that. Oh, Hector, thank goodness you have got it safely."

"There's a great deal more in it which I haven't time to tell you now," Hector said. "What you have got to remember, Iona, is this. The Duchess is intriguing against the Duke; for all we know she may be in touch with London. At any rate she sends this man to watch him, to spy on him, and there may be others. Besides that, there's your own safety to be considered. If she suspects you of being a Jacobite. . . ."

". . . as well as an impostor!" Iona finished. "All right, Hector, you need not say any more."

"Then I will be on my way."

He got to his feet and Iona rose too.

"Must you go to Skye?" she asked wistfully. "I would feel so much happier if you went back to France and warned the Colonel."

"I go on the Prince's behalf."

Hector's face was solemn for a moment and then his smile flashed out. "Pray do not worry about me, Iona."

"Be careful of the book," she said.

"I had thought to leave it here and pick it up on my return," Hector said, "but I may find a French ship at Portree. In which case if my work is finished, I shall be off to France. In any case it is unlikely that I shall see you again until we meet in Paris."

"Then God keep you," Iona said softly.

"And you," Hector replied.

He raised her hand to his lips and called to Dughall.

"Take the lady back to the castle, Dughall, and remember you are to befriend her if she comes to you in trouble."

"I'm nae lik' tae forg't, Master Hector," Dughall replied in his slow, deep voice.

Iona looked at Hector and raised her eyebrows.

"Master?" she queried.

"Dughall was keeper on my father's estate until he came here as forester. He is a MacCraggan, but I love him as if he were a MacGregor."

"Theer's naught wrang wi' the MacCraggans—well, nae wi' sum o' them," Dughall said, and Hector clapped a hand on the man's shoulder.

"There's nothing wrong with you, Dughall, at any rate!" he said. "Away with you now."

"Aye," Dughall replied and started off through the wood.

Iona waved to Hector and followed him. They were moving quickly but Iona found the way was easier downhill.

"Have you known Mr. MacGregor since he was a little boy?" she asked after they had walked for several minutes in silence.

"Aye," Dughall replied, "but I lef' the MacGregors wheen I wed an' came back tae Skaig tae mak' a hame for masel. But ma wifie deid an' ma auld mither came tae keep hoose."

He put out his hand as he spoke to prevent a long thorny briar from catching in Iona's skirts. As he did so, she saw that he had a deep and terrible scar running across the back of his hand from the fingers to the wrist.

"Is that a wound on your hand?" she asked.

He nodded.

"Culloden," he said grimly.

"It must have been a terrible battle!"

"It was tha' richt enough."

"But I thought the MacCraggans took no part in the Rising," Iona remarked.

"Nae in the Rising, for the auld Duke lay a-dyin' an' theer wasna' onybody tae lead us. But nigh on fifty o' us gaed frae here tae join the Prince at Culloden."

"Were there many of them killed?" Iona asked.

"Fourteen deid by the hand o' the English tha' black day," Dughall replied; "an' but for the intervention o' Heaven we wad aul hae been struck doon."

"The intervention of Heaven?" Iona queried.

"Aye, it wae tha'. 'Tis an unco strange tale but ye'll nae wish tae be hearin' it the noo."

"Oh but do tell me," Iona said. "If you only knew how often I have listened to tales of Prestonpans, Falkirk and Culloden, and yet I could never hear enough. It makes them seem more real now that I am here in Scotland. Yes indeed, I have heard many stories but please tell me what happened to you."

Without slackening his pace in any way Dughall's words came slowly from his lips.

"N'ane o' us gaed south wi' the Prince," he said, "but wheen we heard he wae nigh Inverness, we set oot, fifty strong, tae join him. We haed nae leader an' we dinna ken if the auld Duke wae for or agin the Prince. But we ken fine, each mon o' us, whit we should dae. Weel, we joined the Prince's Army at dawn an' found everythin' verry confused. Clans waur arguin' wheer they should stand in battle. The MacDonalds waur awfu' mad for their richtfu' place haed been gi'en tae the men o' Atholl. We haed naebody tae speak for us an' we found oursels placed in a wee marshy hollow. Wheen the battle began, we soon ken' tha' the ither clans tae the right an' the left o' us haed fled an' we waur alane. It wae hand tae hand fightin' an' it looked as if theer waur nae hope o' ony o' us comin' oot alive, wheen all o' a sudden there appeared MacCraggan Mor himsel' wearin' his white sporran an' the three white eagle feathers in his bonnet!"

Dughall paused impressively and Iona asked:

"Who was he?"

"MacCraggan Mor wa' His Grace's great great gran'-father," Dughall answered. "He made the Clan strong an' powerfu'. He wa' a grand mon whom his people luved an' whom his enemies feart. He put the three white eagle feathers in his bonnet. Them that followed him as Chieftain wore eagle's feathers but nae white anes. 'Wheen ye see ma white feathers in the thick o' battle,' he said, 'put your trust in me.' Sae wheen I seed MacCraggan Mor stride intae the midst o' the fight I ken weel tha' he haed come tae save his ain. 'Follow me!' His voice rang out, an' we followed him.

"He turned an' struck doon the English an' niver hae I seed a mon fight like him. He led us oot o' that treacherous hollow an' oop on tae the high ground. We ken theen tha' we waur defeated, for those o' the Prince's men wasna' lyin' deid or wounded waur runnin' awa'. MacCraggan Mor lookit round. 'Theer's no mair we can dae', he says sadly. He brocht us a wee bittie further an' theen he pointed west. 'Hurry hame,' he says, 'an' dinna speak o' wheer ye hae been this day. If theer's a chance o' fightin' agin for the Prince, I'll come for ye,' We came hame, but fourteen o' us waur left behind—those who waur no deid tae be tortured an' stripped naked by the English. It wae only wheen we gets back amang our ain families tha' we ken exactly whit hae happened. MacCraggan Mor haed come bac' frae the grave tae save us!"

Dughall's voice died away. Ahead Iona could see the silver water of the loch.

"That was a wonderful story," she said. "Thank you for telling it to me."

She said nothing more until they were in the boat, and then as Dughall drew out from the shore she asked:

"Do you think the present Duke knows that you went to fight for the Prince?"

"Nay, it wad hae been fulish tae blether o' sic things," Dughall answered. "The auld Duke deid the followin' night. We heard the bell tollin' an' gathered at the castle."

"Was the present Duke there?" Iona asked.

"Nae, he didna come hame for nigh on three week. He wae in foreign parts whaur he haed been for two year or mair. Wheen he returned, he cauled us taegether an' tauld us tha' as we haed tak'n nae part in the Risin', we wad no be punished by the English. Those o' us who haed been tae Culloden hauld a' tongues as ye can guess. We haed heard whit wa' happenin' in ither parts o' the country. Asides, we cad dae nothin' tae help the Prince, for he wae in hidin'."

"But many of you must have helped him," Iona said, "for it was around here that he lay hidden for so long."

"Aye, we helped him, but 'tis wise tae say naethin' o' whit wae done, for theer a' those who wad tak pleasure in persecutin' the Clan the noo."

Dughall had lowered his voice when they were on the water until it was little more than a whisper. Now he said:

" 'Tis best tae keep silent, mistress."

They reached the stone steps and Dughall sprang ashore. He helped Iona from the boat, raised his hand in a salute as she whispered her thanks, and began to row swiftly back the way they had come.

Iona hurried up the steps and across the terrace to the oak door. She fitted the key in the lock. It turned easily and a second later she was in the castle. She closed the door behind her and ran down the empty passage. Now she had only to regain her bedroom without being seen and no one would question where she had been.

She found her way to the little winding staircase down which Cathy had led her from the upper floors and climbed swiftly up it. She was within sight of the security of her bedroom when she saw someone approaching down the broad passage which led from the main staircase. Instinctively she slackened her pace and slipped the shawl back from her head. She only had time to wonder whether she looked dishevelled and if her shoes showed signs of mud when she came face to face with Lord Niall.

"So this is where you have been hiding," he said, "I wondered which room had been allotted to you."

"It is there, my lord," Iona said, trying to speak calmly and pointing to a door a few paces ahead of them.

He looked first in the direction of her hand, then back at her. His eyes travelled slowly from her flushed face and windswept curls to the shawl over her shoulders and down to the dusty hem of her gown. He smiled and she was suddenly more frightened than if he had spat at her.

"I came to ask you whether we could talk together for a short while," Lord Niall said softly. "I think we have much to say to each other—you and I."

7

Beatrice Wrexham looked out of the coach window as the horses began to move slowly downhill. Below she saw Skaig Castle and the evening mist rising from the loch, so that the battlements and pinnacled turrets seemed to be but a figment of the imagination which might vanish at any moment and become but one with the mists.

Beatrice had seen too many castles for the magnificence or beauties of Skaig to move her or awake any emotion other than a sense of relief that the end of her long journey was in sight. The habitations of people never aroused her curiosity, were they palaces or cottages. It was the people who lived in them in whom her interest was centred and more particularly of course the men. As she thought of Niall MacCraggan her eyelids drooped a little and her red lips were curved in a faint smile.

It had been an amusing interlude with a touch of piquancy about it, due principally to its unexpectedness. And it had been pleasant, after she had spent so many hours alone, to be admired and courted with such an impetuous and unbridled passion. Of one thing she was assured—that neither her face nor her body had lost the power to arouse desire.

She and Lord Niall had lingered for two nights at the little hotel at Aviemore and it was with difficulty that Beatrice had been able to persuade Niall that their sojourn should not continue indefinitely. His wild protestations of love had flattered her, his attitude towards his half-brother and his frankness regarding his own ambitions had intrigued her interest.

Beatrice was eager to reach Skaig, but she was shrewd enough to realise that a weapon had been placed in her hands which could be turned to her own advantage. Here was an easy approach to the problem that the Marquis had set her, and she was well aware that it would serve his purpose, should she find enough evidence of Jacobite leanings to depose the present Duke, if she could install his half-brother as Chieftain of the Clan. So long as the Dukedom of Arkrae was loyal to the English King, it would matter little who bore the title.

Niall would make a handsome Duke, Beatrice thought, and it might be entertaining to be instrumental in placing him in such a position. As she thought of his ardency, of the fierce strength of his arms and the possessive hunger of his kisses, she stretched herself and felt the warmth of her own response steal over her to quicken her pulses.

Journeys did not always have such pleasant respites, she told herself, and remembered that on her arrival at Skaig Castle she and Lord Niall were to meet as strangers. He had told her that he had planned to intercept her on the road because ever since he had first fallen in love with her, he had wondered how he could compel her interest. He had been sensible enough to realise he had little chance of doing this in London, where he would be in competition with the Marquis. When he learnt that Beatrice was to visit Skaig he had known that here was a unique opportunity to further both his love and his ambition. Once he had guessed why she was journeying north, he was anxious to leave her in no doubt as to where his sympathies were placed.

Beatrice, while appreciating that Niall needed her help materially, was quite prepared to believe that he spoke the truth when he said he loved her. She was at the same time well aware that, had she been infinitely less attractive, he would to further his plans still have made an effort to seduce her. But she was experienced enough to know that, ambitious or not, desire for her had finally swept him off his feet.

She was too well versed in hearing men talk of love not to recognise sincerity when she met it; and when Niall had driven away from the inn at Aviemore, she knew that he was both her captive and her slave. At the same time it was obvious that he was uneasily aware that his stepmother would make trouble should she learn where he had been or have the slightest inkling that his affections were deeply involved.

It was therefore imperative that they should not arrive at the castle together and Lord Niall had gone ahead with the intention of breaking his journey the following night not in Inverness but at an inn on the outskirts of the town.

"It would not be wise for us both to stay in Inverness," he told Beatrice. "More beautiful than the stars in Heaven, wherever you go, you are bound to excite comment and someone would doubtless sooner or later repeat that they had seen us togehter."

"You sound as if you were afraid of your stepmother," Beatrice teased and noted that Lord Niall looked uncomfortable.

"She is inordinately fond of me," he said at length.

"And you—of her?" Beatrice asked.

"When I was very young, I found her not unattractive," he replied. "I had seen few women, and she was certainly nearer my age than that of my father."

Beatrice laughed.

"The story has a familiar ring," she mocked. "Pretty young stepmother and a handsome, lonely stepson."

There was something provocative in her tone and Lord Niall drew nearer to her to gaze hungrily at her curved lips which parted to show the pearly perfection of her teeth and the tip of a crimson pointed tongue.

"All women for all time will look hags now that I have seen you," he said thickly.

Beatrice smiled and her eyes gleamed enticingly beneath the dark lashes which bordered the heavy lids.

"How can I believe that?" she pouted. "Memories are short and when I have gone south again, doubtless someone else will hear those very words."

"Do you doubt me?" Lord Niall asked fiercely. "I could kill you so that no one else could tell you of your beauty."

He caught her almost brutally in his arms, but she laughed as her head went back against his shoulder. His lips were hard against the whiteness of her neck and after a while her laughter died away. . . .

Yes, Lord Niall had been bewitched by her beauty; but now, as the wheels of the coach rumbled over the bridge leading into the castle, Beatrice wondered if the ardency of his love might not prove a trifle fatiguing.

It was always the same where she was concerned. A new love, a new adventure, she swept into it eagerly and excitedly until all too soon the thrill and ecstasy vanished, leaving her bored and impatient with the whole affair. A lover was like an orange she thought, when it was sucked dry, one's thirst was quenched and there was nothing to do but to throw away the empty rind.

The horses drew up in front of the Castle. Beatrice gave

a last look into the hand-mirror which her maid held for her. Despite the long drive from Inverness there was not a hair out of place beneath her feather-trimmed hat of black velvet and her eyes were bright and unwearied. She wore her most elaborate travelling gown of azure blue velvet trimmed with ermine, and she carried a tiny muff of the same fur.

As the footmen hurried forward to open the coach door and draw aside the heavy fur rug which had covered her, Beatrice paused before descending, well aware that several figures were waiting for her at the top of the steps which led to the great oak door.

At last she stepped from the coach, two footmen assisting her descent, her maid hurriedly arranging the folds of her velvet gown. Then very slowly, her golden head held high, Beatrice moved up the steps. The Duchess was waiting for her just inside the door, and Beatrice surprised a look of chagrin in her eyes and knew it was due to a very feminine pang of envy.

The two women kissed, then the Duchess turned to the tall figure standing by her side.

"May I present my stepson," she asked, "the Duke of Arkrae?"

"We are indeed honoured by your visit, Lady Wrexham," a deep voice said. "Permit me to welcome you to Skaig Castle."

Beatrice felt his lips brush her fingers, then as she rose from her curtsy, she looked deep into his eyes and felt something strange happen to her. She was not sure what it was; a sensation half of pain and half of pleasure seemed to strike her suddenly and leave her weak and quivering, a frailty she had never known before.

She was only half conscious of the Duchess's chattering voice:

"You must be tired, my dear Lady Wrexham, for in truth it is a tiresome, exhausting journey. I vow that the last time I drove to London I was prostrate for weeks after my arrival. But let us repair to the salon. You will need a glass of wine to revive you, but I swear you look as if you have but stepped from your bed-chamber."

Beatrice followed her hostess and now she was able to notice the furnishing of the castle and feel relieved at its luxury. She had been half afraid she would find everything exceedingly uncomfortable, for she had been told in London that the Scots were little better than animals without even the most primitive ideas of civilisation. But one glance at the elegance of the Duke's exquisitely cut and heavily embroidered coat, at the diamonds which glittered at his throat and the formality of his powdered hair had been enough to reassure her that at Skaig the Scots were not without their graces.

She moved beside the Duchess up the broad staircase, their dresses sweeping against the carved oak balustrade, their silk petticoats rustling over the carpet. Beatrice was conscious all the time of the man who followed them. Never had she imagined for one instance that the Duke would be so handsome or indeed so attractive. No, he was more than that; there was something unique about him, something she had never encountered before. She was not sure what it was, and when they reached the top of the staircase, she turned round, making some trivial question an excuse to look at him again.

He answered her courteously and she noticed with a sudden sense of disquietude that he appeared quite unmoved by her beauty and his eyes were cold. She was accustomed to a change in men's faces when they first beheld her, to seeing their faces darken, the pupils dilate a little. She could feel excitement radiate from them, reaching out towards her, drawing her irresistibly as if towards the warmth of a fire. But in the Duke's expression there was only polite interest; and for perhaps the first time in her life Beatrice wondered if her mirror had played her false.

The Duchess was speaking.

"Where is Niall?" she demanded. "I sent a footman to tell him that Lady Wrexham was arriving and that we were waiting to greet her. He can never have received the message or he would have been beside us. Where do you think he can be, Ewan?"

"I have not the least idea of Niall's whereabouts," the Duke replied.

A footman standing sentinel on the landing stepped forward. "His lordship is in the Chinese Room, Your Grace."

"What can he be doing there?" the Duchess asked sharply. "I will call him."

She crossed the landing towards a pair of wide mahogany doors on the far side. The footman hastened to open them for her. They swung open and it was easy for Beatrice and the Duke standing at the top of the staircase to see into the interior of the room.

Lord Niall was leaning against the mantelpiece in a

negligent attitude, one hand raised as he played with his diamond-ringed quizzing-glass. Standing in front of him, her slim, tense figure somehow conveying an impression of defiance, was Iona. In her hands she held a woollen shawl, the corner of which trailed on the ground. Her face was very white, her eyes wide and dark, but her chin was high, the vivid red of her hair a flag of unvanquished courage.

As the door opened, Lord Niall looked round with an expression of irritation, but it was obvious that the interruption came as a relief to Iona.

"Niall, why are you here?" The Duchess's voice was almost shrill. "Lady Wrexham has arrived and you were not there to greet her."

Lord Niall glanced from his stepmother's face towards the landing and he moved unhurriedly towards the door.

"No one informed me that her ladyship's arrival was imminent," he said and, passing the Duchess, moved to Beatrice's side. He took her hand and she felt the warm insistent pressure of his lips.

"My deepest apologies for not being the first to welcome you," he said. "Nevertheless it gives me unbounded pleasure to meet your ladyship."

"I thank your lordship," Beatrice said, and there was a hint of laughter in her tone.

The Duchess turned to Iona.

"Your hair needs attention," she said icily, "and a shawl is hardly the correct wear for the salon. It would be best for you to retire and tidy yourself before being presented to Lady Wrexham."

Iona curtsied but said nothing, and the Duchess swept away leading Beatrice towards the salon, the two men following in their wake. Swiftly Iona picked up her shawl and hurrying from the Chinese Room sped upstairs.

Her heart was still fluttering and her hands were cold with fear. It had been a relief beyond all words that the Duchess should have interrupted her interview with Lord Niall, and yet she was embarrassed that they should have been discovered *téte-à-téte* and she wondered what the Duke would think. In her bedroom, Cathy was waiting and as Iona entered, she went towards her.

"Is all weel, mistress?"

"I got back safely and no one saw me enter the castle," Iona said: "but unfortunately I met Lord Niall in the passage. He was looking for me."

She felt her heart throb again as she remembered that almost agonising moment when Lord Niall had said that he must speak with her. She had been too agitated to make excuses, and miserably conscious of her muddy shoes and stained dress she had followed him downstairs to the Chinese Room.

It was a charming little drawing-room decorated with strange and colourful hangings of exotic birds and flowers; but Iona had no eyes for the room, only for the dark secretive face of Lord Niall.

He closed the door, walked across to the writing-desk and sat himself on the edge of it; then he looked her up and down, playing with his quizzing-glass the while as if it were a weapon he held in his hand.

"You might be my sister," he said at length, "though we are not alike."

She knew he was taunting her and she answered him bravely.

"Surely you are the unusual one. I thought all MacCraggans had red hair."

"Indeed not! Have you ever heard the rhyme which our clansmen repeat when a child is born?:

"MacCraggan red, oh happy day!
MacCraggan black, then kneel and pray."

"The black MacCraggans are the bad ones, and they are also—dangerous."

Iona recognised the implication of the last word.

"I am not afraid of you," she said quietly.

"No?" He raised his eyebrows. "And yet why should you be? I might find a sister useful."

Iona said nothing. His eyes scrutinised her very closely.

"Was it enjoyable?" he asked at length.

The question seemed to Iona to have no sense.

"Enjoyable?" she repeated. "To what are you referring?"

"The night you spent in Inverness," he replied, and she felt the embarrassed colour run swiftly into her cheeks.

She had already decided what her explanation was to be. Keeping her eyes on his, with almost pathetic dignity she said quietly.

"What your lordship supposes is not the truth. The ship which brought me from France made its first port of call at Yarmouth. Two passengers disembarked, another came

98

aboard. The latter was the gentleman whose bedchamber was opposite your own in the hotel at Inverness. He was kind to me on board, for the ship's company were rough and it was not too pleasant to be a woman travelling alone and unprotected. I was in great fear that my possessions, poor though they were, might be stolen from me, and so I gave to the gentleman for safe keeping most of my money and the packet containing the proofs of my identity. He was gracious enough to guard these for me; but unfortunately when we arrived at Inverness, he went ashore before I had time to ask for the return of my valuables. He did not come to the hotel until after I had retired to bed, and I was therefore forced to wake him early in the morning before I left on the stage-coach."

To Iona's own ears the story sounded plausible enough, but she was well aware that the mocking suspicion was still apparent in Lord Niall's eyes.

"And the gentleman's name?" he inquired.

"Thomson," Iona stammered. "Mr. Hugo Thomson."

She made up the name at random, at the same time regretting that she had not been sensible enough to inquire of Hector what name he had actually used at the hotel. She half expected Lord Niall to tell her that she lied; but he said nothing and with a sense of relief she guessed that he was not in a position to know if she was telling the truth or not.

"So that is your story," he said at length; "Yet you would be surprised if I was fool enough to credit it."

"I am not aware that I have given your lordship any reason to doubt my word," Iona said.

Lord Niall laughed. It was not a pleasant laugh and Iona was aware that he enjoyed torturing her. She made every effort to keep her voice clear and steady, to control the quivering of her fingers, the sudden trembling of her lips. But she could not prevent the colour rising in her cheeks or the way it would suddenly ebb away leaving her pale and a little faint.

Lord Niall walked across the room to stand with his back to the mantelpiece.

"Come here," he said suddenly.

Iona drew a step nearer to him, still keeping instinctively out of arm's reach.

"There are many things I might say to you," he said, and his voice was suddenly silky. "Firstly that Mr. Thom-

99

son—if that is indeed his name—was a damned fortunate fellow, and secondly that you are far too pretty to be my sister."

Iona's lips tightened for a moment and he added:

"But you don't like my saying either of these things, do you? Shall I add something else? It is that I am a trifle suspicous of young women who come from Paris just now for the purpose of getting into communication with the Duke of Arkrae."

Here was danger! Now Iona's embarrassment had vanished. She felt instead alert and watchful, and in a voice of puzzled surprise she asked:

"Perhaps your lordship will explain what you mean."

"Why should I bother? You are not so simple as you appear. Besides, I might prove a better friend than an enemy. Why not trust me?"

"With what?" Iona's eyes were wide and innocent.

"Your reason for coming here."

"But surely that is obvious," Iona parried. "You have doubtless seen the letter containing Jeannie MacLeod's last confession."

"I am not interested in that," Lord Niall replied. "I am only interested in you and perhaps a trifle in the gentleman called—Hugo Thomson."

There was a definite menace in his slow tones, yet now Iona was aware that he had nothing definite with which to threaten her. He was but feeling his way, suspicious, uncertain; and while she was afraid of him, she knew that for the moment he was weaponless.

Lord Niall looked down at his quizzing-glass swinging pendulum-like from the thumb and finger of his left hand.

"You are, of course," he said softly, "an ardent Jacobite?"

His words were so unexpected that Iona felt her heart give a frightened leap and the blood drain away from her cheeks; then as he looked at her and waited for her answer, the door opened and she was rescued.

Now in her own room she was well aware that the respite would be but a short one. Lord Niall was dangerous, she was well aware of that. It was not only because he had caught her at a disadvantage in Inverness that she distrusted him, it was something deeper and more fundamental than anything he had ever done or said. It was the instinctive reaction of every sense in her body. He was not trustworthy, there was something horrible and treacherous

100

about him, something which affected her sub-consciously so that she knew with absolute clarity that here was a real and malevolent danger.

"How white ye are, mistress!" Cathy said breaking into Iona's thoughts.

Iona sat down on a chair.

"I'm all right, Cathy," she said a little unsteadily.

"Ye are faint. May I fetch ye a glass o' wine?"

"I shall be all right in a minute," Iona murmured, putting her head down in her hands.

Without waiting for permission Cathy sped downstairs and a few minutes later came back with a glass of brandy which she held to Iona's lips.

"Tak a sup, mistress," she insisted, and because Iona felt too weak to argue she took a sip or two and felt the liquid run like fire through her body.

"Thank you, Cathy," she said at last. "I am better now and ashamed of my own weakness."

"Dinna fash aboot being weak," Cathy answered. "Let me unlace ye an' lie ye doon until it is time for dinner."

Iona did as Cathy suggested and, though she had no idea of sleeping, the long walk through the woods and the emotional disturbance of her interview with Lord Niall had taken their toll and she fell into a fitful slumber.

She was wakened by Cathy bringing her hot water with which to wash and laying out her evening gown.

"Ye must hurry, mistress," Cathy said. "I guessed ye were asleep an' left ye as long as I dare, but it will be wise no tae be late."

"Worse than that, it would be exceedingly rude," Iona said, and slipped off the bed.

She washed and then as she turned towards the dressing table Cathy said:

"There's a deal o' talk doonstairs the noo."

"Of what?" Iona asked.

"O' ma Lady Wrexham. The servants hae been gossipin' with her ladyship's coachman an' grooms an' noo I hear tell that her ladyship has come here tae spy."

"How do they know that?" Iona asked.

"Saving yer pardon, mistress, but her ladyship's servants were boasting that she is under the protection o' the Marquis o' Severn."

"And who is he?" Iona asked.

"Weel, we ken right enough that the Marquis is the enemy o' Scotland. The cruelty o' the English soldiers has

101

his approval an' more, while ane o' her ladyship's footmen avows that the Marquis has sworn afore mony months hae passed that Prince Charles's head shall lie in its blood on Tower Hill."

Iona shivered.

"Is this true, Cathy?"

"I can only tell ye whit they're sayin', mistress."

"Thank you for telling me," Iona said at last. "Hear all you can, Cathy."

"Indeed I'll dae ma best, mistress."

"But be careful," Iona admonished. "You must run no risks. Are you the only one in the castle loyal to the Prince?"

"Nay, mistress, but we dinna speak aboot it, even amang oursels for the Duchess is English an' the Governors o' Fort Augustus an' Fort William often call here."

"I understand," Iona said. "And the Duke?"

"We dinna ken what His Grace feels. If the English come tae the castle, he is polite tae them—but this English lady hae come the noo an' she's awfu' bonny."

Iona understood only too well the implication in Cathy's words. She had had but the merest glimpse of Lady Wrexham through the open door of the Chinese Room, but it had been enough. Beautiful and the mistress of the Marquis of Severn, why should Lady Wrexham have come north unless her reason was much the same as her own?

There was something dramatic in the situation, Iona thought suddenly. Two women arriving within a few days of each other at Skaig Castle, one from France and one from London, each with her instructions, each determined on the success of her assignment.

Iona could see the situation so clearly that it was almost as if she watched herself and the personages at Skaig upon a stage and saw a plot unfolding act by act.

The Duke stood as it were at the cross-roads. Which way would he turn? Which woman would succeed in gaining his support? Iona thought of the Prince far away in France, waiting for her return, hoping almost against hope that she might succeed where others had failed, and then she remembered that quick glimpse she had had of Lady Wrexham—an impression of beauty, of glamour, of youth, of loveliness and with it all the poise of an experienced woman of the world.

What chance had she against such weapons? And then Iona remembered with a sudden thankfulness that the ideals for which she battled were greater by far than the wiles of any woman, however desirable. It was the Cause that mattered, and it was impossible that the fate of Scotland should be altered by the contour of a woman's face.

"I will not be afraid," Iona told herself. "Lord Niall is bad and wicked, but the Duke is good."

She was surprised at her own conviction that this was so. Only this morning she had not been sure, unable to make any complete diagnosis of His Grace's character and personality. But now she knew with a conviction that could not be denied that the Duke, whatever his political sympathies, was good at heart.

Quite unexpectedly Iona's depression left her. She felt revived and fortified. She felt also ready to fight for what she believed, however great the odds against her. She remembered Hector hiding in the woods and sent up a prayer for his safety. Strangely enough, it was comforting to know that he was not so far away. It gave her a sense of danger shared, of a renewed comradeship after she had felt so very much alone.

Cathy robed her in a gown of ivory satin. It was trimmed very simply with rows of narrow lace, but it had been cut by a French seamstress with the skill and dexterity of her race. Iona had no jewels, but her eyes seemed to blaze like emeralds and her white neck had the sheen of precious pearls. Cathy offered to powder her hair but Iona refused. She had never aped the fashions of the nobility and she knew it was safer to remain humble and unpretentious. Besides, she was feminine enough to realise that her hair was in fact lovelier unadorned.

She came slowly down the stairs, for despite Cathy's fears it was not yet the hour for dinner. She reached the first floor and was about to enter the Crimson Salon when she heard voices below in the Great Hall. Curiously Iona paused to listen. A group of men were standing in the centre of the Hall, talking loudly. She leant over the stairs to look closer at them. Then her hands gripped the banister and it was with the utmost difficulty that she prevented herself from giving a cry of horror!

Standing in the midst of the men, his arms bound behind him, was Hector.

8

Without considering what she was doing, impelled only by her own horror at seeing Hector in such a plight, Iona ran down the staircase. She had, however, set but one foot on the stone floor of the Great Hall when a stern voice asked:

"What is all this?"

The men who were gathered round Hector and talking amongst themselves turned hastily towards the Duke who unobserved had entered the Hall from a door on the far side. Iona stood still. She was nearer to Hector than the Duke and with a kind of hypnotised fascination she watched his approach. Dressed for dinner in a satin coat of silver grey embroidered with pearls, he was in strange contrast to Hector who was tousled and dirty, his coat torn, his stockings ripped from knee to ankle. Yet Hector faced the Duke fearlessly, his head held high, his shoulders braced despite the tightness of the rope which was cutting painfully into his wrists.

The clansmen bowed awkwardly but with an inborn reverence as the Duke approached. One amongst them who appeared to be better dressed and slightly more refined moved forward as their spokesman. He had a thin, cadaverous face and his eyes, in one of which there was an unsightly cast, were too close togeher.

The Duke glanced at him.

"Well, Sime," he said sharply, "What is the explanation of this?"

"We found yon mon, Yer Grace, lurkin' in the woods on the east shore. Wheen he saw us approachin' he tried tae escape an' fought lik a wild cat 'til we overcame him."

The Duke looked not at Hector but at the men surrounding him.

"Why were you in the woods?"

"His lordship's orders, Yer Grace," Sime explained. "He sent for me but twa hours back an' told me he haed suspicions tha' there wae a stranger abroad. 'Bring whoever ye may find tae the castle,' his lordship says, an' here we are, Yer Grace—wi' the prisoner."

He jerked his head at Hector. Iona, listening, felt paralysed with horror. The man had said that it was two hours ago that he had been sent for by Lord Niall. That would be after her interview with his lordship in the Chinese Room. She was sure now that he had guessed from where she had come when he had met her walking down the passage. He had noticed her windswept hair, the mud on her shoes, the dusty hem of her dress and had drawn his own conclusions. At any rate, his suspicions had been aroused enough for him to send his men to make a search of the woods.

Wildly Iona wondered what she could do, clasping her hands together in her agitation until the knuckles showed white and her nails dug into the soft palms.

Now the Duke was looking at Hector. For a moment the eyes of the two men met and then the Duke said quietly:

"Unloose this gentleman's bonds!"

The clansmen looked astonished and Sime protested:

"He's a dangerous mon, Yer Grace, an' exceedin' powerful. It took half a dozen o' us tae bind him, an' Andrew's jaw is broke frae the blow he gied him."

"Obey me!"

The Duke's command seemed to echo round the Hall. Sullenly Sime took a knife from his belt and cut the thick rope. Hector shook himself, the ends fell to the floor, and he began to chafe the blood back into his wrists.

"I thank your Grace."

His voice was resonant and light.

"You were in my woods?" the Duke asked.

"I was."

"And your reason for being there?"

"I am on the way to Skye. I prefer to walk over the hills than trudge along the road."

Hector's tone was calm. He might have been conversing with the Duke from the comfort of an armchair.

"That sounds reasonable enough," the Duke commented.

"If I have trespassed," Hector said, "I owe Your Grace an apology. I was not aware that you had closed your territories to wayfarers."

"I have not," the Duke replied. "I have no objection to people passing over my land so long as they do no damage."

105

"It would then be gracious of Your Grace to permit me to continue my journey," Hector said: "these men sprang upon me unawares."

"It appears that I should apologise for their action," the Duke said.

"I see no reason for you to do that," a voice said suddenly from the foot of the stairs, "for they are not your men, my dear Ewan—but mine."

Iona started and turned round. Standing just behind her, so close that he was almost touching her, was Lord Niall. She had not heard him approach and had no idea that he had been listening. Now he passed her without a glance and moved with a kind of languid grace towards the Duke.

All faces were turned towards him and Iona realised that at his coming the whole atmosphere changed. The clansmen seemed to stiffen, their embarrassment, which had been very obvious when the Duke was questioning their action in capturing Hector, vanished. Once again they believed themselves justified, and Sime moved forward to say:

"We found a mon as yer lordship anticipated. We bound him an' brocht him here as yer lordship commanded."

"You behaved correctly," Lord Niall said.

He raised his quizzing-glass and looked Hector up and down in an unpleasant manner, then very quietly in a tone which Iona knew well he used when he was most dangerous, he said:

"Perhaps the prisoner would care to tell us his name?"

It was then that Iona knew that she must act and act quickly before Hector could reply. She sped forward and reached Lord Niall's side.

"This, my lord," she said in a clear voice, "is the gentleman who travelled in the same ship with me and who was kind enough to take charge of my possessions until we reached Inverness. His name, as I have already told your lordship, is Mr. Hugo Thomson."

She was well aware as she spoke of the changing expressions on Hector's face. First she had seen a look of warning in his eyes and knew that he admonished her wordlessly to disclaim his acquaintance, to take no part in what was happening; now that was superseded by a look of astonishment. At the same time she knew that he would be quick enough to understand that she had a reason for her interference.

"Mr. Hugo Thomson," Lord Niall repeated, his lips

106

curving in a sneer which made the words almost an insult. "Yes, of course, and now I recall your face, sir, though I did but see it for a second in somewhat unfortunate circumstances."

"I have already told his lordship," Iona said quickly, speaking to Hector, "of your kindness to me on the ship after you came aboard at Yarmouth. I told him how, for safe keeping, I gave you my money and possessions which were of great value to me. Unfortunately on our arrival in Inverness you did not return to the hotel until after I had retired for the night. I was therefore forced to visit your bedchamber before the stage-coach left and ask you to return to me my property."

Iona's voice died away breathlessly, and then she was conscious that the Duke was at her side.

"I think, Niall," he said, in a voice of cold authority, "these personal matters which concern Miss Iona and this gentleman need not be discussed further. Your men have my permission to go and it would be inhospitable not to offer Mr. Thomson a glass of wine before he proceeds on his journey."

Iona felt both relief and gratitude, and she saw too, the sudden light in Hector's eyes. But Lord Niall was too formidable an enemy to be so easily vanquished.

"I am afraid we are not in agreement, Ewan," he said. "I have not yet finished questioning this fugitive, and my men will take him on my instructions to the dungeons."

Iona gave a little gasp of horror and fright. Lord Niall turned to her and she shrank from the glittering darkness of his eyes.

"Hugo Thomson, did you say?" he asked. "Really, my dear Miss Iona, you must pardon my scepticism, but no Scot ever owned such an English-sounding name."

Iona could only stare at him despairingly.

"Perhaps you would be kind enough to tell me what crime I have committed other than that of trespass?" Hector asked angrily.

"That is one of the points on which I shall question you," Lord Niall said. "I have, of course, several ideas on the subject and it will be interesting to see if they coincide with yours. It is sad, of course, that your liberty should be curtailed so soon after your return to Scotland."

"Return? What do you mean by that?" Hector demanded.

"I may, of course, be mistaken," Lord Niall said, "but

107

that too we shall discover in time. I said we—and I refer to the help I shall receive from the English governor at Fort Augustus. Major Johnstone is particularly adept at interrogation."

Hector squared his jaw but said nothing.

"But why should you do this?" Iona asked wildly. "It is unjust, it is . . ."

She felt the sudden pressure of the Duke's fingers on her arm and arrested her words to turn her face despairingly towards him. He was not looking at her but at his halfbrother:

"I fail to understand your reasons for this, Niall," he said frigidly.

Lord Niall smiled secretly as if at some joke which only he could understand.

"Why trouble yourself, Ewan?" he asked. "Let me assure you that my reasons are good ones and prompted only by my unswerving loyalty to King George."

"I can well believe that," the Duke replied; "but though, as you have reminded me, these men are your servants, this castle is mine and I do not permit gentlemen against whom no crime has been proven to be placed in the dungeons."

"In that case," Lord Niall retorted, "perhaps it would be better if I had him escorted forthwith to Fort Augustus."

"As you will," the Duke said indifferently, "but it is late, and I suggest instead that he is housed in the guard room of the Keep."

Lord Niall hesitated, then appeared to capitulate.

"If it salves your hospitable conscience, my dear brother, let it be as you say." He waved a languid hand towards Sime. "Take this man away," he commanded. "Give him neither food nor drink until after I have had time to question him in the morning."

"Very guid, m'lord."

There was an air of triumph about the man as he moved towards Hector and put a rough hand on his shoulder. With a sinking heart Iona watched Hector being marched away between the clansmen; then as they disappeared from sight Lord Niall laughed:

"You were nearly deceived by that rogue, Ewan," he said. "If you are in a gambling mood, I don't mind wagering you a monkey to a hundred pounds that he will prove to be a Jacobite, and if, as I suspicion, there is a price on his head, I will spend some of it on a gift for Miss Iona."

"Do you think I would accept blood money?" Iona asked angrily. She felt the tears prick her eyes and added in a tone of contempt and utter scorn: "I didn't believe that one Scot would betray another to their English masters."

Blinded now, she turned towards the stairs, but only as she reached them was she aware that someone stood there barring her way. Hastily wiping her eyes, Iona looked up at the Duchess, resplendent in a gown of black velvet. She was standing about three steps up from the Great Hall, her fingers entwined in a diamond cross which she wore suspended from her neck on a chain of pearls. Iona curtsied, then realised that the Duchess had not even seen her. She was looking across the Hall, her eyes fixed on Lord Niall as he and the Duke came slowly towards the stairs. Only as they reached them did the men perceive the Duchess and realise by her silence and the expression on her face that something was wrong.

"I am afraid we have kept Your Grace waiting for dinner," the Duke began courteously but the Duchess seemed not to hear him.

Still staring at Lord Niall, she said in a strangled voice which seemed to burst tempestuously from between her thin lips:

"Why did you tell me you had not been to Inverness?"

If Lord Nial was discomfited, he showed no signs of it.

"My dear *Belle-mère* . . ." he began, but the Duchess interrupted him.

"Answer me," she said. "Why did you lie?"

Now her voice was shrill and instinctively Iona looked up to see if anyone was listening on the landing overhead. It was the Duke who took command of the situation. He walked up the stairs to the Duchess's side and held out his arm.

"Our guest will be waiting for us in the salon," he said sternly. "Niall can answer your question after dinner."

There was an authority in his voice which forced the Duchess to obey him. As if with an effort she turned her eyes from Lord Niall's face and took the Duke's arm. In a silence pregnant with repressed emotion they moved slowly up the stairs. Iona followed with Lord Niall at her side and after a moment she realised that his eyes were searching her face as if he would ferret out her innermost secrets.

"You should have trusted me," he said in a low voice. "I warned you that I was a dangerous enemy."

"I am still not afraid of you, my lord," Iona replied de-

fiantly, but even as she spoke the words she knew that they
were untrue.

She was afraid of him, not for herself but for Hector—Hector who was now a prisoner and in this evil man's
power.

As she sat through the long meal which followed, as
course succeeded course, she had no idea what she ate or
drank. She could remember only the tales she had heard of
English cruelties, of the tortures they inflicted on
prisoners, of the horrors and privations of English prisons.
How could she save Hector? The question presented itself
to her over and over again as she sat at the table
white-faced and silent.

On the Duke's right hand Beatrice Wrexham, glittering
with jewels, talked brilliantly, her laugh ringing out and
proving so infectious that the men laughed with her. But
the Duchess was almost as silent as Iona, her nervous
fingers crumbling the bread which was placed beside her
plate while her eyes seldom strayed from Lord Niall's face
as he listened absorbedly to Lady Wrexham.

Beatrice was exerting herself to the full. Her beauty in
the light of the great gold candelabra was almost
breathtaking. Tonight her golden hair was powdered and arranged high in the very latest fashion. A chain of tur-
quoises and diamonds was looped around her curls and the
vivid blue of the stones seemed to echo the brillance of her
eyes. Similar stones set in a magnificent necklace encircled
her neck while her shoulders and bosom were milky white
against a low cut gown of rich brocade.

Yet nothing that Beatrice wore was of particular importance. The sinuous grace of her soft body was apparent
beneath the most rigid hoops, bones and lacings. However
elaborately gowned, ornamented, and bejewelled, she still
made men think of her naked. When she was most formal,
she yet managed to convey an impression of incontinence.
There was a natural voluptuousness about her movements
and a lasciviousness in the very perfection of her beauty.

It was obvious to anyone tonight that she was intent on
capturing the attentions of the Duke. She leant against the
arm of his chair so that the sweet intoxicating fragrance of
her perfume rose from her hair and the rustling laces of
her bodice. More than once she laid her long fingers,
weighted down with many rings, on his arm as she accentuated some point in the conversation or laughed with him
at some joke.

As she sipped her wine, she raised her eyes to his and no man could have mistaken the invitation in them or in the sensual fullness of her red lips. The Duke laughed and talked with her, but there was nothing more than a polished courtesy in the pressure of his fingers as he returned the tiny handkerchief she dropped deliberately as she rose from the table.

"Shall I see Your Grace again?" she asked in a low voice, as the ladies moved towards the door.

"My brother and I will not linger over our port," the Duke replied. His tone was one of conventional politeness and Beatrice's eyes were hard as she swept from the room.

Too miserable to think of anything but Hector hungry and thirsty in the Keep, Iona followed the Duchess and Lady Wrexham from the dining-room; but when they entered the salon, she slipped away. There was a fire in the ante-room and she went there wanting only to be alone. It was a room which adjoined the Grand Salon and was used by the members of the household in the morning for writing letters.

Through the double doors which led into the salon Iona could hear Lady Wrexham's voice and rippling laughter. She could not hear what was being said, but there was something intolerable in the mere sound of laughter when Hector was in danger.

Iona sat down on the hearthrug, her white dress billowing out around her. Hector was here in this castle and yet she could think of nothing that she could do to help him. Should she go for Dughall? But even as the idea came to her she knew it was impossible. In all probability it was to save Dughall that Hector had taken to the woods. Perhaps he had seen Lord Niall's men approaching, heard them searching among the trees.

Iona knew now that Lord Niall suspected both her and Hector of being Jacobites, and bitterly she accused herself of ruining everything by one act of carelessness, one moment of forgetfulness. Fool that she had been to go to Hector's bedchamber, more foolish still to have forgotten the letter and the packet in the first place!

Round and round in Iona's head went her thoughts. She must find a way of escape for Hector, but how? And who could assist her?

She heard the gentlemen cross the landing from the dining-room and enter the salon. She heard more laughter, then the sound of music and of a voice singing a love song.

111

She pressed her fingers against her temples striving to shut out any distraction from the problem which confronted her.

At length, weary and despondent, she told herself that the only possible chance was to see if Cathy could help her. Maybe she could bribe one of Lord Niall's men, but then Iona remembered how little money she had left after her journey. She was well aware that Hector would be angry with her for trying to help him, and she knew that she should not jeopardise her own usefulness in an attempt to save him. But at this moment it seemed to her that nothing was of greater consequence than that Hector should not be handed over to English justice.

She wondered what tortures they would use on him. She thought of the thumbscrew, of the rack, and the dreaded instrument which, clamped down on a man's forehead, could be screwed tighter and tighter until he screamed in agony! She started to her feet in terror. She could not bear it, she could not. She must do something, but what she had no idea.

She was suddenly fearful that the Duchess or Lord Niall might send someone in search of her. Her hands would be tied if she was forced to join the company in the salon and then later retire to bed when they did. She went from the ante-room out on to the landing. She crossed it and passing the Chinese Room went down the passage which lay beyond.

She had only been this way once before, when she had interviewed the Duke's attorney in the library. But Cathy had told her that the Duke's private sitting-room also lay in this direction. The passage was lighted by candles in huge silver scones. Iona walked slowly. Though she half expected to encounter a servant who might stare at her curiously, there was no one in sight.

She came to the library door, hesitated for a moment and then saw further down the passage that the door of another room was open. There was a fire burning brightly in the fireplace and the candles were lit. On tiptoe she crept towards the door. She peeped in, but there was no one there. She guessed that this was the Duke's own private room. There were many books, a massive writing-table piled with papers, and many little intimate objects which showed that it was a room which was in frequent use and the familiar background of one particular person.

Her heart beating fast, Iona stood looking round her.

She did not know exactly what she had expected to find, but somehow she felt there might be something here which would help her save Hector. She glanced at the writing-table and saw there the miniature she had brought with her from France. It lay in the centre of a big leather blotter. Beside it was the bracelet which had belonged to Lady Elspeth. Leaning over the Duke's high writing-chair, Iona stared down at the two objects.

She was so intent that she did not for the moment hear someone enter the room and only at the sound of the door being closed did she turn, startled and frightened, her hand going to her breast. The Duke looked across the room at her.

"You wish to speak with me?" he inquired gravely.

"Yes, I. . . ." Iona began then wondered wildly what she could say. If she pleaded for Hector, would she betray herself? Resolutely she summoned up her courage. "I. . . hoped Your Grace . . . would hear me."

"But of course," the Duke replied graciously. "Won't you sit down?"

He indicated a big armchair beside the fireplace. It was so large that Iona was almost swallowed in it. Her heart-shaped face seemed very small against the background of dark velvet and there was something childlike in her attitude, her hands resting primly in her lap. She was silent for some minutes, then realised that the Duke was waiting for her to speak.

"It is about . . . the gentleman in the Keep," she said. "I am worried about him. He was kind to me on the voyage, Your Grace, and I would not have him tortured by the English."

"I can understand that," the Duke said, "but as you heard, Lord Niall claims him."

"Yes, yes, I know," Iona answered, "but I cannot understand why Lord Niall should wish to injure an innocent man, someone who has never done him any personal harm."

"My brother seldom does anything without a reason," the Duke replied.

"I think his lordship believes Mr. . . . Mr. Thomson to be a Jacobite," Iona faltered; "but even if he is, surely that is no reason why one of his own countrymen should give him up to the authorities? The Prince with a price of thirty thousand pounds on his head hid in these parts and no one betrayed him."

"Many suffered for it, though," the Duke said quietly. "There is a woman who lives but a short distance from the castle who was reported to the Governor of Fort Augustus as having given the Prince a cup of milk when he passed her croft. The English cut off both her hands and her crippled son was dragged out of bed and shot against the wall of the house. You can see the marks of the bullets if you are interested."

Iona gave a little cry.

"Spare me!" she cried. "It is too cruel, too wicked even to contemplate."

"I agree," the Duke said quietly, "but I would have you know that the Scots have suffered for their allegiance to the Stuarts."

"And yet . . . I hear that many of them are still loyal," Iona whispered.

The Duke glanced at her quickly, then looked away again.

"That may be true," he said, "but there are also others who think that it is best for our tortured land to acknowledge the English King and accept the justice of our conquerors."

Iona sighed.

"Two opinions, and to enforce either one or the other more men must be tortured and imprisoned. Does cruelty ever solve a problem?"

"I have often asked myself the same question," the Duke replied, "and I confess I have not yet discovered an answer. Like you I hate to see people suffer unnecessarily."

He looked down at her bent head.

"You are young," he said. "It would be best for you to concern yourself with the joys and light-hearted gaieties of youth. Maybe you were unwise to leave Paris."

"I assure Your Grace I experienced few joys or gaieties in Paris," Iona replied.

"I am sorry to hear that."

"Gaieties require money," Iona explained. "Joys come, I imagine, from being with those you love and who love you."

"There must have been many people in the latter category," the Duke remarked drily.

"Not in the last two years," Iona said wistfully, thinking of her guardian and forgetting to be on her guard in speaking of the past.

The Duke watched her face in the firelight; the delicate outline of her tiny nose, the soft droop of the sensitive lips, the pain in the big eyes.

"So you lost your lover!" he said, and his voice was surprisingly harsh.

Iona was startled from her reverie. She looked up at him, her expression transparently innocent until the meaning of his question percolated into her consciousness and a blush transfused her cheeks.

"No! No! . . . not . . . not a lover," she stammered. "I have never . . . been loved . . . like that."

"I apologise for the suggestion," the Duke said gravely: "but I find it hard to believe that anyone as lovely as you . . ."

"Please, stop. . . ." Iona interrupted him, her voice a little breathless. "I beg Your Grace not to say such things to me. I realise they are but the meaningless phrases of fashionable conversation, but I . . . I am not fashionable. I am only a simple girl who prefers . . . sincerity."

There was no doubting the sincerity with which she spoke or the honesty of her expression. The Duke seemed to consider her words while his eyes never left her face.

Iona was suddenly aware of his extraordinary good looks. His clear-cut features were classic, his perfectly proportioned body had a grace which made one forget his unusual height and the tremendous width of his shoulders. He might be a Duke, she thought, but he was also a man and it was easy to imagine that, where he led, men would be proud to follow him.

"Why are you called Iona?" the Duke asked unexpectedly.

"Because I was born on the island of that name," Iona replied unthinkingly and then was aware of the enormity of her indiscretion. Hastily she tried to cover her mistake and faltered. "At . . . at least . . . that was what I was told . . . by my nurse . . . it may of course have been untrue . . . a fairy tale to keep me . . . amused."

"Iona is a beautiful little island which has a magic of its own," the Duke said.

Iona wondered if he deliberately ignored her confusion or was unaware of it. At any rate he obviously did not intend to question her further and after a few seconds she felt the frightened fluttering of her pulses subside and her breath come more easily.

The clock on the mantelpiece struck the hour. Iona remembered Hector languishing in the Deep and chid herself for having forgotten him even for a minute.

"Your Grace will recall that I came here to ask . . . your help," she hesitated.

"I had not forgotten," the Duke replied. "Unfortunately it is not easy for me to interfere with what my brother clearly believes to be his duty."

He glanced at the clock.

"Will you wait here?" he asked.

He went from the room and Iona was left alone. For a long time after the door was closed behind him she stared at it, puzzled by his sudden disappearance, wondering where he had gone and why. Yet while they had talked she had been conscious that her fear of him had vanished. She realised he had been unexpectedly sympathetic and intent on what she had been saying. It was only now that she wondered at her own daring in approaching him, in speaking with him so frankly and without subterfuge. Yet had she learned anything of consequence? She must answer the question in the negative.

The Duke was a puzzling person. He had been cold and unbending since the first moment of their meeting, yet some instinct told Iona irrefutably that this was a poise. Underneath that proud, arrogant mask there was a man who had unswerving loyalties, strong enthusiasms and an infinite capacity for love and hatred.

How she knew this and on what foundation her convictions were based Iona did not ask herself. She only knew and thought now that she had known it always, that the Duke was to be trusted. She was as sure of this as she was sure that her feelings for Lord Niall were correct. She hated him and he was evil, vile and a traitor to his own country.

The Duchess was by no means as formidable. She was English, and it was natural that her sympathies should be with the English. She might be intriguing against the Duke, she might be spying for the English, but Iona knew that in this as in other things she would be ineffective and incompetent. She was merely a neurotic, love-sick woman of middle-age for whom life held only one interest—her stepson.

Iona was still sitting by the fire when the Duke returned. As he came into the room, she saw with a sudden leap of her heart that he held a key in his hand. It was a big iron key and he set it down on his writing-table. Then he turned

116

and walked towards the fire. He put his hand on the mantelpiece and stood staring down at the flames.

"I have made inquiries about the prisoner," he said at length. "And I have given instructions that despite my brother's orders to the contrary food and wine shall be taken to him immediately. His gaoler has gone to fetch food from the kitchen, and as the Keep is thus left unguarded I have taken charge of the key so that there can be no question of the prisoner being able to escape."

Iona sat very still, but her heart was beating almost suffocatingly. What did this portend? She felt there was some hidden meaning behind the Duke's kindness, but so far it was not clear. She sat forward in her chair, every muscle tense, every nerve strained. The Duke did not look at her and after a moment he continued;

"I think that your friend will not find the Keep too uncomfortable. When I saw him to be of gentle birth, I saw no reason for him to be subjected to the durance of the dungeons."

"It was exceeding kind of Your Grace," Iona said breathlessly.

The Duke raised his head.

"Kind?" he questioned. "To constrain a free man?"

Iona did not know how to answer him. The Duke sighed.

"You shrink from the thought of cruelty, of unnecessary suffering, of a man betraying his own blood," he said. "In all these things we are agreed. All I ask for my people is peace."

There was a depth in his voice that Iona had never heard before; then, as he looked down into her wide eyes, he added: "Yes, peace."

He walked across to the writing-table, took up the key and stared at it intently.

"It is strange," he said with a complete change of tone, "but I never realised until now that the locks on both the Keeps of this castle are identical. They were added, of course, at a later date than the doors. Originally only bolts were used or a wooden bar supported by staves. The guardroom of the West Keep, in which your friend is imprisoned, has been left very much as it was when the castle was first built. In the other I keep certain trophies of the chase—such as a stag's head which I shot when I was quite young but which was not considered good enough to be hung in the Great Hall, the skin of a wolf which I killed on the hillside when I was twelve years old, and the skin of a wild cat which attacked my dog once when I was riding in the woods. Yes, there are some quite interesting things in the East Keep, and one day perhaps you will be interested in seeing them. It is strange I never realised before this that the keys were interchangeable."

The Duke opened a drawer.

"Here is my own key. You can see the cut is the same."

He put the second key back in the drawer of his desk and laid the other down on the table. Then after a second or two he took it up again.

"I think I hear the guard with the prisoner's food," he said.

He went out into the passage, leaving the door only slightly ajar. A moment later Iona heard him speaking to someone. Swiftly she moved from her chair across to the writing-table and took the second key from the drawer. She placed it in the bosom of her dress and felt the iron strike cold against her skin. She had re-seated herself in the chair and remained motionless for some seconds before the Duke returned.

"I have seen to it that the prisoner has both meat and wine," he said. "My brother will doubtless declare that I am soft-hearted, but it is distasteful to me that a gentleman who has befriended you should suffer unnecessarily from hunger and thirst."

Iona rose to her feet.

"Your Grace is indeed gracious," she said in a low voice. "Have I your permission to retire?"

She dared not look up at him, she was too conscious of the heavy key pressing against her breasts. She swept to the floor in a low curtsey and the Duke crossed the room to open the door for her.

"Good night," he said with an impersonal courtesy. "I hope you sleep well."

"I thank Your Grace."

Iona met his eyes for one fleeting second and then she was gone, moving swiftly down the passage on feet winged with hope.

9

Cathy was kneeling on the hearth rug replenishing the fire when Iona burst into the bedchamber, closed the door behind her and stood for a moment with her back to it, breathless from the speed with which she had run upstairs. Cathy started to her feet and dropped a respectful curtsy: but when she saw Iona's excited face, she forgot all formality and cried out:

"Whit has happened tae ye, mistress?"

In answer Iona drew from the bosom of her gown the big iron key of the Keep. Cathy's eyes widened.

"A key!" she exclaimed in a low voice. "Is it . . . ?"

"The key to the Keep," Iona answered, and although the words came pantingly from between her lips, they were nevertheless spoken in an unmistakable tone of triumph.

She put one hand to her breasts as if to still the tumultuous beating of her heart; then walked slowly across the room to Cathy's side.

"The key of the Keep!" she repeated: "but oh, Cathy, how are we to rescue him? You know who he is? He is Mr. Hector MacGregor, the gentleman your uncle took me to see this afternoon, but I've told Lord Niall his name is Hugo Thomson."

"I jaloused it maun be Mr. Hector," Cathy replied. "But I'll mind he's Mr. Hugo Thomson an' I hae niver seen him afore the noo."

"But how am I to set him free, Cathy?" Iona asked. "Only you can help me!"

Cathy clasped her hands together and her smooth brow was wrinkled in thought.

"I'm a-thinkin', mistress," she said.

There was silence while Iona watched Cathy's face.

"I hae indeed been puzzlin' aul a' the evenin' of how tae rescue the poor gentlemon," Cathy muttered at last. "Noo that ye hae the key it shouldna be impossible; but there are guards an' . . ."

Cathy broke off suddenly and her face cleared as she gave an exclamation:

"*Dhé,* but I had forgotten that 'tis Eachann who is on guard. I met him but a short while ago wheen I were fetchin' wood for the fire. He was carryin' food for the prisoner, or sae he told me."

"That was true enough," Iona said hastily. "His Grace gave instructions that Mr. MacGregor was to be fed despite his lordship's command that he should go both hungry and thirsty until tomorrow."

"Aweel, if Eachann is on guard alane," Cathy said, her eyes widening, "it shouldna be difficult tae find a way. . . ."

"What do you mean?" Iona asked. "Would he help us?" Cathy shook her head.

"Nay, never that. Eachann is ane o' Lord Niall's men an' no tae be trusted, but . . . ."

Cathy paused and looked down, the colour coming into her cheeks.

"Yes, go on," Iona prompted.

"Eachann hae a fondness fae me," Cathy said shyly, her cheeks crimson now with embarrassment.

"In that at least he shows good taste," Iona said. "Do you think you could entice him away from the door? But it might be dangerous."

"Nay, I couldna dae that," Cathy replied. "He'd suspect an' besides, I ken weel he wouldna desert his post."

"Then what do you suggest?" Iona asked a trifle impatiently.

" 'Tis but an idea, mistress," Cathy said humbly, "but I thocht that if I went doon an' talked wi' Eachann an' took him a bottle o' wine, he wouldna tak it amiss; an' if the wine were tae mak him sleep, weel then, we'd hae the chance tae rescue Mister MacGregor."

"Cathy, that is a brilliant plan!" Iona exclaimed; "but what shall we put in the wine? I have no laudanum, for I have never needed anything to help me to sleep."

"I ken where Her Grace's maid keeps a bottle hid."

"We could take some without being found out, I suppose," Iona said reflectively; "but oh, Cathy, I cannot allow you to involve yourself in this even for Mr. MacGregor's sake. If it were discovered that you were a

Jacobite, you might be imprisoned and your uncle with you."

"I'm no feart, mistress," Cathy said stoutly, "an' what I can dae I'll dae gladly. Ma Uncle hae always luved Mister Hector an' ye may be sure he'll be a-wantin' tae help himself. But he canna enter the Castle, so I maun dae what I can."

Cathy spoke simply and yet with so much courage that Iona felt the tears come into her eyes. She bent forward and kissed the girl's cheek and then felt half ashamed at the look of admiration and affection which Cathy gave her in return. Resolutely Iona returned to the task which lay ahead of them.

"It is growing late," she said. "We will wait until everyone has retired to bed and then you must guide me to the Keep."

"Aye, I'll dae that," Cathy replied, "but first I'll gang an' beg a bottle o' wine frae the butler. I'll nae say 'tis fae ye, mistress, but for the housekeeper, an' indeed she ofttimes bids me ask for wine wheen her legs are bad an' the pain o' them keeps her awake."

"Yes, it is best if they think the wine is for the housekeeper," Iona agreed, but reluctantly for she hated this tangle of lies and subterfuge, and wondered where it would all end.

But as Cathy hurried from the room, she envied her having something active to do rather than be forced to wait impatiently, companioned only by fears and apprehensions, for the time to pass.

The minutes indeed seemed to tick by incredibly slowly when Iona was alone. She sat looking at the key of the Keep, wondering if it would enable her to rescue Hector or whether the attempt to use it would only arouse suspicions, if not worse, about Cathy and herself. It seemed to her that Cathy had been gone a long time, and then she realised that only five minutes had passed since the girl had left the room.

Iona remembered hearing someone say that time was relative, and knew this was the truth. When she was happy, the hours flew as if they were on wings; but now every second was a long drawnout aeon of anxiety.

To distract her mind she moved across the room and in doing so caught a glimpse of her reflection in the mirror. Nothing, she thought, could be more inappropriate for what lay ahead than her gown of ivory satin. Whatever part she had to play in the rescue of Hector, it would obviously be essential for her to be inconspicuous. Going to the wardrobe, Iona took out her morning robe of grey muslin. Quickly she divested herself of the evening gown and slipped on the muslin and its soft hue, mysterious as the evening mist on the loch, made her almost invisible when she moved beyond the golden circle of light thrown by the tall candles on the dressing-table.

But Iona was still not satisfied. Her neck and arms gleamed white in the shadows and her shining curls seemed to attract every glimmer of radiance from the candles and the leaping flames in the fireplace. She could see in the mirror the pale oval of her face and above it the shimmer of her hair. From a drawer in the bureau she drew out a shawl of fine black lace. It had been a Christmas present from her guardian and at the time she had been slightly disappointed with the gift, knowing that while it was both beautiful and valuable it was too old for her years and should in reality have been worn by someone more mature.

She was glad now that she had not disposed of the shawl when badly pressed for money. She flung it over her head and it fell in graceful folds over her shoulders, the points of it reaching nearly to her knees. Once again she consulted the mirror and with satisfaction realised that she was practically invisible.

Still Cathy had not returned. Iona's imagination began to frighten her. Perhaps Cathy had aroused suspicion by her request; perhaps she had been taken to Lord Niall and had broken down under cross-examination and revealed everything.

Iona went to the bedroom door, opened it quietly and looked out, but there was no one in sight. There was only darkness and silence—the heavy, pulsating silence of a house which sleeps after the noise and bustle of a busy day. Iona closed the door again, to pace to and fro across the room, every nerve and muscle of her body tense as she strained her ears for the sound of Cathy's footsteps.

At last, when she felt despair flooding over her, the door opened quietly and Cathy slipped into the room. Iona ran towards her.

"Is everything all right?" she cried. "Oh, Cathy, I thought something must have happened when you were so long!"

"Naething is wrong, mistress," Cathy answered, drawing out a bottle from beneath her apron where she had carried it somewhat inadequately concealed.

"It wasna the butler who detained me," she explained. "He wae exceedin' affable an' gied me the wine at once. He hae been drinkin' himsel' an' there wae a glass o' brandy at his elbow, so I doot if he'll ken ought about ma visit in the morn. But Her Grace's maid was awake, an' as the cupboard wheer the laudanum is kept is just ootside her room, I hae tae wait until she had extinguished her taper an' I heard her snorin' afore I dared tae open the cupboard."

"You have put the laudanum into the wine?" Iona asked.

Cathy nodded.

"A decent drap, mistress, an' I gied the bottle a guid shake. Eachann will no taste it, and I swear that wine would mak an army sleep the noo. . . ."

"Are you sure that Eachann is the only one on guard?" Iona asked anxiously. "His lordship may have placed two men outside the door of the Keep."

"Nay, Eachann is alane," Cathy replied, "for I heard frae anither maid there was an awfu' argument aboot it, an' Sime said that, as Eachann wae the youngest, he maun keep watch for the ither men who were tired. 'Tis always Eachann who has the dirty work tae do."

"We may be grateful for that," Iona said. "Shall we go now—or is it too soon?"

"I ken everybody is asleep," Cathy replied, "for the footmen hae snuffed the candles in the passages. 'Tis lucky that I brocht a lantern oop here this verry eve an' hid it in the bottom o' the wardrobe. I wae thinkin' that ye micht wish tae visit me uncle some time wheen ither folks waur asleep. That was, o' course, afore I heard that poor Mister Hector had been caught by his lordship's men."

"It was I who betrayed him," Iona said miserably. "Lord Niall met me coming down the passage and insisted on talking with me. He saw my dusty dress, my muddy shoes and the shawl over my head. He knew I had been outside and had returned on the east side of the castle. He was shrewd enough to put two and two together and guess that I had been in the woods to meet someone—so he had them searched."

Cathy's eyes darkened.

"Theer's little that escapes his lordship," she said bitterly.

123

"He'll be suspectin' me uncle after this, but he'll bide his time, watchin' him like a cat watches a mouse sae that he can pounce wheen a body dinna expect it."

"Oh dear, I am sorry I have drawn you into all this," Iona said.

Cathy flashed a smile at her.

"Dinna fret, mistress," she answered. "I'd rather suffer for the sake o' our Prince than grow fat an' rich in the company o' them as turns traitor tae their ain flesh an' blood."

Cathy spoke passionately and Iona felt there was nothing adequate that she could say in reply. She pressed the other girl's hand while a smile of complete understanding passed between them, then Cathy lit the candle in the lantern and blew out the tapers on the dressing-table.

The two women stood for a moment almost in darkness as the light in the lantern flickered a little, appeared to go out and then rekindled itself with an effort. Cathy watched it anxiously until it began to burn brightly, then she straightened her shoulders.

"Are ye ready, mistress?" she asked.

"Yes, I'm ready," Iona replied, "but wouldn't it be wise for you to take off your apron and your cape? Being white, they would easily be seen."

Cathy considered for a moment, then shook her head.

"Nay, mistress, it wouldna be wise. If we meet onybody they'll think naught but I'm fetchin' a hot-brick or a glass o' milk for a leddy who is indisposed or canna sleep. But if I'm wi'oot ma cap an' apron, they micht be suspicious, thinkin' I hae some unco reason for wanderin' aboot the castle at nicht."

"Yes, you are right," Iona agreed. "Above all things we must not arouse anyone's suspicions, but—pray Heaven that we do not meet anyone."

"Amen tae that, mistress," Cathy said and without further words turned towards the door.

Iona picked up the key of the Keep from her dressing-table and pulled her lace shawl closer around her. She opened and closed the door of the bedchamber for Cathy carried both the lantern and the bottle of wine. As she had anticipated, Cathy avoided the main part of the castle and first led the way up a flight of stairs to the third floor; then wending their way down a long labyrinth of passages, they came to the west side of the great building where they discovered another small twisting staircase almost the twin of the one on the east side which they had crept down earlier in the day.

Cathy moved slowly, for it was imperative for them to go silently and it was also difficult for Iona to keep within the small circle of light from the lantern. More than once she stumbled and it was with the utmost difficulty that she refrained from crying out on feeling herself fall forward into nothingness or bumping painfully against a wall or a piece of furniture.

At last after what seemed to her a very long time they reached the ground floor and entered a high, broad passage. Here the walls were unplastered and they walked on bare stone so that every movement they made, however cautious, seemed to echo and re-echo into the chilly darkness. Not speaking a word, Cathy went ahead on tiptoe until unexpectedly she stopped abruptly. A little way ahead of them the passage curved.

Cathy appeared to be listening; then after a moment she turned and flashed Iona a warning glance before she opened the lantern and blew out the candle. For a few seconds Iona could see nothing, but as her eyes grew used to the darkness she perceived a faint light ahead. She heard Cathy put down the lantern on the floor, then she felt her fingers gripping hers to draw her forward. Hardly daring to breathe, Iona allowed herself to be led slowly along, her body close against the wall, until the light ahead grew brighter and brighter, and the two women concealed from it only by a stone buttress. Very cautiously first Cathy and then Iona peeped round it.

A dozen yards away a big lantern had been set on a wooden bench. Beside it sat a big broad-shouldered youth of perhaps twenty-two years of age whittling at a piece of wood with a knife. His lips were pursed and as he worked he whistled tunelessly. His hair was long and fell untidily around his face. He had thrown off his coat and his shirt was open to the waist, showing a stalwart, hairy chest. This, Iona knew, must be Eachann.

Beyond him was the Keep, its solid oak door with heavy iron hinges and a square lock reached by two stone steps. The surrounding walls, constructed of big square stones, were formidably massive. This part of the castle had been built as a fortress and had never been used as anything else.

Cathy took a deep breath and Iona knew that she was about to step forward and speak to Eachann, when suddenly there was the sound of footsteps. Quietly purposeful they approached the Keep from the other direction. There was the sharp clink of heels on a stone floor growing louder and louder and Iona guessed that someone was crossing the Great Hall. Desperately she put out her hands and clung to Cathy. Both women pressed themselves close against the buttress so that Iona could feel the sharpness of the roughly hewn stone bruising her skin through the thin material which covered her.

Eachann, who had looked up unexpectedly when he heard the footsteps, suddenly sprang to his feet. Someone came forward into the light of the lantern and Iona saw that it was Lord Niall.

The diamond buttons on his coat of puce satin glimmered and glittered in the light from the lantern. He carried a candle-stick of polished silver and the wax trickled thickly and lopsidedly over the stand. His face, dark and satanic, seemed strangely at variance with his powdered hair and the jabot of exquisite lace at his chin. The very gaiety of his clothes and the sparkle of his jewels seemed out of place because of an aura of virulence and venom about him. It seemed as if Eachann felt this, for he took a step backwards and there was something sheepish, yet apprehensive in his attitude as with lowered head he watched Lord Niall from under his eyebrows.

Lord Niall set his candle-stick down on the wooden bench, then he glanced round, his eyes finally resting on Eachann.

"Has the prisoner asked for anything?" he inquired.

"Nay, m'lawd."

"Has he called out, attempted to talk with you?"

"Nay, m'lawd."

"The prisoner is securely housed? It is impossible for him to escape?"

"Aye, m'lawd."

"I will look for myself."

Lord Niall walked to the door of the Keep and Iona saw him slide back the wooden shutter of a peephole heavily barred with iron. His lordship stared through it for some seconds, then he closed the shutter again.

"Asleep," he said, "or pretending to be. You are quite certain he has not asked you for anything?"

"Nay, m'lawd."

"There is always a possibility that a man of that sort might have friends in the neighbourhood or for that matter

126

in the castle itself. If he asks for anyone, be sure to remember the name correctly and bring me word of what he has said first thing in the morning."

"Aye, m'lawd."

Lord Niall put his hand to his chin and appeared to be considering something. After quite a long pause he said:

"You have the key safely?"

"Aye, m'lawd."

Eachann drew it from his belt and held it up. Lord Niall put out his hand.

"I think it would be safer if I relieved you of this. As I have already said there is always the chance of someone trying to rescue a Jacobite."

He took the key and moved once again up the steps to the door of the Keep. He tried it in the lock, and having made certain that the door was firmly shut, slipped the key into the pocket of his coat.

"Keep a good watch, Eachann," he admonished, and picking up his candle he walked off in the direction from which he had come.

Iona and Cathy heard his footsteps growing fainter and fainter until at last they could hear them no more. Eachann sat down on the bench and took up his knife and the piece of wood on which he had been working. He looked at it, gave a great yawn, stretched himself and put down both the knife and the carving. He yawned again, his breath expelling itself in noisy gusts. It was then that Cathy stepped forward.

She had advanced several yards towards him before Eachann, opening his eyes after his tremendous yawn, caught sight of her. Her mouth remained open in a ludicrous expression of astonishment. Cathy advanced steadily until she was standing beside him, then she smiled.

"I was sorry for ye doon here in the cold, Eachann."

"Hoots, Cathy, but ye gied me an' awfu' fright," he exclaimed. "I thocht ye wae a ghost comin' oot o' the dark sae silent-lik."

"I hae no wish tae scare ye, Eachann," Cathy answered. "I was only tryin' tae dae ye a kindness."

"Aweel, an' whit sort o' kindness micht that be?" Eachann asked, catching sight of the bottle.

Cathy held it out to him with a smile.

"Wine?" he queried greedily.

"Aye, an' guid wine at that," Cathy answered. "The housekeeper sent me for it, but I was ower long an' wheen

I got back she wae fast asleep. It seemed a pity tae waste
the wine an' I thought o' ye doon here all alane. It will
warm ye, for 'tis a cold nicht."

"That's awfu' guid o' ye, Cathy," Eachann said. "I
wouldna hae expected it o' ye, indeed I wouldna. Ye hae
been reel cruel tae me this twelve month. I swear ye hae
e'en turned yer heid awa' wheen I looked at ye."

"I have nae doot o' it," Cathy said severely. "Ye are tae
pleased with yersel', Eachann, that's what's wrang with ye.
But mind ye, I'm a friend an' 'tis sorry I am that ye hae tae
spend the nicht in a place like this. Upon my saul, it gives
me the creeps!"

Eachann looked around him.

" 'Tis no whit ye'd ca' a gey place!"

"Gey?" Cathy echoed. "It is doonrich fearfu', that's what
it is. Why, I'd as soon spend the nicht in a graveyard."

"Hoots, I'm no feart," Eachann laughed.

"Aye, ye're a brave laddie, I'll say that for ye," Cathy
said. "But I've heard tell that the ghost o' MacCraggan
Mor walks here at nicht. Ye can see his white sporran
swingin' in the darkness an' his white feathers at the side o'
his bonnet."

She whispered the last words and her tone was eerie.
Eachann shivered.

"Put a loc' on yer tongue, Cathy. 'Tis a fule ye'll be
makin' o' me. I'm no supersteetious an' if MacCraggan
Mor iss walkin' thiss nicht, he'll no harm a puir Heiland
laddie."

"Dinna ye be tae sure o' that," Cathy replied sharply. "If
MacCraggan Mor ken some o' the things that happen in
the castle, it's nae wonder he rises frae oot o' his grave."

"An' whit ca' ye mean by tha', Cathy?" Eachann asked,
but he could not meet her eyes.

"Ye ken full weel, Eachann mon, what I mean," Cathy
said. "Ye an' Sime an' those ithers as make friends with the
English should be ashamed. I heard tell as yersel' were
seen with ane o' they redcoats ootside o' the Fort last Saturday."

"Gawd's maircy, but who told ye tha', Cathy?" Eachann
expostulated. " 'Twas waitin' for his lordship we weer an'
the redcoat but proffered me a wee drappie."

"Then shame on ye for takin' it!"

"An' what harm ca' tha' dae?" Eachann asked defiantly.

"That's for ye tae answer," Cathy said, "an' dinna fash

128

tae explain yersel tae me. Keep yer excuses for MacCraggan Mor if he visits ye in the sma' hours."

Eachann shivered again.

"Stop bletherin', Cathy," he said, "an' gie us a kiss. 'Tis gratefu' I am for the wine."

"Then show yer gratitude by keepin' yer kisses to yerself," Cathy retorted. "I maun get back oopstairs. If onyone finds I hae been here, 'tis a fine talkin' tae I'd get an' nae mistak."

She took a few steps away from him, but Eachann jumped up.

"Nay, Cathy, bide a wee."

"I canna," Cathy said, shaking her head. "Ye wouldna get me sent awa', Eachann, would ye?"

"Indeed I wouldna, ye wee darlin'," he answered.

He put out his arms to catch her, but she was too quick for him. She ran a few steps, then stopped and looked back, realising that he was about to follow her. She pointed to the bench.

"Gang back tae yer post, Eachann," she said. "If there's trouble brewin' for me, there wad be far worse trouble frae his lordship if ye lef' the prisoner unguarded."

"Aye, I mak nae doot o' that," Eachann muttered, and his face fell. "But dinna gang awa'."

"I maun," she whispered, and she hurried away while he stared after her, torn between his desire to follow and his fear of leaving the Keep.

Cathy swung round the buttress and joined Iona in the shadows. For a moment they were both tense for fear that Eachann might come lumbering down the passage; but duty won and he sat down on his bench. His hand went out towards the bottle of wine. He picked it up, looked at it appreciatively, wetted his lips with his tongue then took a long drink.

It was evidently most enjoyable for he smacked his lips loudly and immediately took another pull at the bottle. Iona and Cathy waited. Iona was conscious now of being intensely cold. She could feel the damp seeping up through the soles of her thin satin shoes, but it was not only the cold which made her fingers seem almost too stiff to move and which kept her so tense that she felt as if she too had turned to stone. Suppose they failed, her mind queried; suppose the laudanum did not work on Eachann; suppose the wine merely revived him or else he dozed so fitfully that he heard them when they approached the Keep.

129

She knew that Cathy was anxious too, but there was nothing they could do but wait and go on waiting while Eachann drank. At last the bottle was finished, drained to the very last drop and reluctantly he set it down under the bench. Now he was yawning again, this time drowsily and with not so much vigour. His eyelids were closing, his head nodding a little. His chin touched his chest and startled him so that he awoke with a jerk. He was yawning again, but weakly as if the effort was too much.

It was evidently uncomfortable on the bench for he moved to seat himself on the floor, his back to the wall which faced the door of the Keep.

"I'm keepin' watch," he said aloud in a slurred, somnolent voice. "I'm keepin' watch, ghosties or no ghosties."

His legs were outstretched in front of him, but his head slipped a little sideways, then quite suddenly he keeled over. His head struck the floor, he grunted, pillowed his head in his arms, but did not open his eyes. Slowly his body adjusted itself to a more comfortable position, his knees bent, his back curved. He gave a sudden snort, which echoed round the walls, then he was asleep and snoring in the slow, thick manner of someone who has been drugged.

Still Iona and Cathy waited until after about five minutes, re-assured by the round of Eachann's rhythmic snores they crept forward into the light. All the way to the door of the Keep they watched Eachann, but it was obvious that the laudanum had done its work effectively. It would be many hours before he would be troubled by anything.

Iona ran up the steps and fitted the key into the lock. Her hand was shaking and for one awful moment she thought that she had been tricked and that it would not fit. But it was only stiff and with an effort she managed to turn it. Hardly daring to breathe she pushed the heavy door with both hands.

There was a lantern hanging from the roof of a high circular room. The only furniture was a rough wooden couch covered with a blanket. Lying on it apparently asleep was Hector, but as the door opened he sat up, instantly alert. When he saw who stood there, his eyes widened and he sprang to his feet, but did not speak.

"The guard is drugged," Iona whispered, "but come quickly."

In answer Hector picked up his belt which he had loosened and which had fallen on the couch. He fastened it

130

round his waist and knelt to tie his shoes. Then he glanced round to be sure he had left nothing behind.

"Ready," he murmured.

Cathy was waiting in the passage; Hector joined her and Iona locked the door of the Keep. Then all three slipped past the sleeping Eachann to where Cathy had left the lantern. Cathy picked it up.

"Wait here, mistress," she said in a low voice.

She sped back again to light her little candle from the lantern on Eachann's bench. It was but a second or two before she joined them, but in that moment Hector had reached out his arms towards Iona and pulled her close. She could feel his heart beating with excitement.

"How did you manage it, you wonderful girl?" he whispered.

"It was the Duke," Iona replied. "Oh, Hector, I am sure, quite sure, that he is on our side. But we cannot talk here, we must get you away at once."

"I have no desire to linger," Hector replied, "but if what you say is true about Arkrae—it's splendid news."

Cathy joined them at that moment and without wasting time in further speech they set off quickly down the passage, Cathy leading the way, her lantern bobbing ahead like a will-o'-the-wisp. They passed the stairs down which she and Iona had come from the upper floors and about two minutes later came to a door in the outer wall. Here Cathy stopped.

"Ye had best gang oot this way, Mister Hector."

"Where does it lead to?" he asked.

"Straight on tae the loch," she replied. "Ma uncle may be below wi' his boat but if he's no theer, can you swim?"

"Like a fish," Hector replied.

Cathy raised the lantern and Iona saw there were big bolts on the door and a wooden bar stretched across it. It could not have been used for some time, for the bolts were rusty and it took all Hector's strength to draw them and to lift the bar from the staples. But he managed it, the door swung open and the sharp night air blew in on them.

Iona bent forward and looked out. She gave a muffled exclamation, for Cathy had indeed spoken truly when she said that the door led straight on to the loch. There was below the door a sheer drop of perhaps thirty feet into the still dark water. Cathy raised her lantern and waved it slowly then she drew back into the passage.

"If ma uncle is aboot, he'll see the licht an' ken 'tis a

131

signal," she said. "Wait a wee while, Mister Hector, in case he come for ye; but if there's no sign of him, ye'd best gang swift. Ye maun be far frae here afore the dawn breaks, for his lordship'll send his men in search o' ye."

"I know that," Hector answered. "If only I had a horse, I should feel happier."

"Wheen ye reach the ither side o' the loch," Cathy said, "tak the path which leads to the south; wheen it branches gang due west. After aboot a mile ye'll come tae a wee hoose. Ask for Raild the Piper. Tell him who ye are an' if he canna fund ye a horse, he'll keep ye safe. Ye can trust him as ye'd trust yer ain mither."

"Thank you, Cathy," Hector said. "I shall never forget what you have done for me."

"Ye'll wish tae talk wi' ane anither," Cathy said. "I'll wait doon the passage, but ye maunna linger, Mister Hector. Each minute that takes ye awa' frae the castle is a minute on tae yer life."

She moved as she spoke until she was out of earshot. They could see the flickering of her lantern like a tiny eye in the darkness, but in the starlight Iona could still faintly discern the outline of Hector's face.

"There is not time to say much," he said quietly, "and no words that I could find would begin to express my gratitude, Iona. But my escape will cause trouble and it is you I am worrying about. If you are certain Arkrae is for us, waste no time but hurry back to France with the news."

"I had not the slightest idea what His Grace felt until this evening," Iona replied, "when he deliberately showed me a duplicate key of the Keep and made it possible for me to rescue you. It was fine of him, but I have a feeling that he, too, is in danger."

"Arkrae can look after himself—you can't. Get back to France as quickly as you can," Hector said urgently. "Promise me?" He put out his hands and took hold of Iona's. "Promise me?" he repeated.

"I have not yet found the Tears of Torrish," Iona reminded him.

"Arkrae is prize enough," Hector replied impatiently, "and there's one other thing. You will be in France before me; and besides, there's always the chance of my being captured again. Will you take this notebook and see that it reaches Brett as soon as possible?" He drew the little book from inside his coat and put it into Iona's hand. "I had

132

planned to hide it before they handed me over to the English," he said. "The contents are too valuable for it to be destroyed except as a last resource, but at the same time it would be dangerous for it to be discovered in one's possession. If you are not leaving at once try and get it into the keeping of Dr. Farquharson of Inverness."

"Dr. Farquharson," Iona repeated reflectively. "That is the man whom Colonel Brett told me to get in touch with when I was ready to return to France."

"Then he may already have heard of you," Hector said. "Ask him to dispatch the notebook to Paris and, better still, you with it as speedily as can be arranged." He looked out of the open door into the night. "There's no sign of Dughall and in a way I'm glad. He has risked too much for me already. I shall swim for it."

"The water will be very cold," Iona said, realising that she was shivering in the chilly air.

"It will freshen me up and keep me awake," Hector smiled. "Good-bye, my dear."

He put his arms round her and gave her another affectionate, passionless hug. Iona was growing increasingly familiar with this individual form of endearment and it no longer embarrassed her. Instead she clung to him, reluctant to move from the warm shelter of his arms.

"Take care of yourself, my dear."

Hector released her and sat down on the floor. He dangled his legs over the water before lowering himself slowly, finding a foothold here and there until he was halfway down the side of the castle. Then he jumped.

Iona, leaning out of the open door, heard the splash, but it was too dark to see him in the water.

"May God gang wi' him!" Cathy's voice said in her ear.

Iona strained her eyes into the darkness. She could hear a soft movement in the water, then there was silence. The further shore seemed dark and foreboding. She felt Cathy's hand pull her and was obedient to its insistence. There was nothing more she could do, but even as she moved Iona knew with a clear unshakable certainty that Hector was all right. He would win through, serve the Prince and return safely to France. She was as sure of this as she was sure of life itself. Hector would succeed; but for herself there was no such certainty.

With the greatest difficulty, both Iona and Cathy exerting all their strength, they managed to shut home the bolts on the door, and lift the wooden bar into position. As Cathy turned back towards the staircase, Iona remembered the key of the Keep.

"You must take me first to the Duke's sitting-room," she whispered.

The twisting staircase brought them to the first floor. After a few minutes' walking the passages widened, became carpeted and furnished and Iona recognised where she was. Moving silently, they reached the Duke's sitting-room and found it in darkness save for the glow from a few flickering embers left in the dying fire. It took Iona only a second to slip the key back into the drawer of the writing-table from where she had taken it. But as she closed the drawer, she paused for a moment, conscious that the room was filled with the heavy fragrance of tobacco smoke. As she stood there with her fingers touching the smooth polished wood where his arms had so often rested, it brought her a vivid picture of the Duke, of his grey eyes, cold and almost expressionless, looking down into hers.

Now she was no longer afraid of him. He had saved Hector. He had shown her all too clearly that under that mask of proud indifference he was human—and understanding.

"Thank you, thank you," Iona whispered into the darkness. Then she turned and crept from the room.

10

LADY Wrexham lay on a chaise-longue in the boudoir which led out of her bedroom. It was a big room, light and gay, for the panelling had been painted white and inset with silk brocade and the curtains were of rose damask. The sunshine coming through the closed windows filled the room with a golden radiance, dimming the flames which leapt high from the logs burning in the chimneypiece.

Beatrice lay near the fire, a rug of ermine covering her legs, her head against satin cushions. She was wearing a négligé of Chinese silk, fine as a spider's web and so transparent that few of her voluptuous charms were concealed by its soft folds. Her golden hair, unpowdered and drawn back from her low forehead, was caught simply in a twisted coil at the nape of her neck and held only with two jewelled pins.

Even when she rested, Beatrice wore some of her jewels, and a ruby as big as a pigeon's egg glittered on one hand, on the other there was a sapphire, somnolent as the sea on a calm day. When Beatrice moved her hands, the ruby glittered as if she had awakened some strange fire within it, and after a time she fixed her eyes on it as if it were a crystal which would reveal to her the secrets of the future.

Beatrice's eyelids were heavy over the elysium blue of her eyes, yet she was not tired. She was planning and plotting but for once her scheming had no connection with her instructions from the Marquis of Severn but was solely and completely personal.

Her reverie was interrupted by a loud knocking, but before she could ring the bell by her side and summon her maid, the door opened and Lord Niall came into the room. He was in riding dress, the polish of his high boots reflecting the sunlight as he crossed the room, the chains on his spurs making a jingling musical accompaniment to his footsteps.

135

"There is no sign of the damned fellow," he announced angrily.

Beatrice's expression had not changed at his entry. She had merely raised her eyes from the contemplation of her ring, and now without smiling she asked slowly in a voice that was curiously dull:

"Is it of such consequence that he should be recaptured?"

Lord Niall made a gesture which seemed to combine both astonishment and exasperation.

"You know it is of the utmost import," he replied. "The fellow was a Jacobite, there was no doubt of it, and anything might have been disclosed in an examination of him. But instead, he has vanished—disappeared into thin air. By God, if I can find out how he escaped, I would kill those who helped him with my own hands."

Lord Niall spoke savagely and the fury in his eyes was murderous. Beatrice gave a tiny yawn.

"Why perturb yourself unduly? He may not have been as significant as you think."

" 'Pon my soul, you amaze me, Beatrice," Lord Niall exclaimed. "That man is without doubt, an exile who has slipped back to Scotland to sow dissension and discontent; and what is more, I am convinced that under torture we should have learnt that Ewan is in league with him. It was an opportunity we may never have again; and now without any evidence of how it has been contrived the prisoner disappears overnight from the Keep. I'll swear that Ewan must have had a hand in this, but the Devil knows how I am to prove it."

"If the Duke let him out," Beatrice suggested, "it must surely have been through the door or a window."

"There are no windows," Lord Niall said sullenly, "only arrow slits which one could not squeeze a rat through, let alone a grown man."

"Then the door?"

"I had the key of the door."

"You?"

For the first time since Lord Niall had come into the room Beatrice smiled, then she laughed.

"You had the key! Oh, poor Niall, I do see how exasperating it must be for you."

"Exasperating! It's enough to send me crazed," Lord Niall cried.

Like a spoilt child he flung himself down on the armchair, his face sullen and puckered with discontent.

"Have you inquired of the Duke if he has any explanation of this mystery?" Beatrice asked.

"Yes, I have asked him," Lord Niall replied, "and he admits that on his orders the prisoner was given food and wine. But to make certain that the rascal should not escape while his gaoler was absent Ewan took charge of the key. That information is of little help when I myself went down to the Keep later in the evening, inspected the prisoner through the peephole in the door and took the key away with me."

"It was with you all night?" Beatrice asked.

"All night," Lord Niall answered, "and I slept alone, you will remember." He looked at her and his face softened. "I did not sleep well," he added, "and you know the reason."

Beatrice met his eyes for a second, then returned to the contemplation of her ruby ring.

"We must be careful, Niall," she said. "I have warned you more than once that you are too possessive—and too familiar—in your attitude towards me."

"Can you wonder at it," he aked quickly, "when I ache to hold you, when my lips burn for the touch of yours?"

"I beg of you to be more careful."

"Oh, hell, what does it matter?" Lord Niall inquired. "If only things would go right, if only I could have a modicum of good fortune on my side, I would be able to take you in my arms and let the whole damned world see me do it. When I think that this swine who has escaped might have been instrumental in incriminating Ewan, I could in sheer rage pull the whole damned place down about our ears."

"You cannot be certain the Duke was in league with him," Beatrice argued. "After all, you have nothing to go on; and even if he were a Jacobite, there are plenty of them about. Most of them are slinking around in fear of their lives, of danger to no one but themselves. Suppose we admit that this Hugo Thomson or whatever he called himself was a returned exile, what proof have we that he had made contact with the Duke?"

"I have no actual proof," Lord Niall admitted sullenly, "but I am convinced he would not have come here and risked recognition had he not wished to convey information of some sort to Ewan. He was with the girl at the hotel in Inverness—I told you how I surprised them there—and she met him again in the woods yesterday afternoon."

"Then I imagine that it is but an ordinary case of frustrated love," Beatrice sneered. "You are exaggerating the whole incident, Niall, and I am ready to wager there is nothing more to it then a lovers' meeting."

Lord Niall jumped to his feet and walked over to the window.

"You are deliberately trying to ridicule me and make me appear a fool," he said angrily. "If you are right, why should the fellow have been in such a hurry to escape? And again, how could he have done so without the assistance of someone inside the castle? Could the girl, a stranger here without money or influence have contrived that? No, it was Ewan, I tell you, Ewan who by some authority or devilish ingenuity of which we know nothing has managed to spirit a grown man out of the Keep and leave no trace of how it was done."

Beatrice yawned again, but her eyes were reflective.

"What does the man who was guarding him say?" she asked at length. "And can you trust him to speak the truth?"

"I would not trust my own shadow at the moment," Lord Niall retorted. "Eachann, the man on guard, is a fool; but I have no reason to suspect him of treachery. He is full of tales of ghosts and spirits and other nonsensical bunkum. These people are ridiculously superstitious. My great great grandfather, MacCraggan Mor, is popularly supposed by the household to have wafted the prisoner through the walls or the keyhole, though why the old gentleman should have wanted to save a Jacobite no one can explain."

"Does anyone pretend to have seen him do it?" Beatrice asked.

"No, of course not. It's all talk and those dolts chatter amongst themselves until they believe anything. Eachann keeps averring that he felt the MacCraggan Mor's presence by the Keep although he will not admit to seeing him. I had him flogged to see if I could learn more, but he swore that no one visited him the whole night, though he confesses to having fallen asleep for an hour or two."

"And so you are back where you started," Beatrice said lightly. "An empty cage and the bird flown."

Lord Niall turned from the window and crossed the room to her side.

"Can you not understand why I mind so greatly?" he asked. "Can you not realise why I pin my hopes on finding that Ewan and this Jacobite were in league?"

"Do you really want me to answer that question?" Beatrice asked.

"No, because you know the answer," he said, his tone suddenly fierce and domineering. "It is because of you that I can wait no longer, because I want you and because the mere sight of you drives me mad."

He dropped down on his knees beside her to look close at her face, his eyes burning as if he were in a fever.

"I want you," he repeated hoarsely. "God, how I want you! All my life I have wished to be the Duke of Arkrae; I have desired the power and prestige that the position would bring me; but now I want it for one reason and one reason alone, and that reason is you, my love—you and only you."

He bent forward to kiss her lips, but Beatrice turned her face aside. For one moment he was still, then his hands went out to grip her bare shoulders and to draw her closer and still closer to him. With a surprising strength Beatrice thrust him away.

"No, Niall, no," she protested. "It is dangerous. Anyone might come in. Besides, you have work to do."

"I have nothing better to do than to swear that I love you," Lord Niall answered.

"Not now," Beatrice answered, and there was a sudden edge to her voice.

Slowly and reluctantly he took his hands from her and rose to his feet.

"Why are you like this?" he asked. "If I thought that you were tired of me, I swear that I would strangle you."

Beatrice closed her eyes for a second, then she said with her voice deliberately weak.

"How can you be so unkind? I am not tired of you, Niall, but I am in truth very tired. I am not a man that I can journey from London to Scotland and not be fatigued by the weariness of the long drive. All I ask is a little consideration until I am strong again."

There was a break in her voice—of frailty or of tears, and instantly Lord Niall's attitude changed.

"Oh, my dear," he said. "I am a brute, forgive me. It is that I love you so desperately. I am crazed for you. There's not a second passes but I yearn to the point of madness for the softness of your body. I am importunate, but patience

139

was never my strongest virtue. Nevertheless, forgive me."

"Of course I forgive you, Niall," Beatrice said, holding out her hand to him; "but you must be sensible and conceal both your feelings and your impatience."

Lord Niall took her hand and kissed it.

"I will try," he promised, "but Heaven knows it will not be easy. When I see you smiling at Ewan, when I watch your eyes looking up into his, I am jealous beyond endurance. One day I shall murder him, not for his heritage but because I cannot bear you even to look at another man."

"How foolish you are," Beatrice scolded, "for it seems that nothing I can do or say is of particular interest to the Duke. If I attempt to entice him, you know it is but—for your sake."

"Yes, yes, I know that," Lord Niall answered, "but the mere fact that you must do so makes me hate him the more. If he were at all responsive, I doubt if I could control myself. Thank God that Ewan has always been a cold fish and, incredible though it may seem, remains so, even though you smile at him."

Beatrice's lips tightened for a moment, then she asked in a voice that was curiously icy.

"The Duke has not lost his heart to any other woman?"

"Not that I am aware of, though I assure you that I know very little about Ewan's private affairs," Lord Niall replied. "He has always been curiously reserved. Hard as nails in some things and soft-hearted as a woman in others. Look at last night—how, despite my express instructions, he had food and drink taken to the prisoner. A ridiculous gesture, but he made it, I believe, to please that red-headed chit because she said the fellow had befriended her."

There was a sudden silence.

"Do you think it was to please—her?" Beatrice asked slowly.

"As like as not," Lord Niall said. "Did you not notice the way Ewan looked at her at dinner when she sat there dumb as a dog, white-faced and on the verge of tears? The man means a great deal to her, that's obvious, and I know, as surely as I know my own name, that Ewan is intriguing with him."

Beatrice threw back the ermine rug which covered her and rose to her feet. She walked across the room and the silk of her loose robe flowed gracefully around her, but the lines of her body were silhouetted clearly against the sunlit windows. She was as perfectly proportioned as a Grecian statue and as she turned Lord Niall went hotly towards her.

"Faith, but you intoxicate me!" he exclaimed thickly.

As he touched her, Beatrice pushed his arms aside with an angry, impulsive gesture which she covered almost instantly by putting her hands to her forehead.

"My head is aching, Niall, I must retire to bed. If I cannot come down to dinner, I will send my apologies to your stepmother. At the moment I feel ready to swoon with fatigue—the chatter of voices would split my poor head open."

"You must indeed rest," Lord Niall said soothingly. "If you are not better tomorrow, I will send for the leech. But if I do not see you at dinner, may I come and say good night?"

"No, no," Beatrice said, her voice almost shrill. "Can you not understand that I must be alone? I will talk with you tomorrow, that I promise, but tonight I want only rest and—privacy."

As if he realised that further arguments or protestations of love would only annoy her, Lord Niall took both Beatrice's hands in his, turned them over, and kissed them softly, his lips lingering in the soft hollow of her palms, then moving to caress her tiny wrists.

At last reluctantly he released her, watching her as she moved across the room to her bedchamber and standing immobile for some minutes after the door had closed behind her. She had not looked back or she would have surprised a look of unbridled savagery on his dark face.

All Lord Niall's life strange fires had burnt within his breast, always he had hated the position he must endure of being the younger son, of having to take second place, of knowing that only the death of his half-brother could give him the authority and power that he craved almost to the point of madness.

It was a hate so strong, so virulent that it seemed at times as if it would consume him; but it enabled him to mask his feelings and to act a part day after day, year after year, because only through such a pretence would he ever gain his ultimate goal. A weaker man would have found such a role impossible. It required strength and an almost superhuman self-control to be courteous and polite to the Duke, to take second place in the household, to speak and behave as if he had no ambitions, no desires beyond a comfortable, luxurious existence as his half-brother's guest. Only his stepmother knew the truth, and perhaps a dozen or so of Lord Niall's personal servants had a vague inkling that one day their loyalty might be richly rewarded.

But now there was an ally, an ally so powerful, so influential that Lord Niall could hardly believe it possible that she should also be the woman he so ardently desired. With Beatrice in the castle, with the thought of her response to him personally like a weapon in his hand, Lord Niall knew that the hour had come in which he must strike to gain both a dukedom and a bride.

It was with an air of defiance that he walked boldly from the boudoir, pulled the door to behind him and walked down the corridor. He half hoped that he would meet his stepmother. For the first time for many years he was not afraid of her reproaches. He saw her for what she was, a middle-aged woman clinging to him pathetically because in losing him she lost the last vestige of her youth. Why had he even been hesitant and afraid of her finding him out? What a fool he had been! Lord Niall gave a little laugh and it was not a pleasant sound.

He went down the main staircase and into the Great Hall. He crossed it and a flunkey hurried to open the front door. Outside the castle his men were waiting, some on horseback, others on foot holding stout sticks in their hands. They were all of fine physique, but at the moment they were hot, dusty and fatigued, for they had been out since early morning searching the woods and moors for miles around in search of the escaped prisoner.

Lord Niall came down the steps. Sime detached himself from a group of men with whom he had been talking and went to meet him.

"Any news of the fugitive?" Lord Niall asked.

Sime shook his head.

"The last twa men hae just got bac', m'lord. They hae seen naught o' the prisoner."

Lord Niall's eyes narrowed.

"You are all either fools or knaves," he said harshly. "He must be hiding somewhere near here. Is it possible for a man to vanish in such a manner and not be found?"

But even as he asked the question, Lord Niall knew the answer. Had not Prince Charles remained hidden for months with half the English Army searching for him? As

142

if he guessed what his men were thinking, Lord Niall turned abruptly on his heel.

"I shall not forget your stupidity," he snarled, and began to walk up the steps to the front door.

"Are we no tae search any maur, m'lord?" Sime asked from behind him.

Lord Niall turned.

"No," he snapped.

"An' Eachann, m'lord?"

"Release him," Lord Niall said, "but keep an eye on him. If I thought that he deceived me, he would suffer for it as will anyone else who stands convicted of the same offence."

He passed through the castle door and out of sight. A sigh of relief seemed to go up from the men outside. Three of them hurried off to release Eachann from the dungeon where he had been thrown after he had been flogged. His back was sore and bleeding, his wrists and ankles raw from the rope which had bound him. But he was smiling as they set him free.

"Didna I tell ye that ye wouldn' find the mon?" he asked when he learnt that their search had been fruitless. "It was MacCraggan Mor himself who tok him awa', an' the Chief wouldna hae done tha' if he hadna been an innocent mon."

In the shadows of the dungeon one of the men crossed himself. The rest avoided each other's eyes. Perhaps Eachann was right and they had committed a crime against someone under the protection of Heaven itself.

Upstairs in her bedchamber Beatrice Wrexham walked backwards and forwards across the room. Now that she was alone, her face showed no signs of fatigue, in fact her eyes were bright and alert, and there was something in her quick, lithe movements which betrayed an inner excitement.

The sun was sinking behind the mountains, the mist was rising on the lake, the shadows of the woods darkening to purple. Soon it would be evening and after that would come the night. Beatrice stopped her restless walking to stare at her own reflection in the oval mirror on the dressing-table. She looked into it for a long time, her thoughts making her nostrils quiver and the pupils of her eyes dilate. Suddenly she put up her hands as if she would tear her robe from off her breasts.

"So this is love!" she said aloud.

She watched the way her lips curved over the words, lips that were suddenly parted with a sensual hunger. "Yes, love," she repeated, and put her elbows on the table to cup her face in her long fingers.

Thank God she was beautiful, so beautiful that never had a man been able to resist her, never had she failed to make one on whom she had set her heart her abject slave. She knew now how ignorant she had been when other women had talked of love, when men had almost deafened her with their protestations of it. She had seen the suffering in their eyes and had not understood it—this ecstacy, this rapture, this pain, this torture! Love! It seemed to tear her apart, to make her feel weak and fragile, strong and resolute all at the same time.

She had never dreamt that like a tempest love would sweep over her in such a manner, to leave her utterly helpless and yet at the same time exhilarated and tinglingly alive with its very buoyancy. With an impetuous gesture she threw out her arms and flung back her head. She could feel the yearning of her whole body for this man who had suddenly entered her life.

Since the first moment when she had looked up into the Duke's eyes as she curtsied to him on entering the castle, Beatrice had known what he must mean to her. She had known it when she felt her heart beating tumultuously against her breast, as she had felt a sudden fire consume her and felt faint at the touch of his hand.

Love had come to her for the first time in her life, for until now she had believed that love, as the poets wrote of it, was but an illusion. But this was real, this was something of which she was half afraid and yet ravished by the very pleasure it evoked within her. She thought of the Duke's handsome face, of his square forehead and firm lips. She thought of the strength of his body and the way he seemed to dwarf everyone else not only in height but in personailty so that it was hard, when he was there, to remember even the existence of other people.

She wondered now how she could ever have thought Lord Niall attractive, how she could have ever countenanced even after a wearisome, boring journey his crude lovemaking. He bored her now to the point of screaming and yet she knew that it was not yet the time to betray him. When the Duke was hers, she would reveal Lord Niall's perfidy and have him flung from the castle. There would be no place for him or for any other man at Skaig once she and the Duke understood each other. They would want to be alone.

She pressed her hands against her face at the thought, and the tips of her fingers were sensuous against her soft skin. How handsome he was, how utterly desirable and together, yes, together, they could enter into all the fullness of life!

How much she could teach him! In her vast experience of men she knew how to tantalise them with her beauty until pleasure and pain were equally mingled in sensations denied to the common herd. She knew how to arouse passion to burning point and beyond it. She could play on the emotions as a musician on an instrument. She was an artist in her own sphere and her art was the oldest in the world, practised first in the Garden of Eden when Lilith tempted Adam and discovered both his weakness and her own.

This moment, Beatrice told herself, was what she had been preparing herself for since she was fifteen. She dismissed the Marquis with but a passing thought. He had never attracted her as a man, only as a personality whose power and prestige had brought her many things that her greed demanded. He might be angry, she thought, when he knew the truth; and yet he had some saving grace of humour which would make him perceive the justice of the situation. Yes, that was how he would see it. That Beatrice, who had been loved by so many men, had at last been forced to surrender her heart, her soul and her whole being into the keeping of one.

Yet even the Marquis would not understand that she gloried in her humility.

"How could I have lived so long and not known that love was like this?" Beatrice asked herself.

She rose from the dressing-table. The room was almost dark, a crimson glow in the sky was the last glimpse of the dying day. She rang her bell imperiously. Her maid, who had been waiting for some time for the summons, came hurrying to the room.

"Pull the curtains," Beatrice commanded. "Light the candles and bring me a fresh nightrobe from the closet."

"Your ladyship will not be going downstairs to dinner?" the maid asked.

"No, I shall dine here," Beatrice replied. "Carry my apologies to the Duchess and order a bottle of claret with

145

my dinner. Afterwards I will have brandy; command the wine butler to serve me the very best. I will not drink a raw spirit, as you well know."

"Yes, m'lady."

The maid glanced at Beatrice curiously with her small, deep-set eyes. She had served her now for nearly five years and she had grown to know the signs when something new was afoot. But her ladyship was in a good temper tonight, and that was one thing for which to be thankful. She gave the messages and came back to find a fresh nightrobe as her ladyship had commanded.

It was not as easy as it sounded. Robe after robe was discarded until at last one was approved of exquisite simplicity, made of lace so fine that it seemed that even a harsh breath would tear it. There was a négligé to match of lace trimmed with ribbons as soft as the petals of a magnolia.

Beatrice slipped off the robe of Chinese silk. Naked as the day she was born, she stood before the mirror. She was perfect; there was no flaw in the exquisite curves of her breasts and thighs tapering downwards to the high-arched insteps of her tiny feet. Her skin was the colour of a pearl, the veins blue in the soft hollows of her arms and knees. She stood before the fire sensuously enjoying the heat, while the flames leaping high turned the cold purity of her pale body to a warm pulsating gold. In the background the maid waited anxiously, hardly daring to move. Her ladyship's moods were as changeable as the weather.

At last with a little sigh Beatrice turned from the fire. A silver basin filled with hot scented water was ready for her; and when she had washed, her maid hurried forward with towels of fine linen bordered with precious lace. There were oils and perfumes, creams and powders to be applied, until at last like the sun slipping behind a cloud Beatrice veiled the beauty of her nakedness with the nightrobe of lace and sprinkled it with the fragrance of tuberoses.

Now her hair must be arranged. A dozen times her maid dressed it, only to be cursed for her ineptness; and the long golden tresses were undone, to be brushed, combed and re-arranged in another style. Finally Beatrice was satisfied. Her fair fell in great hoops on either side of her face, the ends pinned to her head with a comb set with diamonds. It made her very young and very ethereal. There was, too, Beatrice believed, something innocent and unsophisticated both in her appearance and in the expression on her face.

It was, she thought, fitting that it should be so for until this moment was she not indeed innocent of love?

Dinner was brought to her and she ate and drank at a small table by the fireside; then she lay back in the chair, waiting for the hours to pass. She was not impatient; it seemed to her that she had waited all her life for this moment and that everything had led up to it.

At last the hands of the clock pointed to midnight. Far away in the depths of the castle she heard another clock strike and counted each stroke slowly and aloud. Then she rose and, taking one last look at herself in the mirror, lifted up the silver candlestick which had been placed by her bedside. Walking so softly that her feet made no sound and there was only the silky rustle of her robe trailing behind her, Beatrice moved down the passage from her bedroom until she reached the top of the main staircase.

The landing was in darkness and everything was very quiet, so quiet that Beatrice fancied she heard the beating of her own heart. Her maid had discovered the whereabouts of the Duke's suite. It lay, she had told Beatrice, past the Duke's room and down the passage which led to the Library. The light of Beatrice's candle flickered on the walls as she moved forward. There were portraits of bygone ancestors to stare at her as she passed them—a more beautiful apparition than any of them could be in their hauntings.

Beatrice reached the door of the Library. Here she paused and looked down the passage. There was a light coming from under one door and she guessed that it was the Duke's bedchamber, for it lay, as she had been told, adjacent to his private sitting-room.

Very softly she opened the door of the library. The room was in darkness save for the feeble flicker of the dying fire. Setting her candlestick down on a table, Beatrice looked at the books lining the wall. From the shelf nearest her she chose one at random. It was of embossed leather, smelling slightly musty with dust and age.

Beatrice threw it on the floor, her lips parted and she gave a cry of terror and fear. Then precipitately she ran from the Library and burst open the door of the Duke's bedchamber. The candles were lit and the Duke was sitting on an armchair in front of the fire. He had taken off the embroidered coat he had worn at dinner, but he was still in his white lawn shirt with its lace jabot and in satin knee-breeches.

147

He was not reading when Beatrice entered, but was staring into the fire, his red hair, which had been brushed clear of powder, vivid against the dark velvet upholstery. As the door burst open and Beatrice stood there, he started to his feet. Then as she staggered a little, her hands outstretched as if for support, he went towards her.

"Help . . . me!" Beatrice stammered weakly. "Pray . . . help me . . . for . . . I have seen . . . a ghost."

She toppled forward and the Duke caught her in his arms. As he saved her from falling, her head fell back and the jewelled comb released her hair. It fell in a cascade of living gold over her white shoulders, and with a convulsive shudder Beatrice turned her face towards the Duke.

"Save me," she whispered, her voice broken and fearful as a little child's.

11

The Duke carried Beatrice across the room to a sofa near the fire; but when he would have set her down she clung to him, crying:

"Hold me! Keep me safe! I beg of you."

As if he had not heard, he laid her down and extricated himself skilfully from the white arms which sought to encircle his neck.

"I will fetch you a glass of wine, ma'am," he said firmly, and turned to where decanters and glasses stood on a small table. Beatrice peeped at him from under her lashes; then as he carried the wine to her side, she lay still, her eyes closed.

The Duke waited. Beatrice's négligé, caught under her as she lay, was drawn taut against the lovely curves of her body and her hair cascaded over her half-naked shoulders to fall in a glorious golden disarray on the satin cushions of the sofa. After a moment, as the Duke said nothing, Beatrice's eyelids fluttered and she looked up at him in a dazed and helpless fashion.

"Where am I?" she murmured, raising her long fingers to her forehead; and she added falteringly: "I think . . . I must have . . . fainted."

"Will you drink this?" the Duke asked, holding out the glass of wine.

With what appeared a courageous effort Beatrice raised herself on one elbow and, putting out a trembling hand, took the glass from him. She took two or three sips, then gave him a tiny, brave smile.

"I am sorry to be so . . . foolish," she murmured.

"I will ring for your maid," the Duke said, turning towards the mantelpiece beside which hung the bellrope.

"No, no," Beatrice cried, "pray do not do that. The woman is indisposed and I sent her to bed some hours ago.

That was why I was stupid enough to visit the Library myself . . . in search of a book."

"And when you were there, something frightened you?" the Duke asked.

Beatrice nodded; she shuddered and put her hand over her eyes.

"I saw something white and ghastly. Oh, but I cannot speak of it, it was so horrifying."

"I doubt if it was a ghost," the Duke said quietly. "A more possible explanation is that you saw your own reflection in a mirror."

Beatrice raised herself further and her eyes were round.

"Do you mean that I look horrifying?" she asked.

"On the contrary," the Duke replied gravely, "but you evidently did not allow yourself time to examine the apparition very closely. There is a mirror in the Library almost directly opposite the door. I think, when you view the room in the morning light, you will decide that it was that which scared you."

"How sensible you are!" Beatrice said. "And now I am ashamed. You must think that I am exceeding foolish and—stupid."

"No, Lady Wrexham," the Duke replied. "I have the greatest respect for your intelligence."

His tone was dry and Beatrice gave him a sharp glance before, with a little exclamation of horror, she put her hand to her hair, pushing back the heavy tresses from her shoulders.

"My hair is unbound!" she exclaimed. "Oh dear, what a sight I must appear to you! My comb is lost too—where can it be?"

"It is over here," the Duke said; and moving across the room to the place where he had lifted Beatrice in his arms, he picked up the curved tortoise-shell comb. He brought it to Beatrice; and when he held it out to her, her fingers curled not round the comb but round his own.

"You are very kind to me," she said in a soft seductive voice.

The Duke made her a little bow, then he deliberately disengaged his hand from hers. For a moment their eyes met and Beatrice with a gesture of her hand indicated a chair near the sofa.

"Will you not sit down?" she asked. "You are so tall that I vow you almost frighten me. I want to talk to you, and why not now?"

The Duke glanced at the clock on the mantelpiece and his eyes wandered towards the great State bed with its curtains of patterned silk, its ostrich plumage which touched the ceiling and the cipher on the headboard surmounted by a ducal coronet. On the dressing-table and on the mantelpiece the candles were burning low and the shadows in the corners of the room were growing darker and more secretive.

"It is late," the Duke replied after some seconds. "Your ladyship is doubtless upset by your unfortunate experience in the Library. Would it not be wiser to postpone our conversation until tomorrow?"

Beatrice smiled, and the parting of her lips was very enticing.

"Are you afraid of me—or for your reputation?"

"Neither," the Duke replied. "I was thinking entirely of your ladyship's well-being."

"That is very gracious of you," Beatrice replied; "but I still desire that we should talk together now, when there is no hurry, the house is quiet and we are—alone."

Her voice caressed the last word and the Duke without further argument seated himself but a few feet away from her. He crossed one leg over the other, rested his elbows on the arms of the chair and locked his fingers together. The lace at his wrists fell back to reveal his hands, shapely and well-cared for, but giving those who looked closely an impression of unusual strength.

Beatrice watched him and her eyes went from his hands to his face, serious and attentive, but otherwise expressionless. Impulsively she bent forward and laid her hand on his knee.

"What are you thinking?" she asked.

"I was but waiting for your ladyship to speak to me," the Duke replied.

"Are you curious to know what I have to say?"

"Naturally it interests me."

"And if I tell you it concerns yourself?"

"I should still be interested."

"It also concerns me."

"I imagined that was probable," the Duke said.

Beatrice took her hand from off his knee and sat up. She swung her feet in their tiny satin slippers to the ground; then she pulled her négligé around her—a pretty gesture although, if it was an attempt at modesty, it had no effect in

151

making her appear more clothed. She patted the sofa beside her.

"Come and sit here," she said invitingly. "What I have to say cannot be shouted, for indeed it is for your ear alone."

The Duke rose to his feet, but he did not move towards the sofa; instead, he walked to the mantelpiece to stand for an instant looking down at the flames, his back to Beatrice. Then he turned to face her.

"Lady Wrexham," he said, "I have an idea that you are going to speak of what is best left unsaid. You are here as my stepmother's guest, and it is best that politics and things of grave import should not be discussed between us. We might agree on such matters, but on the other hand we might disagree, and I would not have the enjoyment of your visit to Skaig in any way disrupted."

Beatrice laughed. It was a soft musical sound.

"Are you so sure it was of politics I wished to speak tonight?" she asked.

The Duke's eyes met hers steadily.

"I am convinced that was your ladyship's intention," he said; "but the Marquis of Severn's views are, I assure you, well known both to me and to many of my countrymen."

Beatrice sighed.

"For a clever man you are singularly obtuse. The Marquis of Severn does not enter into this conversation."

"On the contrary, I consider him a very important factor in it."

The Duke's words were slow and fraught with meaning. In answer Beatrice bowed her head, her hair gleaming in the firelight, two great rippling strands falling forward almost to touch the floor. Then with a sudden gesture she flung back her head.

"What would you say," she asked, and her voice was young and breathless, "if I told you that the Marquis no longer concerned me personally?"

"I should of course believe you," the Duke replied; "but I should wonder if you were wise in making such a momentous decision."

"Wise?" Beatrice queried.

"Yes, wise," the Duke replied. "For, as you do not need me to tell you, Lady Wrexham, the Marquis is a man of great influence and authority. I should be sorry if anyone, even a woman as beautiful and talented as yourself, incurred the enmity of the most powerful man in England."

"I am not afraid of him," Beatrice said. "Once his opin-

152

ions and approval mattered to me; but something has occurred which has changed everything that I feel, think or care about—yes everything. Can you not guess what that is?"

There was a sudden silence, a silence which Beatrice's shining eyes and parted lips seemed to speak more eloquently than words. The Duke turned towards a chair on the far side of the fireplace and sat down.

"I regret that I am not good at conundrums," he said quietly.

He did not look at Beatrice whose eyes, as they sought his, were burning with a strange hunger. At length in a voice so warm, so tender that it was hard to recognise it, she whispered:

"Oh, you fool, you dear sweet, glorious fool. Would you have me set aside all modesty to speak more plainly?"

The Duke made no reply and she rose to her feet to stand in front of him. She was almost blindingly beautiful in the firelight and her face, transfigured by emotion, was more radiant than it had ever been in her life before.

"I love you," she said. "You are being deliberately obtuse, so I must tell you in words of one syllable. I love you, Ewan."

The words seemed to quiver in the air like sudden music and then there was silence. Beatrice's breath came quickly, her breasts rising and falling beneath the diaphanous lace of her négligé. Still the Duke did not speak but sat utterly motionless, looking not at Beatrice but into the fire.

"Will you not answer me?" she asked at last a little wildly. "Oh, my dearest, can you not see, can you not realise what has happened to me? I have fallen in love; and I never imagined, I never dreamed even in my wildest dreams that love could be like this. Now I have found you, there is such happiness ahead for us both."

She moved forward as she spoke and knelt at his feet, her arms resting on his knees, her lovely face, quivering with passion, raised to his.

"You are mistaken!" The Duke's voice was harsh.

"Mistaken!" Beatrice repeated. "I have never been so sure of anything in my whole life. Oh, my beloved, are you afraid? I promise you there is nothing to fear. The Marquis knows nothing about you—that was why he sent me to Scotland, because he was so ignorant both of your loyalties and your intentions. He may be angry when he hears that I have left him for you; but he can do nothing, nothing, I tell you, because he has no evidence of any kind against you. And there are other ways, too, in which I can help you and save you from your enemies. You are not even aware who they are, but I know, and I can protect you from those who would harm you. Your brother, Niall, for instance, is at this very moment plotting. . . ."

"Stop!"

The word was a command.

The Duke rose from his chair and, as he did so, he seized Beatrice by the wrist and drew her from her knees to stand beside him, his fingers hard against the softness of her skin.

"Understand this, I have no desire to listen to what you are about to tell me," he said. "It concerns no one but my family and myself, and you may rest assured that the honour of the MacCraggans is safe in my keeping. What else you have said tonight in this room is from this moment forgotten. Your ladyship is tired; you may even be suffering from a slight fever which would be understandable after such a long and arduous journey. If you will permit me, I will ring the bell and ask that either your own abigail or one of the other maids shall take you to your bedchamber."

His voice was stern and his eyes were hard as he looked down into Beatrice's startled face. When he had finished speaking, he released her arm and the marks of his fingers were livid against the pearly perfection of her skin. Beatrice stared at him in utter astonishment; then she said in a voice hardly above a whisper:

"Can you mean . . . can it be possible that . . . you do not . . . want me?"

Her incredulity was so obvious and so sincere that for a moment the expression on the Duke's face seemed to soften and he replied in a quiet tone:

"I have already told your ladyship that anything that has been said between us this past hour is now forgotten."

There was no possibility of Beatrice misunderstanding him this time. For a moment she stared; her eyes darkened; her whole air of shrinking fragility appeared to vanish. Her body stiffened, became strong, wiry and virulent.

"You insolent barbarian!"

Despite the venom in her tones her voice broke on a sob. At that moment there came a knock on the door. Both Beatrice and the Duke turned their heads towards it; but before the Duke could speak, the door opened and Lord

Niall stood there, his face contorted with rage, his eyes dark and blazing with an ugly, unbridled fury.

He said nothing, only stood in the doorway looking across the room at Beatrice, taking in every detail of her transparent négligé, of her unbound hair, of her close proximity to the Duke and of the strange expression on both their faces.

The Duke spoke first.

"Did you wish to see me, Niall?" he inquired.

"No!"

The monosyllable rang out decisively.

Lord Niall advanced slowly towards Beatrice. There was something fierce and menacing in the deliberate protraction of his movements, something primitive and uncivilised in the expression on his face.

But Beatrice could manage Lord Niall and all men like him. As he reached her side, she held out both her hands in a gesture of appeal, and there was a note of utter relief in her voice as she cried:

"Oh, Niall, Niall, thank Heaven you have come! Take me away from here, please take me away."

She pressed herself nearer to him and instinctively, almost unaware of his action, Lord Niall put his arm around her waist.

"What does this mean?" he began, but her fingers were against his lips, soft, insistent and caressing.

"Say nothing now," she whispered, her body weak and pliant against his. "I will tell you all later, but for the moment take me away—I beg of you."

Her body was heavy against him. He could feel the soft, yielding warmth of her and his arm tightened fiercely. Some of the anger left his face; but as he turned to the Duke, his eyes were still smouldering with suspicion.

"Lady Wrexham is indisposed, Niall," the Duke said quietly. "Will you escort her to her bedchamber?"

"Very well, but I will deal with you later," Lord Niall snarled. His voice perceptibly altered as he looked down at Beatrice and asked: "Can you walk or shall I carry you?"

"I will walk. Let me take your arm."

Together they turned towards the door and only as they reached it did Beatrice look back. For a moment her eyes met the Duke's. It was for but a split second before she turned away and Lord Niall guided her into the passage and closed the door behind him; but in that instant the Duke knew that he had made an enemy, implacable, bitterly revengeful, who would never rest until he was utterly destroyed.

For a long time he stood looking across the room at the closed door, before his glance wandered to the sofa where Beatrice had lain, the cushions still hollowed by the weight of her head and body. Then he took a deep breath and straightened his shoulders as if he made a sudden decision. His hands reached for the bell rope and he tugged at it impatiently.

In her own bedchamber Beatrice, lying in the big four-poster, her head and shoulders resting against a pile of lace pillows, related to Lord Niall her own version of what had occurred in the Duke's room.

"I had to see him some time," she told him as she ended her story. "There were things on which I had to question him, as you well know."

"But why tonight and half-naked?" Lord Niall inquired brutally.

While she talked, he had stridden up and down the room, his almost insane jealousy making him bite his fingers until they were raw.

"Actually I never thought of how I looked," Beatrice replied simply. "I could not sleep and I thought that here was a good opportunity, when there was no one about and your stepmother was not listening, to talk with the Duke."

"But he might have been in bed and asleep," Lord Niall protested.

"I never thought of that," Beatrice answered, her eyes round and innocent. "I had expected him to be in his sitting-room. You remember he told me the other night how he always works late, reading and writing until the small hours of the morning."

"I have no recollection of his saying anything of the sort." Lord Niall said sullenly.

"Perhaps you were looking at me instead of attending to your half-brother," Beatrice replied, adding: "Oh, Niall, I beg of you, do not be incensed with me, I have had enough to bear tonight. Yes, quite enough."

For a moment her voice was shrill and then she continued: "But of one thing you can rest assured, there is no reason whatsoever for you to be jealous of the Duke. I will tell you this, and swear it on my honour, I hate him, I hate him with all my heart and soul; and I vow on all that I hold

156

most sacred that only my own death shall prevent your becoming the Duke of Arkrae."

There was no misunderstanding the vehemence of Beatrice's voice, and Lord Niall was pacified. He stopped his restless pacing and moving to the bedside, took her hand in his and raised it to his lips.

"I believe you," he said: "but we return to the inevitable question—how can it be accomplished?"

"The way will reveal itself," Beatrice answered; "I have never yet failed in anything I set out to do and I shall not fail to destroy the Duke."

For a moment her lips were tight, then she forced a smile to them and turned her face towards Lord Niall.

"It is growing very late," she said. "Your valet will be waiting for you."

"Let him wait; it is what he is paid for," Lord Niall replied.

"I was not thinking so much of your servant as of you," Beatrice murmured. "You must be tired; that green velvet coat, elegant as it is, must be tight. Why not be comfortable?"

"You mean . . . ?" Lord Niall's eyes were suddenly bright.

"If it pleases you. . . ."

"Oh, my dearest."

His voice was hoarse with desire and he bent towards her, but she put out her hand to ward him off.

"I have not yet forgiven you," she said lightly. "But I will endeavour to forget your spurious misjudgment of me before your return."

Lord Niall laughed softly.

"I will teach you how to forgive me," he said, "but never to forget. I would have you remember me always—even in your dreams."

He kissed the point of her white shoulder, then turned and went from the room without another word.

Alone, Beatrice lay staring up at the canopy over her head. She did not see the clever, skilful stitches in the needlework embroidered so beautifully a hundred years earlier by industrious fingers. She did not see the shadows moving in the room with the flickering of her candle. Her eyes felt hot, her lips were dry, and in her heart there was a pain so agonising that she could hardly believe that she was not wounded unto death. She felt suddenly very old;

for something young, tender and infinitely beautiful, which
had been born within her for but a very short while, was
dead.

It had been murdered, she thought, murdered almost in
the moment of its birth; and now she was crippled and
deformed by the loss of it. Her eyes were hurting her,
burning deep in their sockets until her very brain seemed
on fire. Her heart was dead and she could not cry, for she
was long past tears.

Lord Niall moved swiftly down the passage towards his
own room. His suite was in the most ancient part of the
castle facing north. The rooms were small and the
panelling in them was dark with age, but they had their ad-
vantages and he preferred them. Beatrice's room, which
faced south and overlooked the loch, was not far from the
Duchess's apartments. Big double doors divided those from
the main passage; and as Lord Niall drew near them on his
way to his own wing, the doors opened and his stepmother
came into the passage.

Lord Niall was carrying a candle and his first instinct
was to blow it out so that she would not see him; but
before he could do so, he realised that he was already ob-
served. The Duchess was wearing the gown of stiff yellow
brocade which she had worn at dinner; the wide hoops of
her skirts effectively barred his way; her hair was still
powdered and her neck and wrists heavily bejewelled. As
he drew close to her, Lord Niall saw that her face was
twitching as it invariably did when she was agitated.

"Why, *Belle, mére*," he exclaimed, "it is a very late hour
to find you awake."

"I was waiting for you," she replied in a low voice.
"Come into my sitting-room, I must speak with you."

"It is too late," Lord Niall protested, "you must be tired
and I know I am."

"I must speak with you," the Duchess repeated dully,
"now and at once."

There was something in her face which told him that it
would be unwise to cross her further. Shrugging his shoulders, he said petulantly:

"Very well then, but if you have a *migraine* tomorrow,
do not blame me."

The Duchess made no reply and Lord Niall followed her
through the doors of her suite into the big sitting-room

which opened off an inner passage. Here the tapers in the chandeliers and sconces were guttering low, but the room was still bright. On a needlework stool in front of the fire and on the floor beside it were scattered a number of papers. Lord Niall glanced at them and said impatiently:

"What the devil have you got all these things out for tonight?"

He snuffed his candle and put it down on a side table; then he walked across the room and poured himself out a glass of brandy from a decanter which stood on the wine table in front of one of the windows. The Duchess watched him. She stood in the centre of the room, the twitch of her left eye becoming more pronounced. Lord Niall drank half the brandy and walked towards the fireplace.

"Well, why don't you answer my question?" he said aggressively.

"It is for you to answer my questions," the Duchess replied. "What were you doing in that woman's room?"

Lord Niall's fingers tightened round the stem of his glass and his eyes narrowed.

"So you were spying on me?"

"I was," the Duchess replied. "Have I not the right?"

"No, by God, you have not!" Lord Niall put his glass down on the marble mantelpiece with a decisive bang. "Let us make this clear once and for all. I am not going to be questioned and badgered about my actions, however unusual or unconventional that may appear. Whatever I do, you can be assured I have a good reason for it."

"A good reason!" The Duchess repeated the words and then she laughed, a horrible, cackling sound which died in her throat as if she strangled it. "She is young! She is beautiful! I suppose that is what you call a good reason?"

"She also happens to be the Marquis of Severn's mistress."

"And yours?" the Duchess asked. "Yes, yours too. I am not such a dolt that you can blind me to that. You met her at Inverness, you stayed with her there and you lied to me, yes, lied because you were afraid."

"I was not afraid," Lord Niall contradicted. "I was, if you must know the truth, bored with making explanations to you, bored with your incessant whining, bored with being pestered by your eternal jealousy."

"Pester! You say I pester you!" the Duchess screamed. "Once you loved me; once you craved my favours; but

159

now you dare to speak to me of being pestered. After all I have done for you, after the years I have toiled and schemed and plotted to get you what you want!"

"Without success!" Lord Niall sneered. He looked down at the papers. "A lot of good they have done me, haven't they? It has been money wasted, every penny of it. Your spies are incompetent or else you have not the brains to choose them properly. What have they found, I ask you, what have they discovered after five years of this ineffective tomfoolery?"

The Duchess's hands plucked at her dress and she seemed to shake all over.

"You cad!" she said. "You ungrateful beast! When I have given up everything for you."

"What have you given up?" Lord Niall asked derisively. "Your return to England? You know as well as I do that you have no desire to go back. Who cares for or is interested in the widow of a Scottish Duke—especially one without wealth? My father was none too generous to you, I admit that; but while you live here, you can save every penny of your allowance. In England you would have to put your hand in your pocket; and you would hate that, for you are mean as well as jealous, as I have discovered all too often."

"Mean?" the Duchess said, shaking now as if with an ague. "Mean? When I have poured out my money on spies for you, spies paid to follow Ewan to England, to Edinburgh, to France! Do you think those trips have cost nothing? Look at the bills, read them for yourself and then dare to tell me that I am mean."

The Duchess picked up a big handful of papers from the stool and thrust them into Lord Niall's hands. He took them from her, glanced down at them and made a gesture as if he would throw them into the fire, but he changed his mind and chucked them into a chair.

"All right, all right. You have spent a certain amount of money on me, I will admit that, but it has got us nowhere. I am not the Duke of Arkrae, and if I have to rely on your efforts, I never shall be."

"You think that she will gain you the Dukedom, that woman, that English doxy whose bedroom you have just left?"

"It is indisputably a distinct possibility," Lord Niall replied. "But it will not be very helpful either to her or to me if you create scenes like this, if you are going to turn

160

against her and make things more difficult than they are already."

"So you expect me to help her," the Duchess cried furiously, "help her to take you from me?"

"May the devil hear me," Lord Niall growled. "It is not a question of her taking me away from you or from anyone else for that matter."

"Do you speak the truth?"

The Duchess stepped forward and put her hand on Lord Niall's arm. The pressure was insistent and half reluctantly he turned his face to look down into hers.

"Swear to me, here and now, as on the Bible, that you do not love her, that she means nothing to you but a weapon to gain you the Dukedom, swear to me. . . ." She broke off suddenly and added in a whisper which seemed to come hissing from between her lips. "You dare not swear for you love her. I can see you love her."

With a rough gesture Lord Niall shook himself free of her hand, crossed the room to the wine table.

"In God's name, spare me the dramatics."

The Duchess seemed not to hear him. She stood on the hearthrug and whispered:

"You love her and she will destroy you. Yes, I know it, I know it in my very bones. She will destroy you, she will bring you nothing but death and destruction . . . death and destruction. . . ."

There was something so weird in her words and in the sibilant tones that Lord Niall turned round furiously, the decanter in one hand, a goblet in the other:

"Will you be quiet, you old witch?" he shouted. "You don't scare me with your eerie forebodings any more than you frighten me with your threats."

The Duchess put her hands up to her face. She was shaking all over. Lord Niall took a great gulp of brandy and walked towards her.

"We have got to make this clear here and now," he said roughly. "Whatever has happened in the past, you have no further hold over me. I am a young man. I am my own master. Life is only beginning for me, while you, to put it bluntly, are no longer young. I will brook interference from no one. Whatever I may mean to Beatrice Wrexham or she to me, it has nothing to do with you. I am grateful for what you have tried to do for me, I say 'tried' because you have achieved nothing, absolutely nothing. You have had Ewan watched for all these years; but for all the good it has done, you might just as well have given the money to the nearest Jacobite. But all that is finished, finished for ever as far as I am concerned. I am not ungrateful, but I now have someone else to help me, and I would wager my entire fortune that whatever she attempts will be successful. You have got to be sensible, *Belle-mére*, you have got to face facts. We have had some good times together, you and I, but they are over. Scenes of jealousy and recrimination will help neither of us; you must accept things as they are and make the best of them."

Lord Niall finished his glass and put it down.

"In the morning," he said to the silent, shaking figure beside him, "I suggest that we both forget this ugly scene."

He walked towards the door, took up his candle from the table where he had laid it and lit it from a three-branch candelabrum. "May I bid Your Grace good night?"

His bow was a mocking travesty of the conventional curtsey; but when he had made it, the cruel smile of buffoonery left his lips and, as he looked across the room at the Duchess he hesitated, some half-forgotten decency within him stirred by her quivering anguish. Then, as she did not move or speak, he shrugged his shoulders, went from the room and closed the door behind him.

For some minutes the Duchess stood where she was. Then, as if her knees gave under her, she sank down first on to the stool and then on to the floor. At last, slowly, bitterly, to her twitching, tortured eyes came the relief of tears, the slow ugly tears of old age, the tears of utter despair, for she knew now that her life at Skaig was over and there was nothing for her to do but to return to England.

12

Iona was worried. She sensed that something was wrong, but she was not yet certain what it was or whether it concerned herself.

She had wakened early in the morning feeling unusually happy. For a moment her happiness had been vague, like the lingering memory of some exquisite dream when the sleeper has been transported into a sunlit world and while the details are forgotten, the effect remains clear. But as full consciousness returned and her senses became more alert, Iona knew one reason for happiness.

Hector was safe! She need no longer be distraught with anxiety nor with the terror that had pursued her all the day before—a terror that Lord Niall's men might recapture their prisoner. But night-time had come and with it the news that the chase had been abandoned. Hector appeared to have vanished into thin air and Iona could understand Lord Niall's anger and sense of frustration.

Cathy had wakened her yesterday morning with the news that Hector's escape had been discovered and that Lord Niall's men were in a turmoil of agitation and astonishment. Cursed by his lordship and sent post-haste in search of the escaped prisoner, they were in their heart of hearts, Cathy said, convinced that his escape was due to supernatural aid.

Iona and Cathy had both been distressed at the thought of Eachann being flogged in an attempt to make him confess what part he had played in the disappearance of the fugitive. But there was nothing they could do about it; and when later they learned that he had been released from the dungeon, Cathy vowed she would reward him because he had not mentioned her visit during the night.

"The mon hae a guid heart," she said, "for a' that he is a great fule in followin' his lordship."

"Was he in the Duke's service before he became one of Lord Niall's men?" Iona asked.

Cathy shook her head.

"Nay, for they who sairve His Grace wouldna gang frae him. Eachann an' the others who belong tae Lord Niall came frae a wee island on the west coast. 'Tis his lordship's ain property gi'en tae him by the auld Duke wheen he came o' age. He has a castle there, they say; but 'tis naethin' mair than a ruin an' his lordship much prefers tae dwell here."

Iona could understand that; but at the same time she thought it a poor return for his half-brother's hospitality to live in his house and yet to intrigue against him and challenge his authority. It was easy to understand under the circumstances how many difficulties must arise and how Lord Niall's servants were disliked by the Duke's, and vice-versa. The differences between the two staffs had been very obvious the day before when none of the Duke's clansmen had taken any part in the search for Hector; and the fact that the prisoner had escaped the vigilance of Lord Niall's men was an occasion for much jesting by the members of the ducal household.

" 'Tis in mae heart tae be sorry for Sime," Cathy told Iona. "He's a dour mon an' nae tae be trusted, but he's hard put tae it below stairs tae keep oop his ain heid the noo."

"I thought he looked horrible," Iona said with a little shudder, remembering Sime's shifty expression and the unsightly cast in his left eye.

"Aye, he's that richt enough," Cathy agreed; "but his lordship leads an' the men follow. Ye canna blame them wheen they hae pledged allegiance tae him."

It was very obvious that Cathy thought that the real villain of the piece was Lord Niall, and Iona was not disposed to argue with her. She had managed to keep out of his lordship's way the whole of the previous day. This had meant that, when she was not in her bedchamber she must be constantly in the company of the Duchess.

She guessed, though she had no logical reason for the supposition, that Lord Niall was avoiding his stepmother; and so the easiest way to avoid him was to sit in the Crimson Salon with the Duchess, watching the nervous fluttering of her fingers and listening to her constant and unceasing complaints about the cold and discomfort of Scotland.

But if Iona had wished to avoid Lord Niall, she had also

wanted, above all things, to see the Duke again. It was he who had been instrumental in saving Hector; and while Iona was fully aware that his part in the prisoner's escape must be kept completely secret and never revealed to anyone, not even to Cathy, she was determined to express to the Duke a little of her own overwhelming gratitude. Besides, she was certain now that the way was open for her to approach him on behalf of the Prince. She had only to gain from him but a brief expression of his loyalty and a promise of support should the occasion arise, and then that part of her mission was completed. Even if she were not fortunate enough to track down the Tears of Torrish, she would not return to France empty-handed, for with news of the Duke's allegiance to the Stuart Cause and the little black notebook on which Hector set so much store she could be assured of a warm welcome.

When she thought of France and of the Prince awaiting the outcome of her journey, she felt again the warm glow of satisfaction that she had experienced in Paris when she had realised that His Royal Highness trusted and believed in her. But insidiously against her own inclination came the question of what would happen to her once she had returned and given the Prince the assurances he desired.

Was she to go back to her work in the milliner's shop and to the soul-destroying loneliness of the boardinghouse where by the most frugal economies she could afford the meanest and worst furnished room in the building? Was that all the future held, a future in which she would ever be haunted by the beauties of Skaig?

Although Iona's mind had been incessantly busy with the task which had been set her and with the difficulties and troubles which had arisen over Hector and his capture, she had never ceased to marvel at the comfort and loveliness of her surroundings. Not only was she appreciative by nature, but she had also a real love of everything that was beautiful. From the moment she first opened her eyes in the morning to the moment when she closed them again at night she noticed everything from the softness of the linen sheets on her bed to the ever-changing colours of the loch.

Once Iona had thought that the little house near the north wall of Paris where she had lived with her guardian was all that could be wished for where comfort and charm were concerned. Now at Skaig she began to realise what a home could be like when it was the store-house of centuries and the treasures it contained had been augmented generation after generation by those who understood not only the value of the objects themselves but their place in providing a background for an ancient and honourable family.

Iona would wander through the great rooms of the castle, touching the polished furniture, looking at the paintings with their carved gilt frames, wondering at the tapestries wrought in exquisite detail with a skill that was almost unbelievable, and conscious even as she walked of the softness of the patterned carpets and the fragrance of the pine wood burning in the marble-surrounded fireplaces.

There was so much to see, so much to learn from what she saw. And besides the treasures inside the castle the surrounding landscape left her day after day inarticulate with wonder. Whether the sun shone or the rain beat fiercely against the walls of the castle and its many-paned windows, the moors and mountains were always beautiful and the loch as mysterious as an opal.

Absorbing everything with the breathless excitement of a child, Iona awoke to the fact that she loved Skaig as she had never loved anything else in her whole life before. In such a very short while it had become indivisibly a part of herself, and it was with a sense of misery that she realised the truth, because every day she drew nearer to the moment when she must leave it, never to return.

She thought of Paris, and for the first time in her life she understood what her guardian and other exiles like him had felt when they had known that their lives must be lived out among the frivolity and gaiety of a city which could never really amuse them. It was Scotland for which they longed, for the wide sweep of moor, hill and sea, for the winds fragrant with the perfume of heather blowing down from the north, overwhelming the weak but bringing new life and courage to the strong. No wonder they had grumbled, no wonder they had sighed, no wonder there had always been a haunting melancholy in their eyes and on their faces as if some part of them was absent in unceasing remembrance! Now Iona could understand, now she knew that she, too, would be haunted with memories. No sound, however melodious, no music, however finely orchestrated, could excel the cluck of an old cock-grouse winging its way down the hill; no picture, however artistically executed, could rival the panoramic masterpiece of the sun setting behind Ben Nevis.

Iona chid herself for selfishness and self-seeking, but her sadness at the thought of leaving the castle would not be dispersed. It was always there, sharpening her appreciation of everything, giving her a sense of urgency that she must miss nothing because the sands were running out and the moment of her departure grew inexorably nearer.

And yet happiness could spring to her heart with something near to rapture. Hector was safe! The Duke had been instrumental in setting him free; and more than that, His Grace had not failed Iona's most cherished hopes.

She had not believed it possible, even in her most fearful moments, that the Duke could favour the English. She would have believed anything of Lord Niall from her first moment of meeting him; but though she had for a little while been afraid of the Duke and had been chilled by his coldness and air of arrogance, she had never distrusted him, never thought that he could be anything but loyal to his countrymen.

As she dressed this morning, Iona had thought that perhaps today would bring the opportunity of speaking to him of the Prince, of telling him why she had come to Scotland and how much the future rested with him and his decisions in the matter. Like all women with a difficult task ahead she dressed herself with unusual care, choosing a gown of leaf-green muslin which she was well aware became her more than anything else she possessed. She had purchased the muslin in the Marché in Paris, and the Syrian merchant who had brought it all the way from Damascus had reduced the price a little because Iona had smiled at him and because he knew that it would suit her better than anyone else he had ever seen. Iona had sat late into the night working by the light of two candles to finish the dress before she sailed for Scotland. She remembered now how she had wondered in what circumstances she would wear it and knew that even her wildest imaginations had fallen far short of the truth.

The dress was laced with velvet ribbon and Iona, feeling gay, set a tiny bow of it among the curls of her hair; then, humming a little tune, she went downstairs.

She did not at first realise that anything was wrong, although afterwards she wondered if she had not had a vague premonition of it from the moment she reached the main landing outside the Crimson Salon. At first glance she thought that no one was about; then she saw Lady Wrexham's abigail, a sour-faced, nervous-looking woman, look at her in what she felt was an unpleasant manner as she passed by without a greeting, to disappear down the main staircase.

A few minutes later, as Iona moved restlessly about the Crimson Salon, she saw the maid returning, followed by a flunkey carrying a silver tray on which reposed a decanter of wine and two glasses. Iona wondered at the two glasses and thought perhaps that Lady Wrexham was kind enough to offer her maid some wine when she herself partook of it in her bedchamber.

There was no sign of the Duchess, and after a while Iona thought it would be polite to go to her bedchamber and inquire if she had slept well. Her Grace had seemed strange these past few days and at dinner she had hardly spoken at all, answering the Duke in monosyllables when he addressed her directly. Iona had thought that her silence on previous occasions was due to the fact that she was jealous of Lady Wrexham; but last night her ladyship had sent word that she was indisposed and would dine in her bedchamber. Even in her absence, the Duchess had not been any more cheerful.

Iona had grown to dread the long, drawn-out meals when she was uneasily aware of strange under-currents in the conversation, while their meaning was beyond her comprehension. As she moved down the passage, she wondered what the Duke really thought of Lady Wrexham and if, when they were alone together, he unbent before the honeyed blandishments with which she so obviously tried to entice him.

"I dislike her," Iona said half aloud, and then started, for her ladyship's maid was approaching once again, this time carrying a hooped gown of sprigged brocade with a petticoat of azure blue satin. Iona's simple pleasure in her own dress of green muslin vanished. Suddenly she felt that it was drab and unmodish beside the extravagant elegance of Lady Wrexham's clothes. She thought how she and her ladyship must appear in the Duke's eyes. One a woman poised, brilliant, gorgeously arrayed and expensively bejewelled; the other an unsophisticated, unfledged girl ignorant in so many ways and having very little in her to interest a man of experience, of vast possessions and magnificent traditions.

As if to escape her own thoughts, Iona ran the last steps before she knocked on the door of the Duchess's bedchamber. As she waited for a reply, Iona heard a movement in the sitting-room. The door was ajar and after a second or two she crossed the passage; this time, after she had knocked, a voice bade her enter. She opened the door and uttered an exclamation of astonishment.

The whole room was in disorder. Four large trunks lay open and at one of them knelt the Duchess's maid, packing papers and books and an array of china, enamel boxes, work bags, miniatures, ornaments and pin-trays, all of which were strewn around her on the floor. At the *escritoire* by the window was seated the Duchess. She wore a frilled peignoir of pink muslin over her nightrobe, and her nightcap was made to match. Her skin was wrinkled in the morning light and her eyes were swollen and puffy as if she had spent the night in weeping. She glanced towards Iona, but continued to take out of a drawer of the *escritoire* bundles of letters tied with ribbon.

"Oh, it's you, girl," she said ungraciously. "Come in, you may be of some assistance."

"What is happening?" Iona asked, looking round her in astonishment.

Bureaux were open, drawers lay on the floor, one chair was piled with material of every sort and description. There was velvet, muslin, brocade, satin, several bales of it half unravelled and trailing on the floor.

No one answered her and after a moment Iona asked somewhat stupidly:

"Are you packing to go away?"

"Yes, I am going away," the Duchess said almost angrily, looking up suddenly, and Iona saw there were tears in her eyes. She put her fingers up to her forehead. "I am tired," she said suddenly.

The maid rose from the trunk.

"Shall I fetch Your Grace some wine or a pot of tea?" she asked. "Your Grace never touched a bit of the breakfast I brought you."

"I will have tea," the Duchess answered, "and bring a cup for Miss Iona," she added with a surprising solicitude.

"Very good, Your Grace."

The maid withdrew from the room, shutting the door behind her. The Duchess looked at Iona and made a little gesture with her hands.

"As you see, I am going away," she said.

Her face puckered, accentuating the lines round her thin

lips, and Iona thought for a moment that she looked like a sick monkey. The colour of her skin in contrast to the pink muslin was almost ludicrous.

"Surely this is a very sudden decision?" Iona asked, wondering if the question would seem impertinent and yet feeling somehow that the Duchess expected her to ask it.

The Duchess rose from the chair and walked across the room, and the train of her peignoir, which would have been suitable for a girl of eighteen, trailing behind her, knocked over several china ornaments which had been arranged near another trunk.

"Sudden? Yes, I suppose it is a sudden decision," she said, speaking more to herself than to Iona, "and yet I have always known that the time must come when I must go. I have hated this place, hated it from the first day that I came here, and now it has defeated me. The castle has won, as I always knew it would."

Her hands shook and the twitch in her eye was so violent that it contorted her whole face. Iona suddenly felt sorry for her; however disagreeable she had been to her personally, however unkind, here was a woman who was suffering almost beyond endurance.

"You are tired, ma'am," Iona said. "Come and sit down by the fire. You will feel better after you have had a cup of tea."

"I doubt it," the Duchess said uncompromisingly, but she sat down in the chair Iona pulled forward for her and held out her thin, bony hands to the blaze.

"Where are you going?" Iona asked a little timidly.

"Back to England," the Duchess said. "Back to my home in Kent. Do you think they will be pleased to see me?"

"I am sure they will," Iona said brightly, feeling it was the only possible answer.

"Then you are wrong," the Duchess said. "My father has married again and his new wife has no liking for me. She is my stepmother, yes, my stepmother!" She suddenly gave a high, cackling laugh which was poignant with bitterness and misery. "It is a jest! Yes, a rare jest that I, who am a stepmother, will now have to live with mine. She will hate me, she will intrigue against me and do her best to be rid of me. I have done all those things, haven't I? And now I shall have them done to me."

The Duchess's voice died away, and now the tears were running down her wrinkled cheeks. She made no effort to stop them or to wipe them away. She only sat staring at

170

the fire, and Iona saw that she had bitten her lips until they bled.

"But must you go there—if it will make you so unhappy?" she asked at length, feeling that the Duchess was waiting for her to speak.

"If I do not go home, where is there a place for me?" the Duchess asked. "You know full well that I cannot stay here. No, you do not know it, but never mind, it is of no consequence. You will learn the reason fast enough."

"Does it concern Lord Niall?" Iona asked.

The Duchess grasped the arms of her chair and her face was livid.

"Yes, it concerns him," she hissed. "Lord Niall and that woman he loves, that harlot from St. James's. Well, he is welcome to her, but she will bring him nothing that he needs. Instead she will destroy him. But, oh God, I have loved him so."

Her voice broke. She covered her face with shaking fingers and wept noisily, rocking herself backwards and forwards in the chair as Iona had seen the peasant women do when they were bereaved. She felt there was nothing she could say or do, only sit silent, more sorry than she could say for this broken, miserable woman.

At length the Duchess's sobs ceased and she groped for her handkerchief. Iona retrieved it from where it had fallen to the floor and put it into her hand. The Duchess wiped her eyes.

"I am a fool," she said sharply. "It is a waste of time to grieve, and yet I cannot help myself."

She looked at Iona as if she saw her for the first time.

"You are young and pretty," she said. "Waste little of your youth, for it is gone so quickly and then there is nothing left but regrets."

She gave a deep sigh which seemed to shake her whole body.

"Once I was pretty. You would not think it now. But I was pretty enough to attract men, pretty enough to have them desire me. And then I fell in love. God sent love into this world to torture women, did you know that? People talk as though it were an enviable thing, something to be sought, to be prized, to be treasured. Poor deluded fools, what they seek is a poison, a weapon which will destroy them as completely as if they put a bullet through their brain."

The Duchess paused, her eyes closed for a moment as if

she were thinking back into the past, remembering what had happened, recapturing the pain and torture of that first love.

"How old were you when you fell in love?" Iona asked.

She was not really curious, for it horrified her to hear these revelations and see the agony on the Duchess's face; yet she felt that in some way it relieved the stricken woman to talk the bitterness out of her rather than keep it bottled up.

"I was sixteen when my mother took me to court," the Duchess replied. "My father was proud of me. I was his only daughter and his favourite. To his three sons he was a tyrant, and a hard task-master, but to me he was always lenient and understanding. But I was well aware that I must exert myself to earn his favour.

"I was a success at St. James's, and I came home to Kent with several suitors and the assurance that there would be many more. My father had no intention of letting me be betrothed to anyone he did not consider to be his own equal both in wealth and breeding. He turned my suitors away and as my affections were not engaged, I was content to see them go, knowing that there would be others to take their place. Then on my twentieth birthday I fell in love."

The Duchess put her fingers to her eyes.

"Love, love," she muttered. "What is it? Nothing but a crucifixion for those who succumb to it."

Her words were so wild that Iona said quickly:

"Was he nice, this suitor whom you loved?"

"Who said he was a suitor?" the Duchess asked, taking her hands from her eyes, then staring almost resentfully at Iona. "He was no suitor, girl. He would never have dared raise his eyes in my direction had I not loved him first, had I not encouraged him, had I not told him that I loved him."

The Duchess's voice softened.

"He was dark and very handsome," she said softly. "I have always liked dark men . . . they seem so strong . . . so virile."

"Did he love you?" Iona asked.

"Yes, he loved me," the Duchess answered. "He, the penniless son of a country parson, who had come to my father's house to tutor my younger brother, loved me as I loved him."

The Duchess sat up in the chair, pulled her handkerchief
172

between her fingers, staring at it as if she had never seen it before.

"I know not why I am thinking of this now," she said in a voice which tried pathetically to be light. "I suppose packing up brings back old memories. One finds letters and other things one has treasured and hoarded."

"Oh, please tell me what happened," Iona said, interested now despite herself.

"I will tell you," the Duchess said. "For this story should be a warning to you, a warning never to fall in love. I loved David with all my heart and soul. That was his name, David Dunn, son of an obscure parson. For five years I loved him, refusing all offers for my hand, taking care that no suitors of any import approached my father before I had made it very clear to them that I would under no circumstances become their bride.

"Then my father discovered about David. We had grown careless with the years. First we had been content with looking into each other's eyes, with the touch of each other's hands, a hasty kiss snatched once in a while behind an open door or in the twilit garden. Then we wanted more. It was torture not to be alone. We wanted to talk, to discuss things, and it was heaven to be in each other's arms.

"It was a servant who betrayed us, a maid whom I had dismissed for impertinence. She went to my father. It was not difficult for him to discover the truth. David was sent packing without a reference, without even the salary that was due to him. I was sent to Yorkshire to stay with my uncle; and while I was on the visit, broken-hearted, miserable, yet striving to hide my hurt from the curious eyes of my cousins who had an inkling that I was in disgrace, we had an invitation to visit Edinburgh.

"A friend of the family invited us all to stay—my aunt and her two daughters, myself and one of her sons. There was to be a ball in Edinburgh. My aunt accepted the invitation, principally, I think, because she thought that the distraction would relieve my obvious unhappiness.

"It was at the ball that I met the Duke of Arkrae. He was an old man, but of fine appearance and great import. I was flattered that he paid so much attention to me. Not for a moment did I guess that his interest in me was anything more than the desire of an aged men for the company of a young and pretty girl. When my uncle told me that he had asked for my hand in marriage, I nearly swooned in astonishment. My uncle was delighted. He pressed me to accept the Duke, and because I was afraid to go home, afraid of my father's anger and more afraid than anything of the loneliness and emptiness of the house without David, I did not refuse.

"We were married in Yorkshire. It was a quiet ceremony and my father came north for it. That is how I became the Duchess of Arkrae, the third Duchess to a Duke of over seventy."

The Duchess gave the handkerchief between her fingers a sharp tug. The delicate lace tore and the sound of it seemed to give her a sense of satisfaction, for her lips twisted in a tortured smile.

"Yes, I became a Duchess," she went on. "My cousins were full of envy, my friends wrote me pages of congratulations, but only I knew what marriage to an old man could mean. Difficult and set in his ways, a man with a strange taciturn nature, a man without any tenderness or understanding for the feelings of a young and sensitive girl. I know you are thinking that I ought to have been grateful at making such a good marriage after behaving clandestinely with my brother's tutor; but I wasn't at all grateful. Had the Duke been tender or compassionate, things might have been different; but he was not, and having enjoyed me as he might have enjoyed a good day's hunting or a well-served meal, he forgot my very existence. I was lonely. Scotland seemed big and empty and the castle a severe prison from which I could never escape. I wanted youth and laughter, companionship and . . . and love."

The Duchess got to her feet and, brushing past Iona who was sitting on a low stool by her side, moved across to the window. As she stood there looking out on the loch, the clear morning light revealed every wrinkle and flaw of her unprotected skin. It showed up the twitch of her eye, the discoloured, swollen eyelids and the sagging skin over her jaw. It was the wreck of what had once been a pretty face, a spectre of a long forgotten youth.

"I have stood here so often," the Duchess said in a strange voice. "Once I remember wondering if the waters of the loch were very cold and whether one died quickly when one was drowned, or if such a death was slow and agonising. I shall never stand here again. In a short while, when I look out of the window, I shall see green fields, wide spreading trees and the hedges and meadowland

174

which are always green in the mellow English climate. I shall forget the cruel sharpness of the wind, the long snow-locked winters here when it seems as if the spring will never come. I shall forget how I hated this castle—but shall I forget the rest?"

She turned towards Iona and in a voice of terror asked:

"Shall I forget Niall and all he has meant to me? Shall I forget his face, his hands, the way he comes into a room, the way his hair grows from his forehead?" Once again the tears sprang into her eyes. "Can I forget? Can I forget all that?"

Blindly she groped her way back to the chair she had vacated by the fireside. Iona helped her into it. There was nothing she could say, there was nothing she could do. She was thankful to hear the door open and see the Duchess's maid return. Two footmen entered a moment later carrying a huge silver tray. They set it down on a table by the Duchess's side and she busied herself unlocking the little caddy which contained the tea and spooning it into the big crested pot. The maid knelt down at the trunk and resumed her packing. The moment for confidences was passed. Iona accepted a cup of tea from the Duchess and asked if she might retire.

"If Your Grace will excuse me, I would like to go out into the sunshine."

The Duchess nodded absently. Since her maid's return she had not spoken one word, and Iona knew that she was thinking of the past, remembering other things of Lord Niall or perhaps of David, her first love. There was nothing she could do to help, no soothing potion she could offer to allay her sufferings or bring her forgetfulness.

As she came from the Duchess's suite into the main passage on the first floor, Iona felt as if she escaped from an over-heated greenhouse. The emotions and miseries of the past hour had left her with a feeling of vague unhappiness mingled with a sense of apprehension. While she had listened to the Duchess, while she had heard her bemoaning the loss of Lord Niall's love, a question had sprung into her mind. Why had this happened now and at this moment?

Lord Niall was in love with Lady Wrexham, that was obvious; but why had he been brave enough to admit it to his stepmother? Why, when but a few days earlier he had been ready to lie about his visit to Inverness, had he been so frank now that the Duchess felt it impossible to remain at the castle? Something was happening, Iona thought, and she wondered what it might be.

Reaching the door of the Crimson Salon, she stood still. Two people were in the room, standing at the far end before a window which opened on to the balcony. They had their backs to the door and Iona could see them while they were unaware of her presence.

Lady Wrexham, gorgeously attired in the gown which Iona had seen her maid taking down the passage, had a scarf of ermine draped round her shoulders. Her hair was unpowdered but elaborately arranged, and her hand, glittering with rings, was laid familiarly on Lord Niall's arm.

"There are a vast number of things I should want to alter," she said to him.

"The whole place shall be arranged exactly as you wish, my sweet," Lord Niall replied.

Iona had the feeling that this was the end of their conversation and that they were about to turn from the window. Swiftly she moved away from the door and without really thinking where she was going moved down the passage towards the Library. The door was open and a footman was replenishing the fire.

He glanced up as Iona entered and she recognised him as a flunkey who was often on duty at the top of the main stairs and to whom she usually said good morning and good night. She smiled at him now and he smiled back.

" 'Tis a grand mornin', miss," he said.

"I was thinking of going out," Iona replied, "but I would like to speak with His Grace. Have you any idea where he is?"

"His Grace isna in the castle, miss," the footman replied.

"He has gone riding, I suppose?" Iona questioned.

"Aye, ridin' it is, miss," the footman replied, "an' His Grace started richt early frae wha' I heard."

Iona suddenly felt perturbed.

"Was there some reason for that?" she inquired. "Has His Grace gone on a journey?"

"I dinna ken for sure," the footman replied, "but I heard ane o' the grooms say that His Grace asked for his horse verra early this morn. He took naebody wi' him, but gaed off on his ain. 'Tis strange noo I came tae think on it. I hae niver known His Grace dae tha' afore an' I hae been here for nigh on four year."

"It does seem strange," Iona said.

"But ye dinna hae tae fash aboot His Grace," the footman went on. "He's a fine mon an' he can tak care o' himsel', can His Grace."

There was no doubting the flunkey's admiration for the Duke, but Iona was not reassured. Slowly she left the Library. There was something wrong. Something was happening to everyone; to the Duchess, to the Duke, to Lady Wrexham and to Lord Niall. What it was she did not know, but it overshadowed her, dark and menacing. Suddenly she knew that she was afraid; yes, terribly, inexplicably afraid.

13

"The whole place shall be arranged exactly as you wish, my sweet," Lord Niall replied, and he raised Lady Wrexham's fingers to his lips. They were cold against the hungry warmth of his mouth; but he did not notice it, and after a moment Beatrice turned from the window and took her hand from him.

"I shall re-do this room," she said almost petulantly. "I have always hated that shade of. . . ."

She stopped suddenly; her eyes looking critically round the great Crimson Salon, had fallen on a picture hanging between two of the windows. It was of the Duke and had been painted when he was eighteen. In the portrait, which had been executed skillfully, there was youth and a very young eagerness in the handsome face; his eyes seemed to behold something delectable, for there was a faint smile on the clear-cut lips.

Beatrice stared at the picture and there was a strange expression on her face. She walked towards the fireplace.

"Have you seen the Duke this morning?" she asked Lord Niall over her shoulder.

"No, why should I?" he asked. "Doubtless Ewan is busy with matters which concern the estate. Oh, darling, how long must I wait . . . ?"

"No, no, Niall," Beatrice interrupted. "Let me think."

She threw herself down in a chair by the fire, her fingers to her eyes. She was not really thinking. It was her feelings which concerned her, emotions which had welled up within her at the sight of the Duke's portrait. All the morning she had indulged her fancy by planning how she would alter and re-decorate the castle, were it to become hers. It was a very feminine amusement and if Lord Niall had been fool enough to take her seriously and believe that she might in fact spend the rest of her days with him in this benighted spot, she was not to blame for his stupidity.

But while she talked and while she permitted his caresses, something within herself cried out in agony. She tried not to think of last night and yet the memory of it was inescapable. From the moment when she had left the Duke's bedchamber she had known this pain within herself, an agony which nothing could assuage.

She had believed for a little while that Lord Niall's adoration would help her to forget the humiliation she had suffered, but that too was unforgettable. Sleepless until the first pale fingers of the dawn crept through the curtains, she had lain awake vowing vengeance, plotting her revenge; and now she knew that even that would bring her no relief, no escape from the miserable ache within her heart.

How often she had laughed at other women who were lovelorn, how often she had called them fools wasting their time yearning after a man who did not want them! Now she knew that love was a conqueror and one could only surrender to it. To fight against it was to be completely and utterly defeated.

Before such a love as she experienced now she was weaponless, helpless and utterly without defence; and because she was so unused to finding herself in such circumstances, Beatrice squirmed and fought against her very self—warring within her own person.

For a moment she almost loathed her own body that it could betray her so completely; then, as she thought of the Duke's face as she had last seen it, of his eyes cold and indifferent to her beauty, she knew a devouring jealousy which seemed to burn away her heart within her. If she could not have him, then no other woman would.

Swiftly her mind worked, planning the future for herself and for him. She would destroy him, destroy him utterly, and then return to England to the Marquis of Severn. At St. James's in the world she knew and over which she reigned an uncrowned queen she would forget. Yes, there it would be easy to forget Skaig Castle and the misery it had brought her. If the Duke were dead, she was sure that she would be relieved of this agony within her; if he lived, then never would she know one moment's peace.

Beatrice took her fingers from her eyes. Lord Niall was looking down at her, his dark eyes on her face, sinister and unsmiling, the lines between nose and mouth heavily etched in the morning sunlight. There was something in his expression which made her shudder. She was not sure why, but for a moment he seemed utterly repugnant, over-shadowing her forebodingly. Then the illusion passed, for he went down on one knee beside her to kiss her hand and she remembered that he was but a slave and a man besotted by her beauty.

"Of what were you thinking, my sweet?" he asked as he rose.

"I was thinking," Beatrice replied sharply, sitting down on the sofa, "that things cannot continue as they are much longer. We must act and act swiftly. Either we find enough proof that the Duke is a Jacobite to send him to the block or else he must be disposed of by other means."

Lord Niall's eyes narrowed.

"Do you mean murder?" he asked bluntly.

"Why not?" Beatrice inquired. "I should not have imagined you were so squeamish as to delay as long as you have."

Lord Niall's eyes dropped before hers.

"It is not as easy as it sounds," he replied. "There is still justice in the land—yes, even in Scotland."

Beatrice gave a little laugh.

"Then you are afraid," she taunted. "Poison, a quick stab in the dark—who is to guess that yours is the assailant hand?"

Lord Niall shrugged his shoulders.

"Strange though it seems, Ewan has few enemies and there are those who are well aware that I should not grieve unduly by his death."

"Then you should be more careful in whom you confide."

Beatrice sounded not only corrective but scornful, and Lord Niall turned to take both her hands in his.

"What you bid me do I will do," he said solemnly. "What I strove only for myself, I admit that murder seemed too dangerous a method of dispatch; but now, when your fate is linked with mine, there is nothing I would not do."

Beatrice disengaged her hands from his and rose from the sofa. A sudden anger rose in her so that it was with the utmost difficulty that she prevented the words which seemed to burn her tongue from being spoken impetuously and with violence. It was intolerable that Lord Niall should presume to plan her future with his and imagine conceitedly that she would stoop to become a legal part of him.

For one moment the truth almost overwhelmed her self-control; then caution asserted itself and she remembered that Lord Niall was an instrument which she must use, as she had used other and better men at different times. She walked as far as the window and then swung round to face him.

"What then do you suggest?" she challenged.

Lord Niall took several quick steps towards her.

"You are lovely," he said hotly. "So lovely that I find it hard to think of anything but your beauty."

His tone was hoarse with passion, but with a little gesture she forbade him to touch her.

"I asked you a question," she said quietly.

"Come close to me," he replied. "Let me hold you for one moment. I have a feeling that you have withdrawn from me. Tell me I am imagining it, tell me with your own lips that you love me."

Beatrice's eyes rested for a second on his face, on his outstretched hands, then she turned away.

"There are other matters more important than love," she said stiffly.

Her words ended in a little cry, for Lord Niall had stepped forward to grip her arms above the elbow, to turn her round to face him with a roughness that was brutal. Angrily she looked up into his face, then shrank, almost appalled, from the burning darkness of his eyes and the sight of his teeth bared from his tight lips.

"Tell me you love me," Lord Niall said in a voice she hardly recognised. "Tell me now and at this moment or I swear I will kill you with my bare hands."

His nails dug into the soft flesh of her arms until the pain was almost unbearable. As she did not speak, he drew her nearer and nearer until her head fell back before his and his lips were on her mouth. He kissed her cruelly, bruising her lips in a passion in which there was no tenderness, nothing but a fierce, devouring lust. At last he released her, breathless and shaken, her eyes wide with a sudden fear.

"You had best not drive me too far," he said and watched her raise her lace-edged handkerchief to wipe the blood from her lips.

With an almost superhuman effort Beatrice contrived to speak lightly.

"You forget that I am only a woman," she said and glanced down at the livid marks of his fingers on her arms.

181

"I assure you that I am in no danger of forgetting that," he replied, and again she was afraid, just as someone might be afraid of a wild animal.

Then with one of her bewildering changes of mood which enabled her to captivate any man, however difficult, Beatrice smiled at him, her eyes soft and liquid as she raised them to his, then veiled them with her long dark lashes.

"I have always loved strong men," she murmured. "You will make a strong Duke, Niall."

At her words some of his tension seemed to relax.

"As you know, I am ready to prove myself."

"Then let us make plans." Beatrice clasped her hands together. "I have thought of something!"

"What is that?" Lord Niall asked curiously.

"The girl," Beatrice replied. "You said last night that you thought the Duke had given food to the prisoner because he wished to stand well in that chit's eyes. Had you a reason for such a suspicion?"

Lord Niall shrugged his shoulders.

"There might be something in it."

Beatrice glanced towards the portrait of the Duke between the windows.

"We must not ignore the possibility," she said. "It appears to me, Niall, that we have paid too little attention to 'Miss Iona from France'."

She turned from the portrait, her lips pressed together in a tight line.

"Will you question her?" Lord Niall asked.

"Better than that," Beatrice replied. "Command my maid to come here with my smelling salts. I will instruct her what to do; then you find the girl and bring her to me. But not here, the Duchess might interrupt us. I will talk with her in that room across the landing where we found you both together on the day of my arrival."

"The Chinese Room!" Lord Niall supplied.

"Very well, the Chinese Room. Bring her there, but first I would speak with my maid."

Lord Niall rang the bell and a footman was dispatched in search of the abigail. Beatrice smiled.

"If this fails," she said silkily, "we must trust in your strength, my dear."

Lord Niall met her eyes squarely, and strangely enough after a second her glance fell before his. She bent down to

182

straighten the roses which were bunched under the hoop of her gown. Lord Niall watched her and there was an expression of triumph on his face as if he knew that he was the master.

The door opened and the maid crossed the room, a bottle of smelling salts in her hand.

"Did you wish for these, m'lady?" she asked. Her curtsy was demurely respectful.

Beatrice glanced towards the door to see if it was closed.

"Listen, Pollard," she said. "In a few minutes it will be the hour for the servants' mid-day meal. Go downstairs, but instantly make an excuse to retire. Hurry to the second door to Miss Iona Ward's bedchamber, search it thoroughly and make no mistake on this, for if she is clever, as I suspect, she will conceal anything that needs concealment with forethought and cunning. But I have faith in you, Pollard. There are few places so secret that you cannot suspicion them out. Now hurry and do as I say."

"Yes, m'lady."

The maid's face was expressionless as she curtsied and left the room.

"Can you trust her?" Lord Niall asked.

"She is better than a ferret," Beatrice replied. "This is by no means the first time I have set her such a task."

"I can well believe that," Lord Niall answered, "but never before has there been a task of such import to you and to me."

"But of course not!"

There was a touch of sarcasm in Beatrice's reply, but Lord Niall did not hear it.

"I will go and fetch the girl," he said as if anxious for action.

"I will wait in the Chinese Room."

Lord Niall opened the door and Beatrice swept across the landing, her silk skirts rustling as she moved, her long earrings of pearls and diamonds swinging against her white neck. Lord Niall watched her until the door of the Chinese Room closed behind her, then he drew in a deep breath.

The fire in his eyes had not entirely died away since his outburst in the Crimson Salon. His fingers clenched themselves slowly and cruelly and his mouth was brutal. He seemed to be thinking of the future; with an effort he remembered the present. He glanced round as if wondering in which direction he should go in search of Iona, but at

183

that moment she appeared at the top of the staircase leading from the second floor.

As she began the descent, somewhere in the depths of the castle there was the sound of a great bell. Iona wore a cloak over her shoulders. She did not see Lord Niall at once for, as she descended the stairs, she was intent on putting a small lace handkerchief into a tiny satin reticule which hung from her waist.

She was nearly at the bottom of the stairs before she glanced up and saw who was waiting. For a moment she stumbled and put out her hand to the banister to steady herself. Then she came on slowly, her head held a little higher, her whole body stiff, instinctively defiant.

"Good morning, Iona."

Lord Niall stepped forward and his tone was unexpectedly friendly.

"Good morning, m'lord."

"Are you going out?"

"I had planned to take a short walk."

"Would you first be so obliging as to wait upon Lady Wrexham in the Chinese Room?" Lord Niall asked.

Iona shot a quick glance of suspicion at him.

"Why should Lady Wrexham require my presence?" she inquired.

"Her ladyship was saying but a few minutes ago," Lord Niall replied, "that she had unfortunately found but little chance of talking with you since her arrival. She expressed a wish for your presence; but if you are otherwise engaged, I can, of course, inform her ladyship to that effect."

"No, no, of course not," Iona said quickly, feeling that she had been rude. "I will repair at once to her ladyship. Did you say she was in the Chinese Room?"

She would have turned to cross the landing but Lord Niall barred her path.

"I have not been able to recapture your friend," he said. "Does that give you satisfaction?"

"It does indeed," Iona answered gravely. "He should not have been detained in the first place, as your lordship well knows."

"There you are mistaken," Lord Niall replied. "I was right in what I suspicioned, and one day I shall be able to prove it. The only thing I would like to know is, what magic did you use to transport him from the Keep?"

Iona smiled.

"I am not a witch, my lord, though there are times when I wish I were."

"Indeed! Would it be indiscreet to ask you on what particular occasions you would use your superhuman powers?"

"It would not be difficult for me to answer that question, but it would be unwise," Iona said. "I will leave your lordship to guess where my sympathies lie."

She knew she was being daring in speaking to Lord Niall in such a manner, yet somehow at this moment she was not afraid of him. She merely despised him for his cruelty to the Duchess, for his intrigue with Lady Wrexham and for his allegiance to the English Throne. Yet when she looked at him again, she knew that she must not underestimate his power to hurt her and beneath her momentary bravado every instinct in her body told her to beware of him.

As if he half guessed what she was thinking, Lord Niall gave a short laugh then stepped aside to let her pass.

"Her ladyship will be waiting," he said in tones of exaggerated courtesy.

"I will go to her at once," Iona replied and moved swiftly towards the door of the Chinese Room.

She entered the room to find Beatrice sitting in the wide window-seat, her profile exquisite against the blue sky outside. She turned her head as Iona entered and gave her a friendly smile of welcome.

"So his lordship found you?" she said in a soft voice. "Come and talk to me, for there has not been a moment until now when we could make each other's acquaintance."

Slowly Iona crossed the room to the older woman's side. Her intuition warned her all too clearly that this friendliness was a trap of which she must be very much on her guard. Beatrice put out her hand.

"Sit here," she said, patting the padded cushion on the window seat. "How pretty your hair is, but, of course, many people have told you that before."

"I thank your ladyship for the compliment."

"Must we be so formal?" Lady Wrexham said. "My name is Beatrice and yours, I know, is Iona. We are both strangers in this castle, a frightening place too, do you not agree?"

"Frightening?" Iona queried.

Beatrice gave a little shiver.

"Yes, indeed, but all Scotland is the same with their feuds and risings and spyings one upon the other. I vow that I feel the very stones taking note of what I say."

"Then your ladyship is English," Iona said, "I suppose one feels different when one is a Scot."

"Like yourself!" Beatrice smiled. "But are you so sure that you are in fact of this land? I understood from Lord Niall that you claimed to be his sister."

"Whether I am proved a MacCraggan or not," Iona replied stiffly, "I shall still be of Scottish blood. I am as sure of that as I am sure there is a God above us."

Beatrice gave a little laugh.

"So vehement! Oh, what it is to be young and full of enthusiasm! I am growing old and tired, and I find myself convinced of very little. But let us not talk about me, let us talk of you. Tell me what you think of the Duke?"

"His Grace has been kind enough to offer me the hospitality of the castle."

"And I am sure he has been kind in other ways."

But Iona did not reply and after a moment Beatrice added:

"He is extremely handsome, do you not think so?"

"Yes . . . yes, indeed."

Iona's tone was cold to the point of indifference. Beatrice glanced over her shoulder, then she whispered.

"I hear tell in London that he is a Jacobite; what think you of that?"

"His Grace has not confided in me, ma'am."

"But you have your suspicions nevertheless," Beatrice added with a smile, "and you suspect me of being in the other camp. My dear, how blind you are! If you but knew the truth, it would surprise you."

"I doubt it, ma'am," Iona replied.

Beatrice's eyes narrowed.

"You put no trust in me," she said. "I can understand that. Well, keep your secrets to yourself; but one day you may need my friendship for who knows what tomorrow will bring forth, or today for that matter?"

"Who indeed?" Iona replied. She rose to her feet. "If you will excuse me I would like to go for a walk."

"I have no wish to keep you," Lady Wrexham said, and her voice was sharp.

Iona curtsied and went towards the door. As she reached it, she looked back. Beatrice Wrexham was looking out of the window, her profile exquisite against the blue sky. With

186

a sudden impetus of hurry Iona slipped through the door, closed it behind her and ran downstairs.

She felt as if she had gone through a terrific ordeal. What it was she did not know, she was only conscious that her heart was beating too quickly and she felt suffocated. On the steps outside the front door she stood still for a moment drawing in deep breaths of fresh air. She welcomed the wind that came sweeping round the corner, blowing her hair into confusion and whipping her skirts round her body. Its very roughness was somehow comforting, for there was something unhealthy and noxious in the Chinese Room which reminded her of a twisting serpent.

She ran down the steps and started to walk towards the bridge. Beyond it were the moors, wild and empty, the heather bright purple in the sunshine. Iona had a sudden longing to be alone, in a world empty of human beings and with only the loveliness of Nature as a companion.

From the window of the Chinese Room Beatrice Wrexham watched her go, saw the sunshine turn her hair to burning gold, the wind outlining the sweet curves of her young figure. As she watched, Beatrice was suddenly aware that her fingers had torn her lace handkerchief into ribbons. With an angry gesture she threw the pieces from her into the corner of the room. She had risen to her feet when the door opened and her maid came in.

"Have you found anything?" Beatrice asked eagerly.

Pollard closed the door behind her and came close to her ladyship without speaking.

"Have you found anything, woman?" Beatrice demanded again.

In answer Pollard brought out from the back of her apron a small black notebook.

"Only this, and I had a rare search for that, m'lady. I looked in all the usual places such as the top of the wardrobe, inside the shoes, under the mattress, in the lining of every bonnet and in every drawer and cupboard; then just as I was thinking your ladyship must be mistaken and there was nothing to find, I thought to look in the cover of the young lady's Bible. It was there by her bedside and as soon as I touched it, I could feel there was something between the black embroidered cover and the Good Book itself."

Beatrice was not listening to Pollard's explanation. At the first sight of the black notebook she had snatched it from her and was quickly turning over the pages. The entries evidently puzzled her until she turned again to the

187

beginning and her fingers stopped at July the 5th. Then she gave a little cry of pleasure.

"Now I understand," she said. "Fetch his lordship, Pollard."

"I have found what your ladyship required?" Pollard asked stiffly, obviously hurt at not being thanked.

Beatrice glanced at her and gave a short laugh of understanding.

"Yes indeed, Pollard," she said. "As you well know, you have found me exactly what I wanted. Have I ever known you to fail? Remind me to give you ten guineas tonight when I come up to my bedchamber."

Pollard was all smiles.

"I thank your ladyship. That is indeed generous. I will fetch his lordship immediately."

Beatrice shut the little notebook and patted it lovingly.

"Exactly what I wanted," she said aloud, "and that disposes of Miss Iona Ward."

Iona walked for nearly an hour. High up on the moors she looked back at the castle, grey against the silver of the lake, the castellated battlements in contrast to the sharply pinnacled turrets with the Duke's flag fluttering above them in the breeze. People moving in the courtyard were as tiny as children's dolls. Here, when she was free of the enclosing walls, nothing seemed so overpowering or frightening. It was only when she was in close proximity to Lord Niall and Lady Wrexham and the Duchess that she felt so ineffectual, so small and helpless that she doubted her own capacity to carry through the task she had been set.

Now, feeling calm and unhurried, she knew that she had advanced a long way since her arrival. If she left tonight, she would have much to tell the Prince which would be of service to him. But she must know more, she must be absolutely certain of the Duke's allegiance before she returned to France. And yet, she asked herself, was she not in truth certain already?

He had shown all too clearly that his sympathies were with Hector; and even if he were not as convinced as Lord Niall had been that Hector was a Jacobite, he must have had his suspicions.

There were, too, the "Tears of Torrish" to be discovered. Iona had questioned Cathy again about them, but the girl

188

really knew nothing. She had only heard talk of their being lost at Culloden, and Dughall knew as little as she did. Iona longed to talk with him again, but she knew that for his sake she must not make any attempt to see him in case Lord Niall or his men were watching the little croft. She must do nothing more to draw suspicion on Dughall. It was bad enough that Hector had been discovered near his house. Lord Niall was not likely to overlook that fact.

For a long time Iona sat in the heather looking down at the castle and trying to sort out her ideas and impressions of the people who lived in it. As she thought of the Duke, it seemed as if a warm glow spread over her whole being. She began to guess now a little of what he had endured and suffered in these past years. He must have been aware that his stepmother was intriguing against him; he must have known that she loved his half-brother and longed for him to inherit the Dukedom. It must have been hard to live a life of utter loneliness surrounded by enemies who were his own kith and kin.

Always his expression was masked, always there was a proud indifference in him to everybody and everything; and yet he had remained true to his own ideals, uninfluenced by anything save his own conscience and sense of integrity. Iona thought of him with deep respect and also with a sense of wonder. He must indeed be very strong and of great character to endure so much.

The wind suddenly blew chilly as if it came from the snow on the summit of Ben Nevis. She rose and started to wend her way back towards the castle. As she came down over the hillside, she glanced at the road which led to Fort Augustus. She half hoped to see the Duke riding along it, but it was empty. She wondered then where he was, why he had been gone so long and for what reason.

Her sense of danger returned to her. Lady Wrexham and Lord Niall were plotting together. Had they been already successful in driving the Duke away?

It was with this question in her mind that Iona finally reached the bottom of the hill and crossed the bridge. As she did so, she heard horses' hoofs behind her and looked round to see a man come riding swiftly down the road. As she drew nearer, she recognised him. It was Sime. Iona walked on quickly. When she reached the steps to the front door, Sime, having dismounted and left his horse in charge of a groom, was waiting at the top of them for the door to be opened.

"Good afternoon," Iona said, feeling it would be ill-bred to ignore a servant in the castle, even if he served Lord Niall.

"Guid day!"

Sime's response was grudging. Iona saw that his face was dusty, his legs spattered with mud.

"It has been a nice day for riding," she said.

Sime looked at her in a strange manner.

"I hae been tae Fort Augustus," he said, and Iona imagined there was something threatening in his tone.

The front door was opened by a footman and she entered. As she crossed the Great Hall, she head Sime say:

"I wad see his lordship this verra instant."

Quickly Iona ran up the stairs. She had no desire to meet Lord Niall. With a sudden sense of panic she ran the whole way to her bedchamber. When she reached it and had closed the door behind her, she laughed at her own sense of urgency. How stupid she was to be frightened by Sime's rudeness! He doubtless disliked her because he thought that she had something to do with Hector's disappearance. It was fortunate that he did not know the truth.

There was a knock on the door and Cathy entered.

"I hae been worritin' aboot ye, mistress," she said. "Are ye no hungry?"

"I am indeed," Iona answered.

"I thought sae, an' I brought ye something tae eat an' a pot o' tea," Cathy said in triumph and fetched the tray from outside the door.

"Has the Duke returned?" Iona asked as she poured out the tea.

"Nay, not that I ken, mistress. Should I ask below?"

"No indeed," Iona replied. "I but wondered where His Grace had gone."

"His Grace will no run awa'," Cathy smiled.

Iona left her food untouched and rising from the chair, walked across to the window. Below her lay the loch and beyond the silver water rose the mountains. She found her eyes scanning their barren sides as if she thought to see someone moving there. Cathy watched her with an anxious expression on her face.

"The tea will get awfu' cold, mistress," she said at length, but timidly as if she felt it presumptuous of her to interrupt Iona's thoughts.

"It matters little," Iona replied. "I was but wondering. . . ."

She stopped suddenly, the sentence left unfinished. Quite suddenly she knew why she was wondering, why she was thinking so intently and so anxiously of the Duke. It came to her with the suddenness of a blinding flash as if the heavens had opened and revealed all too clearly the truth.

She loved him! She knew it now by the sudden startled beating of her heart, by the warm blood which crept into her cheeks, by the joy and ecstasy which seemed to flood over her whole body, bringing to her for the moment such rapture, such a sense of wonder that she thought she must swoon before the glory of it. She loved him!

Why had she not known of her love before? And yet perhaps her heart had been aware of it. It was for this reason that she had been restless the whole day through; this was why she had been afraid and had sought the solitude of the moors. Yes, all these things—because her heart was crying out for the recognition of her love and her brain would not acknowledge it. She loved him! She thought now she must have loved him from that first moment in the streets of Paris when he had stood there commanding her wordlessly to leave him and she had perforce to do his bidding. Now it was understandable why she had thought of that stranger so often, why the incident, insignificant in itself, had returned to her mind night after night, day after day.

She remembered how she had puzzled over the stranger's identity, wondering if he were a Scot or an Englishman and feeling sad, although at the time she had thought it but a ridiculous fancy, that she would not see him again.

Then, when she had found him again, when he had entered the Crimson Salon magnificently garbed and bejeweled and she had recognised him, she might have known by the quickened beating of her heart that it was love she felt for the man on whom she had come to spy. But blinded by the gigantic task which she had been set by the Prince, she had thought not of her personal feelings but only of the problems she must solve.

Now Iona understood why the thought of returning to France had been repugnant to her, why, when Hector had told her to hurry back, she had almost resented his solicitude, why she had been glad of the excuse that her search for the "Tears of Torrish" must keep her in Scotland and at Skaig.

191

Iona bent forward to press her hand on the window sill. She felt that she must touch the castle, must know it tangible and real and love it not for itself but because it belonged to the Duke. Until this instant it had seemed a great and beautiful edifice with almost a personality of its own; but now she knew it was but a background for a great man, a man of character for whom she had so much respect that she wanted to kneel at his feet.

"I love him!"

Iona's lips formed the words, but she did not speak them aloud; she turned towards Cathy and her face was as bright as the sunshine outside.

"I will finish my tea," she said, sensing the anxiety in the girl's face, "and then I would like to lie down until dinner time."

"I'll gang an' get a warming pan, mistress, an' I hae no doubt that the rest will dae ye guid."

Cathy bustled from the room.

Alone, Iona turned once again towards the window.

"Tonight I shall see him," her heart told her. She felt her pulses quicken at the very thought.

Iona was sure, as she descended the stairs a few minutes before the hour of dinner, that she would find the Duke waiting in the Crimson Salon. But when she entered the room dressed in her gown of ivory satin, it was to find Lady Wrexham and Lord Niall the only occupants. Iona thought that they both looked at her curiously and it was with an effort that she managed to curtsey politely and move across to the fireside, making no effort to speak until she was addressed.

"It appears we shall be a very small party tonight," Beatrice said to Lord Niall.

"The Duchess is dining in her own room," he replied, "and Ewan has not yet returned. As you say, we shall be a small but very select company."

Beatrice raised her eyebrows.

"And what has happened to His Grace?"

"I have not the least idea," Lord Niall replied. "His horse may have lamed itself in which case he must walk home. If so, it is his own fault, for I personally prefer to ride with grooms and attendants. I have often told Ewan that it is unbecoming to his position to ride alone."

"Why not, when you tell me he has so few enemies?" Lady Wrexham asked.

Lord Niall muttered something under his breath, but Iona did not hear what it was. She was aware then that they were fencing with each other and that there was a hidden meaning beneath the formality of their words. The door at the far end of the room opened.

"Dinner is served, m'lord," the butler announced.

Lord Niall offered his arm to Lady Wrexham. She looked towards Iona for the first time.

"I regret we have no one to partner you, Miss Iona from France."

"It will not be for long," Lord Niall said quietly before Iona could reply.

Lady Wrexham looked at him and they both laughed.

Iona could find no meaning either in Lord Niall's words or in their joint merriment; but as she followd them towards the dining-room, she wished that, like the Duchess, she had commanded dinner in her own bedchamber. But now it was too late. They seated themselves at the table, Lord Niall taking the Duke's place, Lady Wrexham on his right and Iona on his left. The big polished table seemed to stretch away endlessly and there was something ominous in its very emptiness.

Footmen hurried in with the dishes. A butler filled the crystal goblets with sparkling wine. Beatrice Wrexham's red lips just touched the glass, then she looked across the table at Iona and raised it.

"To your secret ambitions," she said and sipped the wine.

Iona did not know what to reply; the toast was ironical; she knew that, for her ladyship's eyes gleamed maliciously.

There was a sudden sound of voices outside and the door opened.

"Captain Robert Moore, m'lord," a footman announced.

An officer strode into the room and two soldiers took up their positions just inside the door. The light of the candles shone on their red coats, white breeches and polished buttons. There was a sword hanging by the officer's side and he carried his hat.

Lord Niall rose.

"Good evening, Captain Moore. Your visit is a surprise, but a pleasant one."

"I come on duty, my lord," Captain Moore said, his hard English voice seeming to echo round the walls.

"On duty?" Lord Niall queried.

Captain Moore drew out a paper. He studied it and then said abruptly:

"I am instructed to arrest a young woman staying in this castle—calling herself Iona Ward."

14

Iona rose from the table, her face very white.

"I am Iona Ward," she said in a low voice.

"Then I must request you, ma'am, to accompany me immediately to Fort Augustus," the captain replied sharply.

Iona looked over his shoulder at the two soldiers standing stiffly at attention but with their eyes fixed on hers. For a moment the room seemed to swim round her and she turned back towards Lord Niall.

"Can you account for . . . this, my lord?" she stammered.

It was a cry of help although she would not humiliate herself to make it; but even as the words came from her lips, she saw the expression on Lord Niall's face and the glint in his eyes and knew the answer.

Yes, indeed, he could account for it, though she had not meant her question to be answered so literally. He was responsible for her arrest, he and Lady Wrexham, who was watching her with a smile twisting her red lips. It was they who had had her arrested, they who had been plotting against her. For a moment Iona stared at them and then her momentary faintness and hesitation were gone. She pulled herself up to her full height and there was an expression of utter contempt and disdain on her face as she said quietly:

"I understand."

"What do you understand?" Lady Wrexham asked curiously. "Oh, poor Miss Ward, I cannot tell you how distressed we are that this unfortunate situation should have arisen. But doubtless it is only a mistake."

"Your ladyship does not deceive me," Iona said, her voice cool and clear.

For a moment, she faced the older woman proudly and then she swept to the ground in a curtsy.

"I will bid your ladyship good night,' she said. "Good night, my lord."

195

She rose to her feet.

"I am ready to accompany you, sir," she said to the English Captain. "May I ask for a travelling cloak to put over my evening gown?"

"Most certainly," Captain Moore replied.

He glanced towards one of the footmen, but hesitated as if wondering whether it would be correct for him to give the order. Iona saw his hesitation and spoke first.

"Send for Cathy," she said, "and tell her to bring me my grey cloak."

"Very good, miss."

The footman left the room.

"I will wait, if it pleases you, sir, in the Great Hall," Iona said quietly to Captain Moore. "I have no desire to further disturb his lordship's dinner."

Without waiting for permission she moved towards the doorway, her head held high as if it wore a crown, and passed between the two soldiers. She led the way to the Great Hall, the Captain following her, the soldiers behind him. The log fire had been lit in the big open fireplace at the far end and the candles were burning brightly in the sconces; but even so the huge place was cold and drear and the shadows in the arched roof and in the far corner by the Chair of Justice were dark and foreboding.

Iona remembered how Hector had stood in this hall, bound and threatened with an examination at Fort Augustus. He had escaped, but now it was her turn and there was no one to rescue her. Her whole being cried out for the Duke. Then with a sudden sense of panic she wondered if he too had already been apprehended. Her anxiety for him was so intense that she felt she must make certain; but just as she was about to speak to the Captain she heard the patter of feet down the staircase and looking round she saw Cathy approaching with her cloak. The girl ran forward and there were tears running unchecked down her cheeks.

"Oh, mistress, mistress!" she exclaimed. "This canna be, it canna. . . ."

"Do not distress yourself, Cathy," Iona said quietly. "There had undoubtedly been a mistake and I am sure that it will soon be explained. Has the Duke returned?"

"Nay, mistress, but canna ye wait for His Grace tae come hame? He wadna allow ane o' his guests tae be treated in such a way, I ken weel."

"You are certain His Grace has not yet returned?" Iona insisted.

Cathy shook her head.

"Nay, mistress, for I inquired o' the footman who told me tae come tae ye."

"Then wait for His Grace, Cathy, and inform him what has occurred the instant he returns."

"Aye, I'll dae that," Cathy said; then she bent down suddenly and kissed Iona's hand. "God keep ye, mistress."

Iona put her arms round the girl's shoulder and kissed her cheek.

"Thank you, Cathy, and be sure and tell His Grace where I have been taken.'

She looked then at the English Captain, conscious that he had been unexpectedly courteous and considerate in allowing her to talk with Cathy without interruption. For the first time she noticed that he was a very young man and that he held himself stiffly as if half afraid that he would not do the right thing. His features were well-formed and there was an air of breeding about him.

"I am ready, sir," Iona said, her eyes meeting his firmly.

It was he who looked away.

"There is a coach outside, ma'am," he remarked, and his voice held a forced note as if he deliberately made it abrupt.

"I am indeed relieved that I will not have to walk to Fort Augustus," Iona smiled.

She moved with an almost regal grace across the Great Hall, conscious at the same time of the military clang of the soldiers following her, their muskets on their shoulders.

Outside the door a coach was waiting. It was a large vehicle painted black and sparsely cushioned, but nevertheless it was well sprung and Iona stepped into it with a feeling of relief. She had expected something much more austere.

Captain Moore seated himself beside her. The door was shut behind them and they heard one soldier scramble up beside the coachman and the other take his place behind where ordinarily a footman would have travelled. There was a sudden awkward movement amongst the team of horses and then they were off. Iona bent forward to have a last glimpse of the great oak doorway of the castle, of the footmen standing there in their claret-coloured livery, of the massive grey walls and pinnacled towers dimly discernible in the twilight; and then the coach had turned and they were passing over the bridge and away from the castle.

Again she felt a wave of panic sweep over her, not of fear for where she was being taken, but a fear that she might never see Skaig again. It held everything, she thought, that meant anything to her. It was the home of the man she loved, a place, strangely enough, which in a very few days she had grown to think of as home. Now she was leaving it. When, if ever, would she return?

With a tremendous effort at self-control she forced herself to concentrate on the ordeal which lay before her. She would need all her wits, all her good sense if she were to face an examination by the Commander of the Fort and come through it unscathed. What could he have against her, she wondered? But whatever it was, she was certain that Lord Niall and Lady Wrexham had provided the evidence and that Sime had carried it to the Fort that very afternoon.

"What could they have said?" Iona asked herself.

Suddenly she felt as if her heart had stopped in the sheer agony of knowing the answer. They must have found the notebook which Hector had given her for sake-keeping. She remembered that last night before she had slept she had read her Bible as was her usual custom. The notebook had been there then. Now she guessed that during the day someone had discovered it. Perhaps it had not been a wise place to put anything so precious, but she could think of nowhere better.

She had indeed often wondered if she should give the notebook to Cathy, but she had felt that it was not fair to ask the girl to take any more risks than she had taken already. Inside the cover of her Bible was by no means a place of complete safety, yet who would search her room?

Iona knew the answer to that question. It would have been Lady Wrexham's idea. And might she not have chosen a moment to send one of her servants to do the dirty work when she knew that Iona was out or engaged with her in conversation?

Very slowly, like the pieces of a puzzle, the whole plot fell into place. A deep sigh escaped Iona involuntarily. This was an ignominious ending to the high hopes she had entertained such a short while ago of fulfilling the Prince's faith in her. Now perhaps she would never see Paris again, the Prince would never know where the Duke's allegiance lay, and the English spy watching Colonel Brett would never be discovered.

If only she were a man, she thought quickly, and could fling herself upon the Captain sitting opposite her, overpower him and make a dash across the moors. It might be easy in such circumstances to get to Inverness and set sail for France. But she was only a woman hampered by the wide hoops of her satin dress and by her heavy travelling cloak. There was nothing she could do and again she sighed.

A voice came out of the darkness.

"I regret, ma'am. . . ." Captain Moore began; but before he could say more, the horses were suddenly pulled up with a jerk. "What has happened?" he exclaimed in a very different voice.

One of the soldiers scrambled down from the box and opened the door.

"There's a body lyin' across th' road, sir."

"A body?"

"Yea, an' us reckons 'tis a woman. Shall us be after movin' it, sir, or will yer 'ave a look at it?"

"I had best see for myself," the Captain said.

He would have moved from the coach, but Iona put out her hand and stopped him.

"If it is a woman in trouble, may I come with you?"

The officer hesitated for a moment and as if her offer were some relief to him, he said hastily:

"Yes! Yes, you might be of service, for I cannot understand why a woman should be lying in the road."

He descended from the coach. Iona allowed her hand to rest for an instant in his as she, too, stepped down on to the road. It was cold and very nearly dark and the wind had risen. It seemed to whistle round them bitingly. One of the soldiers lifted one of the lanterns from off the side of the coach and, carrying it ahead, led them to where a woman lay in the roadway. The horses had stopped but a few feet from her, and Iona saw that she was sprawled out, the fingers of one hand almost touching the high bank of heather, her feet deep in the mud of a cart track.

The soldier held the lantern above her head. A black shawl covered her; but it was Iona who noticed first the curious position of her arm and of a bundle cuddled against her breast beneath the black shawl.

"There is a baby here!" she exclaimed.

She knelt down on the roadway and pulled back the shawl from the woman's face. The eyes were closed. For a moment Iona thought that the woman had but fallen asleep, tired out, when something in the rigidity of the features and the pallor of the skin told her the truth. The woman was dead.

Very gently Iona tried to draw aside the rags which covered the bundle in her arms. Even in death the woman held it tightly and when at last the tiny head was disclosed there was not an instant's doubt that the baby was dead too.

Iona drew it from the mother's grasp. The rags that covered it fell away and revealed the tiny naked body of a very young child. It was little more than skin and bone, so thin and wizened that it was almost a skeleton. Quickly Iona covered it again and, still holding it in her arms, looked up at the Captain.

"This child and its mother, too, from all appearance have died of starvation," she said coldly.

The soldier holding the lantern bent down, took a look at the woman's face, then straightened himself again.

"Oi can tell yer who this woman be, sir," he said gruffly.

"Who is she?" Captain Moore asked.

"Her be one o' the women from th' crofts twenty mile away that us burns a week ago."

"Do you mean the crofts near Invercannich?" the Captain asked.

"That be them, sir. I 'member th' woman made a terrible to-do her did when us found a couple o' swords in th' thatch. We 'ad information, if yer 'member sir, that they was a-hidin' weapons in that place. Us searched an' found 'em, shot th' men and burnt th' roof over th' heads o' th' others."

"You shot them?" the Captain said. "I thought men were sent for transportation if they were discovered with weapons in their possession?"

"Aye, that's th' law," the soldier said. "But there was some resistance o' a kind among th' men an' th' Major says ter shoot th' devils and have done with it. Tis less trouble in th' long run, but 'tis cruel 'ard on th' women an' children. I 'ear as 'ow folk are afraid to give 'em food an' lodgin' round 'ere when they 'ave been burnt out."

"The woman must have been walking to Skaig for help," Iona said. "That is why she is on this road. Look at her feet."

She pointed to the woman's feet, which, cut and covered with congealed blood, were bare save for a few rags.

"Yus, that's one o' th' women right enough," the soldier remarked.

He raised his lantern and looked at the Captain. Iona's eyes were on him too. It was with an effort that he seemed to come to a decision.

"Move the woman to the side of the road. We can do nothing for her. I will send some men to bury her tomorrow."

"No, you can do nothing more for her," Iona said stiffly.

She waited while the two soldiers lifted the pitiably light body and laid it by the side of the road; then she placed the baby in the crook of its mother's arm again. She whispered a prayer and turned away quickly to hide her tears. After Captain Moore had joined her in the coach, they journeyed for some minutes in silence and then he said a little awkwardly:

"There are always tragedies of this sort when there are wars, ma'am. It is impossible to prevent such happenings."

"Impossible," Iona queried, "when you heard the soldier say that the men of the households were shot?"

"They offered resistance," Captain Moore said quickly.

"Resistance!" Iona said scornfully. "How could they resist against trained soldiers? The weapons you searched for were in the thatch, but the men resisted with their fists. Bare fists against muskets, is that the English idea of fair play?"

"It is not a question of fair play," Captain Moore retorted. "These people are rebels; they strike our men down in the dark. All the time they are plotting, ready to rise again just as soon as the opportunity occurs. We bring peace and justice to Scotland, but it must be at the expense of those who break the law."

"And so you think that peace and justice can be gained by shooting defenceless men, by leaving their women and children to starve?" Iona said sarcastically. "You must be a great idealist, Captain Moore."

"That is unfair!" Captain Moore's voice was young and impetuous. "If you think that I can see such a sight unmoved, you are mistaken. I hate many of the things we have to do here. It is not a man's job to fight women."

"I agree with you."

"But Scottish women are as treacherous and wily as their men, and I assure you that it is not easy to stamp out their worship of the Stuart Kings."

"And replace it with an allegiance to a German usurper," Iona finished. "No, I can understand that."

Even as she spoke, she realised that she had been indiscreet. Her words seemed to bring a sudden silence to the jolting coach and after a moment Captain Moore spoke in a very different voice.

"If you have such sentiments, ma'am," he said, "may I warn you not to express them in front of the Governor of the Fort?"

His words sent a sudden chill through Iona and she remembered the way Lord Niall had spoken of Major Johnstone. But she knew that Captain Moore's warning was spoken in a friendly manner.

"Why have I been arrested?" she asked.

"To be honest, I have no idea," Captain Moore replied. "I am but carrying out the orders given to me by my superior officer."

"Of course, I should not have asked you that question. I apologise."

"Pray do not. I must admit I was astonished and surprised when I saw you. I was expecting an older woman, a hardened, elderly Jacobite. It does not seem possible that you, who are so young, could have done anything which might be considered dangerous, but I do beg you to guard your tongue."

Despite her instinctive antagonism to anything that was English, Iona could not resist the friendliness and sincerity in the young man's tones."

"I am grateful for your advice, sir," she said.

The Captain made a sudden movement in the darkness.

"I wish we had not encountered that woman," he said. "It has distressed you and I swear it will haunt me. You have spoken frankly to me, ma'am, and I will be frank with you and say that I have already asked for a transfer to the South. I cannot stand it here, the work we have to do, the poverty and suffering, and the feeling that one is hated wherever one goes. There are enemies behind every clump of heather, lurking in every pile of stones."

There was no mistaking the raw suffering in his voice and Iona felt her enmity and anger melt away.

"I will respect your confidences, sir," she said. "I am glad to hear that there are amongst the English those who are not deaf to humanity and to the cries of injustice."

"Things seem so very different when you are not mixed up with them. When I was at home, the Rising seemed a stupid, insane action on the part of the Young Pretender. I thought it was just because he was ambitious for personal power. I did not understand then what the Scots feel about their rightful king, how bitterly they resent the thought of being ruled by someone of German blood, and how willingly they will lay down their lives for what they believe to be right."

"You can say all that," Iona said softly, "and yet you continue to persecute us?"

"Not me personally," Captain Moore said. "As I have already told you, I have asked for a transfer."

"But your countrymen will go on butchering the Scots, imprisoning them and torturing them. Have you not heard how the Duke of Cumberland's troops behaved after Culloden? Can you imagine that such treatment of a vanquished enemy could ever be wiped out by anything but the spilling of blood and more blood?"

"The Duke had his reason for what orders he gave, ma'am," the young officer answered. "I was too young to be present at Culloden, but I have heard other officers explain what happened. I feel no good will come of our discussing it, for after all what was done then has been done. . . ."

". . . and will never be forgotten," Iona said softly. "One day after we are dead, when history comes to be written, I believe that the English will be ashamed of their behaviour that day, and indeed of the behaviour of their troops now. And yet despite all that, despite the persecution, the suffering, the horror of it all, you will never be able to stamp out and destroy the love of the Scots for their rightful King James III and for his son, Prince Charles."

Her voice rang out and then before Captain Moore could answer her, the horses drew up with a jerk, there was the sound of voices and the flashing of a light outside the window. They had reached the Fort.

In the light of the raised lanterns Iona saw Captain Moore's face. He was looking towards her and the expression on his face was of a man moved to the very depths of his being. Their eyes met and he just had time to whisper almost beneath his breath, "Take care of what you say", when the door was flung open. Captain Moore rose from his seat and stepped out. A voice roared an order and there was the crash of men presenting arms.

"Allow me to assist you to alight, ma'am," Captain Moore's voice was now cool and detached. Iona gave him her hand and stepped from the carriage.

She had a quick impression of curious faces and a gaudy predominance of red coats and shining buttons, of a long, uncarpeted passage, and then the door of a room was opened.

"Miss Ward, sir, from Skaig Castle."

Captain Moore's voice was curt and military and in curious contrast to the man Iona saw facing her. She realised at once that she had been taken to Major Johnstone's private sitting-room. It was a big room with a bright fire burning in the fireplace, and well-furnished in a somewhat masculine manner. In a big wing-backed chair Major Johnstone sprawled before the fire. His coat was unbuttoned, showing a stained white shirt. There was a glass of red wine in his hand. His face was crimson, the purple veins predominant on the huge swollen nose. It was the face of a gross liver, a coarse character. His wig was pushed sideways on his head and he still wore his riding-boots, dirty and mud-spattered from the day's riding.

He made no effort to rise, but sprawled in his chair regarding Iona from the top of her head downwards. His glance was somehow lewd and indelicate and despite all her resolutions she found herself flushing a little under his scrutiny.

"Gawd's truth!" he said at length in a thick voice. "So this is the filly they suspect of being a damned Jacobite. Well, gal what have you to say for yourself?"

He raised his glass to his lips and took a great gulp of wine; and as he rolled it round his mouth, he waited for Iona to answer. When she did not, he swallowed the wine and shouted:

"Have you lost your tongue? Answer, can't you?"

"Are you speaking to me, sir?"

"Who the hell else did you think I was addressing?" the Major thundered.

"As a guest of the Duke of Arkrae," Iona answered, "I must request that you give me an explanation of why I have been brought here."

"You request! Gad, that's rich!" Major Johnstone said.

He gave a deep and what purposed to be an ironic laugh but which turned instead into a belch.

"Let's get this straight, my girl," he said. "You may have been the guest of all the blood-stained Scottish Dukes in Christendom; but if you are a Jacobite—and it's up to me to decide whether you are or not—it's lucky if you keep your head."

"Am I not correct, sir, in believing that by English law a man or woman for that matter is innocent until proved guilty?" Iona asked.

The Major glared at her; but as he did not answer, she went on:

"I would but ask you, sir, for proofs of my guilt, for I have no knowledge of them."

The Major looked her up and down.

"You've got guts, I'll say that," he remarked. "Take that cloak off and let's have a better look at you."

His tone was coarse and the look in his eyes frightening, but Iona thought it best to comply with his request. Besides, the room was very hot and the air almost suffocating with the stench of spirit and stale tobacco. She was relieved to slip the heavy cloak from her shoulders and the hood from her head. Captain Moore stepped forward and took it from her.

"That's better," the Major said approvingly. "And now, Moore, sit down, pour yourself a drink and we'll have some fun."

Captain Moore put down Iona's cloak on a chair near the fire and hesitated.

"You heard me you young jackanapes," roared the Major.

"The lady, sir, shall I fetch her a chair?"

The Major glared at him.

"A chair for a prisoner! Has the sun turned what little brain you had?" He glanced at Iona. "Ah, ah . . . now I understand! A pretty face and they become a lady. If she was plain as a pikestaff, she'd be just a woman and a prisoner. All men are the same; I know 'em; and all females are the same under their airs and graces and—their gowns. I know 'em too. Sit down, man, and do as you're told. If you don't want a glass of wine, then that leaves the more for me."

There was nothing for Captain Moore to do but to cross the room to the chair on the other side of the hearthrug.

205

He seated himself while Iona stood between them, her face almost as white as her dress, but her head with its rebellious curls remained high.

"Ve-ry pretty, ve-ry pretty," the Major drawled, his eyes taking in every detail of the low-cut gown, the curve of breast and waist and the grace of Iona's bare arms.

"Now then," he said sharply, "tell me in your own words, and no lies mark you, I want the truth—what you're doing in Scotland?"

"As you have doubtless been informed," Iona said quietly, "I came here but a short while ago from Paris with papers which sought to prove that I was the Duke's half sister, the Lady Elspeth MacCraggan."

"And did they believe you?" the Major asked. "Not on your life! You damned Jacobites are up to any trick and always ready to pretend to something or other like those rascally Stuarts! We've had the Old Pretender, the Young Pretender, and now they have got a Woman Pretender. Who the hell is going to believe you? Not me, at any rate."

"It would, of course, be impossible for you, sir, to come to any decision on the matter without seeing the proofs that I brought with me," Iona said.

The Major glared at her and his lower lip stuck out in ugly fashion.

"Are you being impertinent or trying to teach me my business?" he asked. "I know what I shall believe and what I won't believe. Now, when did you last see that imposter, Charles Stuart?"

"Do you mean the Prince?" Iona asked.

"Prince? He's no more a Prince than I am," the Major growled. "I'll call him the Young Pretender, if you like it better; but Charles Stuart is his name and you know full well of whom I speak. Now then, gal, speak up—when did you last see him?"

Iona took a deep breath.

"I think you are making a mistake sir. I have already asked you to give me your reasons for bringing me here and for subjecting me to this examination. Until I receive a satisfactory reply to that request, I cannot acknowledge that you have the right to question me in any matters appertaining to my private life."

The Major set down his glass on the table with such violence that the wine was spilled over his hand and on to the floor.

"Zounds!" he exclaimed. "Dare you defy me and speak to me in such a manner? Do you realise, you cheeky wench, that I have the authority to have you taken from this room and thrown into the deepest dungeon in this Fort? Or better still, give you over to my men for their amusement?"

Iona's chin, if possible, was raised a little higher.

"I must ask your pardon, sir, if I was mistaken, but I understood that you represented here in the Highlands the justice of the English throne."

The veins seemed to swell on the Major's face and he grew so crimson that it almost seemed as if he must burst a blood vessel.

"You Jacobite baggage," he said, the words coming so forcibly from his lips that he literally spat them out. "I'll teach you to speak to me in such a manner, I'll . . ."

The door was suddenly opened. Iona who had been watching the Major's horrifying expression of mounting anger, turned her head slowly. Her heart gave a wild leap, for in the doorway, seeming immeasurably taller, broader, and more awe-inspiring than ever before, stood the Duke. He was wearing his riding-coat, his boots were spattered with mud, but he moved with his usual unhurried air of innate dignity.

As he walked slowly into the room, the whole atmosphere seemed to change perceptibly. Captain Moore got to his feet, and with an effort, groaning as he did so, Major Johnstone rose unsteadily to his.

"Good evening, Major! Good evening, Captain!"

The Duke's voice was quiet and authoritative.

"Good evening, Your Grace."

The Duke looked at Iona. His eyes came to rest on her for one brief moment, taking in her pallor and tightly clasped hands, and also the sudden joy and relief in her eyes and the excitement of her parted lips. The Duke put his riding-whip down on the table.

"I have been from home all day," he said. "When I returned, I learned with some consternation that a guest of mine had been arrested during dinner and brought here for questioning. May I ask, Major, on whose authority this was done?"

The Major seemed about to answer him gruffly, but changed his mind.

"I have a paper here," he said disagreeably.

He felt in one pocket and then in the other, and at last brought out a rather crumpled sheet of paper. He unfolded it and glanced at it uncertainly.

"May I see?"

The Duke's hand was on the paper and had taken it from the Major before he was aware of what was happening. His Grace read it aloud:

"On behalf of the Most Noble, the Marquis of Severn, and in the name of His Most Gracious Majesty King George I authorise you to arrest Iona Ward, Jacobite, who is staying at Skaig Castle.

Signed: Beatrice Wrexham.

The Duke folded the paper and handed it back to the Major.

"I am astonished, Major," he said, "that the English Army should take orders from a strumpet, however influential her protector."

The Major looked uncomfortable.

"It is signed with the Marquis's own seal," he snarled.

The Duke gave a little laugh.

"How often are gentlemen's rings purloined from them by such women in moments of weakness!" he said ironically and then added in a sharper tone: "Is this the only evidence you have of this lady's guilt?"

"Lord Niall sent word that he would bring the proofs of the woman's infamy over to me tomorrow morning," the Major snapped.

"I fear, Major, that you have been hoaxed," the Duke said lightly. "This lady, who is under my protection and a guest at my castle, has been brought here on a charge which can very easily be proved both false and ridiculous. I must regret that you have been inconvenienced in such a way. You will, I am sure, permit me to escort her back to the castle?"

Iona gave a little gasp of relief and without thinking of what she was doing stepped forward until she stood beside the Duke, her eyes glowing as she looked up at him. The Major had hesitated and seemed about to accede to the Duke's wishes, but now his expression hardened.

"On the contrary, Duke," he said, "This woman has been arrested and must stay here the night until his lordship's appearance in the morning. The seal of the Marquis of Severn is, I assure you, enough authority for me to act on and to act correctly in my position as Commander of the Fort."

The Major's voice was truculent and as the Duke did not answer for the moment, he added:

"You may be the Duke of Arkrae and own a slice of this damned country, but here in this Fort I'm the boss and you're on English soil. Good night to you, my lord Duke; you can leave the woman behind."

"I think not!"

The Duke's voice was very quiet. He continued:

"You were authorised, Major, to arrest Iona Ward. Is that not correct?"

"You have seen the paper," the Major snarled.

"But you have in fact arrested somebody very different," the Duke said. "It has, it is true, been a secret until now, so that you are not entirely at fault. This lady is not Iona Ward, but my wife—the Duchess of Arkrae."

Iona gave a little gasp as she felt the Duke take her hand and set it on his arm. She was conscious of the pressure of his fingers, and then of the Major's bloodshot eyes staring into hers and of his raw and angry voice as of an animal which has been deprived of his prey, asking:

"Is this the truth?"

Again Iona felt the Duke's fingers press hers.

"Yes . . . yes," she faltered.

"You're his wife?"

"Yes."

The Duke turned towards the chair by the door. He took up Iona's cloak and set it round her shoulders.

"We will bid you good night, Major," he said.

His hand was on the latch when the Major stopped him.

"Blister it," he swore. "But how the hell am I to know this is true? If you are wed, as you say, where were you married and when?"

"Surely that is immaterial," the Duke queried. He looked down at Iona and drew her a little nearer to the door. "Besides, Major, with your vast knowledge of English law you must not forget our Scottish ones."

"What the deuce do you mean by that?"

"I mean," the Duke replied and his voice was light, "that if this lady were not already my wife, she would in fact be so from this very moment. Marriage by declaration before witnesses is in Scotland, as you well know, entirely valid and absolutely binding. Good night to you, Major."

He drew Iona through the door and closed it behind him. There was the thunder of fearsome, resounding oaths and the crash of glass; but Iona was conscious of only one thing—of the Duke's hand on hers, of his fingers, strong, warm and resolute, taking her swiftly to freedom.

15

The Duke's horse, a magnificent black stallion, was waiting, held by a soldier, in the courtyard. It was obvious
from the animal's demeanour and its mud-splashed, sweating flanks that it had been ridden hard and long, and the
fiery spirit which had made it temperamental and difficult
to handle earlier in the day was now subdued into a
peaceful docility.

The Duke and Iona walked quickly across the courtyard. As they reached the stallion, the Duke looked down at
Iona with one of his rare smiles and said quietly:

"I can offer you speed but not much comfort, I am
afraid."

"All I ask, Your Grace, is to be taken from here with
all possible speed," Iona replied in a low voice.

The Duke put his hands on her waist and lifted her on
to the saddle. She was conscious of his great strength, of
the ease with which he swung her on the horse's back as if
she in truth weighed no more than the proverbial feather,
and then before she had time to do more than steady herself the Duke had sprung into the saddle behind her. She
felt his left arm go round her and found herself held
securely and closely against him, while he gathered up the
reins in his right hand.

The solider let go of the horse's bridle and at a sharp
trot they rode from the yard. The soldiers who were on
sentry duty or wandering around with little to occupy them
stared with curious eyes but did nothing to delay their
departure.

Outside the Fort the stallion moved forward with a
quicker gait. Instinctively Iona put out her hand and found
herself laying it on the Duke's shoulder just below his
neck. His arm tightened about her and she was cradled
against him, her head pillowed against his broad chest.
There was a faint fragrance about his riding coat, a per-

fume to which she could not put a name but it had the sweetness of the heather-laden wind blowing over the moors. She fancied she could hear the beating of his heart, and her own began to thump madly. There was an ecstasy in this close proximity, a joy beyond anything she had ever known before.

Iona shut her eyes. If only, she thought, she need never open them again and the future could hold only this wonderful contentment at finding herself in the Duke's arms and knowing that for the moment at any rate his strength and protection afforded her a harbour of security. Never, she thought to herself, had she known such happiness as this. Then with a sudden pang of misery she remembered that it must end.

She opened her eyes to glance upwards at the Duke's face. He was staring ahead, his chin square and set, his expression stern, his lips pressed together in a firm line. A tiny sigh escaped Iona and he must have heard it, for swiftly he looked down at her cradled against him.

"You are uncomfortable?" he questioned.

"No indeed, Your Grace," Iona replied, and the Duke urged the stallion forward.

They were climbing uphill all the way, riding along the familiar road which led to the castle. But before they reached the summit, the Duke turned along a bridle track and after a little while, when the village of Fort Augustus was out of sight he reined in the stallion to a standstill. The moon was rising and it had not come to its fullness but beneath the great stretch of open sky Iona could see the Duke's face clearly as he looked down at her. But his eyes were dark and fathomless, and she was uncertain what expression they held in their steel-grey depths.

The Duke stared at her. His eyes seemed to be searching the exquisite oval of her face, lingering on the sensitive curve of her parted lips, on the red curls pressed forward in sweet confusion beneath the fur which edged her hood.

Suddenly Iona felt a shyness which swept her long dark lashes against her cheeks, and then, compelled by a wordless command, she raised them again, her eyes meeting the Duke's and being held compellingly, mesmerically while something within her trembled with a strange, unaccountable sweetness. For a long, long moment they looked at one another and Iona became aware that her whole body was quivering within his hold. At last the Duke spoke, his voice very low and deep.

"And now, *m'eudail*, we can talk together."

To cover her embarrassment, both afraid and ashamed that he might notice it, Iona replied:

"What does that mean, that word you have just used?"

"It is Gaelic," he replied. "It means 'my darling'."

For a moment she was utterly still. She was astonished by his reply as if the very stars had fallen from the heavens; then she felt his other arm go round her, knew that he lifted her a little higher against his breast and his lips came down to meet hers. The world stood still and Iona was conscious only of a flame rising within her body till it seemed as if it must utterly consume her, the Duke's mouth on hers was both tender and possessive. It demanded the utter surrender of herself, and yet at the same time he asked rather than compelled her subservience.

She felt a happiness that was almost too great to be borne, and just when her very being seemed about to faint at the wonder of it, the Duke set her free. As he took his mouth from hers, she gave a little inarticulate murmur and hid her face against his neck. Her hood had fallen back from her hair; tenderly he touched the shining curls, smoothing them, stroking them, but all the time holding her so closely to him that their hearts were beating in unison and she felt that they were indivisibly joined to one another.

"Did you not know that I loved you?" he said softly at length. "Heart of my heart, I thought you must have guessed it a long while ago."

She made no answer and at length he asked:

"Look at me, my little darling!"

Because of her shyness Iona could not move; she could only cling to him, her face hidden because she was afraid that, if he looked again into her eyes, her innermost secrets would be revealed to him. Masterfully and with an insistence which could not be denied he put his hand under her chin and turned her face up to his. His eyes searched hers and now nothing could hide the love that shone there; and as he looked, his own face softened and was transformed. The hardness and arrogance vanished, the mask of pride and reserve were laid side and Iona saw him as he should have been, a man young both in heart and in years, pulsatingly alive with the joy of living, a beauty in his expression which for the first time was compatible with the classic mobility of his features. Then as his mouth, tender and curved with the softness of love, came near to hers, he said:

"Tell me that you love me. I want to hear it from your own lips even as I dreamt that you might say it. Tell me, beloved, that I am not mistaken."

For a moment Iona could only tremble. It was so hard to speak, so difficult to set aside her shyness even though now her fear of him had gone for ever. At length, so softly that he must bend his head to hear them, the words came fluttering from between her lips:

"I . . . love Your Grace."

Then their lips were joined again in a kiss that was both sacred and divine so that even while she responded to it Iona felt a wordless prayer of thankfulness rising up from within her to the God she worshipped.

"M'eudail!" the Duke said again, and now his voice was resonant with a rising passion. His arms about her were like bands of steel, holding her so fiercely that for a moment she feared that the very breath might be squeezed from her body. "You are mine, mine! I defy anyone, man or woman, to take you from me."

"They will try?" Iona asked, suddenly afraid.

"Yes, they will try," the Duke answered soberly, a little of the glory leaving his face as the dangers surrounding them came back to his mind. He put out his right hand and gathered up the reins from the stallion's neck. "We must go on, my little love; there is much for us to do this night."

"What have we to do?" Iona asked.

Her voice was faint, for already they were moving swiftly forward; and as the Duke did not reply, she did not repeat the question. She would know all in his good time, she was sure of that, and she was content to trust him utterly, to ask nothing more than that he should control and guide her actions. She wished only to obey what he should command, and the wonder of what had occurred swept over her again like a flood-tide so that in very happiness she must hide her face against him and not even watch where they were going.

This was no time for talk, and Iona felt that words were meaningless and unimportant when all that was essential could be said by the closeness of their bodies, by the strength of the Duke's arm around her and by the throbbing of his heart against hers. This was happiness, this was a loveliness beyond anything she had ever imagined. Even more than that—this was being alive.

Never, she thought, had she felt so vividly, so throbbingly alive as she did now. She knew instinctively that there was danger ahead. They had enemies behind them, in front of them, and for all she knew around them. But at this moment she was supremely unafraid and she knew with an unquestionable clairvoyance that the Duke would win through whatever the odds against him.

He drew the stallion to a standstill. Iona raised her head. Behind them was moorland stretching up to where it joined the darkness of the sky, ahead were the abrupt, rough sides of a mountain. Where they stood there were a few scattered trees, while the ground was rough and stony with an occasional boulder.

Swinging himself down from the saddle, the Duke held out his arms to Iona. For a second she waited, savouring the delicious moment before he should take her, before she would feel her breasts crushed against his. Then she leant forward and she was in his strong grasp.

"You are so small," he whispered softly, "so tiny that I am half afraid to touch you, and yet you are big enough to fill my whole world."

His lips were against her hair before he set her free. As he did so, Iona gave a little cry of terror. A dark shadow moved by some bushes and she saw it was a man. Instantly the Duke's arm came out to protect her.

"Do not be frightened, my love," he said. "It is only Raild whom you can trust as I have always done."

"Theer's nae doot aboot that, Yer Grace," a voice replied.

A man came forward in the moonlight and Iona saw that he was elderly, his shaggy hair and heavy eyebrows white against a lined weather-beaten face. He was wearing a kilt and there was a dirk at his waist and a knife in his stocking.

He reached out to take the bridle of the black stallion and the horse nuzzled its nose against him as if it asked for a caress.

"Sae ye remember me?" Raild said, rubbing his hand against the horse's nose.

"Thunderer, like myself, has a long memory, Raild," the Duke said. "Will you tether him to one of the trees, for we must not linger here."

"Aye, Yer Grace, I'll dae that," Raild replied and led the horse away into the shadow of the trees.

Iona looked at the Duke inquiringly. He was staring at

the great pile of stones ahead of him and now he went towards them. Wonderingly and in silence she followed him. She thought for a moment he was about to climb the side of the mountain till she saw him brush aside some briars of a straggling bush and bend down. He must have set some hidden mechanism in motion, for almost immediately there was a slow grating sound as a great boulder of rock moved sideways and a dark, gaping hole appeared where it had stood.

There were quick footsteps from behind them and Raild came swiftly from the trees. Without saying a word he bent his head and entered the dark aperture in the mountainside; Iona heard the sound of a tinder box in use and a moment later there was the yellow flare of a light. It flickered in the darkness and she perceived that Raild had kindled a candle in a lantern. He picked it up and held it above his head. As he did so, the Duke put out his hand to Iona.

"Come," he said, "and there is no need to be afraid."

"I am not! I am with you," she replied simply and felt the answering response of his fingers.

She had to bend her head to pass through the opening in the rock, but once she had done so she found that the ceiling was high and it was easy not only for her but also for the Duke to stand upright. Ahead lay a flight of roughly hewn stone steps, while behind her Iona heard the rumble of the stone which covered the entrance being set back in its place.

Raild started up the stairs, the lantern throwing a wide circle of light which made it easy for Iona and the Duke to follow him. Up, up they climbed until the steps were succeeded by a passage also sloping upwards, beyond which they came to another flight of steps.

It was cool inside the passage, but the air was sweet. Although she wondered where it would lead them, Iona asked no questions for both men were silent. But her curiosity was aroused as they climbed higher and higher until at length the passage widened into a vast vaulted chamber, a cavern in what she thought must be the very heart of the mountain.

The roof was so high that the light of the lantern only flickered on it uncertainly, but round the walls, roughhewn, glittering and shining in the light, were stacked a number of articles. Raild stopped in the cavern. He set down the lantern on a bench close to the wall and took down another from where it was hanging on a strong nail.

"I'll gang an' see if onybody iss tha' the noo, Yer Grace," he said. "Wait ye here wi' the leddy!"

"Yes, we will wait here," the Duke said. "Be careful not to show a light."

"Nay, I'll pit doon the lantern i' the inner cave," Raild answered. "Theer'll be moonlight on the rock."

Having kindled the second lantern from the first he moved away and disappeared through an opening at the far end of the chamber. Iona turned to the Duke.

"Where are we?" she asked.

"This is the Chief's Cavern," he said. "It is a secret known only to the Head of the Clan and revealed by him to one or two of his most trusted servants. It is actually a natural formation of rock and at one time could be reached only from the caves leading directly on to the Black Rock, which was originally the Judgment Seat of the Mac-Craggan Clan."

His words awoke a vague memory in Iona's mind. The Black Rock! She remembered now she had seen it from the Duke's Library, jutting out almost at the top of the mountain which bordered the west side of the loch.

"The steps we have just climbed," the Duke continued, "were made by my great great grandfather, MacCraggan Mor, and it was his idea to make the Chief's Cavern a refuge and a hiding place for those in trouble. It has served both me and my forebears."

"It is an amazing place," Iona said, looking around her and putting out her hand to touch the walls themselves. They sparkled as if they were frosted, from the minute particles of quartz embedded in the granite, giving the whole place a strange, almost ethereal beauty.

"I can understand what a splendid hiding place it must be," Iona said and as she turned from the walls intending to move towards the Duke, she glanced down at the things which lay piled on the floor.

There were weapons of all sorts and descriptions. There were broadswords, claymores, dirks and muskets, and beside them a pile of tartan plaids, philibegs, and shoulderbelts stacked in a tidy pile.

"Why are those here?" Iona asked and knew the answer even before the Duke replied.

"Weapons and articles of Highland dress are forbidden to my people. They are therefore stored here in safety until the day that we are free again both to carry arms and to wear our national costume."

It was then that Iona would have asked him the question for which she had come all the way from France; but as the words came to her lips, as she turned her eyes away from the weapons and tartans, she saw something else by the light of the lantern. It was a long box, resting on the very bench on which Raild had set down the light. In shape it was not unlike a coffin; but it had a glass top and through the transparency of the glass something attracted Iona's attention and made her look more closely. What she saw held her spellbound and she lifted the lantern to be quite certain she was not mistaken.

In the box was a kilt and jacket, and lying on top of them was a white sporran, the silver clasp gleaming in the light of the lantern; above it, laid neatly on the breast of the jacket, was a bonnet, trimmed with three white eagle feathers. Iona set down the lantern; she turned to the Duke, who was standing in the centre of the cave watching her, a faint smile on his lips.

"Whose clothes are these?" she asked and there was a tremor of excitement in her voice.

"They belonged to my great great grandfather," he said, "the MacCraggan Mor, of whom I have just spoken."

"Who knows they are here?" Iona asked.

"No one save myself and Raild," the Duke replied, an expression of surprise on his face at the urgency of her question. "They were placed here in my great great grandfather's time and have remained here ever since."

"Then it was you who wore them at Culloden!"

Iona's voice was low, yet its vibration seemed to echo round the vast cavern.

"Who told you that?"

"Dughall told me of how your men, fifty of them, went to Culloden. They had no leader and they would all have been killed had not MacCraggan Mor come back from the grave to save them. They recognised the white sporran and the three eagle feathers in his bonnet. He led them to safety and then vanished. Now I know who was there, fighting as they had never seen a man fight before. It was you!"

The Duke took three steps towards Iona and put his hands on her shoulders.

"Yes, my darling," he said quietly, "I was there, but I came too late to help our Prince. He was already defeated."

Iona's eyes were suddenly full of tears.

"Oh, I am glad," she whispered, "glad beyond words

that you were loyal, that you did what you could to help him—our beloved Prince."

The Duke took his hands from her shoulders.

"I was too late," he said and there was the sharpness of pain in his voice.

He took a few steps across the cavern and then walked back again.

"I did not hear of the Rising until the Prince was already in retreat. I was in Italy, for I had been travelling abroad for two years, doing a grand tour of Europe and buying pictures and furniture, at my father's request, for the castle. It was interesting at the time, but I bitterly regretted later that I was not here in Scotland when the Prince landed. As soon as I heard what had occurred, I set sail for home. We were held up by storms and I did not reach Moraig on the West Coast until April the 14th. I bought a horse and rode as fast as the poor beast could carry me towards home. Five miles from the castle on the outskirts of my father's territory is Raild's croft. I arrived there late at night and as my horse was almost too exhausted to go farther without a rest, I stopped and asked Raild for food for myself and attention of the animal.

"It was fortunate I did so, for Raild was able to tell me what was occurring at the castle. I learnt that my father was dying, that my stepmother was openly in favour of the English and that my half-brother, who was always in attendance on her, was also of her way of thinking.

"Raild told me, too, of the position of the Prince's army and of the English forces, which were at Nairn. There was no time for argument or even for me to go to the castle if I were to help the Prince. I had neither clothes nor weapons with me, having left all my luggage on the quay at Moraig. Then I remembered that my great great grandfather's kilt was in the Chief's Cavern. My father had revealed the secret of it to me before I went abroad, being aware that he was an old man and might not live to see my return. Raild and I came here that very night. I dressed myself in Mac-Craggan Mor's clothes, armed myself and mounting a fresh horse I set out with all possible speed towards Nairn. You know what happened at Culloden. I arrived when the fate of the battle had already been decided. The clans were running away and the English with their fresh, well-fed, well-trained men were sweeping everything before them.

"With the greatest of good fortune I found the little band of MacCraggans fighting against overwhelming odds, surrounded and in danger of being completely annihilated. I managed to extricate the majority of them and lead them to a place of safety. One of them addressed me as Mac-Craggan Mor and I realised then that they mistook me for the ghost of my great great grandfather.

"I decided it would be best for me to disappear as mysteriously as I had appeared. I set the clansmen on their homeward way and rode back by a different route to find Raild waiting for me at the foot of the mountain where he was waiting tonight. I had been wounded in the battle, my leg was bleeding from a sword cut, and I had lost a lot of blood. Raild brought me here to the Chief's Cavern and while he was binding up my wound I told him what had happened. When he heard that the clansmen had not recognised me, he begged me to lie hidden, for already tales were being told abroad of the cruelty being inflicted by the English on the Highlanders who had taken part in the Rising. Raild persuaded me that I must keep myself hidden until my wound was healed. I was safe enough here and no one but he knew of my return to Scotland.

"I remained here for over three weeks and by that time I had learned that the Prince was in hiding and that the sufferings of those who had been loyal to his Cause were almost beyond endurance. I knew then that I could do little good in declaring myself to be a Jacobite, for not only would my own head be forfeit but, because my father had died in the meantime, my people would be killed and tortured, their houses burned over their heads, my castle and lands confiscated. I had been too late to help the Prince personally but at least I could try to save those who had served him as I had longed to do. With Raild's help I went back to Moraig, repaired to the local inn and then sent word to the castle of my arrival. A coach, outriders and servants were sent to meet me. No one had any idea that I had not just arrived from Italy.

"I took up my position as Duke and Chief of the Mac-Craggans, aware that it was a precarious throne. My stepmother and my half-brother hated me. Niall wished to be Duke and they had already agreed that the easiest way to achieve this was to incriminate me as being a Jacobite. These past five years have been long and tortuous. Every moment I have had to be on my guard; every word I have uttered, every action I have done has had to be considered and examined cautiously lest they should betray me. It is not my own skin I have been intent on saving; I swear to you that I am not in the least afraid for myself. But if I am implicated, my people will be punished with me, for most of them hold allegiance to one person and one person only, our rightful and most beloved Prince—Charles Stuart."

The tears were streaming down Iona's cheeks as the Duke stopped speaking. Impulsively she swayed towards him, her arms outstretched.

"Thank God you can say that," she breathed.

The Duke held her closely; but before he could speak, there was the sound of footsteps at the other end of the cavern and they saw the light of Raild's lantern. They drew apart, but the Duke still held Iona's hand in his.

"Theer be many a-comin' the noo, Yer Grace," Raild said.

Iona turned to the Duke, a question on her lips.

"Things have happened," he explained quickly, "which have led me to think that my people will invite the suspicions of the English. Despite the most drastic penalties of transportation and death the majority of them still have weapons or articles of Highland dress hidden in their crofts. Since the early hours of this morning I have been riding round the estate stopping at every croft, speaking to the head of each family and bidding them bring me here this very night everything which is forbidden and for which they will suffer dire punishment should it be found in their possession. They will come to the Black Rock, as the MacCraggans have come since the beginning of time; and when they have gone. Raild and I will hide what they have left behind in the Chief's Cavern."

Even as the Duke was speaking, he drew Iona forward towards the passage where Raild was waiting. Once again the lantern lit the way for Iona's feet. There were more steps leading upwards, some of them so sharp and so steep that she was breathless when she reached the top, where a big stone, manipulated by a pulley, had been moved aside to reveal a small opening into a low cave.

The cave was dark and dirty. There was, too, the pungent scent of fox as if that animal had sheltered there the previous night. The first cave led by a narrow aperture into a larger and higher one, and as they stepped into it, Raild extinguished the lantern.

Now by the light of the moon Iona saw that they had reached the Black Rock. It was wide and flat, a natural platform formed of black granite. The Duke led Iona forward until they stood at the end of the cave, the rock stretching before them to where it jutted out over the loch, the water of which shimmered silver hundreds of feet below. There was a path on the edge of the mountain-side, winding up to the Black Rock. It was a narrow, dangerous path, seeming to afford hardly enough foothold for a sheep, and yet coming up it sure-footed and in silence was a band of men.

It was hard to see them in the darkness for they seemed a part of the grey mountain itself; but every now and then the moonlight glinted on something that shone like steel, something which they carried beneath their arms or tucked securely into their belts. Instinctively Iona looked towards the castle. There was a blaze of light in almost every window and the reflection of them glittered like a multitude of fallen stars in the water beneath. It was lovely beyond words and yet Iona felt that at this moment its beauty was menacing.

Here on the windswept mountain the loyalty and sacred tradition of the Clan was centred in its leader—a man whom they could trust and who trusted them. In the castle there were enemies, their minds twisted and warped with hate and envy. Iona shivered. Instinctively she moved a little nearer to the Duke. She had a sudden sense of danger, a premonition so acute and strong that impulsively she turned to speak of it, to beg him to be careful. But even as she did so, the first clansman stepped on to the Rock, a rugged giant of a man, a grey beard hanging over his chest, a plaid thrown over his shoulders, two naked broadswords in his hands.

The Duke stepped forward. The clansman made a respectful obeisance, then he gave the swords into Raild's keeping.

Another clansman appeared and another, and soon there was a continuous stream of them stepping out of the darkness on to the Black Rock, advancing towards the Duke, making obeisance, then handing the weapons they carried to Raild who took them away into the inner fastness of the cave.

At length there were no more arrivals. By this time the Rock was closely packed with clansmen standing facing the Duke in a silence which seemed to hold a strange tension and yet at the same time a sense of comradeship as in a danger shared. Then the Duke looked at those around him, and in the moonlight which was gradually brightening, his expression seemed softer and strangely tender.

"My people," he said quietly, "I asked you to come here tonight because we live in times of grave danger. You have answered my call and trusted me with what is to many of you your most treasured possessions. I will guard them well until the day comes when we shall walk proudly as free men again, free to wear our own tartan and to carry weapons for the protection of our homes and families. There are many things I would like to say to you at this moment, but there is not time. It is dangerous for us to linger even on this spot hallowed by long tradition and in itself a part of the history of our clan."

The Duke paused and at that moment two people came up the path and appeared at the edge of the Rock. Several heads turned in their direction and Iona saw that the late arrivals were Dughall and the old woman who had offered her a drink when she had visited the croft.

"Good evening, Dughall," the Duke said, "I feared that you were prevented from joining us here tonight."

"Nay, Yer Grace, I came as ye commanded an' brocht wi' me ma claymore. 'Tis vexed I am tae part wi' it, fae it hae gi'en guid sairvice but I mak nae doot the day'll come wheen I'll wield it agin."

"I believe it will," the Duke said; "and this is your mother?"

He looked down into the wrinkled, wizened face of the old woman peeping up at him from under the folds of her black woollen shawl.

"Aye, Yer Grace," Dughall replied. "Her wad come wi' me an' naught would keep her awa'. She hae someat tha' she wishes tae place for safe keepin' intae Yer Grace's ain hands."

"Tha's richt," the old woman piped up. "wha' I hae I'll gie tae Yer Grace an' nae ither."

Dughall's mother moved her shawl and Iona saw that she carried a small, roughly made wooden box.

"Whatever you give me," the Duke said quietly, "I will endeavour to preserve until such times as you can take it again into the safety of your own home. The only assurance I can give you in taking charge of your treasures is that I will guard them as if they were my own, and if necessary with my life."

His words were simple and so sincere that Iona felt an almost overwhelming pride well up in her heart.

"Those be braw words, Yer Grace," the old woman said. "An' wha' I hae iss worthy o' them. It wae gied me, Yer

Grace, by ma nephie's wifie after he haed been killit at the Battle o' Culloden. 'Tis a brae lassie she is, an' wheen he didna come bac' that black day she gaed tae look fae him. Wi' only Gawd tae protect her she gaed alane amang the deid an' dyin' an' by the maircy o' Heaven she fund her mon, my nephie, wheen she hed thocht tae gie up the sairch. Tha' wae but a wee breath lef' in him, puir laddie, fae his wounds wa terrible an' theer wae little she cud dae tae succour him. But he haed maur tae think o' at tha' moment than his ain pain.

"Wi' death itsel' dimmin' his ee he drew summat frae the bosom o' his jacket an' gied it intae her hands. 'Guard it weel, wifie,' he said, an' he told her whit it weer. He deid in her arms an' the next day she came walkin' ower the moors tae ma ain hame, an' she tellit me wha' haed happenit. 'They'll be searchin' ma hoose, auntie,' she says, 'fae they ken weel tha' Jock hae followit the Prince. Keepit this safe, fae it wa wi' his last breath tha' Jock handit it tae me.' An' I hae guardit it weel thees four years, Yer Grace. Noo I gie it tae ye."

The old woman lifted the box and set it in the Duke's hand. He looked down at it.

"Will you tell me what it is?" he asked quietly.

"Lift ye the lid, Yer Grace, an' see fae yersel," the old woman replied.

The Duke did so. He looked down into the box, then put his hand in to touch something soft.

"A bonnet?" he asked.

"Aye," Dughall's mother replied. "A bonnet, Yer Grace, an' it was Prince Charlie's ain, tha' flew frae his blessit heed wheen he rode frae the battlefield."

Iona gave a little gasp of astonishment and it was echoed by the clansmen standing round. They pressed forward, straining their necks to see the precious relic of the Prince they loved.

"Prince Charles's bonnet!" The Duke said in astonishment.

"His ain, Yer Grace."

"Then we will indeed keep it safe," the Duke said proudly, "until such time as His Royal Highness shall return—to claim it."

He closed the lid of the box. Iona moved forward and touched his arm.

"Please," she said, "may I say something?"

He looked down at her and a tender smile curved his lips.

"If you will."

Iona turned towards the clansmen.

"I came here but a short while ago from Paris," she said, her voice low but clear so that even those standing farthest away could hear her. "Before I left that city, I saw our Prince; I spoke with him; and among other things he asked me, when I was in Scotland, to discover if I could if there was any trace of his bonnet which had blown from his head after the Battle of Culloden. The reason he was so interested in this article of clothing was that the night before he went into the battle His Royal Highness was given by a lady of title a valuable collet of diamonds. These diamonds were sewn for safety into the Prince's bonnet and when he lost it he lost them, too."

Iona turned towards Dughall's mother.

"Will you allow me," she asked, "to look inside this bonnet you have kept so carefully all these years and see if the diamonds are still there?"

"Aye, look ye, mistress."

The Duke raised the lid of the box and held it out to Iona. Very carefully and with reverence she drew from its hiding place the blue bonnet with the white cockade. For a moment she held it high in her hands and the clansmen pressed forward to look. Then she felt within the broad band. For a moment her fingers encountered nothing; then they discovered a hard, round lump, another and yet another.

With a sense of mounting excitement Iona's fingers explored further. The stitches which had held the diamonds in place had grown rotten with the years, and with a small tug they fell apart so that the necklace was free. In the moonlight, the diamonds sparkled like tiny stars as she drew the whole chain from the bonnet and held it high in the air so that all could see what she held. A deep sound went up from the little throng.

"The Tears of Torrish!" Iona said, and her voice was shaking with excitement. "These are what our Prince asked me to find for him."

"But fortunately he will never receive them," someone snarled.

Everyone turned. Standing on the rock at the head of the path was Lord Niall and at his side stood Beatrice

Wrexham. For a moment it seemed as if everyone was turned to stone. Lord Niall's interruption was so unexpected and as he and Beatrice stood there, their very appearance in the moonlight seemed to make them unreal— the fancy of a distorted mind.

Lord Niall was wearing a coat of ruby velvet embroidered in silver. There were diamonds at his throat and diamonds glistening on his fingers, but his face beneath his white powdered hair was dark and sardonic. His eyes glittered and there was an expression of evil in them which held Iona spellbound so that she could neither move nor cry out.

Slowly and with a menacing deliberation Lord Niall took several steps forward on to the Black Rock. Beatrice moved beside him, the wide skirts of her yellow satin gown sweeping against the rough clothes and bare knees of the clansmen.

Lord Niall drew near to the Duke, raised his quizzing-glass, looked at his half-brother and laughed.

"So, my dear brother," he said, "at last we know the truth; at last we see you in your true colours as a Jacobite and a traitor. I have indeed suspected it for some time and tonight, when I learnt that the clansmen were gathering at the Black Rock, I knew that my moment had come, the moment for which I have waited so long and so patiently."

He dropped his quizzing-glass and looked away from the Duke to the clansmen standing around. Their rough faces were expressionless and no one had made any movement or sound while he was speaking.

"As for you," Lord Niall said to them, his voice as biting and as scornful as if he had used a whip, "are you fools that you do not realise when you are well off, or has this man who calls himself your Chief bewitched you? Of all the clans in the North we alone have not suffered at the hands of the English. Are you crazed enough at this moment when the Pretender is defeated and driven into exile to invite martyrdom—for it will be little else? The English are our masters; let us face facts and make friends with them while we can.

"I have been wise and astute enough to do this and in consequence the English trust me as I trust them. But the Duke, beguiled by the promises of a King without a throne, would have you throw away your comfort and security and lastly your lives in a lost cause. There is only one way to treat Chieftains who deliberately betray their people. The Duke's head is forfeit; but we will leave it to the English to judge him and to carry out the sentence as he well deserves. I will be Chief of our clan. I will lead you with common sense; and under my rule we will follow no upstart Prince, no Jacobite Pretender to a throne that is already amply and ably filled. Down on your knees, you dolts, and pay me the allegiance that is my due as your Chieftain and your new Duke."

Lord Niall's last words rang out like a command, his voice echoing eerily in the cave behind them; and then, as he finished, Beatrice moved swiftly forward. Before Iona knew what she was about to do, she snatched at the chain of diamonds which still dangled from her fingers. Quick and unexpected though the movement was, Iona instinctively tightened her hold on the chain. For one moment the two women faced each other, each pulling against the other's strength; then with a sudden tug Beatrice was the victor and three-quarters of the collet were clasped in her hand.

At last Iona found her voice.

"No, no," she gasped, "you shall not have them!"

But it was too late. With a laugh of triumph Beatrice turned away, the diamonds in her hand. Then something happened!

Afterwards Iona could never remember exactly what had occurred; but suddenly, as if obeying an unspoken word of command or an irresistible impulse which affected them all at the same moment, the clansmen began to move. They neither raised their arms nor appeared in any way violent or unrestrained. They only walked, man close against man, away from the Duke and Iona standing in the mouth of the cave, across the Black Rock to where it jutted out over the loch. Slowly, peacefully they moved and yet relentlessly they advanced, their faces set and strangely frightening in their very lack of expression.

Instinctively Lord Niall and Beatrice backed before them, until after a few steps Lord Niall realised the danger.

"Stop!" he cried. "Stop, I command you"

His voice ceased and changed into the frightened snarl of an animal that has been trapped, to be followed almost immediately by the high, piercing scream of a woman—a scream of sheer terror.

Then there was silence. The clansmen stood still, for they had come to the very edge of the Black Rock.

16

Iona found herself clinging to the Duke's arm, trembling all over; but she was conscious of his calm strength and that he had neither moved nor spoken since the moment of Lord Niall's arrival.

At his other side Raild spoke in a low voice:

"Nane ca' fall frae the Rock, Yer Grace, an' live."

It was a statement of fact. The clansmen turned again to face the Duke, and his voice rang out steady and unhurried.

"You will go at once to your homes," he said. "You have none of you any knowledge of what has happened here this evening, nor will you speak of it again even amongst yourselves. In the morning those who are working by the loch side will find the bodies of his lordship and the lady who has been staying at the castle. They will bring me news of their discovery, but it will concern no one else. Go now, and God be with you all."

The clansman with the long white beard who had been first to arrive made an obeisance.

"Aye, we'll dae as air Chief bids," he said and led the way from the Rock.

Quickly, swiftly and silently, the others followed him and almost before it seemed possible the clansmen had gone, vanishing into the shadows as secretly as they had come.

Then at last the Duke drew a deep breath and turning to Raild, he laid the box containing the Prince's bonnet in his hands. Raild looked down at it for a moment, then pressed his lips reverently to the unpolished wood. It was a spontaneous gesture and a simple-hearted way of showing a feeling and a devotion that could never be expressed in words.

The Duke turned to Iona.

"Come, my dear, we must go home," he said.

And now for the first time she looked down at what she

held in her hand. Three diamonds only remained of the "Tears of Torrish", three stones twinkling brightly in the moonlight—all that was left of the lovely precious chain. Iona would have spoken, but the Duke put his arm round her and drew her into the cave.

"We must get home," he said, and there was an urgency in his voice which made her bite back the words which trembled on her lips.

Raild had kindled the lantern so that they could see their way through the small entrance into the inner cave, and there he set in motion the mechanism which revealed the steps leading down to the Chief's cavern. Down down, they went, the golden circle of light guiding their feet.

Now Iona felt a complete and utter exhaustion sweep over her, and more than once she would have fallen had it not been for the Duke's supporting arm. It seemed to her that it took an immeasurable time to negotiate the steps, until at last they came to the end of them and were again at the foot of the mountain. The Duke helped Iona out and she felt the rising wind blowing through her hair as Raild ran to the trees to come hurrying back with the black stallion. Quickly and in silence the Duke lifted Iona on to the saddle and sprang up behind her.

"Good night, Raild."

His voice was hardly above a whisper, and Raild only raised his hand in response. Then they were hurrying away, the stallion seeming after his rest fresh and no longer tired, unless it were that instinctively he knew the comfort of the stable lay ahead.

Almost immediately they began climbing the hill, and even through her weariness Iona sensed that they were not going direct to the castle. She raised her head and the Duke understood the unspoken question.

"You must remember we are supposed to have come straight from Fort Augustus," he explained. "By this path we join the road at the top of the hill."

"I understand."

Iona barely whispered the words and without slackening speed the Duke glanced down at her.

"Shut your eyes, my dear," he said softly. "You have had much to endure and there are still difficulties ahead of us."

She obeyed him without argument, thankful that for the moment she need to make no effort but could relax against him, happy despite everything because he was close, because his arm encircled her. At last they were trotting downhill and the lights of the castle drew nearer and nearer.

Suddenly Iona was afraid. If only she could lie like this for ever. Already tomorrow menaced them: but for a few seconds more she need not think of anything save him whom she loved.

The Duke reined in his horse, grooms came running, the front door of the castle was opened and flunkeys hurried down the steps to help Iona alight. Her feet touched the ground but she felt as if her legs did not belong to her. She stood there swaying a little uncertainly, a sudden dizziness making it impossible for her to see the way. Then just when she thought she must faint, she felt herself caught up in strong arms and the Duke carried her up the steps and into the Great Hall.

A butler hurried forward to offer assistance, but His Grace brushed him on one side. Holding Iona close, he carried her up the main staircase and up the next flight to her own bedchamber. Cathy was at the door and as she opened it the Duke crossed the room to set Iona down on the bed, her head sinking weakly against the pillows. Before he let her go, his lips lingered for one moment against her hair; then he straightened himself.

"Put your mistress to bed," he said to Cathy, "and see that she is not troubled until she has rested."

"Aye, Your Grace."

Cathy curtsied as the Duke went from the room without looking back.

Iona was barely conscious that Cathy undressed her; her faintness had passed, but she was weary almost beyond endurance; and when at last she could slip between the cool linen sheets faintly perfumed with lavender, she fell at once into a deep and dreamless sleep.

She was not aware that Cathy brought food and warm milk from downstairs only to find that it was impossible to waken her. She was indeed aware of nothing until her eyes opened to find the sunshine peeping from between the curtains and the hands of the clock nearing eight o'clock.

For a moment she lay half asleep, half awake; then she remembered everything. She sat up in bed and throwing back the clothes, crossed to the window and drew back the curtains. Even as she did so, her eyes instinctively avoided the loch. She could not look at the shining, silver water.

It was then she saw lying on her dressing-table, sparkling and shining with a brilliance which made them almost appear alive, the three remaining "Tears of Torrish". Iona looked at them and after a long moment she raised her fingers to her eyes. Her mission was accomplished and she had done all that she had been sent to do.

The seconds ticked past. Iona walked across the room to the bed. On the table beside it stood her Bible. She lifted it in her hands and found, as she had expected, that the notebook had gone. She had known that it must be so and it was with a sense of fatality that she sat down on the edge of the bed, her Bible still in her hands. The notebook was lost, and yet how much else she had accomplished!

It was then that there flashed into Iona's mind a fact of which subconsciously she had been aware all the time. She knew quite clearly that she must go away. The Duke had said he loved her, and only her heart knew how much she loved him in return, but it was impossible for her to stay. She had not lived at the castle, had not come in contact with the Duke and those who served him without realising what a great and proud heritage it was to be the Duke of Akrae, Chieftain of the Clan MacCraggan; and although the Duke might lose his heart to an unknown young woman who had come to spy on him at the request of a Royal Prince, it was obvious that it would be impossible and indeed unthinkable for him to marry such a person and make her his Duchess.

Now that Iona faced the position frankly and without the distracting wonder of the Duke's presence, she knew that the glory and rapture of their happiness together last night must remain only a sweet interlude in a night of adventure and horror. Thinking of him, of his height and breadth of shoulder and his arrestingly handsome face, Iona knew that never could she confess to him that not only had she come from France with forged papers, but also that she was in fact of such inconsequence that she did not even have a name.

It was obvious, of course, that the Duke had not believed her story of being the Lady Elspeth MacCraggan. It was not as a half-brother that he had kissed her last night and told her that he loved her; but even if he had disbelieved her story, it was impossible for her to admit that she had known it untrue from the very moment when it emanated from the ingenious brain of Colonel Brett.

Yet were she brave enough to confess that she was both a liar and a pretender, there was something else—something far more important. Family pride was a very real thing, and

Iona had known what it meant to the Scottish from the very first years of her life. How often had she heard her guardian boast of the Drummonds, how often she had listened to other exiles speaking of their clans, their forebears and the part their ancestors had played in the History of Scotland. But sometimes there would be some scathing reference to a child who had been born out of wedlock, or to a base-born or illegitimate offspring of some great man who had caused trouble to other members of his family and brought an honoured name into disgrace.

Iona knew that never could she tolerate being spoken of like that by the generations to come. She loved the Duke, she would love him with her whole heart and soul all her life. She could never forget him. Her love for him was not only inescapable, it was eternal, it would remain with her to her death and beyond; but she would never hurt his pride or do anything to injure or defame his family.

Iona set her Bible down by her bedside; and as she did so, the door opened and Cathy came in, an early morning cup of chocolate in her hand.

"Sae ye are awake, mistress," she exclaimed, "an' I'm hopin' it is a guid nicht ye have passed, for it wae tired tae death ye were wheen I disrobed ye."

"Yes, I was tired," Iona replied, "but now I am myself again."

Her voice was strange and Cathy glanced at her with a sudden solicitude in her eyes. As Iona did not look at her, she said.

"Theer's strange happenin's this morn, mistress. Are ye weel enough tae hear tell o' them?"

"Tell me everything," Iona replied quickly.

" 'Twas at dawn this morn," Cathy began, "that twa o' the woodmen saw sommat unco strange on the lock. They oot wi' theer boat an' found it wae the bodies o' his lordship an' ma Lady Wrexham."

Cathy paused impressively.

"Go on," Iona said.

"They brocht word tae His Grace who sent ithers tae bring back the bodies. They are lyin' the noo in the Great Hall an' His Grace is askin' fae the minister."

Iona took a deep breath and rose to her feet.

"Listen, Cathy," she said. "I want your help. There is no time now for explanations, but I must leave the castle at once."

"Ye wad gang awa, mistress?"

232

Cathy's words were a cry.

"At once!" Iona answered firmly. "But I cannot do it unless you help me. His Grace must not know. You understand, on no account must he know that I am leaving. Somehow I must get away, and only you can help me."

"Theer's anither strange happenin' I must tell ye, mistress—Her Grace gaed this morn at dawn."

"Before the bodies were recovered?" Iona asked.

Cathy nodded.

"Aye, an' maybe 'tis fae the best for Her Grace wad hae been grievin' fae his lordship, I make nae doot o' it."

Iona pressed her fingers together.

"I must get to Inverness at once, Cathy, but first there is something of the utmost import—a little black notebook. Mr. Hector gave it into my keeping but it was stolen from me by either Lady Wrexham or Lord Niall."

"To incriminate ye wi' the English, mistress?"

"Yes, Cathy, but it is also of value to the Prince. Could you find it, do you think?"

"I ca' but try, mistress," Cathy replied. "Her ladyship's maid is in the housekeeper's room awailin' to wak' the deid. His lordship's valet is doonstairs the noo."

"Then this is your opportunity. Oh, Cathy, please contrive to discover it—a small black book which has been used as a diary."

"I'll dae ma best, mistress!"

Cathy slipped from the room. Iona listened to the minutes ticking past. Soon the room would be empty and she would be gone. She felt her heart contract at the thought, followed by a pain like a physical wound beneath her breasts. Then she no longer heard the clock; she was living again those moments when the Duke had told her of his love. Her lips were parted, her eyes soft with happiness. . . .

Cathy came hurrying into the room and Iona was startled from her reverie. Then tense and alert her anxious face asked a question wordlessly.

"Is this it, mistress?" Cathy asked and held up the little black notebook.

"It is indeed! Oh, Cathy, how clever you are. Where did you find it?"

"In the drawer o' her ladyship's dressing-table wi' some ither papers an' a great gold seal, mistress," Cathy smiled.

Iona took the notebook in her hands. She looked at it for a moment without speaking then raised her head and her voice was resolute as she said:

"Now I must get away at once. But, Cathy, how can we manage it?"

"Drink ye the cup o' chocolate," Cathy replied, "for 'tis cauld it's gettin'; and whilst ye sup I'll run doonstairs tae see if I can hear aught o' anybody leavin' the castle."

"Yes, please do that," Iona said; "but remember, say nothing."

"Ye ken weel I'll dae as ye say," Cathy replied. "But oh, mistress, it breaks ma heart fae ye tae gang awa'."

There were tears in the girl's eyes as she closed the door. Iona took a few sips of the chocolate and began to dress. She was in her travelling gown and putting her things together ready for packing when Cathy reappeared.

"What news?" Iona asked quickly as the girl came into the room and closed the door behind her.

"Bad news, mistress," Cathy replied. "Theer is but ane person leavin' this morn, an' he is ridin' tae Inverness wi' a message tae some relatives o' His Grace regardin' the death o' his lordship."

"Riding?" Iona said. "Could I not ride pillion?"

"Oh, mistress, ye couldna dae that?" Cathy cried.

"Why not?" Iona said. "If it is the only way of leaving the castle, I must take it. Go quickly, Cathy, find out if the man will take me, and above all things swear him to secrecy."

"But, mistress. . . ." Cathy began, only to be silenced by Iona who said almost sharply:

"Do as I ask, Cathy, I beg of you. This is no whim but something of the utmost import."

Without further ado Cathy did as she was told, and half an hour later Iona was on her way. Fortunately Jamie, the stout, good-humoured youth who had been persuaded by Cathy to take a passenger on his journey, had managed to obtain a double saddle and Iona, perched behind him on a spirited roan mare, was not too uncomfortable. The only luggage she had been able to bring with her was a bundle done up in a small shawl, and this she balanced precariously between herself and Jamie.

It had not been easy to avoid the curiosity of the grooms, but Cathy as usual had contrived to get Iona out of the castle without being seen and Jamie had picked her up outside the stables. As they galloped across the bridge, Iona pulled the hood of her travelling cloak well down over her head and no one seeing Jamie would have thought that he had anyone more interesting on his pillion than a country woman accompanying him to market.

It was only when they reached the summit of the hill and Iona felt safe that she looked back. There was no one in pursuit, there was only the beauty of the castle in the early morning sun to bring the quick tears to her eyes. She saw it dancing iridescently beneath her, and she turned away, knowing that the pain which seemed to stab her through and through was something which would grow worse with every successive mile.

It was a long and wearisome ride to Inverness. Jamie changed horses at a half-way inn and Iona was able to rest her aching limbs and force herself to eat and drink something although what it was she had no idea. Her sense of unhappiness was aching within her now until she felt as if the misery of it was almost unbearable and at any moment in sheer weakness she would ask Jamie to turn round and take her back to Skaig. But when she thought of the Duke, she knew that she could never bear to see those proud eyes look contemptuously at her, could not live and know that he either despised or pitied her.

For some moments before she left she had hesitated whether she should write to him; then she had known that she had nothing to say. There was no explanation to make and had she taken up her pen she would have written—"I love you, I love you, I love you. . . ." down the page until there was no more space left. And finally she had decided that she would go as she had come, unexpectedly and without warning, and perhaps in that way he would remember her with a fondness which would not be dimmed or spoilt by explanations.

As the horse jogged along, Jamie sometimes singing or whistling a tune, Iona thought only of last night and of that ecstatic, wonderful moment when the Duke's lips had held hers. Once again she could hear the warm secrecy of his voice as he spoke of his love, once again she felt the fierce strength of his arms as he cried out: "You are mine!"

Yes, she was his—for ever! The tears gathered in Iona's eyes, but she would not let them fall. Unknown though her parents might be, she was certain of one thing only—that Scottish blood ran in her veins. She would therefore be proud, as every Scot is proud, and contemptuous of any show of weakness. What she had to bear she would bear with fortitude and without self-pity.

At last, when every bone in Iona's body seemed to be aching from the discomfort of her position on the saddle, they reached the outskirts of Inverness and at the sight of the town she recalled vividly her first impression of the grey houses and grey roofs against a grey sky the morning after she had landed from France. Now the sky was blue and the sunshine made the roofs seem silver rather than grey, and the waters of the Ness were silver too, while the hills on the far side of the river were beautiful and gay with colour.

In the market place Jamie stopped to set her down. When Iona thanked him, he refused the small sum in silver which she offered him for his trouble.

"I'll dae aul I can fae a friend o' Cathy's, mistress," he said. "Ye keepit yer siller, fae ye may hae need o' it wi' a long journey ahead o' ye."

She tried to thank him, but he looked embarrassed and rode away as quickly as he could. Iona watched him until he was out of sight and then, picking up her bundle and putting it under her arm, she set off in search of Dr. Farquharson.

It was a little time before she found his house for it lay off the main street. Several times she had to ask her way finding it difficult to understand the very broad Scottish in which she was answered. When finally she reached the house, it was to find a poor, rather dirty place, and the door was opened by a slatternly maid-servant who regarded her with suspicion.

The Doctor was out, Iona was informed, and it was with a grudging air that she was told she might wait in a cold room without a fire. Feeling justifiably despondent, Iona sat down on a hard chair, wondering what she would do if the Doctor refused to help her; but when finally he arrived and she saw his good-humoured, cheery smile above a long, red beard, Iona's spirits rose. He took her into his warm study, set her down by the fire and sent for tea and cold meats, then listened attentively while she told him as much of her story as she thought it necessary for him to know.

She made no mention of the Duke's sympathies, feeling it was not fair to involve him in any way. She told the Doctor of Hector and what information there had been in the little black notebook which had been unfortunately lost, and how the Prince had sent her on another mission which was now accomplished.

"So you want to return to France?" Dr. Farquharson stated rather than asked, rising from his armchair and standing with his back to the fireplace.

"As soon as possible if you can manage it, sir," Iona replied.

"If only you had come yesterday or the day before, it would have been easy," Dr. Farquharson said. "A French ship was in harbour until midnight, but she sailed with the tide and Heaven alone knows when there will be another."

"Then what can I do?" Iona asked in dismay, remembering what little money she had left and feeling it would be impossible to spend several weeks waiting in Inverness with the Duke not so very far away.

"I've thought of something," the Doctor said suddenly. "Wait you here, lassie, and I'll be back as quick as I can."

He went from the room and Iona heard the front door slam behind him. So she waited, at first sitting primly on the edge of her chair, tense and anxious; then, after a while, sitting back comfortably, feeling a drowsiness from the heat of the fire creeping over her and with it the memory of last night warming her heart with a little echo of the joy and rapture that had been hers. Once again she remembered the Duke's face looking down into hers, the strange sound in his voice as he called her *"m'eudail"*.

She was asleep when Dr. Farquharson returned, bursting into the room breezily, his heavy footsteps making the ornaments tinkle on the mantelpiece.

Iona awoke with a start.

"I'm afraid I've been asleep."

"The best thing you could do," the Doctor smiled, "and I have good news for you."

"A French ship?" Iona queried.

"No, not as good as that," the Doctor replied, "but good enough. A friend of mine, an honest-hearted man, is leaving within the hour for York. He is a salesman of wool and he has his own waggon, so when I explained the position to him, he said he would take you and welcome."

"To York?" Iona said. "But how will that help me?"

"When you get to York, you can take the stage-coach straight through to London," the Doctor explained. "They go every day I've heard tell, and I'll give you the address of a gentleman in London who will find you a ship at the docks or send you through to Dover so that you can cross the Channel by that route."

"It is so very kind of you to take all this trouble," Iona said.

She tried to sound more enthusiastic; but the idea of such a long journey, with its inevitable dangers and hazards, was somehow infinitely frightening. The Doctor crossed to his writing-table.

"I'll write down the name of the gentleman. He will look after you in London," he said. "He's a Scot like myself and you can trust him with all you have told me, but I should not confide too deeply in Willie Hogswell—that's my friend from Yorkshire. He's a good man, is Willie, but I'm not too sure of his politics."

"I'll be careful," Iona promised. "How . . . how soon do I go?"

"There's time for another cup of tea," the Doctor replied. "And a bit of food as well. You'll be needing to keep up your strength for such a long journey and Willie hopes to be ten miles away before it is dark."

Iona ate and drank as the Doctor suggested and then he led her through the narrow streets to where Willie Hogswell was waiting. Two large grey horses and a well-built waggon were standing in the yard of an inn. When Iona entered the courtyard, she recognised it. It was the inn where she and Hector had stayed on the eventful night of her arrival. But there was no time for reminiscences, no time to recall the past, for Willie Hogswell's big rough hand was clasping hers and there was a welcome on his fat, good-natured face.

With a broad Yorkshire accent he told her that he would be glad of her company and that she was putting him to no trouble. Then almost before Iona had time to thank the Doctor, Willie whipped up the grey horses and with the wooden wheels rumbling noisily over the cobbles the waggon moved slowly out of the yard and they turned their faces towards the south.

17

The fat woman beside Iona rambled on with the apparently endless story of her illnesses.

" 'Twas real queer I was taken that Wednesday—the very morning when m' daughter was a-coming to stay—and he says to me, he says, 'Mrs. Muggins, you've been over-doing it again', and I says to him, 'Doctor, I swear to you I have sat here quiet as a mouse and never a thing have I done contrary to your suggestions'. Then he says to me. . . ."

But Iona was not listening. Dimly through the windows misty with the fug inside the coach, she could see houses, churches and shops. It was London at last. It seemed to her that she had been travelling for years rather than weeks; and although she had not yet reached the end of her journey, it was something to know that the first part had been completed.

Looking back at the time it had taken to come from York, she had not believed that anything could move as slowly as the stage-coach except Willie Hogswell's horses, which had appeared to crawl like snails between Inverness and York. Iona had sat beside Willie in the front of the waggon and felt herself torn in half by conflicting desires. One half, which was weak and vulnerable, wanted them to be slow, because there was just a chance in a million that the Duke might come after her and ask her to return. The other half, which was stern and matter-of-fact, wanted the horses to move quicker and still quicker, so that Skaig would be left far behind and she could force herself resolutely to start her life again in other surroundings.

When they reached York, Iona had thanked Willie fervently for his kindness; but he brushed aside her thanks and almost brusquely bade her God speed. He had been extraordinarily kind, and under other circumstances Iona would have enjoyed listening to his drawling Yorkshire voice as they wandered up hill and down dale through wonderful scenery in all sorts and conditions of weather. But while Willie talked, her ears were hearing another voice, a voice that could be both firm and commanding, soft and tender. While Willie pointed out the beauty of the Lowlands of Scotland and the northern counties of England, Iona could only see Skaig, its grey walls proud against moor, sky and water.

She found it hard to eat and Willie chid her in a friendly fashion about her appetite, striving to entice her with huge pastries which he himself thought the most delectable food on earth. To please him Iona tried to force the food between her lips, but after a time her eating became only a pretence and her face grew thin. Her gown hung loosely and her eyes were enormous and dark-shadowed. And yet her suffering only seemed to increase her beauty. There was something almost transparent about her little face, as if the gallant spirit within was showing through the walls of the flesh as a light might shine through a thinly curtained window.

At York Iona had taken the stage-coach, a big unwieldy affair drawn by four horses which, although changed at frequent intervals, never appeared to exert themselves unduly.

And now at last she had reached London. Anxiously she felt in the pocket of her dress to see if the piece of paper Dr. Farquharson had given her was safe. If she had lost that, she would be lost indeed, for she had but a few shillings left in her purse. It was humiliating to realise that she would have to ask a stranger, however warm his sympathies might be to the Jacobite Cause, for the loan of her fare to France. But somehow, Iona thought, she would contrive to pay him back, however long it took her to earn it.

At the back of her mind was a tiny aching fear that the gentleman whose name Dr. Farquharson had given her might be no longer there! Suppose he had gone away, suppose after all he had changed his mind and fugitive Jacobites could no longer be certain of his assistance. But as the torturing thoughts arose within her, Iona's wholesome common sense managed to thrust them away. Fate had looked after her so far and it would not fail her now.

The man sitting opposite her in the coach was, she had learned, connected with a Bank. Now he pulled a big gold watch from his pocket.

"Nigh on three o'clock," he announced. "This plaguey coach is five hours late again. I shall protest, as I have protested before. 'Tis disgraceful that they can't run them to better time."

"You're lucky it isn't five days late," someone said languidly from a far corner.

"Lucky indeed!" the gentleman in banking snorted. "In these days of improved travelling facilities, when I make an appointment in London for 16th September, I expect to keep it."

So it was 16th September, Iona thought. She had lost count of the days, for one had seemed very like another since she left Skaig. She wondered on what date she would arrive in Paris, and then decided with a sudden unusual bitterness it would matter very little to anyone save herself.

"We're nearing the old Bedford, we are," the fat woman said suddenly, bending forward to rub a large puffy hand against the window. "And 'tis glad I'll be to see it. The ale they sell there is the best in London; and if I says that, I knows what I'm talking about, I can assure you."

The other passengers paid no attention to her. They were gathering their belongings together, settting their hats on their heads, buttoning their gloves and generally titivating themselves in an effort to improve their travel-stained untidiness.

Iona pulled her grey cloak over her shoulders and tied the ribbons at her neck. She was well aware that her gown was sadly creased after all its journeyings. She had done her best to clean it every night and to start the day with a spotless muslin fichu round her shoulders, but nothing could really improve its shabbiness. She had often regretted that she had not brought more gowns with her from Skaig. One dress was a pitiably poor wardrobe when one was journeying for such a wearisome length of time.

"Here we are!" the fat woman cried and, turning to Iona, she added: "Good-bye, my ducks; take care of yourself. I hope there's someone meeting you. You oughtn't to be walking about London with a pretty face like yours."

Iona smiled at her reassuringly; but at the same time she felt an aching loneliness at the thought that no one would be meeting her and she alone of everyone in the coach was unsure where she would lay her head that night.

The horses drew up; ostlers came running to their heads; the doors were opened, steps let down, and everyone pushed and shoved in their haste to descend. Iona was almost the last to leave the coach. She was in no particular hurry, so she sat back while the others hustled past her, and then, carrying her small bundle, she descended slowly and with a dignity that was an intrinsic part of her.

Several coaches were drawn up outside the Bedford Inn. Some were just departing and their conductors had already raised the long brass horns to their lips, while the coachmen, red-faced and foul-mouthed, were whipping up the leaders. Others were arriving, the horses sweating and dusty, the passengers tired and disagreeable. It was a scene of turmoil and confusion and for a moment Iona, watching bustling ostlers, sweating porters and the embarking and disembarking passengers, felt bewildered and lost. Suddenly beside her a voice said:

"At last! I knew, if I waited long enough, you would come."

She started violently and the last vestige of colour was drained from her already pale cheeks. Looking down at her, seeming immeasurably taller and bigger, stood the Duke.

Speechlessly she started at him and realised that he was smiling. She had never before seen him so happy. He bent down, took her hand in his, and raised it very gently to his lips.

"I have waited for two weeks," he said. "Where have you been? I was half afraid I would never find you again."

"I have been . . . been coming . . . here," Iona replied; "but why, oh why, have you been waiting for me?"

"Do you really want me to answer that question?" the Duke asked, and something in his tone made her drop her eyes before his and sent the colour rushing tumultuously back into her cheeks.

"My carriage is waiting," the Duke said; "but first, you must be hungry. I have a private room in the hotel. Shall we repair there?"

Without waiting for her permission he took her arm and escorted her through the mêlée of horses and pedestrians into the hotel. There he led the way to a small room at the back away from the noise of the bars and overlooking a well-kept garden.

A fire was burning brightly in an open fireplace, and the dark oak panelling was a perfect background to Iona's shining head as she pushed back her hood. A waiter appeared and the Duke gave an order. The door shut behind him and they were alone.

For a moment the Duke stood looking at Iona, making no effort to move to her side, only watching her intently from where he stood, his eyes taking in the sharpened lines of her heart-shaped face and the soft shadows beneath her eyes.

After a moment Iona quivered beneath his regard; her hands went first to her hair, then to her dress in a vain effort to smooth the creases from it.

"I am untidy, Your Grace," she said in a quick, breathless little voice. "I would not have you see me in such a state. But why have you come? You make it so much, much more . . . difficult."

There was a break in her voice and she turned half away from him towards the fire.

"What do I make more difficult?" the Duke asked quietly.

"For me to go away," Iona answered miserably, almost as if she spoke to herself; and then with a great effort she raised her head and faced him squarely. "Can Your Grace not understand that I must go, that it is impossible for me to stay with you even if you would have me?"

The Duke took several steps to her side, but there he stood silent, his eyes searching her averted face. At his coming Iona trembled and was conscious of a sudden flame leaping within herself so that she dropped her head and dared not look at him. The Duke waited a few seconds and then he said softly:

"Will you not look at me, Iona?"

She did not move or reply, and after a second he said:

"Look at me!"

This time his words were a command, and in answer Iona flung back her head suddenly. Her expression was strained, her lips tight-pressed against each other, and her eyes tragic. For a long, long moment the Duke looked down at her then he said:

"Oh, my darling, did you think I would ever let you go?"

At the words Iona swayed a little and would have fallen if he had not put out his arms and held her steady. As he did so, she cried out, her hands warding him off with an almost pitiful effort.

"It is impossible, quite impossible," she cried. "Please believe this and do not humiliate me by forcing me to tell you more. Only know that I cannot be yours. . . . Never!

243

Never! . . . for your sake—for the sake of all you honour and hold most sacred."

It was as if the Duke had not heard her, for slowly, tenderly and with a strength she could not withstand, he overcame her resistance until at last she was encircled by his arms, her body close against his, her head against his shoulder. She felt a sudden joy invade her, yet still she strove against surrender, holding herself stiff and tense even while every nerve in her body cried out to her to let his love sweep her away in a flood-tide of ecstasy.

"Is there really anything you are afraid to tell me?" the Duke asked.

"Not afraid," Iona answered in a whisper, "but ashamed. Let me go!"

"No!"

His answer seemed to ring out and desperately, driven by her conscience and by her sense of honour, Iona made one last attempt at resistance. With a sudden movement she wrenched herself free from the Duke and, retreating from him, stood behind a wing-backed chair.

"Listen to me," she said. "You have got to listen . . . but if you touch me again I . . . cannot tell you . . . for I love you—love you with all my heart and soul . . . but it is because I love you so . . . so deeply that I cannot do . . . what you ask."

Her voice faltered for a moment and then she went on:

"Your Grace has a great position, you have a name respected and honoured throughout the length and breadth of Scotland. People look up to you and honour you as . . . indeed I do . . . and because of such things, and . . . because you are who you are . . . I can never be your wife."

"And why not?"

For a moment Iona shut her eyes. For one despairing moment she wished she might die before she need answer the question she had most dreaded to hear from his lips. Then, not looking at him, her long lashes veiling her eyes as they stared unseeingly at her hands gripping the back of the chair, she stammered:

"I have no name . . . I have never had one . . . I was brought up by my guardian, Major James Drummond. . . . When I was old enough to understand, he told me that he could never reveal to me . . . the name of my parents. All that he could tell me was . . . that I was of Scottish blood and that . . . I had been christened Iona."

Iona's voice broke completely and then wildly she cried out through her tears; "Now go . . . and go . . . quickly."

Her hands went up to her eyes. She stood there trembling all over, fighting against the tempest of her tears which threatened to overwhelm her; and even as she strove for self-control, she listened for the sound of the Duke's footsteps retreating, the sound of the door closing as he went out of her life.

Then suddenly she heard him make a movement and almost despite herself she looked from between her fingers. She had a glimpse of his face almost transfigured by the tenderness of his expression as he went down on one knee beside her and raising the hem of her dusty, creased gown, kissed it reverently. For a moment he knelt there; then he rose to his feet and drawing her hands from her face held them tightly in both of his.

"My dear, foolish, little love," he said very softly. "Have you forgotten that you are already my wife?"

Iona's fingers quivered in his, but he would not release them.

"But that . . . that was not . . . binding," she said. "It was just an expedient . . . to allow me to escape . . . from the hands of the English."

"Expedient or not," the Duke replied firmly, "according to the law of Scotland . . . your law and mine, my darling . . . we are married."

"But . . . but . . ." Iona faltered.

"There is no but," the Duke said masterfully. "You are mine and nothing that you can say or do will ever persuade me to let you go."

Now it was impossible for Iona to hide the happiness which enveloped her and left her speechless, lighting her eyes until they shone like stars, parting her lips through which her breath came quickly. The Duke drew her towards him; once again she was in his arms; and this time his mouth sought hers and found her lips.

She felt him take possession of her, felt a wonder and a magic sweep over her in utter and complete surrender of herself. She clung to him; for a moment the world was lost and forgotten and she was carried into a heaven of sweet contentment where there was only the Duke and her overwhelming love for him.

When he released her, she felt for a moment dazed and hardly conscious of where she was. She awoke to reality at

245

a knock on the door. The waiter had returned with the food the Duke had ordered.

What she ate or drank Iona had no idea. She could only sit beside the Duke, her hand in his, and know that her life had changed from one of drab uncertainty into a golden rapture which she was half afraid to question. They ate almost in silence until after a while the Duke, drawing her to her feet and wrapping her cloak around her, said:

"We must go now, my love, for there is much to do before night falls."

"What have we to do?" Iona asked wonderingly.

But he only smiled at her reassuringly and answered:

"You will see!"

He threw a guinea on the table and led Iona from the quietness of the little room at the back of the hotel into the tumult and noise outside, where a coach of claret and silver with the Ducal coat of arms emblazoned on the door, drawn by a pair of horses and attended by a coachman and two footmen, stood waiting. The Duke handed her inside and Iona sank back against the satin-padded cushions, comparing it with the hard discomfort of the stagecoach.

They drove off and she bent forward eagerly, looking through the windows at the streets of London, at the houses of wood and plaster with their square-paned windows, at the fine churches raising their great spires to the sky and the labyrinth of streets, lanes, alleys, courts and yards. There were Sedan chairs with their attendants often arrayed in gorgeous liveries; there were coaches dazzlingly painted and gilded, their footmen watching disdainfully the passers-by being splashed by the muck thrown up by the wheels and horses' hoofs, from the gutters in the centre of the streets. But to Iona the most extraordinary thing about London was the music of its bells. Not only church bells ringing out joyfully, but the bells rung by the dustmen, the sweeps, the knife-grinders, muffin men, old clothes men and postmen. Bells mingling with the street cries of "Chairs to mend," "Scissors to grind", and the haunting high notes of "Sweet Lavender".

"I always wondered what London would be like," Iona exclaimed, entranced by all she saw and heard.

"I will show you all you wish to see, my darling," the Duke answered, "and then I shall take you back to Skaig. I wish above all things to be alone with you there."

The implication in his voice made her flush, but her lips smiled as she answered:

"And I too would like that . . . above all things."

He drew her close to him and everything was forgotten; the horses trotted on, passing the famous clubs of St. James's Street, fine squares, elegant shops, a man standing in the pillory, three women being flogged through the streets; but Iona had eyes only for the Duke and ears only for the sweet things he was whispering to her. She was startled when finally the coach drew up outside a house.

"Where are we?" she asked a little apprehensively.

"We are in Berkeley Square," the Duke replied, "and this is the house of my aunt."

Iona looked apprehensive and he added understandingly:

"Do not be afraid, dear heart; I wish her to meet you."

The door of the coach was opened and the Duke assisted Iona to alight. When she entered the big hall with its pillars of green marble and its wide bronzed and gilt staircase, she felt both awed and overpowered. They walked on a thick rose-tinted carpet up the stairway and Iona was miserably conscious of her shabby and travel-stained appearance. For the first time she noticed the Duke's elegance, the exquisite cut of his pearl-grey velvet coat with its sapphire and diamond buttons which matched his ring and the pin in his lace cravat.

She had a glimpse of herself in the mirrors which decorated the brocade-panelled walls of the wide landing at the top of the stairs, and knew that though her hair gleamed brightly and her eyes were huge with excitement, her gown and cloak were unworthy of a lady's drawingroom.

The footman flung open a pair of double doors.

"The Duke and Duchess of Arkrae, m'lady," he announced in stentorian tones.

Iona had no time to recover from the surprise of hearing her title for the first time, for at the other end of an enormous, over-furnished room sat a most formidable old lady. She was white-haired, sharp-nosed, and obviously of a great age; but her glance was shrewd and penetrating as the Duke bent to kiss the claw-like hand she held out to him.

"This is a surprise, Ewan," she said in a strangely deep voice. "I had no idea you had come south."

"I have been here some days, Aunt Anne," the Duke replied, "but I have unfortunately not had the opportunity of calling upon you until now."

"And whom have you brought with you?" the old

woman asked, her sharp eyes taking in every detail of Iona's appearance and being well aware of the manner in which she had been announced.

"I have the honour to present my wife," the duke answered. "Iona, this is my aunt, my father's only surviving sister, the Dowager Countess of Tyndrum."

Iona swept to the ground in a low curtsey. The Countess's eyes rested on her red head and she said in a voice which had a strange note in it:

"Why was I not told of your marriage, Ewan? And who are your wife's relations?"

"I will answer those questions one at a time," the Duke replied, "but first permit me to offer my wife a chair. She has been travelling for some days and is, I am afraid, somewhat fatigued."

As he spoke, he drew forward a low chair and set it at the Countess's right hand; then he took up his position on the hearth-rug, his back to the fire. The Countess stared at Iona, who, conscious of her close scrutiny, felt embarrassed and glanced up appealingly at the Duke. But his face was stern and she wondered what had upset him until he said calmly and quietly:

"You asked me two questions Aunt Anne. First, why you had not been informed of my marriage. No one has learned of it until now save two people who were present when it took place; you are the first of the family to be told."

"I suppose I should be flattered at that," the Countess remarked sarcastically.

"Indeed, I think you will be when I tell you a little more," the Duke replied seriously. "It has some bearing upon your second question as to who are my wife's relations; but before I speak of that, I have a tale to unfold which I think will interest both you ladies—you, my aunt, who are a MacCraggan by birth, and Iona, my wife, who now takes her place with me at the head of the family."

"What is this story?" the Countess asked impatiently.

She picked up an ebony stick from beside her chair and held it in her hands as if the feel of it afforded her a sense of protection.

"My story is this," the Duke began. 'When I was a boy, I had a favourite cousin. She was older than I; but Letricia—your only daughter, Aunt Anne—had an ageless charm for everyone who met her. There was, I well believe, never a man, woman or child who, having met Letricia, did not love her; and I was no exception. She was a beautiful creature, and when I went back to Eton after the holidays, I used to dream of her. She was my first love and I have never forgotten her."

The Countess made a restless movement.

"When Letricia died," she said sharply, "few people were brave enough to speak about her—to me."

"Letricia died a long time ago," the Duke answered, "but I have not forgotten her, nor have you, Aunt Anne. No, you could never forget her, and I would remind you now how lovely Letricia looked when she first fell in love. That was about twenty-one years ago, wasn't it? When she fell in love with Roderick Cameron and you forbade her ever to see him again."

The Countess thumped her stick on the floor.

"Stop!" she said. "How dare you? Be silent! These things shall not be talked of now."

"That is where you are mistaken," the Duke replied. "These things must be talked of; they can remain secret no longer, Aunt Anne, and I do not ask that you listen to me I insist that you do so."

His words were so authoritative that the old woman sank back in her chair, but her face was grim as the Duke continued:

"You forbade Letricia to see Roderick Cameron; but she loved him, and one day when you were away they were married secretly. You knew nothing of the marriage until six months later when Roderick was killed in a sword fight and Letricia, broken-hearted and unable to conceal her misery, confessed the truth. You were incensed at her deception and even more perturbed by the knowledge that Letricia was with child. You had always been ambitious, Aunt Anne, and now you were at your wit's end to know what to do when your daughter, whose beauty you had valued so highly, was not only the widow of a penniless second son, but also about to become a mother. You were determined that her chance of social success should not be endangered. With shrewd ingenuity you made arrangements for Letricia to take a holiday in Iona.

"You had inherited a small castle there, an isolated place which no one ever visited. Letricia's child was born there. It was a girl and was christened by the only name she was ever to own—Iona."

The Duke's glance rested for one second on Iona. Her hands were clasped together, her face as she stared up at him as white as the fichu round her neck, her eyes wide with astonishment.

"After Iona was born," the Duke went on, "you sent Letricia back to Edinburgh; and taking the baby, you set sail for France. It was an arduous journey; but driven by your determination to save the daughter you loved from what you thought was a feckless, insane marriage, you were prepared to endure any discomfort, to surmount any difficulty. You reached France and went to Paris where your cousin, James Drummond, lived in exile—you had always been fond of one another, he had once wished to marry you, and persuaded by your distress, he agreed to take the child and bring her up. Before you left, you made him vow by all that he held most sacred that he would never reveal to your grand-daughter who she was or who were her parents.

"You returned to Scotland. Within a year you had contrived to marry Letricia, who was too miserable to care what happened to her, to the Marquis of Kinbrace. A year after that she died in childbirth and her baby with her. And so you lost your second grandchild, Aunt Anne."

There was a pause, a pause in which neither the Countess nor Iona moved; then the Duke went on:

"When I first saw Iona, my wife, she reminded me of someone. For a short while I could not think who it was; and then I remembered only one MacCraggan who had that peculiar combination of red hair and green eyes. It was obvious, when I compared the two, that Iona was a MacCraggan, but of which branch of the family I was not sure. But when she told me inadvertently that she had been born in Iona, I stumbled on my first clue to the truth. You had covered your tracks skilfully, Aunt Anne, but servants have long memories. Not far from Skaig there lives an old couple who were at one time caretakers in your castle at Iona. I talked to them. They were loyal, but they were not clever enough to deceive me, and I pretended to know a lot more than I did. Gradually the whole story revealed itself.

"When I was in Paris a short time ago, I visited a lady who had devoted many years of her life to looking after Rory MacCraggan. He was a first cousin of yours and I am sure you remember him well. I went to Paris to collect some heirlooms which he had taken into exile and which I considered should be brought back to Skaig. The woman with whom Rory had lived spoke to me of James Drummond. She was but recounting tales of other exiles who had fled to France after the Rising in '15. She happened to mention that James Drummond was dead and she wondered what had happened to his ward—a pretty girl with red hair and green eyes who had always seemed so devoted to him. It was not very difficult to piece the story together, Aunt Anne; the story of Letricia, your daughter—and the story of Iona, your grand-daughter."

The Duke's voice died away but seemed to linger in the very atmosphere. Unable to control herself, Iona started to her feet.

"Is this true?" she asked in a bewildered voice: "really true?"

"You must ask your grandmother that question," the Duke answered softly.

Iona looked down at the old lady. The Countess's knuckles were white and she gripped her ebony stick with all the strength that was left in her. For a moment Iona thought she was about to cry out and denounce the Duke as a fabricator of lies; then she saw that the old lady was crying. Impulsively, with a lovely unhesitating gesture, Iona knelt down beside her chair.

"Am I really your grand-daughter?" she asked, and her voice trembled.

The tears ran slowly down the Countess's wrinkled cheeks. She put up her hand and touched Iona's cheek. For a moment she could not speak; and when she could, she said brokenly:

"You are very like Letricia, my dear."

For a moment the two women clung to each other and both their faces were wet with tears, then the Duke drew Iona to her feet. He held her within the shelter of his arm.

"There are two things I would ask, Aunt Anne. One is that we may stay here tonight, and the other that tomorrow you will have a reception at which you will present Iona to your friends."

The Countess looked up at him and wiped her eyes with a lace-edged handkerchief.

"It shall be as you wish, Ewan," she said. "I am too old to fight against you or anyone else. It shall be as you wish."

The Duke drew a watch from his waistcoat pocket.

"And now for a short while we must leave you," he said. "We will return for dinner, but before then we have another call to make."

251

Instinctively Iona looked down at her dress and the Duke said with a smile:

"If you hurry you have time to change."

"Change?" Iona questioned.

The Duke nodded.

"I brought your trunk with me and Cathy too, in case you should need her. When we arrived here, I sent the coach to fetch her from the hotel where I have been staying pending your arrival. If I am not mistaken, she will at this moment be downstairs in the Hall waiting to hear if Aunt Anne will accept us as her guests or if we must repair to an hotel."

"You must both stay here, of course," the Countess said, and for a moment a faint wintry smile twisted her lips. "You meant to have your way, whatever I might say to the contrary. You don't deceive me, my boy."

"I'm glad of that," the Duke replied and bent to help the Countess to rise from her chair.

With one hand she supported herself on her ebony stick, with the other she reached up and touched Iona's red curls.

"You are very like Letricia," she said again, "and I loved my daughter. Make what arrangements you wish, children; I am going to bed. I have a feeling that you should prefer the house to yourselves. I must gather my strength for the morrow when I shall present my grand-daughter . . . my only grandchild . . . to the *beau-monde*."

She went slowly across the room. The Duke opened the door and turned to Iona.

"Change quickly," he said. "I can allow you but twenty minutes. Can you manage in that time?"

"Of course I can," Iona smiled.

But it was difficult because there was so much she wanted to tell Cathy. It was almost like coming home to see her sweet honest face again, to hear her soft Highland voice. But in twenty minutes Iona's hair was skilfully arranged and she was arrayed in a gown of blue muslin sprigged with flowers. It was not an elaborate dress but it became her; and her reflection in the mirror told her that the Duke would find her beautiful. She was just about ready to descend the stairs in order to join him when there came a knock on the door. The Countess's maid stood outside.

"Her ladyship's compliments," she said to Cathy, "and she thought Her Grace might wish to borrow a fur cape as the evenings are growing cold. She also asked me to inform Her Grace that she has ordered her dressmaker to call early

252

tomorrow morning, for her ladyship is sure Her Grace will require many gowns for her trousseau."

Cathy brought the wrap to Iona who gave a little cry of pleasure at the sight of it. Of sapphire blue velvet, it was lined with sable which framed her shoulders. Excited and thrilled beyond measure she ran downstairs. There the Duke was waiting.

"You are very punctual, my darling," he said and added: "There is one thing I wanted to ask you before we leave. Have you the 'Tears of Torrish' in your possession?"

Iona nodded.

"Indeed I have," she replied, "for I have worn them next my skin for fear they should be stolen from me."

She drew them from her bosom and the Duke looked down at the three diamonds gleaming in the palm of her hand.

"Bring them with you," he said, and before she could ask him any questions he led the way to the coach outside.

As they drove off, the Duke put his arm round Iona and felt the softness of the sable cloak.

"Sables? You are getting very grand," he teased.

"Your aunt . . . I mean, my grandmother . . . lent them to me. Was it not kind of her?"

"There are so many things that I want to give you," the Duke said, holding Iona a little closer to him. "Furs and jewellery among them. There are some family diamonds which will become you well and we shall have to give a ball especially so that I can see you wearing the emerald tiara."

"Do not say too much," Iona begged him, "it frightens me. I only feel safe and secure when I am alone with you; but oh, when I think that I need no longer hide my head in shame, that I have a name at last . . . ."

"You have indeed," the Duke answered. "You are the Duchess of Arkrae."

"And I am also a Cameron," Iona answered, "and half a MacCraggan—your second cousin! At times I feel as if my heart would burst with the excitement of it all."

"Just because you have a name?" the Duke asked.

"No, more than that," Iona replied, "because of you—oh, but you know that."

"Yes, I know it," the Duke answered and pressed his cheek against hers.

For a moment she was still, then she turned impulsively towards him.

"You are sure you love me," she asked, "quite, quite sure? You are so clever and I am so ignorant; you have great traditions behind you, I have nothing."

In answer he drew her into his arms with an almost fierce strength, and his lips were on hers.

"You are all I ask for in the whole world," he said. "Is that nothing?"

She had still found no words to answer him when the coach drew up at a house in Pall Mall. It was a big house and the windows were shuttered; there was somehow, Iona thought as the door opened into a dimly lit hall, an air of secrecy about it.

The Duke spoke to a flunkey who led them down a long passage. He opened the door of a room at the end of it and announced:

"The Duke and Duchess of Arkrae, m'lord."

For a moment Iona thought she had been here before. There was a little company of gentlemen seated round the table and the room was lit with but a few candles. The shutters were closed, the shadows dark and mysterious. Then Iona saw a face she knew.

"Colonel Brett!" she ejaculated in astonishment and looked round to see who else was there.

She saw a figure seated in a chair at the far end of the table. He rose and came forward to her. As Iona sank to the ground in a deep curtsey, he extended his hand.

"Oh sir, sir," she muttered.

"You had not thought to see me here?" the Prince asked. "And I had not expected to see you, Arkrae."

The Duke bowed.

"My wife, sir, has something to impart to Your Royal Highness."

Silently Iona held out the three "Tears of Torrish".

"Those are all that are left, sir. I found them, but . . . I could do no better."

The Prince looked down into her hand.

"The 'Tears of Torrish', by Gad! But only three. Who is fortunate enough to have the rest?"

Iona glanced at the Duke. Understanding the appeal in her eyes, he told the Prince briefly what had occurred.

"I must count myself lucky that all were not lost," the Prince said, "but what is more important is that you have brought me not only diamonds, but your husband, my dear." His hand rested for a moment on Iona's arm, then he turned towards the Duke. "I am sadly in need of your help, Arkrae," he said. "I have been talking here with His Grace of Beaufort and my Lord Westmorland. I have asked them for five thousand men, that is all; but they tell me they cannot provide me with even five hundred at this moment. Can you be of greater service?"

The Duke drew a deep breath. Quietly he replied:

"If it were possible, sir, I would give you fifty thousand and myself at the head of them; but I could on my own land raise but a hundred or so, and we can be certain of no support from the other clans. They are scattered and ruined, our people tortured, imprisoned, disarmed and transported. The Highlands are still loyal to you in their hearts, but we cannot fight without men, without weapons. Time may enable us to tell another tale; but if you ask me to speak for Scotland, sir, I can but tell you the truth—bitter though it may be."

The Prince put his hand up to his eyes as if he would hide the disappointment on his face. He turned and looked at the men seated round the table.

"Arkrae says the same as you, my lords. There is nothing for me but to return to France."

His voice was so sad that Iona felt that she must cry at the very misery in it; then the Prince smiled and so irresistible was his smile that she felt herself smile at him in return. He turned towards her and holding the three "Tears of Torrish" between his fingers, placed them in the palm of her hand.

"You found these for me in Scotland," he said; "that is where they belong. Use them as you and your husband think fit to help those who have suffered, to succour those who are in need because they have followed a Stuart."

"Oh, sir, that is indeed generous," Iona exclaimed.

The Prince shook his head.

"I only ask that sometimes when you are in Scotland," he said, "you will remember a man whose happiest time of his life was spent there—hunted and pursued, yet loved by the people who helped him. Yes, I ask only that those in Scotland should remember me, for I can never forget Scotland."

The Prince's voice was deep with emotion, and Iona's eyes were blinded with tears as he walked away from her across the room.

Back in the coach Iona hid her face against the Duke's shoulder.

"There is nothing more we can do, my darling," he said gently.

Then after a moment he put his fingers under her chin and turned her little face up to his.

"We have other things to consider," he said softly.

"What are they?" she enquired innocently.

"The most important," he replied, "is that you are—my wife."

The deep passion in his voice made her tremble, and the colour rose in her cheeks.

"Are you afraid of me, my Dearest Heart?" he asked.

"No . . . no," she stammered, "it . . . is . . . just . . . that . . . I love . . . you so much . . . I am . . . afraid it is only . . . a dream."

He swept her close to his breast.

"It is true, my wife, my darling, my precious little love. You are mine now and for ever."

His lips were against her mouth, but he did not kiss her.

"Tell me again, my adorable Little Pretender," he insisted, "that you belong to me. I want to hear you say it, so that I too can be sure—of you."

It was hard for Iona to speak because she felt as though she was being carried away on the wings of ecstasy. There was a flame rising within her, and she quivered not with fear but with a strange new excitement she could not name. Then so softly he could hardly hear, she whispered:

"I . . . love . . . you . . . my . . . husband . . . I am . . . yours."